I0702402

For my dad, who always wanted to see these stories made into a proper book. This one is for you. Thank you for always supporting me and being so vocal about how proud you were of me. I love you, and I really, really miss you.

Broken Gears Chronology

The Continent Of
Invarnis
Duskwood
Springhaven
(Formerly Prism)
Cobalt
Bay
Dogwood
Lane
Bone
Port
Bone
Bay

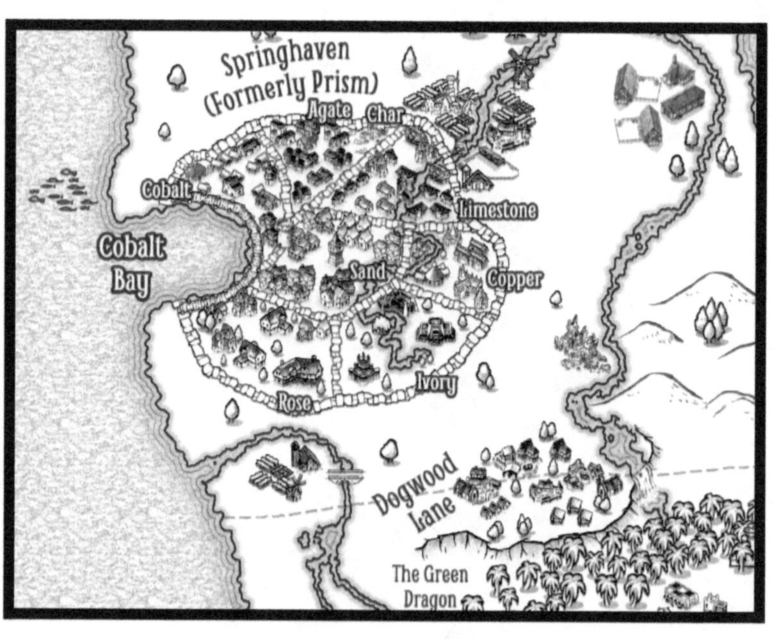

Springhaven
(Formerly Prism)
Agate
Char
Cobalt
Cobalt
Bay
Limestone
Sand
Copper
Ivory
Rose
Dogwood
Lane
The Green
Dragon

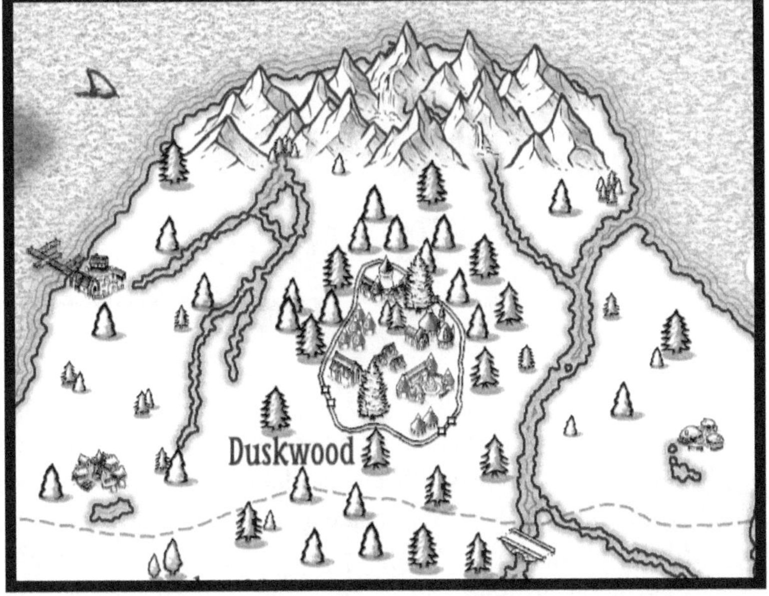

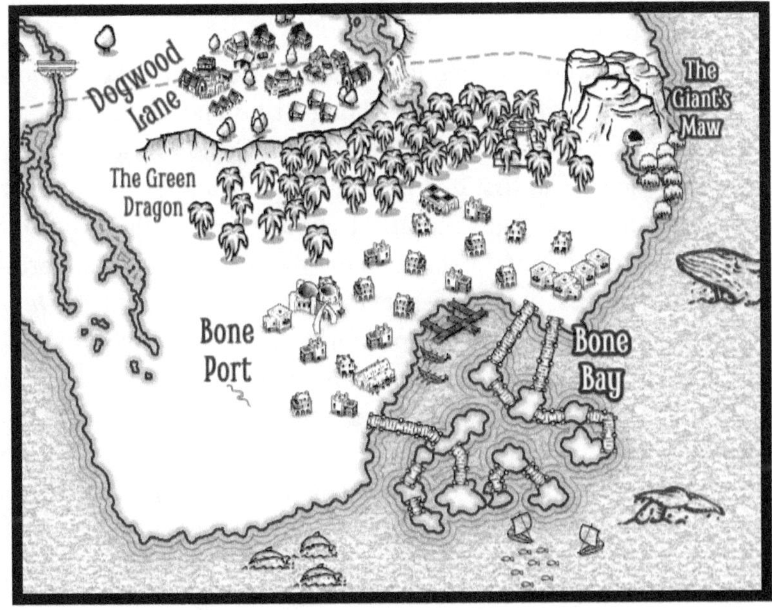

Duskwood
Dogwood Lane
The Green Dragon
Bone Port
The Giant's Maw
Bone Bay

PREFACE

So why did I write this book? After all, most of these stories are still, as they've always been, available for free reading on my website, www.WordsByDana.com, though a few were written specifically for this book. Simply put, because books are awesome. They feel good, to hold and to have and to discuss and to relive again and again. So it just makes sense that these stories eventually became a book.

It's also worth noting that these stories are an evolutionary record in my writing journey (though I've chosen to order them following the chronology of the Broken Gears world rather than their creation). The first one I wrote, *New Year's Gifts*, was written five years ago, way back in 2017. I wrote it for no other reason than for fun. At which point I should mention that some of them are, for lack of a better phrase, especially larky. *O Harried Night* and *Check, Please* are good examples of this. They're never referenced in any of the books. *Check, Please* exists almost entirely in a vacuum, save for happening sometime after the events of *Across the Ice*.

That being said, some of these, such as *The Butterfly Effect* and *Salty Siblings*, were born out of passing mentions in the Broken Gears novels. The stories were just too good not to tell, but it just wasn't feasible in those books.

And then, of course, there are the stories that show either how characters got to be who they are, as with *Monsters Inside*; who they eventually become—*Death Cults and Taxes (Addendum)*—and what big moves we all were kind of expecting them to make but just hadn't yet gotten to see—*A Modest Proposal*.

These aren't the end, though. I still have loads of story ideas waiting for their turn in my planner. I'll keep gifting them to my VIP newsletter subscribers as I write them. And there are still more Broken Gears novels to be written as well. In the meantime, however, I hope you enjoy these little behind-the-scenes scenes. And, as always, thanks for reading!

Pigs and Fae

"Of all the perils I had to face in the Dragon, I never expected one of them would be Fae." Set before the events of *Raven's Cry*. No spoilers.

~~~

Our foray into the Green Dragon, which is what we call the jungle just beyond my home city of Bone Port, began normally enough. My best friend and guardswoman, Basira; my guardsman and friend, Eduardo; my Uncle Ducky; and I had left my home early that morning to go hunting. Ducky wanted to bag a panther to add to his collection of trophies, and there was no way I was going to let him try without the best team available. That, and my parents—the Count and Countess of the Bone Port and Bone Bay territories—were hosting a luncheon that day for some business associates. I would rather face off against an angry panther than make small talk for an entire afternoon. Thus, I left my older brother, the future count, to deal with all that unpleasantness.

"It's wretched in here, Cali," Ducky grumbled as we picked our way through the dense underbrush. He slapped at yet another

~~~

mosquito. "How do you stand it?"

"Bathing in lemongrass oil," I replied, smirking at him.

There was a very good reason my uncle had yet to bring down a panther. He and the jungle do not get along.

The air inside the Green Dragon doesn't move. It just sits there, collecting heat from all the life within and the sun shining overhead. The thick tree canopy traps moisture from the swampy ground, and it sticks to you as if you're moving through soup. Though Uncle Ducky can move quite stealthily for a man of his size—I've seen him sneak up on many a deer—he somehow loses that skill as soon as he steps into the Green Dragon.

Ducky wiped his brow on his already damp sleeve. "It's barely sunup. How is it already so bloody hot?"

"Shhhh," Basira scolded, chopping away a clump of broad leaves with her machete. "Do you want to scare off every living thing?"

Ducky had been complaining about the heat all morning.

"I don't understand why we couldn't have come in at night, when it's cooler," Ducky mumbled under his breath. He pulled a hip flask from his belt and took a swig.

"Because that's a madman's game, Duke Richard," Eduardo whispered, sidling up next to him. "They'd have you dead and up a tree without you ever having heard or seen them."

I raised my brows in agreement. The jungle was even more dangerous at night. By stalking panthers in the early morning, we hoped to find one tired after a night of hunting. I waited as Eduardo completed a small circuit around us, Basira keeping her eyes ahead. I didn't mention that he didn't take such precautions when it was a group of us native Bone Portis. The fact that he'd barely made any jokes this morning told me how nervous he was with Ducky as his charge. Eduardo was rarely without a broad, bright smile, but this morning the best he'd done was smirk.

Eduardo finally nodded to me and said, "Lady Calandra."

With this signal, I moved ahead. We'd known each other so long, words were often unnecessary between us, doubly so when hunting. I did my own visual sweep of the area. Not that I didn't trust Eduardo—quite the contrary—but I meant to keep my skills sharp, and more pairs of eyes are always better than one in that verdant, dangerously beautiful place.

Finding tracks in the soft, loamy soil was easy. Following them offered the real challenge. Moving quietly through heavy underbrush without spooking lethally venomous snakes—such as spearheads, which hid both on the ground and in trees—was like walking on the edge of a knife. Basira led the way. She was almost snakelike herself, in all the best ways, and therefore sharp enough to avoid them. Eduardo took up the rear behind me, while Ducky did his best to copy Basira's graceful path through the jungle. He looked more like a drunken capybara.

When Basira stopped and held out her hand, I assumed she'd spotted our prey. The slow tilt of her head a moment later, however, changed my mind. I crept forward to see what held her attention. Eduardo stuck close like a guardian shadow.

"Sir, my lady," he said, addressing Ducky and me in order of rank. "Be cautious."

I succeeded in smothering a teasing smile, wondering whether it would have been more fun to rib Eduardo for his mothering or Ducky for being mothered. Granted, the rolling hills of the Southern Plains where Ducky lived and had done most of his hunting were vastly different from our jungle; the man had faced off against more than one furious bear! Then again, I couldn't blame Eduardo for fretting over how we might explain it if Ducky got eaten.

When I drew even with Basira, she extended her arm with the grace of a dancer and pointed to a large strangler fig. All across the ground fluttered small sulfur-cloud butterflies. These were not strange, as they often congregated en masse wherever they found food. Within the maze of the strangler fig's exposed roots, however, tiny lights flashed and danced like oversized dust motes in sunlight. The light was dim here, however. The luminescence came from the things themselves, whatever they were.

I took a step forward. Eduardo whispered protests behind me as Ducky moved to follow, his foot crunching down loudly on leaf litter and twigs beneath us. The lights beyond flashed together as a high-pitched cry—like a tiny, laughing squeal—rang out, and they shot for us.

"Bugger all!" bellowed Ducky. "They're Fae!"

Basira swore and raised her machete, and I briefly wondered what on earth she planned to do with it.

"Be still! Be still!" I hissed, laying my hands on Basira and Ducky, who were both primed to fight.

Eduardo fell in line with me. The other two followed suit, but I felt their muscles twitching beneath their skin. I kept my eyes glued to the tiny, glittering horde, which wobbled and flashed erratically as it made its way towards us. The speed of the Faes' initial takeoff had dropped sharply as the cloud listed to the side. It looked as if the group was fighting with itself as to which direction to go.

"My lady," Eduardo breathed, watching the Fae approach, "what are we doing?"

"Making ourselves uninteresting," I explained. "Cover your ears and close your noses. Then don't move. If they want to take something, let them have it."

"I hope you're not making this up as you go." Ducky peered at me from the side of his eyes as he scrunched up his face, closing off his nostrils.

"Fae are like miniature, dangerous toddlers," I recited, my voice nasally as I matched my expression to Ducky's. "The best method for dealing with them is to bore them."

I could practically hear Basira roll her eyes. I couldn't see her, but her voice told me she, too, had followed my directions. "That's from another one of your books, isn't it, Cali?"

"It's in my bag," I admitted.

"Why would you bring a book on a hunting trip?! When…"

She let her voice trail off as the swarm of Fae reached us. Closer now, I could make out the Faes' individual forms. Each one stood about half the height of my thumb. They resembled humans in that they had two arms, two legs, and a head, but that was where the similarity ended. Each bore four tiny, diaphanous wings and two feathery antennae. Their bodies were androgynous, their fingers and toes long and pointed, and each gave off a soft white glow.

We all clamped our mouths shut and scrunched our faces harder, pressing our hands tightly over our ears. The Fae tittered and chirped, wobbling through the air around us. I ran through scenarios in my head. Best case, they'd get bored and move on. Worst case, they'd get angry and set fire to the jungle around us. Fae possessed various elemental abilities, and I sincerely hoped these weren't feeling particularly petulant today.

Fae are sharp-eyed and excellent flyers, I recalled from the book. Seeing them totter and lurch back and forth around us made me nervous. If the book had been wrong about that, what else might it have gotten wrong? The author had observed them in open areas. Maybe these had different habits.

Wait a second. Hadn't the author also said Fae don't inhabit the jungle because there were too many predators? I knew we Bone Portis rarely came across the little creatures, but I hadn't put together the reasons for it until I'd read that passage. If that was true, why were these here? I swallowed hard as I suddenly suspected everything in it had been tripe.

The Fae pulled at my hair, which I'd twisted around and piled on top of my head to keep off my neck. They bounced and swam through Eduardo's, which was cut short but very thick. Basira's hair was braided tightly against her scalp, so the Fae only played with the loose end, swinging it this way and that.

I heard Ducky make a soft choking noise next to me, and I slid my eyes to see three Fae playing around his nose. They pulled at the tiny hairs sticking out of his nostrils, and more played with the wiry strands of his beard. I suddenly wondered how much happier his face might be in the heat if he'd shaved the thing off. Not that he ever would; he'd had a full beard at least my entire life. He looked back at me, panic in his eyes. I saw the moment he passed the point of no return. His nose wrinkled, his throat tightened, and he sneezed.

The Fae playing around his face flew back, spinning end over end through the air, their tiny gossamer wings desperately flapping against the gust. We all stiffened, waiting for their next move. One of the Fae, upright and hovering again, shook its teeny head. Then what I can only guess was laughter erupted from its mouth. The others joined in, and I worried it might be the Fae version of an evil cackle.

They flew back at Ducky's face, pulling at him and giggling. My uncle's composure broke, and he swatted them away, cursing and spinning in his spot. The entire horde flew at him, and I waved my hands at them, trying to distract them from their new toy. Basira and Eduardo copied me, and within moments the entire flock of Fae were buzzing frenetically all around us, squealing in their tiny voices.

"Retreat!" Ducky called, and he took off in the wrong direction towards the strangler fig.

"Wrong way!" I shouted, following him. "Ducky! Wrong way!"

True to their name, billows of the sulfur-cloud butterflies flew up from the ground in a confusion of panic and wings. As I pursued Ducky, I stepped on soft, squishy things, which made disgusting squelching noises beneath my feet. Warm, sickly sweet-smelling juice and goo oozed into my sandals and slipped between my toes.

Ducky slipped mid-stride and landed with a heavy *oof!* onto his back, sending up more clouds of the butterflies. As I stooped to help him up, I heard Basira and Eduardo calling after us and swearing at all the flying creatures. Those Fae closest to Ducky stopped in their airborne tracks and chittered in a way I could only interpret as more laughter, especially as they doubled over and leaned on one another for support.

"What the blazes am I lying in?" Ducky demanded. He looked with disgust at his hand, which was covered in the same sticky slime collecting in my sandals.

I looked to the ground and answered with growing realization: "Figs."

Rotting figs, to be exact. They were *everywhere*! That explained the swarms of butterflies. And I suspected the Fae, wherever they had come from, couldn't resist the sweet, sticky fruits lying thick upon the ground and ready for the taking. I felt tiny bodies smack into the back of my head and turned to see a few Fae unsteadily catch themselves midair. Another came hurtling towards me and slammed into my forehead, sticking there. It was like being hit with a soggy leaf.

"They're drunk!" I called back to Basira and Eduardo.

I turned back to Ducky, who had levered himself into a kneeling position.

"You've got a bit of... uh." He motioned to my forehead where the Fae was still stuck.

Thankfully, the little creature was already hard at work peeling its sticky little body off my skin. I didn't want to risk hurting it, especially with so many others of its kind around. Once free, I watched as it made odd gestures towards me. The sharp, wild gesticulations made me think it was angry and trying to use its magic against me.

"Do you suppose alcohol inhibits their powers somehow?" I asked Ducky, peering more closely at the Fae.

Ducky stood and took me by the arm, lifting me to my feet. "Not really the time, Cali."

The Fae continued to harass us, pulling our hair, grabbing our ears, and reaching into our noses. One even flew into Basira's mouth, which she spit out, sending it shooting at Eduardo's chest.

"You said they're drunk?" Ducky yelled through the swarm.

I opened my mouth to reply, but spotted a Fae heading straight for it, so I pressed my lips together and nodded so hard I thought I might pull a muscle. Ducky nodded back and pulled his flask from his belt. Untwisting the cap, he waved it around and tromped back towards the strangler fig, waving Fae and butterflies out of his path with the same gusto Basira had when she cut away leaves with her machete. Reaching the tree, he bent over a little well several of the twisting roots had created.

"Come and get it, you rotten little buggers!" Ducky called, pouring the contents of his flask into the well.

Within moments, the Fae converged on the treat, dancing beneath the tawny stream and trying to climb inside the flask before being washed back out like a spider in a drainpipe. Ducky shook off the last hanger-on and screwed the lid closed again. Butterflies still clouded all around us, but the Fae were now single-mindedly focused on the liquor pool.

"I hope you drown," Ducky grumbled, glowering at the amassed Fae.

I grabbed his arm, and we trudged back the way we came, sticky, sweaty, and empty-handed.

"Cali," Ducky said as we emerged into full sunlight, a sure sign we were out of the jungle and nearing civilization again.

"Yes, Uncle Ducky?" I sighed.

"I'll make you a deal. You ever bag a panther, let me put it in my trophy hall and I promise I'll show it to everyone who comes through and tell them my favorite niece, the greatest hunter of all time, fought the Green Dragon for it."

I chuckled. "Deal."

Basira looked back at me and asked, "Ocean?"

"Stars, yes!"

"What's this now?" Ducky asked.

Edaurdo looked back at him and explained, "We're going to go cool off in the bay. Would you like to join us, Duke Richard?"

"Heavens, no! Not when there's perfectly good running water back at Cali's family estate. If anyone needs me, don't bother."

"You're going to crash their luncheon," I told him.

Ducky pointed to his scowling countenance and asked, "Does this look like a face that cares?" He then grinned and added, "Besides, I like to make an entrance."

"Suit yourself." I laughed, running off with Basira.

Despite my uncle's protests, Eduardo escorted Ducky back to my family's overwater residence. He agreed to meet Basira and I in one of our favorite swimming spots afterward, and Ducky shook his head at the lot of us.

THE DEATH-SPEAKER

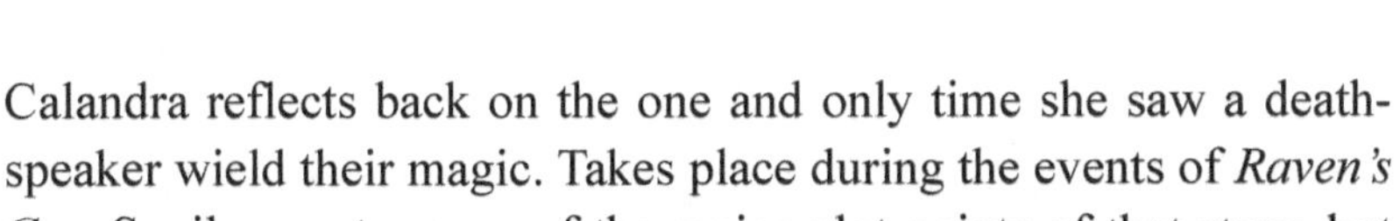

Calandra reflects back on the one and only time she saw a death-speaker wield their magic. Takes place during the events of *Raven's Cry*. Spoilers as to some of the major plot points of that story, but to be honest, this story is mostly for the spooky vibes.

~~~

Water dripped from somewhere nearby, though the ancient stone walls of the room multiplied the sound and threw it back and forth… back and forth. The room was dim too; naught but a few scant tapers provided the only illumination around us now.

We were somewhere deep beneath the manor, though I didn't know this area. It certainly wasn't for storing root vegetables and the like. I was in my raven form, and though I'd been forced to wear a hood most of the way down from my prison, I could feel that sunset was still hours off.

Previously, before we'd descended into these depths, Nicodemus had removed my hood just before we'd joined the rest of our party, which had gathered at the top of a stone staircase, spiraling downward. The way down had glowed almost pitch-
~~~

black, as if the darkness of the stairway consumed whatever light it could reach. I wasn't familiar with the landing area we had gathered at either, and I'd wondered how many secret nooks and crannies my uncle's old manor hid.

Nicodemus had me tied securely to his wrist, of course, but nevertheless I was on the lookout for an escape. I may have once mentioned that he never failed to have me with him during especially aggrandizing daytime events. Thus, the feeling of heavy anticipation from the other waiting attendees didn't surprise me.

There were about twenty or so people in our gathering—mostly magi, but a few non-magical nobles as well, given their dress. They had spoken in hushed tones to one another as we'd waited at the top of the stairs in that desolate, hidden place.

"Do you suppose it will require a sacrifice?" asked a noblewoman with a veiled, double-coned sort of headdress. She'd pronounced *sacrifice* like the word itself might be magic. Of course, her tone had also communicated that, as is the way with the privileged and wealthy, she feared not a whit for her own safety, sacrifice being required or no.

A sour-faced magus had asked one of his cohorts, "What's taking so long? There's a very slim window of time during which the ritual can be performed, you know."

Two other nobles, a young man and an older woman who looked like she might be his direct relative of some kind, had conferred quietly with Nicodemus near the back of the group.

"What if they can't, you know, do it?" asked the man. He had looked afraid, though I couldn't guess of what. And he'd clearly been reticent to speak aloud what *it* actually was.

His companion had shot a glare at Nicodemus and snipped, "Then we'll get our money back, won't we?"

Nicodemus' current host-body was a tall, handsome gent just shy of his forties. In response to the woman's comment, he had given a smile that would appear utterly charming to anyone who didn't know what a snake he was. Which, I assumed, meant the entire crowd.

"Fear not, good lady," he'd crooned. "The death-speakers know their business well."

The woman sniffed, but I saw her blush a little as a smile whispered across her pinched mouth. I would have rolled my eyes if ravens had that ability.

Eventually, a smell like wet earth began to waft towards us. Up from the cellars below. I'd barely had time to wonder why when a figure appeared out of the engulfing darkness—a pale young man dressed in the synod's servant garb. Dark hollows stood out from under his eyes, and he was covered in what could only be freshly turned soil. He had looked blankly at our group gathered before him.

"This way, please," was all he'd said before turning and leading the way downstairs.

Members of the party exchanged glances. Someone had giggled stupidly, like this was some kind of game. Someone else went pale. We followed the servant, Nicodemus leading. As we'd made our way down, down, down and around the spiral staircase, into the depths of the manor, Nicodemus began to give instructions in an affectedly weighty tone.

"I trust you all have followed my instructions to leave any and all mirrors behind. Even a small handheld one can ruin the ritual."

He'd looked back over his followers, which surprised me. This wasn't for show. Having known him for so many years, I could tell he was genuinely scanning for contraband.

When he'd been satisfied, he'd added, "Likewise, no one is to conjure any additional light."

The list of rules went on. No one was to touch the death-speaker and no one but he, Nicodemus, was permitted to address it. No one but the death-speaker must speak the name of the dead. And no matter what anyone saw or heard or felt or smelled, they were to remain calm and in place.

Death-speakers were extremely rare. And those few that existed kept to themselves, away from the rest of the magi community. I had never seen one, despite all my years being trapped at the synod. Rumors surrounded their existence, each one more unbelievable than the next.

They were not actually human, but born of the dead themselves, formed by magic and moonlight, crawling out from chest cavities like giant worms.

They could only perform their magic via blood sacrifices from unwilling souls.

They could speak directly to the Dritch, and the Dritch spoke back.

When we'd finally arrived at the end of our journey into the cellars' depths, we'd gathered into the large, dim room with the few candle tapers and nearby dripping water.

There was space enough for every member of our party to spread out if they wished, but they huddled close to one another instead. The servant lad stood silently behind us, next to the door. An aura of… wrongness filled the place. It felt cloying and sticky. I fluttered my wings to try and shake off the feeling, and Nicodemus gripped my foot with a thumb in warning.

He hissed close to my head. "Behave, now, or I might feed you to the death-speaker. I hear they take their meals raw and still living."

Whether or not that was true of the death-speakers, I didn't doubt he would try. Given everything else he'd subjected me to.

"I prefer pigs, if you're offering." The voice was low, rasping, like bones rubbing and clicking together. And it seemed to fill the entire room.

Even Nicodemus jumped as it wreathed its way around us. A noise like wind through dry leaves followed the statement, and it took me a moment to realize the sound was that of laughter.

In a corner, shrouded in both darkness and black, tattered robes, a hooded figure shuddered, not unlike the candle flames around us. A long black beaked mask stuck out from under the hood. The room's wan light barely limned the figure, but I saw all too well as it raised a black-gloved hand and pointed at Nicodemus.

"You are the Grand Magus, I assume?" it asked.

How could the death-speaker not know? Didn't all magi answer to him? Wouldn't any of them give their right arm to meet him?

"I am," Nicodemus replied. And though his answer was confident, I felt him shake ever so slightly.

The death-speaker took in a rattling breath. "Then let us begin. There is little time. Where are the bereaved?"

The older woman and her young companion stepped forward, the woman with far more self-assurance than the man.

"We are here. The deceased's sister and son."

The death-speaker extended its hands. "I will need your names."

The young man's eyes widened. He looked to his aunt and began shaking his head. I couldn't blame him. It sounded for all the world as if the death-speaker was actually going to take their names from them. His aunt, however, shook him from where he was gripping her arm and replied in a tone loud enough to make their names echo off the stone walls.

"Baroness Liana Poppleton. And this—" She yanked her nephew forward. "—is Lord Rhett Poppleton."

"Very good." The death-speaker kept its hands extended. "Each of you, take one of my hands. The rest of you…"

If a silent crowd could fall into something beyond silence, the rest of our party did.

"The rest of you, form a circle around the body. Iah, close the door."

The body? As the sound of the servant pulling the door closed behind us echoed, I looked but failed to see anything for a long moment. Then, as if by the death-speaker's will, I saw it there. A body, an old man, covered in splotches of dark soil. At least, I hoped it was soil. It lay dressed in the fine garments of nobility, wrinkled now and spoiled by stains. The body looked fresh, as if it hadn't been dead for more than a few hours. And it was curled in a ball on the stone floor of the room. Or rather, no…

I reared back, and this time Nicodemus didn't scold me. The hands and feet of the body had been tied. Why would someone need to tie up a corpse?!

Nicodemus' eyes were on the body. I'd seen that sort of hunger in his eyes before. Where this horrific tableau revolted me, he leaned towards it. He wanted the knowledge it offered. He stepped towards the deceased, extended his free hand towards it. And then… could no longer progress forward. I could feel him strain against some unseen force. That same dry-leaves-and-wind sound from before rattled from the corner; the death-speaker was laughing again.

"This body is under my protection," it said.

Nicodemus looked at the death-speaker, eyes alight with the dark fire I knew all too well.

"How? How do you do what you do?"

The beaked mask shook slowly back and forth. "This is not your gift, therefore the lore is not for you to know, Grand Magus."

Nicodemus grinned, but it was feral and threatening. "And if I —"

The death-speaker cut him off not with a word, but a noise. A chattering noise growing from its throat like the sound of beetle carapaces and segmented legs. The noise grew and grew until the walls seemed to shake with it. I was trembling and I didn't care who saw. That sound, it was like a physical sensation, like insects crawling all over my body. I could see the others in the group felt the same. They cried out and squirmed and slapped at their arms and legs. The death-speaker had released Rhett's and Liana's hands and was instead gripping the arms of the chair it sat in. Rhett scuttled to the far side of the room. Meanwhile, Liana held her ground, but looked as if she was regretting every decision she'd ever made. The feeling of wrongness grew in the room while the noise reverberated, and I realized that disturbed miasma was emanating off the death-speaker itself. One of our group was even pulling at the handle of the closed door, which refused to move.

Finally, mercifully, the noise died, and with it the horribly clawing, itchy feeling.

The death-speaker looked around the room at our frightened party. "Calm yourselves. It is for your protection that I wield my power so freely."

The group quieted, though it was clear they only complied out of fear. Nicodemus' muscles were tense beneath my feet, but he said nothing.

"If I did not suffer for my power, then all of you would."

What does that mean? I couldn't help thinking.

But the death-speaker was already moving us on. It instructed us again to join hands around the body lying on the floor. Rhett took some corralling by his aunt, and with much trembling, the others followed suit.

"Good," the death-speaker said at last. "Now, remain still and silent as the dead. We must trick the deceased. He must not know he's returning to the land of the living." A feeling of apprehension and questioning rolled through the room then, to which the death-speaker said, "Fear not. I have taken all necessary precautions to protect us."

Being tethered to Nicodemus, I could do nothing but perch on his wrist and wait. Did those protections extend to birds not actually taking part in the ritual? I was suddenly, and perversely, pleased the corpse was tied up.

The death-speaker took in another rattling breath. And then

began, "Rutherford Poppleton."

Again, its voice echoed off the walls, but this time was different. This time, it became a sustained whisper, filling the room until it was a susurration of power. The echoes were the death-speaker's magic at work, though I couldn't guess its purpose.

The death-speaker must have tightened its grip on Rhett and Liana's hands, because the former tensed, looking as if he wanted to jerk away. A pained look overtook Rhett's face, while Liana began to grit her teeth.

"As still and silent as the dead," the death-speaker had said. Our party was surprisingly successful, given their fear. The death-speaker, however…

It hunched forward, shaking and drawing in deep, gasping breaths. Its back heaved harder and harder, until I was afraid it might actually be having a fit of some sort. And then, in a moment, it stilled. The noise dropped away to pure silence. It was as if time had frozen.

Then, without warning, the death-speaker reared, slamming its spine against the back of the chair, squeezing the baroness and young lord's hands so hard they both cried out in pain. Rhett sank to one knee, still gripping the hand on his other side. The death-speaker's head flew backwards, and the noise that erupted from its throat was nothing of this world.

A squeal, the sound of metal tearing, and a thousand fleshy wings beating themselves to death.

Through a slit in the death-speaker's hood, I saw a sliver of the skin at its throat. The flesh was desiccated, pulled taught across the lower jaw and voice box. It looked deeply scarred too, though it was difficult to make out, for a light was building behind the thin, stretched skin. Behind the death-speaker's larynx, an orb of light grew and then pushed outward, as if extruding itself through cracks in the flesh. When it emerged, the death-speaker let out an audible, crackling sigh. The sphere of light seemed to look around at us, though it had no discernible eyes, before landing its strange gaze onto the body.

In a split second, the death-speaker's head snapped back up. The sphere shot towards the corpse on the ground. A circle of symbols lit up beneath our feet, throwing a sickly, brownish-red light around the room. Stars, was the summoning circle drawn in… in blood?

The sphere disappeared inside the corpse and then seemed to explode as light shot out from the eyes.

And the mouth, as it gaped open wide.

People cried out and jumped back, but the death-speaker's voice was there. "Remain linked. The circle must not be broken." Whether it was aloud or in our heads, I couldn't tell, but the people listened. It might have only been out of a deep sense of self-preservation, but everyone held fast to their neighbors' hands.

We watched in dumbstruck terror as the body lifted its head, its movements jerky, like a broken marionette.

The corpse—Rutherford Poppleton, I assumed—tried to stretch out and, failing that, looked down to his bound hands and feet. From his position on the floor, he leveled an angry glare at our group.

"Rutherford," said the death-speaker in a tone that sounded more like a mother consoling a child. "Rutherford, forgive our deceit, but your loved ones have a great need, one only you can address."

Rutherford jerked his head up towards the death-speaker, stretching farther than what would be comfortable for a living person.

"My loved ones?" he asked. His voice was surprisingly smooth for having come from a dead body. I guessed it was similar to how he'd sounded in life.

The death-speaker looked to Baroness Liana and nodded. She looked unabashedly apprehensive now, but crouched low and tried to mimic the death-speaker's soothing tone.

"That's right. We're here, Liana and Rhett. Say hello, Rhett."

"H-hello, Father," Rhett managed to stammer out.

Rutherford looked from his sister to his son and back again, his neck still craning at an angle I was worried would snap sinews.

"I'm dead," Rutherford said at last. His eyes were clear, and I saw something like understanding dawn in them. "I died."

"Yes," Liana said. "This afternoon, you passed. Quietly, in your study."

"I was writing," he replied thoughtfully. "And drinking."

Rhett managed a tremulous smile. "That's right. Your favorite port. Do you… Do you remember what you were writing?"

"I was getting my affairs in order, at the advice of… of my…" And then Rutherford began to laugh. It was not a nice laugh either. "That charlatan you were bedding. Did you really think I was stupid enough to fall for that little act you two put on?"

Liana's face, already tinged red by the summoning circle, twisted into a snarl. "You didn't know anything. There's nothing to know. I…"

"I did," Rutherford crowed through his laughter, talking over Liana. "I knew the whole time. I only pretended to string you along. Like an idiot cat with a piece of yarn."

Liana stood again, gripping the other person's hand in hers so tightly that her knuckles lightened in the dirty red light. "Even in death, you're a miserable, miserable cretin. Do you know that, Rutherford?"

Her brother only cackled in response, and the light emanating from his eyes and mouth grew brighter at her mention of his name.

Meanwhile, Rhett's eyes flicked between his aunt and his father. "But, Father, you have… done it, haven't you? Gotten your affairs in order?"

Rutherford laughed harder, so hard his body was racked with coughs. The light shining out of his eyes and mouth juddered. I looked to the death-speaker, but it only sat silently, face hidden behind its mask.

The light steadied as the cough subsided, and the gathered party remained still, watching this disaster unfold, but I could feel their attention focus tightly on the forthcoming answer.

"No," Rutherford chuckled at last. "I never intended to. You pack of backbiters can tear yourself to shreds fighting over my estate."

Rhett's eyes widened in panic. "No, Father, you can't mean that! You—"

"I can do what I like," Rutherford snapped. "Now more than ever. Perhaps if you hadn't been such a disappointment, I might have considered. But you, sniveling little milksop that you are? Pah! Good luck."

Now Rhett's face twisted, and he sneered, "I'm glad I poisoned your drink. How's that for being a milksop?"

Rutherford gave a derisive snort. "Poison? That's a coward's murder weapon. Didn't even have the balls to bludgeon me properly."

Rhett's lips pulled back into a snarl, and he leapt for Rutherford's corpse. The moment the circle broke, the light went out inside of Rutherford, and the sphere flew out from his chest. It circled Rhett as the death-speaker ordered the young lord to retake his place, but Rhett was too busy trying to catch the sphere to listen. He grabbed at it like a child clumsily pursuing a damselfly. The death-speaker had just begun to rise from its seat when the light zipped around the back of Rhett again, and this time flew straight at him.

Rutherford's light flew through Rhett's shoulder and out the other side. The sound of bones cracking and flesh ripping splintered through the room as the light flashed momentarily, and then dimmed to less than half its former brightness. Rhett screamed in pain and grabbed his injured shoulder, which now hung lifeless at his side. Blood was already beginning to seep through the fine velvet of Rhett's sleeve.

"Hold." The word echoed through the room, stopping us all in whatever panicked tracks we might have been just about to make. That had been the death-speaker. From behind the dimmed light sphere, it extended its gloved hands and carefully cupped the sphere between them. "No more mischief from you, please." Again, its voice had changed to one, clicking and rasping though it was, full of care.

"Mischief?" snarled Rhett. "Mischief?! He broke my bloody arm!"

"You are lucky he didn't do worse. Because he could have. And what law would have punished him?"

"You!" Rhett replied. "You could have."

"Do not presume to tell me my business, boy!"

The insult cracked like a whip in that large, glowing stone room. We all watched with rapt attention for what would happen next. Even Liana looked keen, though given what we'd heard I suspected she cared little for her nephew's fate now that the truth was out.

"We do not control the dead. We are their guardians, and you…" The death-speaker turned its gaze onto Liana now too. "And you will consider yourselves fortunate nothing worse befell you here today, given your transgressions."

I wondered what worse things were possible, and suspected the death-speaker itself had the ability to enact some of them.

It looked back down at the glowing orb in its hands. "Begone, all of you. I must shepherd this one home before it is too weak to make the journey."

The door behind us creaked open, and Iah, the servant lad from before, entered to escort us out. Nicodemus said nothing as we left, but he waited for everyone else to go in order to follow at the back. I turned as we were making our way out, just in time to catch a glimpse of the death-speaker tipping its mask up, just far enough to reveal its mouth.

The lips were thin and stretched and pale. It opened them wide, revealing teeth sharpened down to points. Its tongue, purple and rotted, like that of a corpse, flicked out, and the death-speaker noiselessly swallowed the sphere.

I never saw another death-speaker after that. Never in my time, throughout the adventures I would later have, did I hear of them again. Not beyond the usual rumors anyway. I can only assume they continued to be as reclusive as ever, if not more so after that debacle. I have seen that magic is not dead, though, not entirely. And I cannot help but wonder if there aren't a few death-speakers still out there… somewhere.

Monsters Inside

A look into Felicia and Lowell's past. Spoilers for their backstory.

~~

Part 1

Thank the stars it was summer. Escaping a mob frothing at the mouth from fear would have been impossible in the harsh Duskwood winter. Pins and needles sparked in Felicia's legs while she and Lowell hunched down in the hollow of a dead tree. In the onyx sky above, the moon shone bright as a pearl. It threw down harsh planes of light, which the twins'd had to avoid while they fled. Felicia looked down at Lowell. In the gloom of their hiding place, she could just see the sheen of tears on his face. They dribbled out from beneath the masked side of his face and flowed freely from the uncovered half. In truth, she wanted to cry too. The urge became almost irrepressible when thoughts of her parents snuck back to the forefront of her mind. Though she'd only just turned eight, she'd had lots of practice suppressing her tears. She pushed the temptation away again. Now wasn't the time. Not until they were away from Timbergreen, their village, and the sound of the villagers searching for them had faded into silence. And she needed to be strong for Lowell.

Felicia scowled up at the sky, cursing the moon. If it weren't for that cold celestial matron, they might have been able to keep moving. As shouts echoed towards them from farther off in the forest, she cursed her fellow villagers too. She cursed the pigs that had fallen ill, which had spread their sickness to the people. She cursed the heavy rains that had come before, which had drowned a good portion of crops.

Lowell shifted against her, sharpening the pins and needles in Felicia's legs to barbs. He let out a little whimper. She bit her lip and tensed against the pain, pointing her thoughts towards escape and success. He hiccupped softly and shifted again. Lowell's false leg—barely more than a couple of sticks trussed together—stuck out ahead of him like a signpost. At least the retired axe handle it was made from still mostly resembled an ordinary branch, despite its years of service.

The memory of seeing their father's own axe turned on him gusted to the front of Felicia's mind. A sob surged up her throat. She barely choked it back down, though a few tears eked from her eyes. Lowell hid his face in her shoulder and cried harder. Their father's sacrifice had given their mother enough time to push the twins out the back door of their little cottage and towards the bloody sunset.

"Take care of your brother," she'd said, just before dropping a hurried kiss onto each of their heads. "I love you. Now go!"

Then she'd slammed the door shut. Felicia had heard the bolt shoot home. She'd almost tried to pull it open again anyway when a *bang!* thundered from within—the sound of an inside door being kicked open and slamming against the wall.

"There's no need for this," came their mother's muffled voice from within. Always a peacemaker to the end, even though she too had seen their fellow villagers sink the blade of Father's favored tool into his head. Mother tried sensibility again. Felicia and Lowell had stood frozen during those horrendous seconds. "Please, don't!" The clang of metal against metal. Felicia imagined their mother had tried using one of the iron kitchen tools to defend herself. A cry, cut short. And a definitive thump.

"Take her to the village center," growled a voice within. Felicia thought she recognized it as one of their neighbors. A man who'd chopped timber by their father's side for years, though she couldn't be certain. "The boys are settin' up a stake there. Tie her up. We'll burn her good."

"Shouldn't we wait until she wakes up?" asked another voice. This one, Felicia didn't know.

"Better to do it while she's out. Can't use her magic that way. Now be quick."

The last spark of hope had sputtered out in Felicia then. Her mother's final directive screamed in her mind. Felicia tugged at her twin brother, whose eyes were pinned to the closed door.

She tugged harder and said, "We hafta run!"

Fear climbed up her throat, knowing running would be brutally difficult for Lowell. Pushing past pity, she yanked on his arm, nearly toppling him. She steadied Lowell and ushered him forward while his eyes strayed back to the door.

"Run! Or we're gonna die." Felicia hated herself for the fear that seeped into Lowell's gaze. Still, he finally looked forward, so she said it again. That got him moving, though he winced with every uneven stride.

They'd hobbled together through the woods as the lowering sun watched their progress. Felicia felt it was deliberately taking its time, either to help the villagers in their search or to watch the twins' inevitable demise. Less than a half hour later, they hadn't made enough progress to escape the tortured screams echoing across the trees. Nor were they able to outrun the haze of smoke that followed not long after.

A few hours later, Lowell was grimacing with every step. Tears ran from his eyes, but he never complained. That was when they'd found their hiding spot. Felicia had hoped the people of Timbergreen would be satisfied with two deaths on their hands. The distant sound of a search party hounded the twins, however.

Tucked in the tree hollow, Lowell cried harder. Felicia regretted thinking on the horrors of the last few hours. She hugged him, and his sobs muffled into her shoulder. Sweat prickled on Felicia's forehead. Summers this far north were mild but a touch humid. And though she tended to "run hot," as her mother had always phrased it, neither were the reason for Felicia's perspiration. Indecision and fear whipped her heart into a gallop. Perhaps they should try to find a good tree to climb while they could. Though neither of the twins was particularly athletic, all lumber-town children learned to climb trees shortly after walking. Timbergreen had more cats than dogs, and the few dogs around were for pig herding. Thank heavens the village didn't boast any great hunters, but some still had decent tracking skills. Felicia risked peeking her head out to look at the sky. A wispy set of clouds drifted languidly towards the moon, still haughtily high in the sky. When they covered her shining face, they'd move.

Felicia readied herself and encouraged Lowell to do the same. At least the strange connection they shared also made stealthy communication easier. They'd need to move the moment the clouds provided them some measure of safe passage. Lowell nodded without a word having to be said.

Morning was hardly kinder. Though Felicia and Lowell had found good concealment in summer's fulsome leaf cover, sleep evaded them both. The sounds of fear-fueled bloodlust had persisted until an hour or so before dawn. They'd used the last dregs of night's shelter to make what progress they could, but the sun rose all too soon. It blared its brightness down with all the fervor of an Old World Inquisitor searching for rebellious Lamplighters. Cries more distant but no less angry followed the sun's appearance.

The earth took pity where the sky persecuted. The twins soon found a karstic spring from which to drink. Fissures and small caves dotted a nearby ridge. Lowell found some blackberry bushes, dandelions, and even some chanterelles. Their mother had long ago taught them to identify the hearty mushrooms from poisonous doppelgängers. He also found a nest of four eggs but only took three and apologized to the bird family. Meanwhile, Felicia stabbed at some fish in a shallow end of the spring with a rudimentary spear Lowell had fashioned from a stick, a rock, and a bit of sacrificed clothing. She failed with the fish but managed to kill a fat frog. It tasted vile but eased the pangs in their bellies. She also scared off a wildcat just after it had caught a fish for itself, which she took for herself and Lowell.

For the first day, the two focused on rest and recuperation. The tasks of survival provided a distraction from recent memories. They spoke little, and most of what was said came from Lowell. He spun fanciful musings about Old World Kelpies and Fae. Where those creatures, if they weren't extinct, might make their homes nearby and what Lowell would do if he ran into one. Felicia's heart warmed at her brother's attempt to divert her attention from their circumstances. After the second day, however, the stories faded into silence. Even though she couldn't read him the way he could her, Felicia knew what Lowell must be thinking.

"We hafta move on," she said during their second night.

They sat before a meager dinner of dandelion leaves and bulrush. The roots of the latter were nicer when roasted, but they didn't want to risk lighting a fire unless absolutely necessary.

"I know," was Lowell's only response.

"Tomorrow."

Lowell poked their dinner with a stick and said, "Yeah."

Felicia closed her eyes and forced herself to think of nothing. It resulted in her simply repeating, *don't think*, over and over in her mind, but it did the job.

Lowell dipped his head. "I don't mean to hear you."

"I know you don't," Felicia replied.

Quiet stretched between them before Lowell said, "You don't hafta protect me."

Felicia gave him a sad smile. She'd always protected him. That certainly wasn't about to change. He didn't address that line of thought. Instead, he returned them to their previous discussion.

"Where'll we go?"

Felicia had been giving that subject a lot of thought, though she'd tried to do so out of Lowell's… hearing, for lack of a better word. Lowell gave no indication whether she'd been successful. It didn't seem fair that the connection between them only went one way. Then again, her own ability extended to everyone *except* Lowell, so perhaps that was a sort of balance.

"The seaside," Felicia said, turning her thoughts back to the issue at hand.

Lowell smiled weakly. "Mama and Papa always wanted to visit the seaside."

Felicia nodded, tried to smile back, and crumpled. The last two days cascaded down on her as heavy as the rock walls around them. She wrapped her arms around her knees and hid her face. Lowell pulled her close and wrapped the gnarled fingers at the end of his bad arm around her shoulder. He cried with her and, just for a little while, they allowed themselves to be the orphaned, grieving eight-year-olds they truly were.

☠

The trip to the coast went easier than expected. Lowell and Felicia didn't know whether they'd simply been very lucky or if the people of Timbergreen had given up finding them. The most frightening part had been visiting another village in order to steal supplies. Lowell had provided a distraction while Felicia took what bits they needed—fishing line, hooks, dried meat—and hid them under her clothes. They traveled mostly dusk through dawn, resting during the day, and arrived at the seaside dirty but in better shape than they could have hoped for.

The town of Halibut Harbor had established itself as a haven for all manner of tourist activities. No zeppelins graced its boundaries, but gleaming steam engines belching smoke arrived daily to deliver and take away both people and goods. Middle-class holidaymakers brought in the most money. Dressed in bathing costumes, they swam and splashed in a little cove where boats were not permitted. The boardwalk offered shopping, restaurants and cafés covered every type of cuisine, and steamboat tours took sightseers out to view nature's bounty from the comfort of decks and cabins.

A sign at the local pier crowed, *Newly built! Beats Brineton's Quixotic Quay by over thirty feet!* It offered games of both chance and skill all along its length, as well as booths offering taffy and fudge and other seaside treats. As clock towers didn't really fit on piers, the designers had instead installed a wooden waterless facsimile of a fountain. On the hour every hour, clockwork fish and gulls emerged to gambol through their dry playground. Petrolsene lamps lit the pier long into the night, throwing shards of light down through the boards to Felicia and Lowell's first hiding place beneath. Unfortunately, as they both quickly learned, beneath the pier also served as a place for employees of the Tawdry Tuna to pick up extra clients. Not to mention other clandestine meetings. The twins quickly moved on and found a sheltered spot in the crawl space beneath a shop. They made sure to only go in after night had fallen and leave before sunrise, always on the lookout for witnesses.

While the earth had been kind and the sky cruel, the sea seemed merely capricious. Neither Felicia nor Lowell were good swimmers, and she forbade him from going in past his knee. She, however, was determined to improve. The ocean offered all manner of food, but the glut of it lay in deeper waters. Even just the kelp forests offered greater abundance than they'd ever known. Felicia practiced around the leeside of a rocky outcropping, tied to a rock with a pilfered length of rope. Lowell did the same when she was gone. When the tide was low, they used that same outcropping to cook food, though they kept their fires small.

Halibut Harbor was rarely quiet. Carousing carried long into the night, and fishermen woke before dawn to head out. Only during the wee hours of the morning could the twins trawl the shoreline for useful bits and bobs. Lowell crafted himself all manner of new false legs from abandoned detritus, testing and improving and testing again. He also built nets and other tools and had an idea that he might make a good deckhand or cabin boy. As soon as he learned women weren't welcome on many vessels—bad luck, according to nautical superstition—he abandoned the idea. He also suggested they might get a job delivering things or helping in a backroom or something.

"We can't trust no one," Felicia said.

"But we might get some money," Lowell argued. "Maybe they'd even let us stay inside somewhere."

"We're gettin' money."

They knew how to fish, and Felicia sold the excess. She had quickly learned how to turn her tender age to her advantage. She gleaned useful details from her targets' minds and spun tales to sell quickly and for a good price. Lowell sometimes helped, but she'd said she didn't like the way people stared at him. So Felicia encouraged him to find less public employment. Thanks to their connection, he quickly sussed out her real motives.

Another day, Lowell tried restarting the same old argument. He'd seen people about the town. Plenty seemed nice.

"People in Timbergreen seemed nice too," Felicia spat. "Until things got bad."

Lowell tried again, weakly. "But—"

"I said no, Lowell!" she said. "We hafta stay hidden to stay safe."

He begrudgingly agreed, and Felicia stomped out of range to be alone for a while.

Autumn's chill tinged the evening air. The throngs of Halibut Harbor visitors that once clogged the boardwalk had trickled down to more of a lazy stream. Soon that would dry up into nothing. The town was entering its slow season. Felicia always kept both a physical and mental ear open for news. Plans to make up for the holidaymakers' absence were on everyone's minds. Felicia too had begun to consider options. Rooms at the Snug Salmon boarding house would be going for cheap, but she doubted that she and Lowell could afford one for the entire winter.

They'd managed to save a little. More than she'd expected, truth be told. She suspected Lowell got up to more than he said when they were apart. Once again, Felicia found it really unfair that the universe had decided their connection should only go one direction.

Given the town's slowdown, she wondered at the arrival of a carnival. They would have done better to come a month ago.

The lights and music immediately entranced Lowell. They both snuck close, peering over a low grassy dune, to watch men and women hoist faded striped tents into the air. Lowell's eyes danced as he took in their construction, murmuring to himself how he could copy the design for himself and Felicia. She scanned the grounds for opportunity. If the carnival pulled in a good crowd, she could slip in and go around to request donations. Maybe for a local children's home or something equally made-up and sympathetic.

The carnival occupied a long stretch of empty beach. It created a rather idyllic atmosphere, what with the waves crashing in the background and an organ piping out jolly tunes.

"Oh, Felly, can we go?" Lowell whispered. "We've done so good. We should have a bit of fun, shouldn't we? Other children get to go to the carnival."

Felicia suppressed a shiver, not wanting to worry him, and huddled farther into the grass. She decided against mentioning they were hardly in the same position as other children. Honestly, sometimes Lowell's perpetual optimism made it seem he'd forgotten they'd been running for their lives less than three months ago. She also decided against mentioning the only children who would be going to the carnival were the local ones. Parents had taken their broods back from whence they came a fortnight ago. Singles, childless couples, and old people were the only visitors left. The glow of excitement in Lowell's eyes was too precious to smother, though. It had been so long since she'd seen that much joy in him.

"Yes," she said. "We can go. We'll hafta clean up, though. Don't want anyone thinkin' we're there to beg."

Even Felicia had to admit the carnival was impressive. And they'd managed to pull in nearly the whole town. The posters plastered all over every lamppost and railing proclaiming *Two nights only!* surely helped. One huge tent in the center hosted acrobatic feats, dancing horses and dogs, and bear taming. Fire-eaters, jugglers, and contortionists gave audiences a taste of their talents before pointing towards smaller tents and promising more inside. Guests could pay a fee to dress up in silly costumes and have their likenesses forever preserved via image-stills. Caramel apple slices on sticks and bright candyfloss marred smiling faces with their sticky leftovers, while the smell of popcorn and roasted nuts wafted through the air.

Spinning panes of colored glass around petrolsene lamps threw rainbows along pathways, tempting guests through mysterious portals. At the end of one, they might find a hall of mirrors that stretched reflections into ridiculous proportions. Or perhaps a murky tent filled with Old World creatures of magic. These, Felicia had discovered, were merely people in elaborate costumes and lighting tricks done with mirrors. Lowell wanted to see *everything*, but Felicia didn't want them getting separated. So they agreed to move methodically through the carnival, allowing Lowell to enjoy each piece while Felicia worked nearby. Of course, he had encouraged her to take time for herself. She'd temporarily appeased him by buying a caramel apple wedge, shoving the whole thing into her mouth, and making a sticky caramel grin at him.

They'd cleaned up as best they could, which wasn't saying much. Though the extra-large bow Felicia had tied into her hair was apparently having a positive effect. The donations bucket she carried did a good job of masking her grubby dress. Lowell had even coached her on batting her eyelashes and smiling prettily. His lessons hadn't really taken, but Felicia was compensating by sprinkling in what extra compliments she could think of. The cheerful crowds seemed happy to donate a little extra money to her finishing school fund. Having realized the locals would likely find it strange if she said she wasn't from around there yet also wasn't back home and in school, she'd gone with the next best lie she could think of. Halibut Harbor wasn't so small that everyone knew everyone, thankfully.

The thoughts swarming from the multitude around her sounded

twice as loud as their chatter. She had learned from a young age not to shout over mental discourse, but it required focus. The headache she was sure to have later would be worth it, though. Her smile could even be described as warm when another couple of coins clinked into her bucket. The hope they produced shocked even her.

"A school, eh?"

Felicia's eyes snapped in the direction of the voice, ready to ply her tale yet again. She could immediately tell by his dress he was no ordinary carnival-goer.

The man peering down at her sported a top hat, a bright red coat, and an enormous mustache. His dark eyes twinkled, which encouraged her. The scars of various shapes and sizes patterned across his walnut skin, however, gave her pause. A joke waited for its chance at the forefront of the man's mind. She wasn't good at making jokes, but providing someone with a setup when you knew the punch line was easier.

"Yes, sir," she replied. "Finishin' school."

The man's mustache smiled with him. "I see. So tell me, do you finish finishing school or does it finish you?"

Felicia smiled back. The joke didn't really do anything for her, but she was optimistic about getting a few extra coins from this one. "You're very funny, sir."

"And where is this finishing school?"

Felicia froze and listened. Thoughts flitted as quickly as damselflies, making them difficult to catch, especially amongst all the others zipping around them. Names of places she'd never heard of whizzed by. She snatched at one.

"Woodlawn," she said. She tried to make her eyelashes do like Lowell had shown her.

The man rubbed his chin. A notch had been taken out of the pointer finger on that hand. "Woodlawn? Never heard of it. And I've been all over. Where's that exactly?"

"South," Felicia blurted.

The man threw back his head and laughed. "Not bad, little miss. Of course, just about everywhere is south of here."

Felicia edged a step back. Another when the man stooped to her level.

"How old are you?"

"Ten anna half, sir." She hoped the lie of an extra two years would convince him she wasn't the idiot child he probably already thought she was. "Oh, that's my parents callin'. Sorry, s'cuse me."

Felicia turned, but the man hooked a pinkie around the handle of her bucket. She tightened her grip and scanned the crowd. Lowell was some distance off, raptly watching an illusionist transform a lacy handkerchief into a dove. The man's thoughts followed her gaze, so she tore her eyes away from Lowell.

"Is that your brother?"

"Who?" she asked as blankly as she could. She fruitlessly tugged at her pail. "Excuse me, sir, but I hafta go."

The man leveled his dark eyes at her. "You think I don't know everything that goes on in my carnival?"

He tightened his grip. The strength in that one finger scared Felicia.

"I saw you and your brother watching us set up," the man added.

Felicia pulled hard enough to make the coins in her bucket rattle. The man lowered his voice into a soothing tone.

"Settle down. There. Now, you've spun some impressive tales this evening. I could take what you've swindled and have you arrested for fraud, or you can come with me."

Felicia's mind raced. She risked a glance back at Lowell. She mentally shouted at him, but he was out of range. Even if he wasn't, he might be too dazzled with the illusionist to hear her.

"I'll let you hang onto the bucket with me," the man offered.

Felicia swallowed hard and tried to listen to his mind over her own screaming fears. She couldn't concentrate. Everything was a buzz. In the mire, no ill intentions reached out slimy fingers. She was all too familiar with the sensation, though its current lack of existence meant nothing for the future. Still, her choices were almost nothing at the moment. She managed to nod, hoping against hope she might weasel her way out of this with her prize intact.

The man nodded once and led her by their shared bucket handle down a path. It led away from Lowell, who Felicia resisted the urge to look back at.

PART 2

"Lowell turned away from the illusionist he'd been watching to call to Felicia. Yes, she was working to earn money for them, but she needed to take some time to enjoy herself too. Everyone did once in a while. And if anyone had earned it, she had. The smile fell from his face, however, when he realized he couldn't sense her anywhere. Their connection meant he could always feel her presence, as long as she was within range of him. Nothing answered back his mental search for that familiar sensation.

"Felly?" he said aloud, as if that might summon her back.

It wouldn't. They'd tested their abilities through various experiments while growing up. Their connection only went one way and was limited by range. He said her name again. She'd never stray far from him in a situation like this. Something must have happened. Lowell swallowed hard and hobbled over to where he'd last seen her spinning her tale. His heart began to pound when she still failed to appear.

Lowell considered taking his mask off. Though he'd used thin muslin to cover the eyehole on the side with his dodgy eye, it still blurred everything, putting the job almost solely on his other one. He shook his head at himself. No. His parents had never let him outside without his mask, and Felicia too had always forbade it.

"Because other people won't understand," was what his and Felicia's father had always said.

Lowell looked to the carnival workers. He could look for Felicia himself—that's what Felicia would want him to do—but he *needed* to find her, to make sure she was okay. What if she'd been injured? If they were separated, how would they find one another again? Hot tears prickled at his eyes as he imagined where Felicia might be. He envisioned the distance between them increasing. How much time would he waste if he tried searching the entire carnival himself? Every moment might steal their ability to find one another again. The illusionist had gone, but nearby was a wandering vendor selling roasted nuts. She had apple cheeks and silver-streaked hair pulled back into a long plait. Like the rest of the carnival staff, she wore a striped outfit that resembled the tents. Lowell headed for her.

"S'cuse me," he said. His voice cracked. The nut-seller looked down at him. He cleared his throat, trying to summon courage. Without Felicia, being brave was up to him. He failed to feel any more hopeful, but his urgency pressed him forward. "I can't find my sister." The admission made his voice wobble. He tried to push back his tears, but they won out and garbled his words. "She was just here and I've lost her and I can't lose her but I don't know where she'd have gone."

"Oh, darlin', don't cry," the nut-seller said. "We'll find your sister. Don't you worry. C'mon. We'll do it together, shall we?"

She extended her hand, and Lowell swallowed back the worst of his sobs. Yes, it would be okay. There were kind people in the world, despite what Felicia said, despite everything they'd seen, and Lowell had just found one.

The man hanging onto the other side of Felicia's donation bucket tried to make conversation as they walked, but Felicia said nothing in return. She scanned his thoughts, looking for advantages. Unfortunately, they mostly jumped from one bit of carnival-related business to the next. Her own kept returning to Lowell. Would he even notice she was gone? He'd been so wrapped up in watching the illusionist, he hadn't even looked her way when the mustachioed man had cornered her. Heat burned behind her eyes, but no tears came. Just anger. Why did Lowell always have to be so fanciful? She looked back to the man on the other side of her bucket. Perhaps Felicia should abandon the money she'd collected and run for it. But they needed something to get them through the winter.

Her mother's words rang in her head: "Take care of your brother."

Felicia swallowed hard. She was going to need to get through this with her prize intact.

"You said this is your carnival?" she said at last.

The man looked sideways at her. The hint of a smile ruffled his mustache. She read in his thoughts that he was pleased she'd spoken, but he was still wary. Through the flitting thoughts that zipped by in his head—*the contortionist crowd looks a little thin; not just mine; need to get that hole patched*—Felicia couldn't catch whether he was onto her tactic. Nevertheless, he was honest when he answered.

"Mine and my brother's."

"It's very impressive," she said. "Which is your favorite part?"

The man chuckled. "That's a bit like choosing children. Every bit is different. Each has its own problems and joys."

Felicia made herself smile, trying to be charming the way Lowell had shown her. She even managed to muster a touch of the enthusiasm he so naturally effused. "Yes, but if you hadta choose *one* bit?"

The man stopped and looked around. The names of people and

different acts buzzed in his mind. A headache was building in Felicia's skull. People milled about in every direction, both visiting and working the carnival. Felicia had gotten good at focusing on one person's thoughts through practice—it was a bit like holding a conversation in a crowded room. It always wore her out, though, and she had been doing it all evening. She tried to ignore the dull thudding behind her ears. Without rest and quiet, it would radiate up to the top of her skull and down the back of her neck. A few times, it had gotten so bad she couldn't bear noise or light. Through sheer force of will, she managed to drive the pain back. It remained enough, however, to let her know she'd pay later.

The man rubbed his chin thoughtfully with those marred fingers. He leaned towards her, she instinctively leaned away, and he spoke in a conspiratorial whisper. "Just between you and me, I especially like the menagerie."

The menagerie had been mostly puppets, both people dressed as animals and hand-controlled ones. Felicia was pleased; the man wanted to garner her trust. Hope glowed in him like soft white light. His grip on the bucket of Felicia's falsely gotten gains loosened. She gave a yank. It came away. Just an inch, but it did. And she turned to run. She'd run straight out of the carnival grounds, stash the money somewhere safe, and run right back for Lowell.

The bucket jerked back so hard the coins within it jangled as if surprised by the sudden hullabaloo. Felicia held on but only just, arm tugging painfully at its socket. Her heart crawled into her throat. She looked back at the man. Though none of the indignant rage she expected rose in him, he fixed her with a hard look. Other mind-voices crowded around her. People were wondering what the little scene had been all about. She tried refocusing on the man's thoughts, but her headache doubled in strength and complained louder than the other noise around her. To ease the pain, lest it overrun her completely, she let go of her concentration and allowed the chatter, both mental and otherwise, to wash over her as one clamor.

The man looked ahead and said, less warmly than before, "Come on then. Let's finish this."

Holding the woman's hand, Lowell looked right, left, and right again. The longer he was separated from Felicia, the more certain he was that something had happened to her. He considered calling out for her. It was one thing for him to attract the attention of one person, though, and another thing completely to attract everyone else's. Carnival-goers passed on all sides with candyfloss and popcorn and bags of nuts in hand. The carnival workers still plied their trades here and there, drawing people towards new attractions.

The world kept going while Lowell's was falling apart.

The once-jolly surroundings suddenly seemed grey and sinister to him. Had one of these people been responsible for whatever had happened to Felicia? He kept his ears open for the sound of her thoughts. If she was conscious, she would try to contact him. He was sure of that.

"What's your sister look like, darlin'?" the nut-seller asked.

"She's got long dark hair in a bow," Lowell said. "And a bucket. She's been collectin' money."

"Money?" said the woman. "What for?"

Lowell wasn't sure which option Felicia had decided on for herself. As she hadn't wanted him to help her—she said his mask, arm, and leg would attract too much attention—she hadn't told him her final scheme. Although, he'd gleaned something about a school from her thoughts.

"Rebuildin' the local schoolhouse."

The woman pursed her lips and squinted her eyes. Lowell wished he had Felicia's abilities just then.

"Why's it need to be rebuilt?" she asked.

Why had he said *rebuilt*? Lowell grappled with himself before blurting, "It burned up."

The woman made another face, this one more certain than the last. She turned a corner and led him between two tents. Its stripes felt like cage bars.

The woman said, "I think I know the best place to look for your sister."

The mustachioed man led Felicia to a tent at the back of the carnival. Over the entrance flap hung a sign that read *Private*. With the hand not holding onto her bucket's handle, he held open the flap for her. Felicia looked back to the carnival. In the distance, the crowds floated from one tent or cart to another. She could still run. In this quiet corner, she could distantly make out the man's thoughts again, but her headache was getting more persistent. They still showed no ill intentions, but that didn't guarantee anything for the future. And once she was inside that tent, getting away would be even harder. Fine. She'd figure out something else for Lowell and her. Felicia's fingers were just loosening on her money pail when a woman in the striped uniform of a carnival worker appeared around the edge of another tent. The sight of Lowell hobbling by her side made Felicia freeze.

"Felly!" Lowell cried.

He pulled away from the woman holding his hand and lurched towards Felicia. Felicia's eyes, however, stayed on where his hand had clasped the woman's. Why had Lowell trusted this stranger? Didn't he know better by now? Felicia didn't move as her brother practically tackled her in a hug. The woman blocked the path out. The man still holding the other side of the bucket blocked any kind of escape the other way. Felicia released the handle of her money

pail. Lowell was sobbing against her shoulder, wittering on about how scared he'd been. There was something in there too about how he felt he hadn't any choice but to look for help, but it mostly garbled into sobs. She'd been frightened too, of course, but she wouldn't show it in front of these people. She patted her brother's back with one hand and spoke firmly in her mind.

Not now, Lowell. We needta get out of here. Pull yourself together.

Lowell hiccupped and pulled back. He wiped a streak of shining snot across his almost ungrubby sleeve. His eye not covered by his mask was pink from crying. The sight softened Felicia. She took his hand in hers.

"Glad to see you've found one another," the man said behind them. "Colleen, thank you for your assistance."

Colleen's face remained pleasant, but she crossed her arms over her chest. "I understand they've been collectin' money for charity." She nodded at the pail. "Would that be their spoils, Mister Hornbeam?"

"Spot on," Mister Hornbeam replied. "Come along, children."

He motioned towards the tent flap, which he still held open. Felicia searched the adults' thoughts. The effort made her headache roar. The darting damselflies of Colleen and Mister Hornbeam's thoughts became buzzing gnats behind the insistent pounding.

"Felly?" Lowell whispered.

She ignored her twin and made herself look at Mister Hornbeam, despite how badly she wanted to close her eyes.

"We'll go, sir," she said. "We'll leave the money and be on our way. Sorry to bother you."

She didn't wait for permission and pulled Lowell along the path, towards Colleen.

"No, no," said Mister Hornbeam. "The three of us need to have a chat. In you come. Colleen, why don't you join us?"

Through the buzzing, Felicia could just sense that Colleen was being included to help corral them. Felicia looked around the woman's skirt, but the gap on either side was too small to make unless the twins were extremely quick. Felicia might be able to do it on her own, but Lowell never would with his bad leg. She looked back to the man and scowled. Trudging into the tent as petulantly as possible, she even dragged her feet. Lowell followed, just without the dramatics, which might have been the first time they'd ever reversed those roles.

Walking into Mister Hornbeam's tent, Lowell was entranced: painted wooden models of acrobats and dancing horses, elephants and lions and monkeys, and shadow figures that transformed depending on the angle hung from the tent's support posts. After nearly losing Felicia, though, he kept an ear open for her thoughts. And he kept hold of her hand. Though he didn't distrust Mister Hornbeam or Colleen the way Felicia did, Lowell looked for escape routes. Unfortunately, nothing presented itself.

Oil lanterns spread a dim glow throughout the tent. Dusk had grown heavy outside since he'd met Colleen. Mister Hornbeam sat at a scuffed, collapsible desk. Colleen stood at the entrance to the tent—a guard against escaping twins. Mister Hornbeam swept a hand towards a steamer trunk, indicating Lowell and Felicia should sit there. Neither did. Felicia was suffering one of her headaches. They always muddled her thoughts, as if he was hearing her talk through water. He wished he could hear what she'd gleaned about the adults.

Mister Hornbeam didn't acknowledge their refusal to sit. Instead, he leaned back in his chair and crossed an ankle over his knee. "You've parted some of my customers from their money. Money they could have spent on my carnival. Does that seem particularly fair to you?"

"It was for a good cause," Lowell said.

"Rebuildin' the local schoolhouse," said Colleen, "which, as I understand it, is doin' perfectly fine."

"Eh?" Mister Hornbeam pointed at Felicia. "This one told me it was to send her to finishing school."

Lowell shifted from foot to false leg and back again under the adults' stares. Felicia stuck out her chin, however. Her eyes twitched, probably against the pain of her headache, but she betrayed no other sign of her pain.

Mister Hornbeam drummed his fingers on the desk. "Where are your parents?"

Lowell lowered his eyes to the floor. A long pause passed.

"I myself don't have any parents," Mister Hornbeam went on. "My brother and I, we're orphans."

Lowell lifted his head again and met Mister Hornbeam's eyes.

"Fever took both Ma and Pop the same winter. The cold nearly took my brother and me." Mister Hornbeam shook his head. "Life's hard enough already. Harder when it's just a couple of youngsters against the world."

Colleen tilted her head to the side, giving him a sideways look. "Where's this goin', Mister Hornbeam?"

He looked back to her. "I'm sure we could offer these two a place if they've nowhere else to go."

Colleen's eyes settled gently on the twins. The gaze hurt Lowell, because it reminded him of the way his parents had looked at him and Felicia. No one had looked at them like that since…

He swallowed a lump in his throat and tried to look back at Colleen as innocently as possible. He didn't allow himself to think about possibilities, only about not getting in any more trouble.

"Do you have anywhere else to go?" Colleen asked.

"Of course we do," Felicia snapped. "What kinda stupid question is that?"

She shot a hard look at Mister Hornbeam, but it didn't last. She winced and closed her eyes. Lowell heard nothing from her mind but a muffled sense of pain. He couldn't remember her headaches being this bad before. Sweat shone on her forehead, and she swayed from foot to foot. Lowell's heart picked up its pace, but he forced himself to take a deep breath. Felicia was about to be very cross with him.

"No," he admitted. "We don't have anywhere else to go."

"Lowell!" Felicia snarled. Then she shut her eyes and sat down on the steamer trunk.

The confused, pain-tinged noise from her mind grew louder, and she pulled her hand from his to cover her eyes.

Though he felt like the worst brother in the history of brothers, Lowell charged forward. "We can earn our keep." Felicia groaned beside him. "We won't work for free, though. We expect to be paid like anyone else. That's only right. We just need a place to sleep."

"Away from everyone else," Felicia put in, her voice strained. She still kept her hands over her eyes.

Mister Hornbeam smirked, cocking an eyebrow at the twins. "That's quite a list of demands. What can you do?"

"I can fix things," Lowell said. "I'm good with tools."

Mister Hornbeam and Colleen turned to Felicia. He asked, "And you, little miss? What do you bring to the table?"

Felicia's slouched back rose and fell as she breathed deep. Lowell distantly heard the echo of Mister Hornbeam's thoughts as she strained to hear them.

"You're wonderin' when you can pull out the flask that's hidin' in your desk," she said.

Then the buzz rushed back in, obscuring Felicia's thoughts again. Through her hands, Lowell caught Felicia squeezing her eyes shut.

Mister Hornbeam laughed and slapped his knee. Meanwhile, Colleen's lips flattened into a thin line. That was more like the looks Lowell was used to seeing, and he hunched his shoulders, physically drawing into himself.

"Clever girl! Cle-ver girl," Mister Hornbeam guffawed. "Looks like we've got a mind reader on our hands."

Felicia shook her head, clenching her jaw. "Fortune teller."

Lowell jumped onto the idea. "People like fortune tellers." Mind reading had the tendency to frighten people. "Fortune tellers make them happy, 'specially when you tell them how to find happiness."

Colleen's face softened, but her eyes never left the twins.

Mister Hornbeam's laughter faded into chuckles. "Fortune teller it is, but you haven't earned your own space yet."

"Then where'll we stay?" Lowell asked. "With you?"

"Oh no!" Mister Hornbeam chortled. "Goodness, no. I'm no one to be responsible for children." He turned to Colleen. "How about with you and Marty?"

Colleen blanched, and she turned bugging eyes onto the carnival owner. "You can't be serious!"

"Haven't you always wanted children?" Mister Hornbeam looked at her with puppy-dog eyes.

She balled her fists at her side. "I told you that in confidence, Gerald!"

He patted the air as a mollifying gesture. "It's only until we find more suitable accommodations for the wee bairns."

Lowell's eyes flicked back and forth between the adults, wishing more than ever for Felicia's ability.

Colleen growled. "Fine, but only until then." She turned back to the twins. "No offense. You seem like lovely children."

Lowell smiled but decided it was best not to reply. Felicia, however, began to hum in her throat. Lowell had seen this before. He scanned for a bucket before landing on the money pail Felicia had been using. It sat a few paces away on Mister Hornbeam's desk. Lowell reached, limped towards it, but Mister Hornbeam pulled it away.

Lowell objected, "I need it for—" Behind him, Felicia wretched. He heard the splat of vomit against the ground and grimaced at their new employer. "—her."

Mister Hornbeam sighed, opened a drawer in his desk, and pulled out a flask. Just as Felicia had said. After taking a swig, he said, "Colleen, would you mind putting them to bed?"

Felicia laid in a bed suspended from ropes attached to the wall of a large wooden caravan. Colleen had led them to her quarters, grumbling dark oaths against Mister Hornbeam. She'd left the twins there for a while, and Lowell had done what he could to ease Felicia's headache. He turned the oil lamps down to almost nothing, save for one, and laid warm wet flannels made from torn bits of his clothes on her head. He warmed them by wrapping them around the glass casing of the one oil lamp he'd left turned up. The pounding in Felicia's head had ebbed, leaving a thinner ache behind. She and Lowell listened to two voices arguing outside the caravan.

"You didn't even ask me, Collie!" said one. A woman.

"Mister Hornbeam didn't give me a choice!" Colleen replied. "And it's only temporary anyway. They don't want to live with us just as much as you don't want them."

"So you *do* want them? Blazes, Collie, is this some roundabout way of getting back at me? Because I don't want children?"

"No! Do you really think I'd do that to you, Marty?" Colleen's voice cracked. "What kind of person do you think I am?"

Indiscernible murmuring followed. Felicia didn't bother to focus, not wanting to feed the last remnants of her headache. And anyway, she didn't need her abilities to know what would follow.

"We'll get our own place here soon enough," she whispered to Lowell.

How long they'd stay with the carnival, she didn't know. Maybe once spring came, they'd have more options. They could always try and nick some money and run, but they'd need to steal quite a lot to hide themselves and survive Duskwood's merciless winter. What might have happened had she not gotten caught? Had Lowell not sought help? Had they somehow gotten away? Did it even matter? They were stuck here now, at least for the time being.

Tears shone in her brother's eyes. "I'm sorry, Felly. I was just tryin' to help. I was worried about you."

"I know," she replied coldly. Her anger wasn't for Lowell. It was for everything else, so she reached a hand towards him. He took it in his gnarled one, and she rubbed the craggy skin there. "Just promise me you won't go trustin' any of these folks. They don't want us. They only care about what they can get from us. Promise me, Lowell."

He sniffed. "I promise."

Colleen's voice piped up outside again. "Mister Hornbeam? What are you doin' here so late?"

Then Marty's voice. "Mister Hornbeam, you can't go in there. Mister Hornbeam!"

The door to the caravan flew open and hit the wall with a *bang*. Felicia shot up from the bed. Her head spun, but she grabbed the bed frame to steady herself. The man she'd met earlier that night—Gerald Hornbeam—was not the one who stood at the other end of the caravan. He looked like Gerald, minus the mustache, scars, and bulk. And his eyes were colder. This scarecrow-like figure was definitely a different sort of person altogether. Colleen and Marty, who Lowell and Felicia had yet to meet, followed him in.

"This is our private home!" Marty said.

She was plump with fair hair cut short like a man's. Also like a man, she wore trousers instead of a dress. Her outfit, like Colleen's, bore the striped pattern of a carnival worker.

"Nowhere is private in my carnival," drawled this Mister

Hornbeam. He turned his gaze onto Lowell and Felicia.

His thoughts made bile rise in Felicia's throat again. Before she could start mentally humming a tune to shield her brother, Lowell shrank against the wall.

"These two are our newest acquisitions?" He approached the bed and bent to examine the twins face-to-face.

"They're the carnival's two newest employees, if that's what you mean by acquisitions," Colleen replied.

"Of course that's what he means," Marty muttered. "Only *he* would refer to people like that."

"Watch your tone, Menagerie Mistress," Mister Hornbeam said. He turned his head back to look at the two women like an Old World automaton: lifeless and precise. Then back to Lowell and Felicia with the same cold precision. He reached out to touch Felicia's bow. She barely restrained herself from smacking his hand. Instead, she opened her mouth wide and heaved vomit-scented breath over his face. She even hissed like a cat to really try and startle him. The man drew back and coughed.

He curled his lip. "I will never understand my brother. Be warned, urchins. We don't abide parasites in this carnival. If you don't perform well, you will be discarded."

He turned on his heel and left. Colleen and Marty watched him go with poison in their gazes.

"Such a charming man," Marty said after he'd gone. She looked at the twins, who clutched each other and returned mistrustful stares. Finally, she looked to Colleen. "At least they're old enough to take care of themselves."

"Yes, we are," Felicia shot back. "As soon as we can afford it, we'll be out of your hair."

"Thank the stars for that," Marty said.

Pain threaded through Colleen's thoughts. Some reconciliation had occurred between the two women, but it hadn't erased the hurt. She turned away from her partner and pulled a blanket down from a shelf that wound its way around the entire caravan wall.

She offered the blanket to the twins. "You can sleep on my side of the bed tonight, but tomorrow we'll have to get you cleaned up and find some fresh clothes."

Marty grumbled something behind her—*It's my bed too. No telling what vermin they're infesting the sheets with,* said her thoughts—but didn't argue.

Lowell and Felicia nodded. They'd enjoy these last few hours in the safety of each other's company before their new life as a fortune teller and whatever Lowell would become began. Felicia just hoped they had as little contact with the second Mister Hornbeam as possible. Lowell nodded in agreement. Felicia squeezed his hand before they settled down to sleep.

PART 3

Felicia scowled down at her new clothes as she sat on the floor of the caravan. They were clean, which was nice. She hadn't had clean clothes since, well… She turned away from that thought, stuffing the pain it brought back down. It didn't bother her that the stripes all down the garments made her look like a huge piece of New Year's candy either. She despised what the clothes represented. She'd failed to take care of herself and Lowell, failed to extract them from the carnival's clutches. Now they were trapped here until she could figure out a way to steal some money and plan an escape.

"Oh, Felly, aren't they great?" Lowell said.

He stood on the other side of the caravan they currently shared with Colleen and Marty—the carnival-working couple had yet to find peace about the twins coming to live with them. The caravan rocked like a steamship on a grumbling sea, and Lowell had to hold onto a handle attached to the polished wood caravan wall to keep from falling over. He balanced on his one leg, having taken off his false one to give the chafed skin where it attached some relief. The one empty leg of his striped trousers hung tied in a knot to keep himself from tripping on it.

Felicia turned her scowl onto her twin. He was part of the reason they were in this mess. He was far too trusting, which Felicia couldn't understand. After everything they'd been through, had he learned nothing? Still, she should have figured something out. She might have had that blasted headache not incapacitated her.

The headache had melted away while she'd slept last night, and Colleen had gotten them fed and cleaned and found them new clothes that morning. There was an oddly small man on staff who had clothes that fit the twins marginally well. Colleen had bargained with the small, gruff man, taking on a portion of his carnival chores in exchange for the garments. The move made Felicia feel strange, as if Colleen wasn't quite as alien and distant as Felicia had initially thought. After all, she and Lowell had often made similar trades back home with…

Again, Felicia banished the thoughts. They managed to needle her heart a few times before she caught herself, but refocusing her anger smothered the pain.

"Stop prancing, Lowell," she snapped. "This ain't a holiday."

Lowell looked up from admiring his stripey new clothes. His expression fell. "I know that. I'm just gladta be wearing something else. My other clothes were getting really uncomfortable."

That was probably due to the tiny bugs crawling through them. Colleen had tutted over the clothes that morning and given them to another carnival worker to be cleaned. Felicia suspected they'd never see the garments again but hadn't said anything. Now that they were alone, however, she let loose.

"You should be uncomfortable. Maybe it'd remind you we needta get out of here instead of pretending these people don't just

wanna use us."

Lowell looked to the ground, still holding onto the handle on the caravan wall. Colleen and Marty were outside on the driver's seat. The carnival had packed up that afternoon and left Halibut Harbor. Marty had hitched up four mules to the caravan and taken up a place near the rear of the colorful procession. Felicia had watched from the window as other caravans like this one had passed. All painted in bright colors, they resembled trundling New Year's ornaments. To where they were headed next, she didn't know, though she had gathered it wasn't back towards Timbergreen, their old village. Good.

The caravan floor dropped from beneath them before jumping back up. Felicia, already being on the floor, just rolled a bit before steadying herself. Lowell stumbled, however, lost his grip on the handle, and fell hard to the floor. He clipped his shoulder against an end table, nailed to the floor, on the way down. Tears filled his eyes as righted himself and rubbed the spot. Felicia's anger took a backseat, and she crawled over to make sure he was alright. She couldn't really look at the injury without him taking off his baggy waistcoat and unbuttoning the equally overlarge shirt, so she gave it a squeeze instead. Lowell winced, but nothing felt broken and no blood stained his shirt.

Serves you right, Felicia thought.

She then mentally jerked back. Lowell may drive her crazy sometimes, but she didn't want him to be hurt. She'd thought she'd forgiven what had happened yesterday; apparently not. She tried to squash the resentful feelings—they frightened her. If she didn't have Lowell, what did she have? When that didn't work, she tried redirecting her ire at Colleen and the two Mister Hornbeams and even Marty, who, truth be told, wanted as little to do with the twins as they wanted to do with her. Her anger towards Lowell remained, however. A burning ember, tiny though it was, burned in her. She then tried the only other thing she could think of: ignore it until it went away.

She looked to Lowell to see if he'd caught her thoughts—mental activity flew so quickly, one really had to focus to snatch individual thoughts. A few tears leaked from Lowell's eyes, though he seemed to be focusing on his injury. He wasn't wearing his mask at the moment either. Both his enlarged eye and the one that was like hers had gone almost entirely pink as he cried.

"You're okay," she said. For some reason, she could not bring herself to comfort him as she knew he would want, with soft words and a smile.

A small window at the front of the caravan slid open. Colleen's round face looked back at them through it from her spot on the driver's seat. "Everything alright back there? The road's getting a bit rocky."

"We're fine," Felicia shot back.

Colleen met her glare and held it for a moment before switching to Lowell. He'd hidden his unmasked face.

"You alright, darlin'?" Colleen pressed. "I thought I heard someone take a tumble."

Lowell nodded and peeked through his shaggy hair, keeping his bad eye hidden. Felicia could hear him trying to hide the wobble in his voice. He failed. "I'm okay. No bleeding."

Colleen gave him a warm smile and put a hand to the side of her mouth. In a stage whisper, she said, "There's a bit of candy in the drawer next to you. Don't tell Marty. She doesn't like me having it. Too much of a sweet tooth, she says."

Marty said something Felicia couldn't discern, as the woman was facing away from them, concentrating on driving the mules over the uneven road. The caravan still rocked beneath them, but it was easier to stay upright now that both twins were on the floor. Colleen winked at Lowell before sliding the panel closed again. His face had lit up, and he scrabbled to find the promised candy. Felicia glowered at the window. She turned away only when Lowell offered her a piece of the candy. A new thought had entered Felicia's head, making the candy taste like sand in her mouth. She could tell from Colleen's thoughts the woman wanted Lowell to like her. She wanted both of them to like her, but Colleen knew she had a better chance with Lowell.

She's tryna lure Lowell into another trap, I just know it, and Lowell is trustin' enough to fall for it.

Lowell was wholly focused on his new treat and didn't even look at her. The ember of resentment inside Felicia burned a little brighter.

Lowell couldn't understand Felicia's continually sour attitude. The carnival was incredible! It traveled slowly, allowing the twins time to get to know it before being thrown into their new responsibilities. Most of the carnival workers lived in and/or worked out of caravans like Marty and Colleen's. The huge tents were erected and recompressed using cranks and winches and steam-powered machines that Lowell desperately wanted to examine more closely. None of the carnival staff, though, even the nicest ones—and there were a few pretty nice ones—would allow an eight-year-old boy with a false leg and gammy arm near the loud, dangerous machines. Failing that, Lowell began trailing Marty, who ran the menagerie.

A few of the animals in this dimly lit tent were real—besides the white horse the carnival staff either painted with black stripes or topped with a slender horn made of paper and paste, it was mostly birds, which had long tethers attached to their legs. Just a few smaller hawks, owls, and corvids, but Lowell didn't mind. The rest were a combination of people in costumes, puppets, and even a few steam-powered creations. These latter ones were covered with either fur or leather and performed with jerky movements. They were often hidden in shadowy corners of the tent and lit so that carnival-goers could be properly fooled and frightened from a distance. Some even had voices, using a perforated strip like in a player piano to create tinny yet eerie calls that looped throughout the night.

Marty, head of this curious troupe, both orchestrated it like a maestro and performed. She herself played the part of a stag. She wore a mask, face paint, antlers, and a full-body puppet that transformed her silhouette from human into the skittish, graceful creature. A huge mountain of a man played the part of a lumbering bear, covered in skins and grunting amiably. Another player dressed entirely in black drove a pack of wolf puppets on wheels. And that was just the Duskwood section of the menagerie tent. The Bone Port section—the great, sweltering swathe of land to the south, full of birds bright and colorful as jewels, verdant jungle, deadly panthers, and venomous snakes—was like walking into a fantasy land. Lowell stuck to Marty like a burr, despite all the times she told him to shove off. Marty had nothing but disdain for the twins, but the bear, who ironically was called Bruin, took pity on the lad. Lowell suspected Bruin wasn't his real name, but it fit the gargantuan, hairy man well enough. Bruin allowed Lowell to examine the puppets and ani-machines, as he called them, though he wouldn't let Lowell actually touch anything. That is, until Lowell started making suggestions.

Lowell couldn't help it. The gears in his brain refused to stop making ideas, blowing them about like so many bubbles. What if they added a device that was connected to the wolves' casters to make them growl or howl as they rolled along, similar to the player piano device in some of the others? Maybe a sort of horn or whistle plus mini-bellows for the howling? Some of Lowell's ideas were outlandish, like the one about building a steam-powered water buffalo that charged around the Bone Port section of the tent. Others, though, like the one about puppeteers waving sticks with fake luna moths attached around the heads of passersby as they wandered through the Duskwood section, were adopted. While Marty still gave him the cold shoulder, the others began to accept him with varying degrees of warmth.

"He's just a child," Lowell overheard Bruin say to Marty one day.

"A child I'm saddled with," Marty had replied.

Lowell tried to ignore the words, to focus on his current project —Bruin had entrusted him with the wolf howl experiment and he didn't want to disappoint the man—but the words *saddled with* rang in Lowell's head anyway.

He and Felicia were earning money slowly. They were each given a small weekly wage, but their own space meant buying a caravan for themselves, which, given how expensive they were, wouldn't happen for years. That, or negotiating to rent a space in a storage caravan, space which could be used to store helpful equipment that didn't require inconveniences like human safety considerations. Not that any specific organization was holding the Hornbeam brothers to much of a safety standard, but child welfare was one of those things that made people nervous, even if those children were a pair of orphans. The newssheets loved to sensationalize, and a carnival was just the sort of place they could easily speculate about.

Felicia at least had the advantage of tips. Gerald Hornbeam, who was by far more pleasant than his brother—they'd learned said brother was called Jeffrey—had even gifted her a pile of colorful scarves. They smelled of cedar wood and spirits.

"Our old fortune teller wore these," Gerald Hornbeam had said as he handed Felicia the scarves. Colleen, who stood by, gave him a sympathetic glance. "I think she would have liked you to have them."

Felicia had frowned but accepted the gift. Lowell could hear the echo of Gerald Hornbeam's thoughts in Felicia's. Someone called Becky, someone dear to him, someone no longer with them.

"What happened to her?" Felicia had pried.

Gerald Hornbeam gave them a sad smile but didn't answer. A brief flash of a woman with dark hair and blue eyes flashed in Lowell's head, lovely and warm and lively. The rest muddled. Lowell could guess. Life was difficult and dark even without people being ugly to each other.

Still frowning, Felicia had thanked him. She too understood how unfair life could be.

When she did her fortune telling act, Felicia wore the scarves around her head, layered like a skirt over her striped trousers, twisted like bracelets around her wrists, whatever would make her look mysterious. Lowell made sure to tell her how nice she looked, not only to make her happy but also because she really did. The vibrant colors paired so well with her dark hair and fair skin. He felt warmth from her at the comment, though there was a strange undercurrent he didn't understand beneath it. It felt prickly and cold and sort of aimed at him, but also muted. Felicia usually only collared her emotions to hide them from other people, never from him.

Lowell could tell from his sister's thoughts that she didn't completely hate her new job. She got a small tent all to herself with a sign outside that read:

Fortunes told! Madame Mystery, child prodigy, reveals your future.

Both Felicia and Lowell had a great laugh at that. It was the first time they'd laughed like that in a long time, and it made Lowell practically glow with joy. Even Felicia felt lighter than she had in a long time. And the carnival-goers loved her. Probably because she always gave them good fortunes. Granted, she tinged them with tantalizing peril—"You must overcome a sinister trial. Beware the holly leaves that catch and cut, but on the other side,

you will find your treasure."—but she always gave people something to look forward to. And happy people generally tipped well. The tips weren't required. A small wooden bowl on the table with a sign beside it pre-thanked visitors for them. It wasn't much, but every little bit helped.

When they traveled, Lowell often rotated between caravans. He spent a good deal of time with Bruin and his wife, Elissa, a tall, elegant Bone Porti woman with onyx skin who always wanted to feed Lowell.

"And take some back to your sister," Elissa would often say. "Maybe a good meal will put a smile on her face."

The caravan workers often had community get-togethers, and Gerald Hornbeam was proud papa to them all. Felicia went out of her way to avoid these as much as possible. She didn't care about being rude and scolded Lowell again and again for joining in.

"You said you wouldn't trust them!" she hissed at him once as he made his way to yet another group event.

That odd, cold feeling pointed at him had grown stronger. Now it was accompanied by an angry mental humming, a sure sign Felicia was working to block her thoughts from him. This was an old argument between them. It was proper deep winter now; they'd been with the carnival a few months.

"They're not all bad," Lowell replied. He'd become more stubborn in his position during their stay. Bruin had begun to trust him with more of the menagerie maintenance; Marty had even answered some of his questions the other day.

"Some of them are bad enough for the rest," Felicia snarled.

An image of Jeffrey Hornbeam sprang up in her mind. Lowell couldn't argue with that. The man radiated malice. Every time he came around the menagerie, the workers made themselves scarce. Doubly so when he had some of his cronies in tow—a handful of blokes from the strongmen act. Being co-owner, Jeffrey held power equal to that of his brother, Gerald. Gerald could only do so much to protect his employees from Jeffrey's machinations, which focused entirely on increasing personal profits and power, always at the expense of the carnival workers. Thank the heavens Gerald oversaw the carnival's accounting. Both the twins had done everything they could to stay away from "the bad Hornbeam," as they called him.

"It's just temporary," Lowell returned petulantly. "I dunno why you get so worked up."

"Is it?" Felicia asked. Disbelief rolled off her. "When the time comes, are you gonna abandon your new friends?"

Lowell pulled a face at her and walked away. Some time apart would be good for them. Nevermind that they'd had plenty of time apart these last few months. Felicia spent much of her free time in the giant, wheeled aviary where the performing birds lived and were cared for. People didn't often linger, as the birds made an awful racket. Despite this, Felicia said she liked the quiet, and Lowell knew what she meant. With this, their separate jobs, and Lowell's visits to other caravans, the twins saw less of each other than they ever had.

Felicia heard the panic in Colleen's thoughts before the woman entered her tent. They'd established a sort of acrimonious understanding, at least on Felicia's end. Colleen knew Felicia didn't like her and had stopped trying to charm her, so Felicia had stopped being so outright nasty. Marty had never tried charming either of the twins, so that was pretty much the same as it always had been. This, though, this was new. The fear broadcasting from Colleen was fresh and raw. Felicia stood, ready to run. When Colleen entered her tent, the woman's eyes were rimmed with red, but her voice was as taut and strong as a violin string.

"Felicia, come with me. Now. Something's happened."

The *something* blared from Colleen's thoughts. Felicia's breath caught, and she took a step back.

"Mister Hornbeam's dead?" she whispered. Gerald Hornbeam, the good one.

Colleen froze. The two stared at one another for a long, silent moment. Felicia had been so shocked, she had shown her hand. She would lie, of course. Maybe there was a chance Colleen would believe she'd heard the news elsewhere, but her shocked expression was a strike against that argument. Colleen's lips thinned, but she collected her wits. Felicia could practically feel the woman shunt her fear and suspicion to the background, behind bigger problems.

"I said now, Felicia. Come on."

Felicia wanted to balk, but Colleen's fear silenced her. That, and she could tell the woman was genuinely trying to protect her, though from what kept zipping out of Felicia's grasp.

Obediently, Felicia followed Colleen through the carnival to the caravan. Felicia noticed they did not take a direct route along the carnival's main thoroughfares. Instead, they skirted the outer edge, obscured by tents. When they arrived, Marty was already there with Lowell. Lowell was crying, his tears soaking into the fabric of his mask.

One look at Lowell and Colleen said, "So you've already heard then."

Lowell nodded, but it was Marty who spoke. "We just got here. I've already stashed the jewelry."

Colleen and Marty didn't have much jewelry, and what they did have was mostly Colleen's, but it was good quality. Not the paste-and-glass costume stuff, but rather some family pieces.

"Thank you," Colleen answered. "Twins, whatever money you've got, give it to me."

"Why?" Felicia asked. Even though she could still hear Colleen's thoughts being protective, handing over what they'd worked so hard to earn was too big an ask.

"We don't have time to argue," Colleen snapped. It was the harshest Felicia had ever heard the woman speak.

A heavy knock on the door silenced them all. Marty snatched the tea tin she and Colleen kept on a high shelf, the tin they kept their savings in, and shoved the entire thing into the large pockets of Colleen's striped dress. Before Felicia and Lowell could take their own action, the door opened and in walked one of Jeffrey Hornbeam's goons. As would be expected of one performing in a strongman act, the man was huge, with pork leg-sized shoulders and hands huge enough to grab and lift each twin by the head.

"Evening, ladies," the man leered, showing a gap-toothed smile. He tipped an invisible hat to Colleen and Marty, ignoring Felicia and Lowell, while his eyes darted around the room.

Colleen and Marty said nothing in response. The man was looking for things of value, to take, and Felicia looked to the mattress. Underneath it hid Lowell's and her money, paltry though it was. She didn't dare get it, but she kept glancing to it, which made Lowell do the same. The man began opening drawers and riffling through them.

"The bereaved Mister Hornbeam thinks it best that he holds onto everyone's valuables going forward," the strongman explained without having been asked a question. He turned another nasty smile onto Colleen and Marty. "Safer that way."

"Safer for him," Marty spat.

Colleen motioned for her partner to keep silent, but rage practically crackled off Marty. Still, she remained where she was and folded her arms across her chest.

Felicia listened to everyone's thoughts as best she could, though it was difficult with all the strong emotions crashing through them, buzzing and coloring and generally making a mess of everything. Lowell kept one eye on her, trying to make sense of the echoes. The only thing Felicia managed to clearly glean was that this change was something Jeffrey had wanted for a long time and was finally getting.

The strongman failed to find much in the way of treasures. The few costume jewelry pieces Colleen and Marty did possess had been left out, and the man scooped these into a leather pouch at his side. He turned over the mattress and found the battered envelope that contained every bit of Lowell and Felicia's stash. He picked it up, making Lowell and Felicia exclaim together.

"That's ours!" Felicia said.

"We earned it!" Lowell added.

The man simpered down at the twins. "Don't you little brats fret. Mister Hornbeam'll take good care of it for you."

"We can take care of it ourselves," Felicia said.

"Shut it!" The man shouted so suddenly, all four of the caravan's tenants jumped.

Felicia and Lowell looked to Colleen and Marty standing behind them. Colleen's face was pained, but Marty might have been carved from stone for all the emotion she betrayed. Why weren't they doing anything?!

"Please don't take our money," Lowell said. He began to cry again.

Felicia put a hand on his arm, both to silence and comfort him. The man turned on them again. The threat of violence thrummed beneath his thoughts, and Felicia took a protective step in front of her brother.

The strongman drew his hand back and said, "One more word outta either of you, and I'll pop you something good."

Lowell's throat bobbed as he swallowed a sob, and Felicia feigned deference, lowering her eyes, though she kept the man in her periphery.

The strongman eventually finished his ransacking of the caravan. He even took the bag of sweets that always lived in the end table. As he made his way out, he growled, "Mister Hornbeam wants everyone to meet at midnight tonight. Be there."

No one moved as the sound of the man's heavy footfalls retreated from the caravan. Only after they had well and truly disappeared did Colleen move. She sank down and gathered the twins in her arms. Felicia and Lowell exchanged a look as neither returned the embrace, arms hanging limply by their sides.

"I'm so sorry, dears." Tears ran down Colleen's face as she spoke. "I'm so sorry."

Another look passed between the twins. Even though Felicia couldn't read Lowell's thoughts, she could read his face well enough. He was thinking the same thing as she, and he voiced that thought a moment later.

"Why didn't you do anything?" Lowell sounded betrayed. Fair dues. He had begun to trust their pseudo-guardian. Felicia wanted an answer because knowing that would determine what they did next.

Colleen squeaked a sob. "Because there's nothing we can do. Mister Hornbeam owns the whole carnival now. With a word, we'd be out in the cold with nothing but the clothes on our back."

"We did try to safeguard yours," Marty added with a sharp look at Felicia, "but someone was too stubborn. Now look where you are."

Felicia glared back, but her strength had left her. They were back to where they had started, and she didn't expect Mister Hornbeam to let them see any more of their wages.

The carnival kept strange hours. Being open late every night meant a midnight meeting was perfectly normal for the carnival staff. Lowell and Felicia had already kept similar hours when they'd been on their own, so it was no great change for them. What was changed, however, was the new miasma of sorrow and misery that pervaded the air. Carnival community events were usually jolly

affairs with chatting and laughter. Lowell had always loved them. Now, the silence hung thick and suffocating.

As he and Felicia walked through the crowd with Marty and Colleen, Lowell heard snatches of the thoughts Felicia managed to glean. Most of them asked the same question: *What now?* He had wondered that too. He and Felicia hadn't had a chance to talk, as Colleen and Marty had remained in the caravan all night, arguing over the same question.

Felicia's own thoughts hadn't been much help either. They'd mostly consisted of, *I told you so!* and warnings that they needed to proceed extra carefully now.

Their little group found Bruin and Elissa and sidled up to them.

"Did they get anything of yours?" Elissa whispered.

Lowell thought it wise that Elissa had taken up whispering responsibilities. Bruin probably couldn't whisper if his life depended on it.

"Not much," Marty whispered back, "but they took the ragamuffins' money."

"Oh, Lowell honey, no," Elissa cooed. "I'm so sorry."

She was sorry, like Colleen, but that was all. Lowell's stomach sank to the ground. He'd thought… family didn't…

Tears pricked his eyes again, but he was tired of crying and wiped them away. He looked to Felicia and tried to be stern and tough like her. Felicia stared forward, eyes on Mister Hornbeam, who stood on a crate in the middle of the gathering. Several of his cronies flanked him.

"My beloved family." Jeffrey Hornbeam spoke in tones like rotting fruit—sickly sweet and revolting all at once. "The loss of my brother, taken by a heart attack earlier today, is a loss for us all. Allow me to comfort you. The carnival will carry on, as Gerald would want. You will all remain in your positions, and we will travel on as planned."

Jeffrey spoke for a while longer, not about anything of

importance and all of it delivered in that disingenuous tone that made Felicia look like she wanted to throw up. Finally, he came around to the matter of money.

"I know some of you were alarmed this afternoon when we collected your valuables. This is for safekeeping. Rest assured, you still have access to them. Every penny and item has been logged, and I will keep it secure in my safe. You are free to withdraw in limited increments as needed."

"And if we decide to leave the carnival?" someone piped up.

Jeffrey gave a smile so slimy it could have been made of worms. "By all means, do. As I said, we have logged how much you have, and it will precisely be returned to you upon your exit."

The smile made Lowell shiver. Around him, people's faces darkened or went agape with shock.

"Consider me not only your new carnival caretaker," finished Jeffrey, "but your friendly banker as well."

PART 4

Felicia gleaned much the night of Gerald Hornbeam's death. Memories of Jeffrey previously campaigning to take control of the carnival workers' money floated through many of the minds around her. For "security," Jeffrey had said, but his brother hadn't allowed it when he'd been alive. Some people hadn't been quick enough, had lost everything of value they owned to the goons. Colleen and Marty were exceptions, though Felicia heard suspicion and malice shot towards them. Jeffrey's goons now had a list of people whose homes had yielded little in the way of wealth.

Loudly and publicly, Marty and Colleen made noise about how expensive the twins were to keep. Granted, they'd begun buying a soothing lotion to treat a large scar along Felicia's leg. The scar became dry and irritated if not cared for properly, but treatment didn't cost nearly the difference between what Marty and Colleen had hidden and what the strongman found in their caravan. Elissa and Bruin had only lost a little as well, though that was because Bruin had happened to be bigger and more imposing than the crony assigned to their caravan. Jeffrey's gang of thugs shot him venomous glares that night, and even Felicia worried for the little family. After all, Elissa always sent food back with Lowell for, as Bruin affectionately referred to her, *the petulant girl.*

Things went exactly as Felicia had expected them to go after that night. Carnival workers were no longer paid in money, but rather in vouchers they could use to withdraw money in, as Jeffrey had said, limited amounts. Again, he promised everyone's records would be kept impeccably.

Felicia couldn't keep a scowl from her face every time she looked at Lowell now. Nor could she hide her resentment. He heard her thoughts and looked at her with pain and regret swimming in his eyes.

"I'm sorry, Felly," he said again and again. "I never..." His voice cracked and his face crumpled. "I thought this might be a good place for us."

"Don't call me Felly," Felicia hissed.

Lowell broke down into sobs.

Colleen and Marty talked through options every day. The goons were always lingering nearby in pairs as the ladies worked and went about their other business. Jeffrey interfered more than his brother ever had too. He berated the carnival staff for mistakes and imagined deficiencies. He docked the staff's pay, entire teams even, for one person's minor error. Colleen told Felicia and Lowell to make themselves as scarce as possible, which they'd already begun to do. Her fear fanned the twins' worries, but Marty's words hardened Felicia's heart even more than before.

"They are not our children, Collie!" Marty whispered from their bed late one night.

Rather, it was the wee hours of the morning. Felicia and Lowell now each had a hammock that hung from the ceiling on the other end of the caravan, giving Colleen and Marty their bed back. It wasn't Marty's whispered words Felicia heard, of course. The woman's thoughts were practically shouting. Felicia saw Lowell wince in his hammock as they echoed in Felicia's mind.

"You can't be suggesting we abandon them," Colleen hissed back.

"Spring will be here soon." Marty was trying to reason now. "They survived on their own for who knows how long, so they're clearly resourceful. They'll be fine."

Anger rolled off Colleen. Covers rustled as she rolled away from Marty in bed. "I cannot believe I'm hearing this."

Felicia peeked over the edge of her hammock. Through the murk, she could just make out Marty's and Colleen's forms. Marty leaned over Colleen from behind her.

"I'm not trying to be heartless, Collie," Marty pleaded, "but we have to think about ourselves. If we leave, we can't afford to take them with us. And we can't afford to stay." Nothing. She tried again. "Remember what you said when they first came? They don't even want to be here. They still don't. You've seen how Felicia acts; she's miserable."

Felicia exchanged a look with Lowell. Hurt and fear stared back at her. Guilt picked a scab on her heart, but she shoved it down.

Colleen continued to ignore Marty. What each had said stewed within them, and nothing was decided. Felicia swallowed hard. Not even she knew where Marty and Colleen had stashed their money. She still made tips, which she squirreled away in a special inner pocket of her trousers that Lowell had designed for her. She always had to leave a little in the bowl, though, to be convincing, making saving slower than ever. She had no idea what they were going to do.

Lowell was at Bruin and Elissa's caravan when Jeffrey's cronies burst in. Four of them, all hulking bricks of muscles with ugly sneers torn across their faces. Bruin stood up from the small fold-down table they'd just been eating dinner around. Elissa too stood and stepped protectively in front of Lowell. He peeked around her, hanging onto her skirts and trembling. The goons lined up in front of the door, the only exit, and crossed their arms over their chests.

"We know you're holding out on us," said one.

"Hand over your money for safekeeping, Bruin," said another, "and we can keep this clean."

Lowell knew what was coming next. He must have started shaking harder, though he didn't realize it, because Elissa slipped a hand behind her back. He took it and held on for dear life. As expected, Bruin refused. The strongmen closed in. They opened their assault with a punch to Bruin's gut. Elissa ran forward to help, ripping her hand from Lowell's grasp, and received a backhand across the face for her trouble. Lowell shrank against the wall as one of the goons punched Bruin, while two others held his arms. Another stood between Elissa and Bruin, flinty eyes promising more pain if she interfered again.

When Bruin was on the floor, covering his face and head with his arms while the three kicked him, Elissa broke. Bruin groaned through blood and broken teeth as she went to the fold-down table and unscrewed one of the feet. Within the carved table foot hid their money, and she handed it over with tears in her eyes but her chin held high. True to their word, the strongmen left after that.

Elissa had to take care of Bruin, so Lowell was left to make his way back to Marty and Colleen's caravan alone. The entire way, he struggled to swallow noisy sobs. They choked him, and every shadow made him jump.

A new nightmare met his eyes when he walked into what had become his home over the last few months. Within the first place that had felt safe since he and Felicia had lost their parents, Jeffrey stood, flanked by two of his thugs. He had six of the large men at his beck and call, plus a handful of more smaller, weasely ones. Marty held Colleen back with an arm around the waist as the latter railed at the men.

"You can't take them!" Colleen shrieked. "Gerald charged *me* with their care."

"Gerald is dead." In that same strange, automaton-like way he had when the twins had first met him, Jeffrey turned his head towards Lowell. "Ah, the other one is here now too. Good."

His expression was flat. Lowell's senses finally caught up with him. He'd been so dazed from the horror in Bruin and Elissa's caravan, he hadn't heard Colleen shouting, nor did he register the warning Felicia's thoughts were broadcasting.

Felly! Lowell's own mind cried. Of course, she couldn't hear that.

One of the strongmen held his sister, a blacksmith's-glove-sized hand clamped on each shoulder.

Fear laced through her thoughts, nearly as loud as Colleen. *Get away, Lowell! Run!*

Not just fear, though. Love. All her resentment and anger that had burned against him for weeks now had disappeared. It kept his feet planted to the spot.

Lowell didn't move, just kept looking at Felicia as the other crony grabbed him by the arm. Colleen doubled her efforts, and Marty had to fight to hang onto the woman.

"Enough with your hysterics," Jeffrey said. "You obviously cannot afford to care for these children, so I must take over."

"No!" Colleen exclaimed. "We can. We have been."

"Then prove it," Jeffrey said.

Colleen closed her mouth, looked back at Marty.

"Collie, don't you dare," Marty hissed.

Colleen hesitated. Before, she'd just been furious. Now, tears filled her eyes.

"Do it and I will *leave* you," Marty added.

Terror flashed in Colleen's face. A sob escaped her throat, and she put a hand over her mouth. Looking back to Felicia and Lowell, tears slipped down her face.

"I'm sorry," Colleen whispered. "I'm so sorry."

Felicia narrowed her eyes while Lowell's breath caught in his throat. He couldn't believe what he'd just heard.

His sister looked at him. "Told ya this'd happen."

Colleen drew back as if struck. She looked to Lowell. "No, Lowell. You didn't think we would…"

Her voice trailed off as Lowell looked to the floor. No, he hadn't thought Colleen would betray them, which made it hurt all the more.

More months passed, and spring languidly returned to northern Invarnis. Jeffrey kept the twins close and had them working for him from breakfast to bedtime. As Gerald had before him, Jeffrey made his home in an especially large caravan, drawn by eight draft horses. It was big enough for a tiny sitting room, a squashed combination kitchen, dining, and entertainment area, and a bedroom. A locked closet served as the twins' room at night. Felicia coped better, as she had never harbored illusions of loyalty from any of the carnival staff. No one came to their defense, not after that horrid night Bruin had been beaten to within an inch of his life. Lowell, however, wept every night for a long time afterward. Felicia tried to comfort him, but there was little she could do to soothe a wound of betrayal like what Colleen and the others had inflicted.

The twins were never entrusted together with anything that took them far from Jeffrey's side. One always stayed behind, close to him, to ensure the other returned. They cleaned for him, brought him food and drink, mended his clothes, and anything else he asked of them. Anything less than immediate and deferential obedience was met with a swift blow to the face or a kick. Lowell struggled with fulfilling his orders as quickly as his new "caretaker" expected. Felicia interceded, though this usually ended with both of them being punished.

"Don't," Lowell told her. "We shouldn't both get hit."

For once, Felicia had no response. She stared at a small bloodstain on Lowell's dirty carnival uniform. Her brother's nose had bled earlier that day after Jeffrey had struck him for spilling a tray of drinks. The skin around Felicia's eye was puffy and sensitive from when she had jumped to Lowell's defense.

Lowell was right, but she couldn't imagine a world where she simply stood by and watched him suffer.

The twins tried to give Jeffrey a wide berth, but they could not avoid his thoughts. Felicia stopped dead in her tracks the day she gleaned a new scheme cooking in his head.

Terrible servants, he thought to himself. *I'm sure someone will pay good money for them. Just need to find buyers…*

That night, as the twins laid down in their little closet-prison, Felicia shared what she'd heard.

"Are you sure he meant us?" Lowell whispered, his voice shaking. "You can't sell people."

"You can if no one stops you," Felicia whispered back.

Lowell's throat bobbed as he swallowed hard. Ever the optimist, he said, "Maybe whoever he sells us to will be nice." Despite his words, he did not sound confident.

"Lowell, he said buyers." Felicia hardened her tone, making herself sound steady, but her stomach churned. "More than one."

Lowell's eyes widened. Felicia's control over her emotions

slipped. Seeing her brother so frightened hurt worse than any hit from Jeffrey could. She began to tremble, and Lowell drew close. He wrapped his arms around her shoulders. She returned the embrace, letting her mind wander to options. She didn't bother trying to mask her thoughts; she needed Lowell's help to think of solutions.

They still had the paltry collection of tips Felicia had managed to earn before Jeffrey had taken her fortune teller job from her. She'd actually been good at it, and she found she would trade nearly anything to be doing it again. Felicia shook her head. Wishing was a waste of time. The tips, still hidden in their special hidden pocket, wouldn't last them a week. The carnival staff's money was all locked up in a safe, to which only Jeffrey knew the combination. The darkness of their closet pressed in around the twins as they realized, once again, they had no options.

The buyers showed up the next week. Three men. Lowell and Felicia removed the guests' muddy boots for them, smearing the twins' clothing in the process. A spring shower the night before had made everything soggy, but the sun shone today like everything was right in the world.

"You see, they are quite obedient," Jeffrey said. The man actually looked pleased for once.

Felicia and Lowell were being on their best behavior because Jeffrey had threatened to break one leg each if they fouled up this meeting. How he expected Lowell to be helpful after that, considering he only had one leg to break, the twins didn't know, nor did they have any wish to find out. He'd delivered the threat directly after telling the twins none of his usual supporters—his goons—would be in attendance. For appearance's sake.

The men's thoughts echoed into Lowell's mind. They sized up

the twins like cattle. None of them were impressed with Lowell, and his stomach twisted as they turned their attention onto his sister. Lowell exchanged a pale-faced glance with Felicia, whose mouth was set in a firm line.

"They're both very strong," Jeffrey said as he led his guests to a table in the kitchen, dining, and entertainment area.

He snapped his fingers. Felicia followed and began to serve drinks. Lowell hadn't been allowed after he'd dropped the drink tray that one time and broken an entire bottle of scotch—cheap scotch, but that distinction hadn't mattered to Jeffrey. Without a task, Lowell lingered near the entrance. Felicia had begun humming in her mind, whether to shield herself or Lowell or both from the men's thoughts, he didn't know, but he didn't like it. Detestable as it was to hear these cretins consider Felicia's capabilities like they would a household appliance—hours of labor per day, strength, how well she matched the rest of the household, liabilities—Lowell knew one of them would walk away today with his sister in tow. He couldn't stop it if he wasn't armed with as much information as possible.

Jeffrey must have noticed the buyers' focus on Felicia. He motioned at Lowell. "I know the lad looks a bit worse for wear, but he's clever enough to compensate."

"Not too clever, I should hope," one of the buyers said.

Jeffrey gave a wormy smile like the one he'd given on the night of his brother's death. "No need to worry there." He snapped his fingers again. "Boy, come here and show them your leg."

Lowell tried exchanging another glance with Felicia, but she didn't meet his eyes. Snatches of thoughts slipped through her humming barrier. The buyers had begun to think about the future, when Felicia was grown. Both the twins' faces heated, their pale skin coloring. Lowell looked back to the table, to the men gathered there, the empty vase sitting atop said table, anything to distract himself from the terror growing in his belly, sliding tendrils up his throat. A new idea began to form, and it turned Lowell's blush to cold paleness.

Obeying Jeffrey's order, Lowell tromped over. His gait, as always, was uneven, but he exaggerated it now. He didn't stop himself from fidgeting, and he let his gaze dart, never landing on anyone for more than a few seconds. Jeffrey's brows dipped in disappointment, but he only motioned to Lowell's false leg, which hid beneath his trouser leg. Without a word, Lowell hiked his trousers to his calf.

Jeffrey tipped his head. "He made that himself. The lad won't require any more care than any other servant."

The buyers' eyes roved over Lowell's false leg. Lowell wasn't shamming when he lowered his eyes to the floor. The sneers on the men's faces stripped away all the pride he'd felt when he'd first made the leg, using bits and pieces he'd filched from around the carnival. A heavy, awkward moment passed.

Jeffrey cleared his throat. "And, as you can see, he's not *too* clever."

The buyers' attention detached itself from Lowell like lampreys moving on to better prey. Now Lowell's eyes burned as well as his face. The idea from before flared brighter as the men looked back to Felicia.

"Girl, go fetch us some flowers for the table, would you?" Jeffrey said. "Your brother will entertain us while you do."

The unspoken threat in Jeffrey's words was all too clear. Felicia gave a sloppy facsimile of a curtsey—as there'd never been any need, she'd never learned to do one correctly—and headed out the door.

"Boy," Jeffrey said, apparently trying a new angle, "come closer."

Inside, Lowell quailed at whatever new humiliation the carnival owner had in store for him, but he obeyed.

"Now, open your mouth and catch." Jeffrey tossed a salted nut at Lowell.

Lowell caught it by pure chance. The buyers leapt onto this new game but didn't seem to think they should take turns. They lobbed nuts in Lowell's direction. The snacks pelted him in the face, one fell down his shirt, and another hit him in the eye. Disoriented, Lowell stumbled and then tripped over his false leg. The men guffawed as the boy went sprawling. A sensation like heat from acid burning through metal flowed across the room, and Lowell looked up to see Felicia returning with flowers in hand. As subtly as he could, Lowell shook his head. His sister was trying to decide between several different reactions—screaming at the men, throwing one of the liquor bottles at them, faking a fit—any of which would land them both in a world of hurt with Jeffrey. Felicia's eyes flashed, but she gave the tiniest nod of her head.

Lowell righted himself and asked, "Can I fetch lunch?" He tried to make himself sound hopeful instead of terrified and nauseated.

Jeffrey turned a baleful glare on him. The man considered whether Lowell was likely to drop it and ruin the meeting.

"I'd like to show our guests what a good job I can do," Lowell added. The words made him want to vomit all over Jeffrey's colorful carpet, but he swallowed the bile back down.

Jeffrey sighed as if Lowell exhausted him and waved a hand. "Very well, but be careful. You wouldn't want to embarrass yourself or your sister, would you?"

Lowell bobbed an awkward bow and left, throwing one last glance at Felicia. She followed him with eyes that said she hoped he would run away and never return.

Lowell had to hobble all the way to the canteen tent on the other side of the carnival. Even though it hurt to, Lowell ran. He needed to make up time because he planned to stop elsewhere first. The sun was so bright, there was no use trying to sneak. Still, Lowell skirted the edge of the carnival and tried to be

inconspicuous… or as inconspicuous as his uneven gait, made worse by running, allowed him to be. The carnival workers were, thankfully, all busy getting set up for that evening. The carnival wouldn't open for another couple of hours, and there was always lots to do.

By the time Lowell got back to Jeffrey's caravan, the man was glowering openly. His guests, meanwhile, had emptied half the bottle of scotch. Lowell was so, *so* careful as he navigated opening and closing the door, remaining upright on the steps, and not tipping the basket he carried too far right or left. Within the basket were jars of piping hot spring soup for a first course, a salad, roasted rabbits, and a bottle of wine. Everything was supposed to be secure inside, but Lowell didn't want to take chances.

"Is everything as I requested?" As he spoke, Jeffrey's expression darkened in the way Lowell and Felicia had learned to recognize as danger.

"Everything," Lowell said. He gave a smile he hoped was proud. It wobbled, but he held it up anyway.

"About time!" The buyer who spoke gulped the rest of his drink. His cheeks and nose were red now, and he pounded the glass on the table.

"Perhaps you'd prefer to have some wine with lunch." Jeffrey's voice was as flat as his expression. He looked at the inebriated man like he would a pesky fly.

"Doesn't make a difference to me," the man replied. He held out his glass to be filled up.

Felicia hurried to help Lowell serve. The scent of the food wrapped around Lowell's stomach and squeezed. Jeffrey hadn't given them breakfast that morning, an "incentive," he'd said, to encourage them to perform well. One of the buyers continued to drink scotch, the rest switched to wine. Except for Jeffrey. He drank only water from a pitcher Felicia brought to the table. As the buyers plowed through their meal, the twins retreated to the far side of the room, ready to be called upon again. Felicia pressed her arm against Lowell's. He felt her warmth more than her actual touch through the tough skin on his bad arm. She was trembling, and Lowell twined his gnarled fingers around her hand, giving it a squeeze. She continued to shake. He tried comforting himself by thinking if his plan didn't work, at least they had this time together. It was not very successful, and his insides twisted tighter.

The soup course passed, then the main. Pudding was simple—individual strawberry and rhubarb pies. As the men tucked into this final course, one started sweating profusely and mopping his face with his napkin.

"Everything alright?" Jeffrey asked.

The man waved him away. "Of course. Was a bit too enthusiastic with the drinks, I suspect."

The other men began to show signs of discomfort as well. One tugged at the collar of his shirt, while another began to down water like a fish. None of them said anything, of course. It would not do for men to go bellyaching about their discomforts like old ladies, or so Lowell heard one of them say to themselves via his connection with Felicia. Jeffrey leaned back in his seat and flapped his jacket, pretending to adjust it. Lowell heard all their private complaints.

What did you do? Felicia asked in her mind.

Lowell refused to even look at her. He didn't trust himself. He just kept his eyes on the floor.

One of the buyers asked for the way to the WC. Jeffery directed him before turning furious eyes onto Lowell. The carnival owner stood, but his legs went out from beneath him. Lowell's eyes were glued to Jeffrey's as the man began to claw his way towards the twins.

"What's the matter with you, man?" another of the buyers asked. He sounded as if he was having trouble breathing.

"His legs must have fallen asleep," Felicia said before anyone else could speak. "They do that sometimes. Bad blood flow. Why don't we head to the sitting room? You all can digest in peace there. Lowell will take care of Mister Hornbeam."

The carnival owner grimaced and gasped. He waved incoherently at his guests, but Felicia was already leading them away—both the remaining buyers wobbled, glassy-eyed, as they went. She glanced back to Lowell while Jeffrey continued his slow, laborious crawl towards the lad. Lowell edged away.

With a great heave of air into his lungs, Jeffrey wheezed, "What the blazes did you do to me?" He reached a sweaty, shaking hand towards Lowell.

Lowell wasn't quite sure, truth be told, but it seemed to be working. He was curious why Jeffrey seemed to be reacting faster than the others. Maybe because the buyers were all heavier set? Or could the alcohol have something to do with it? The questions helped distract Lowell from a tiny voice in the back of his mind, screaming in terror at what he'd done, at what might happen next.

Jeffrey crawled slowly, but rage burned in his eyes. He tried calling for help, but nothing more than a strangled noise came out. His breathing became more ragged. Pain seeped into the rage. Jeffrey scrabbled towards Lowell, hands shaping into crooked talons, but Lowell backed far out of reach. In the tiny sitting room, Lowell heard Felicia encouraging the two buyers there to relax, close their eyes, and recuperate from such a lovely lunch.

Appearing around the corner, she called over her shoulder, "I'll bring you more drinks in just a moment."

She locked eyes with Lowell, then looked in the direction of the WC. Not a sound came from within, and sound traveled very well in such a confined space as the carnival owner's caravan, extra large though it was.

Thud.

Lowell looked back to Jeffrey. His head rested on the floor; not even breath moved him.

The twins looked at one another again. Being extra careful not to alert the men in the sitting room, Lowell held up a finger and moved slowly. He knocked on the door to the WC.

"Sir, everything alright in there?" Lowell called softly. Nothing, so he knocked again. Still nothing.

Lowell swallowed hard, swung his gaze to the ceiling, and turned the door handle. No cry of alarm went up when he opened the door, so he lowered his gaze just until he found the man's head. It tilted back against the wall as the man sat on the toilet. The man's breath too came in shallow wheezes, but his eyes were closed.

"Sir?" Lowell whispered.

No response. Eyes still on the man's head, Lowell placed a hand against the wall for balance and extended his false leg. He found one of the man's ankles and prodded it with the end of his prosthetic. Still no response, so Lowell turned, left, and closed the door. Felicia had disappeared, and Lowell's heart leapt into his throat. A second later, he felt the familiar presence of her mind against his. She was just in the other room again. They were nearly out of range of each other. She emerged from the sitting room a second time and crept over to Lowell.

"They're both out," she whispered.

Lowell jerked his head back towards the WC. "So's he."

"What did you do?"

Lowell reached into his pocket and pulled out an orangey-yellow, horn-shaped mushroom. At first glance, it looked like an ordinary chanterelle. Felicia leaned in for a closer look and raised shocked eyes to Lowell a moment later.

"You added poisonous mushrooms to their food," she said.

Lowell nodded and put the dangerous fungus back into his pocket. "To the soup."

Felicia smiled at him. "Mama would be proud."

Lowell's face fell. He wasn't so sure about that. Their mother had always been a peacemaker. There wasn't time to consider that now, though.

Together, both of them looked at the safe, within which hid enough money to buy them a train ticket to anywhere they liked, lodging, food, and more. They just needed to get inside. Lowell made a beeline for it and set to work examining the lock. It was simple in that it was a basic combination style, but what was the combination? They could guess for years and still not get it right. Felicia was already scanning the caravan for possible combination clues or hiding spots. Before they could even begin to look, however, the door to the caravan opened.

"Mister Hornbeam, there's a problem with the…"

Marty's words trailed off as she took in the scene. Jeffrey Hornbeam lay dead on the floor. From her vantage point, she'd be able to see into the sitting area. Her eyes were already there. She flung the door shut behind her and strode into that room. A moment later, she reemerged, eyes goggling.

"Who are those men?" she demanded. "And why are they dead?"

Lowell shuffled his feet. "They weren't dead a few minutes ago."

Marty's eyes went even wider.

"They were here to see if they wanted to buy us," Felicia said, eyes glinting colder and harder than any child's should.

"To… to buy you?" Marty began. Then she snapped her mouth closed.

Lowell heard the rest of what she might have said aloud echoed from his sister. As human thought was wont to do, especially in moments of confusion, it was quick and jumbled.

Buy? Mister Hornbeam was going to… Well of course he was. But murder? Would you have done the same? Collie isn't going to… No. Not the time.

Marty's eyes focused again. The twins still stood by the safe, and they stared at the woman with bated breath. One scream and they'd be running for their lives with nothing but the clothes on their backs… again. Marty's thoughts spun faster, debating with herself. Lowell couldn't keep up. Felicia was trying, but she winced with the effort.

Suddenly, decisively, Marty marched over to the twins. She rolled up her striped trouser leg and unstrapped a leather strip from around the top of her calf. A pouch hung from the leather, having rested behind Marty's knee. She held it out to the twins.

"Here. It won't last long, but it'll get you far away and then some." The bag jangled a little as Marty held it out, but it bulged with rolled-up bills. "Springhaven is your best bet. Easy to get lost in a city that big, but I hear the Enforcers there aren't like the ones in Duskwood and Bone Port. You'll need papers to live there too, but I suspect resourceful children like yourself can figure something out."

Felicia and Lowell shared a look. Marty was obviously trying to get rid of them, but her thoughts didn't match that conclusion… not exactly anyway. She *was* trying to get rid of them, but only concern painted her thoughts. Not malice or jealously or anything else they'd expected.

Marty shook the bag. "Take it! Colleen will want to keep you, to go on the run if need be." She cast a look at Jeffrey's body on the floor. "I don't know if it'll come to that, but I don't want that for us, and I know you don't want us as your family."

Hope tugged at Lowell's heart, but Colleen's choice rang in his head. She'd chosen Marty; he and Felicia weren't really their children.

Mama and Papa chose us, Lowell thought. Again and again, through all the trials Lowell and Felicia had faced since birth, they had chosen the twins over money and even their own safety. *We deserve someone who will choose us.*

Lowell looked to the safe, as did Felicia.

"That'll take you too long to crack," Marty said. "And what's

in there isn't yours to take."

Felicia turned a scowl onto Marty, letting the woman know just how much she cared for trifles like theft. Marty shook the pouch again.

"Take it and be off." A warning rang in Marty's tone now.

Reluctantly, Lowell did so. Felicia emptied the rest of the salted nuts into her pockets. They felt Marty's eyes on them as they snuck out of the caravan and away from the carnival. Lowell wished he could have said goodbye to Colleen and Bruin and Elissa, even if he was upset with them.

Better this way, he told himself. *Less messy, less chance of getting caught.*

That night, Lowell and Felicia checked themselves into an inn and had a nice dinner delivered to the room. For the right price, the innkeeper didn't make a fuss about two children in odd clothes traveling alone.

"Do you think they've got the safe open yet?" Lowell asked, tucking into his pork pie.

"Probably, if Colleen's involved," Felicia replied. "And if the evil Mister Hornbeam didn't change the combination. She seemed pretty close to the good Mister Hornbeam."

Lowell heard what she didn't say. "Yeah, I think the evil one killed the good one too."

"We'll never really know, not that we need to care." She actually smiled as she shoved a huge piece of pork pie into her mouth.

Lowell managed a smile as well. The food and warm room went a long way to quieting the shadows plaguing his mind. They continued their dinner in silence until Felicia split the slice of cake that came with dinner.

"So what are you thinking?" she asked.

Another smile, warmer and more sure than before, stretched across Lowell's face. Cake certainly helped too. "I think we're going to be okay. I don't know how, but somehow, we will be."

Harvest Festival Haunting

Takes place after the events of *Raven's Cry*. No proper spoilers, but character relationships formed in *Raven's Cry* are present. A special event night at the Raven's Tower turns spooky.

~~~

Crisp leaves of rust, gold, and maroon mounted assaults against the doorway again and again, seemingly determined to gain entry to the warmth and noise within. The bitingly cold air whipped them up around boots and sent them nipping at cloak hems heading inside. Meanwhile, the fireplace across from the door beckoned them to her crackling embrace. Hector, assistant manager of the Raven's Tower, pushed back each volley with a cinnamon-scented broom, leaving eddies of the warm aroma swirling through the air as the fat golden moon looked on.

"Welcome, sir, madam," Hector said as he moved aside for two more guests, tipping his hat to the couple. "Hot mulled cider is available here, the main festivities are upstairs in the barroom, and you can check your coats with Spencer there at the cloakroom."

"He means Specter," said a boy no older than fifteen from behind the cloakroom counter. He raised his hands above his head
~~~

and wailed with a dramatic performance worthy of the worst stage hams in history. "WOOooOooo! Get it? Spencer. Specter."

The couple chuckled and headed over to turn in their coats while Hector swept more incorrigible leaves back out the door. Once the couple disappeared up the curving stairway, Hector turned back to the lad.

"Apologies, Spencer, but that joke is never funny."

"Miss Cali said to play up the spooky factor," Spencer tossed back over his shoulder as he hung up the two new coats.

Hector watched the boy for a moment longer, wondering whether Spencer was even his real name. He'd been around before, doing odd jobs for Calandra, but had usually looked as if he'd been living on the streets. Tonight the lad was washed and dressed in proper clothes, however. Probably Calandra's doing. He didn't press; Hector had learned from his first day working at the Raven's Tower not to ask too many questions. Everyone seemed to get along better that way. The door opened again and in walked two men. One resembled a scarecrow, the other a bearded pumpkin, both wrapped in greatcoats. More leaves rushed in behind them as the wind whipped through the open door.

"We're not late, are we?" came a muffled voice from behind… well, a muffler.

"Sir Allen, welcome!" Hector said, extending his hand. "So glad to have you join us this evening."

"Hello, Hector. As I've said before, please call me Neal."

Hector made a face like Neal had just suggested he cover himself in toffee like an apple. "Hmm, Lord Allen instead?"

"Oh stars, no. Sir, if we have to endure one of them." The bearded pumpkin next to Neal chuckled. "Hector, this is my friend and colleague, Engineer Cooper Richmond."

"Copper will do fine," Copper said, pushing his face out from the collar of his coat.

"Now that I know your official title, Engineer Cooper…" A

playful grimace stretched across Hector's face.

Copper harrumphed back into his coat and slid his eyes towards the steaming mugs of cider behind Hector. "There any booze in those?"

"No, sir, but there's an excellent selection upstairs."

Hector then went through his spiel again, and Spencer made the same joke as before. Neal burst out laughing, and Spencer shot Hector a smug grin.

"That's quite a good one. Perhaps I ought to go by Neal Ah!-llen tonight."

Copper rubbed his face, groaning.

Neal nudged him with his elbow. "Didn't I tell you this place was fun? It's about time you came with me."

"Aye, it'll be more fun once I get a few drinks in me."

Calandra surveyed the barroom with satisfaction. Some regulars, some new folks, and most of them without any relation to Duskwood as far as she could tell. Felicia and Lowell had introduced her to the harvest festival holiday. Lowell really. Felicia had, unsurprisingly, been rather nonplussed about it the first few years, though she'd warmed up eventually and even helped consult for the Tower's celebration when Calandra had introduced it two years ago. It had been an almost instant success.

Garlands of colorful leaves wound around beams and support struts, while lanterns of carved turnips (for the tables) and pumpkins (on the bar and in the windows) glowed with grotesque faces. Gabriel had created some special drinks for tonight, including an absurdly popular creation called a pumpkin spice sling. Calandra always enjoyed watching the behemoth of a man grate tiny nutmegs over them. And the smell of pies both savory and sweet wafted from Laura's kitchen.

Calandra looked down at her note cards for the evening. Every table had available activities listed on the back of the menus and where to find them. Most could be played independent of a judge—Pin the Fangs on the Vampyre, for instance—but the supplies for others had to be replenished. Pumpkin Darts looked like an especially popular one of these.

"Copper, did you read this?" came a familiar voice from the bar. Calandra smiled as she spied Neal reading from the back of the menu. "In Duskwood, on this night it's commonly held that the veil between life and death is thin enough to pass through."

"Aye, but you already knew that, didn't you?" his associate, Copper, grumbled, following Gabriel with a determined gaze.

"Yes, but I wanted to make sure you did too."

"I study the same things you do, you know?"

Copper's focus remained on trying to get Gabriel's attention away from the other patrons who'd arrived before him.

Calandra swept over to them. "Neal, it's so good to see you."

"Calandra! And you!" He shook her hand and motioned towards Copper. "My friend and colleague—"

"Copper will be just fine." He spun as he fired off his words. "If that chap below tells you different, Copper will still do fine."

Calandra laughed. "Hector is nothing if not a stickler. I'm very pleased to meet you, Copper. Any friend of Neal's is more than welcome. I'm Calandra, owner and operator."

"Owner, eh?" Copper's eyebrows bobbed. "What's the fastest way to a drink around here?"

"I'll take care of you." Calandra walked behind the counter and took their orders before helping thin Gabriel's queue.

Hector came upstairs to help out once the river of arrivals slowed to a trickle, leaving Spencer to greet and handle the cloakroom. Wendy and Moira, Laura's teenage daughters, helped serve, made some of the simpler drinks, and generally assisted as needed. As the libations flowed, everyone became more jovial, not to mention loud. Calandra was just thinking this might be her most successful event yet when…

Tsssssssss!

The room dimmed as the light of every petrolsene lamp shrank into nothingness. Silence settled over the room immediately after, whooshing through like a ghost. The faces of the jack-o'-lanterns, now the only sources of light, leered from the darkness. Applause and laughter bubbled up from the cauldron of darkness in which they were all now steeped.

Calandra stood on the opposite side of the room from the bar, and her eyes met Gabriel's. The sort of rapid, silent conversation passed between them that can only be had by two people who'd known each other for years.

Was that supposed to happen?

Nope.

Carry on as usual?

Yup.

Holler if you need anything.

You too.

Calandra flitted between the crowd, smiling and nodding while sweat moistened her palms and her heart drummed inside her chest. She sidled up to Hector, who met her halfway.

"Check the boiler room," she whispered, forcing her smile to stay in place.

"Um, check it for what, please?" Hector replied.

Calandra blinked at him, her smile falling. "For whatever makes the petrolsene go, of course. I can't smell anything, so I don't think there's a leak, but… what?"

Hector's eyes darted around as a few patrons gathered nearby, clearly waiting for an opportunity to talk to Calandra. He said, "I don't know anything about petrolsene lines, assuming that's the right term. Lowell's always been the one to handle that."

Of course he was. Mechanical things were one of those things that always just worked perfectly because Lowell made sure they did, but he wasn't here tonight.

"Miss Calandra," said one of the ladies standing nearby. "This is ever so much fun, but it's a touch dark, don't you think? Could we turn the lights up just a smidge, please?"

Calandra's mouth turned back up into a smile all on its own, a move she had performed her entire life.

"Apologies, ma'am. We seem to be having some… technical difficulties. We will have everything fixed as soon as possible."

The way the expression on the woman's face fell made Calandra's insides twist. Stars, how she wished she could have played this off for just a bit longer. She turned to her companions and relayed the information. It'd be all over the bar within minutes, and her harvest celebration night would cave in on itself like a gourd infested with worms.

"Hector, a free round of drinks for everyone. Non-alcoholic."

Hector nodded and skittered off. Calandra was about to turn away when she saw Laura emerge from the kitchen.

Oh, blazes, Calandra thought as a new thought hit her.

She headed over. Laura might as well have been a specter herself, as covered in flour as she was.

"The ovens?" Calandra asked.

"Yes, ma'am. I can keep things warm in them for now, but we'll lose the heat quick if I have to keep opening them."

Making sure no patrons could see her, Calandra mouthed a colorful swear. She closed her eyes and took a deep breath. "Do whatever you can."

Calandra could still hear laughter from the gaming areas, so not everyone hated this new development. That was a plus.

Oooooooooooooh…

The moan floated up through the floorboards, drenching the room in cold silence again. A few giggles, some more nervous than amused, tittered through the quiet.

"Don't mind him. He's just our friendly pet ghost," Calandra blurted before she knew what she was saying.

More laughter, thank the stars. She made her way to the stairs just as Hector announced the free round of drinks for everyone. They'd be disappointed when they learned the details of this deal, but she couldn't focus on that now.

Darkness coated the stairwell like oil, filling it so completely she could see nothing most of the way down. Calandra almost considered going back up to grab one of the turnip lanterns off the table, but the handrail was here, and soon enough the orange glow of the fireplace stretched its luminescent fingers through the darkness and reached for her.

"Spencer," she called at the foot of the stairs. "Are you alright?"

No answer. Calandra walked to the center of the room. Darkness pressed around her, eager to swallow this room like it had the stairwell. A horrible face with thin eyes and a too-wide mouth gleamed from a pumpkin on the cloakroom counter. The light flickering inside its orange-fleshed skull made the grin appear as if it were growing. Calandra knew from personal experience the world was not all it seemed—Kieran's vampyrism was proof enough of that—and she kept her eyes on the jack-o'-lantern just in case. She crept forward, towards it, and…

"RARGH!"

Something grabbed her arms from behind. Calandra spun, caging her yelp in her throat and raising her hands to fend off her attacker. He had already jumped away and, she just now realized, was laughing so hard he had to lean against the wall for support.

"Spencer?!" she demanded. "What the blazes are you doing? You nearly gave me a heart attack!"

Spencer rubbed the heel of his hand against his eye, wiping away tears. "Nah, you'd of been okay. You're a tough old bird."

"You have no idea," she grumbled. More clearly, she added,

"We heard a moan. Was that you?"

Spencer's laughter picked back up. "What? You think I've got someone down here with me? Nipping back between the coats for a little—"

"Not a moan like that!" Calandra scrunched her eyes shut, pinched the bridge of her nose, and took a deep breath. "You're not hurt then?"

"Nope, right as rain. Bit dark, though."

"We're working on it. Do you know anything about petrolsene lighting systems?"

"Not a clue."

Calandra hurried back towards the stairs, almost tripping up the first one. "If anyone tries to leave, take your time. It's dark back there, right?"

"Dark enough for some sneaky action." Calandra could practically hear Spencer wink at her.

"Just be polite. But also take your time."

Clang! Clang! Clang! Oooooooh...

"What now?" she breathed into the thick darkness wrapping back around her. She focused on her annoyance, trying to smother the frigid squirming in her stomach. The noise had come from somewhere above. It had stopped for the moment, and she headed into the storeroom just below the barroom to investigate.

A single jack-o'-lantern had been placed in here. A bit of festivity behind the scenes, but it appeared more foreboding than festive now as it sat alone in a sea of dark. And not just dark. Being an Old World building, the Tower lacked some of the more modern comforts. Radiators, namely. The fireplace downstairs helped, and having so many people packed above created its own heating system, but the storeroom felt cold as a tomb at the moment.

Calandra crept slowly towards the pumpkin, its toothy maw gaped open in a perpetual scream. It would have to serve as her light for exploring. She banged her knee on a crate and stumbled, loosing a series of oaths against whatever had caused this mess.

Something warm took her hand, and Calandra jumped back. Not far enough to get away, as the presence maintained its hold, but it spoke this time, which stilled her.

"Let me help you."

"I… gah! Kieran!" she whispered-yelled back. "Will everyone please stop doing that?!"

"Apologies. I didn't mean to scare you. Saying that, why are you scared?"

"Sorry for whatever my heart's doing to you at the moment," Calandra said, softening.

She'd spent enough time with Kieran to know the better he knew someone, the less their blood tempted him. Still, it couldn't have been easy for him.

She squeezed the Vampyre's hand, though it somehow felt less like a hand at the moment. "As much as I appreciate the guide, you shouldn't be down here. What if someone sees you?"

"Cali…" Amusement painted every syllable. "I couldn't be more invisible if I tried, and I'm not even trying."

She relaxed. Fair enough. And if some kind of unhappy apparition had crossed over, perhaps a Vampyre provided some protection. "Do you think it's possible for spirits to visit us?"

"I think any number of things are possible."

Before Calandra could respond, as if contributing to the conversation, another wail rose up, followed by more clanging. She turned in the direction of the boiler room, though the door was as hidden as Kieran.

She squeezed his hand, and the Vampyre replied, "It is quite alive from what I can tell."

"Good… I think. I need to get over there."

Kieran led her seamlessly through the maze of chairs, boxes, and other business paraphernalia, placing her hand on the door handle when they arrived. Calandra tried the knob, pulled, but the door only rattled in response.

"Would you like me to take care of it?" Kieran whispered, a warm breeze against her ear.

"No, I need this to look as normal as possible. Will you take me back towards the stairs, please? And then make sure nothing… bizarre happens?"

"I don't know how much help I can be, but I will do my best."

"Thank you."

Kieran led her as far as the entrance to the stairwell. Before releasing Calandra's hand, he said, "Tell me if Neal gets the fangs close to the Vampyre's mouth."

Calandra managed a smile. It faded, however, when she heard the telltale sign of Gabriel having to flex his muscles, quite possibly physically as well as metaphorically.

"Oi!"

A moment later, someone shouted, "Watch where you're pointing those darts!"

Gripping the handrail, Calandra quickened her pace.

The mood in the barroom was palpably different than when she'd left it. The air reeked with discontent. Hector's hair, always so neatly coiffed, had developed a few ducktails as he zipped back and forth to keep customers happy. Someone was frozen mid-reach by the back of the bar, barely illuminated by a family of small scowling pumpkins. He'd been going for one of the bottles stored back there, and Gabriel pinned the man in place with his eyes. Wendy and Moira were lost amongst the crowd at the moment.

Calandra headed for the bar. She was still sifting through options when a familiar voice broke through her thoughts.

"Calandra, there you are!"

She turned and saw Neal and Copper elbowing their way— Copper doing most of the elbowing—through the murk towards her.

"Heard you were having some technical issues," Copper said.

"Would you like a couple of engineers to have a look?"

Calandra could do nothing but stare at them, because forcing herself to not repeatedly slap a hand against her forehead took the rest of her mental faculties. Still, "I'm an idiot" slipped from her mouth. She shook her head and added more sensibly, "I hate to ask you, but we are in a bit of a bind."

"It's no problem," Neal said.

Calandra motioned for them to follow and hurried towards the bar. "Gabriel," she shouted over the din. "Take these two down to the boiler room. The door's stuck. See if they can get us sorted." Then, turning back to the man who'd tried to filch some free liquor, who was still standing in exactly the same place, she said, "Come now, sir. That's no way for a man of your breeding to behave, is it?"

The man slunk off, and Calandra went about soothing as many ruffled feathers as she could. Most of the food prep had been put on hold, so Laura, Moira, and Wendy helped fill drink orders.

Calandra didn't worry about Kieran being discovered. He'd avoided notice in the Tower for years. What did concern her was the small voice asking from the back of her mind questions like, "What if it is a specter? What then? What are you going to do?" Or it made unhelpful suggestions like, "Banshees used to exist. Maybe it's one of those. You've seen stranger things. And it is a full moon out on harvest night."

This voice was gratifyingly muzzled when, not ten minutes after Gabriel had gone off with Neal and Copper, the lights came back on with a pleasing hiss. A cheer went up from the crowd, and Calandra immediately reassessed the room. A few games needed their supplies refreshed, which worked out since she needed to go downstairs anyway.

The lights being back on didn't mean nothing supernatural had happened, her annoying voice pointed out. Though having them back did make Calandra feel much better about facing whatever it was. What met her in the storeroom was nothing like what she'd imagined.

"Is this our poltergeist?" she asked, curling her lip in disapproval.

"Aye," Copper replied.

"I thought it was the loo!" slurred a man, heaped in a chair and resting his head on the table. He still clutched the special copper mug Gabriel served one of their custom drinks in. It looked a bit dented.

"I'm afraid there's a bit of a mess in there," Neal said. "Thankfully, all he did was pull the emergency shut-off valve. Just had to turn it back on."

Gabriel crossed his arms over his expansive chest and grunted, "Door's broken now."

"Oh dear," Calandra sighed. Stepping closer, she asked gently, "Sir, you've had quite a bit to drink tonight, haven't you?"

"S'been a bit. I lost count."

"Alright. Are you here with anyone?"

The man nodded, stretching his cheek back and forth along the wood of the table, and Calandra took the details of his party.

"Gabriel, I'll be back as soon as I can. Please keep our guest company in the meantime. Neal and Copper, I am so sorry for the inconvenience. As a token of my appreciation, please enjoy anything you like tonight on the house."

"Really, Calandra, it was nothing," Neal said. "You don't have to—"

"Thank you kindly, Miss Calandra," Copper interrupted. "We'll be off to enjoy your hospitality now. Just holler if you need anything else." He popped in a bow before practically trotting back upstairs.

The man's friends were found and very sorry about their friend's behavior. When Calandra trudged up the stairs to her flat hours later but much happier, she found Kieran waiting for her with a glass of wine in hand.

"So? All's well in the end?"

"Yes, hauntings and all." She flopped onto her couch, being careful not to spill her wine. "Do you still want to know how Neal did at Pin the Fangs on the Vampyre?"

Kieran folded himself next to her and grinned, showing his own fangs. "Of course."

"Terrible. They ended up in the Vampyre's hair. Though to be fair, it was pretty late into the night and Copper must have spun him at least five times."

Kieran laughed from deep in his belly. "I told you that would be a good game." He mimed tipping a glass towards her. "Happy harvest festival, Cali."

"Happy harvest festival, Kieran." She tipped her real glass towards him. "To locks on doors, new doors, and good friends."

DIFFERENT CAGES, ALL PRISONS

If you've ever wondered how Camilla and Kieran first met, you're in luck! Takes place several years before the events of *Out of the Shadows*. Only very slight spoilers for *Out of the Shadows*.

~~~

K ieran felt like he could sleep for a hundred years. Thank the stars he was finally back… well, not home, but as close as he could get nowadays. A few relaxing weeks with Mina and Neal was just the thing for soothing traveling aches.

"I will rip out his intestines and *feed them to him*!"

In all the years Kieran had known her, he had never heard Mina so upset. He rushed through the kitchen, up the stairs, and burst into Neal's drawing room. The desk and tables were tidy, the books shelved or neatly stacked, and the liquor bottles and glassware all arranged within his open globe bar. He and Mina, however, stood in the center with drawn faces and a multitude of emotions swirling in their eyes. Mina's eyes were red and puffy from crying, and her hands balled into fists at her sides. Neal somehow looked both determined and defeated.

"Kieran," Neal said. A brief flash of happiness lit his

~~~

expression, but it faded when he looked back to his wife.

She looked away, spine stiff. Kieran knew that posture well. He'd seen it plenty of times when he and Mina had attended medical school together. She was struggling to keep herself composed.

He approached gently. "My friends, what has happened?"

Mina wrapped her arms around herself, and Neal placed a hand on her shoulder.

"Adelle… she…" Mina pressed a shaking hand to her mouth. Neal drew closer while Kieran took her free hand in his. She looked at him, and tears slipped down her cheeks. In a cracking whisper, she said, "Adelle has been arrested for stealing. She's in the Halls of Justice."

The admission broke her. Mina covered her face with her hand and wept. She curled into Neal's embrace and did not seem to notice Kieran lift her other hand, still grasped in his, to his heart.

The Halls of Justice? Adelle? Stealing? Kieran would have been less surprised if they'd told him a giant hole had opened up in the earth and swallowed half the city overnight. Had Mina's touch not tethered him in place, he might have fallen over.

There were no trials in Springhaven. There were only accusations and punishments. Rather, one punishment. A life of imprisonment and torture. The latter was, so the party line went, to extract information about possible other criminal activity—for all criminals surely knew others. That, and to punish those who, through their criminality, had threatened other citizens' safety.

Accusations, Kieran thought.

"Who?" he asked. He didn't need to specify further.

"William," Neal answered. Mina was still sobbing in his arms. "Fifth Hawkins."

Kieran's jaw dropped, showing his fangs. "How? Why?" He shook himself. "Adelle would never."

Adelle, Mina's sister, was one of the kindest people Kieran had ever had the good fortune to know. Before he had been turned into a Vampyre, back when he and Mina had been courting, he and Adelle had shared quite a rapport. Protectiveness of her sister had eventually turned to gratitude for Kieran's constant support of the doctor-in-training. Medical school had not been easy for Mina, what with her being one of the only women in attendance and certain classmates thinking they had any right to be cruel. Since Kieran's turning, Adelle, like most everyone else, believed him to be dead. Mina and Neal had kept the Vampyre abreast of their old circle's news, however, and he looked in on old friends and family when he could.

"We know," Neal replied. "The report says it was over jewelry."

"Jewelry!" Mina snarled, head snapping up. Rage had come back to replace sorrow. "Of all the absurd notions! She never cared for jewelry. That gib-faced cockroach! I know he's framed her. I just know it! Probably hoping it'll get him promoted to Fourth, the snake."

Kieran nodded slowly. He'd never met William Hawkins, but he'd watched from the shadows for years. William, a Fifth in the Enforcer order, had always been a proud man, but he'd been enamored with Adelle since they'd started courting. And their happiness had continued up until she'd had…

"What about Camilla?" he asked.

That stilled Mina, who looked ready to make good on her evisceration promise.

"She's coming to live with us," Neal said. His voice was resolved, but his eyes expressed heavy worries.

A courier delivered Camilla as if she was just another parcel. For three days, the ten-year-old girl had been in the care of a city-

approved governess. This woman, sharp-eyed and built like a brick, attended the handoff as both witness and judge. As Fifth Hawkins had given up guardianship of his only child, the subsequent paperwork and processing time put the poor thing in limbo. Neal, who rather despised his position as a magistrate, had tried to use his limited power and contacts to hurry the process along, but the city was firm. No rush. And the governess would return several times during the next few weeks to check on Camilla's adjustment. Child welfare was too important.

"Tell that to all the children packed into orphanages," Mina had sneered.

At least she and Neal had been able to use their wealth (and history of charitable donations to said orphanages) to procure private care for Camilla.

He and Mina arranged their schedules so they would both be home when their niece arrived. Exactly like receiving a parcel, the couple had to sign papers to complete the transfer. They all stood in the Allens' receiving hall before the grand stairway. The late afternoon sun spilled buckets of light over them. Mina couldn't decide if she liked this or thought it was in poor taste on the sun's part. All the while, the governess described Camilla and her situation to them as if they were strangers. And as if Camilla was not standing right there.

"She is my niece," Mina said, perhaps a touch too sharply. "I am well aware of her temperament." To be fair, the governess had the audacity to describe Camilla as aloof. Mina opened her mouth and then closed it like she'd had more to say on the matter before thinking better of it.

"I am only doing my job, Mrs. Allen," the governess said.

"*Doctor* Allen." This time, Mina really did snap. The governess raised a disapproving eyebrow at her. Mina took a deep breath through her nose and added more gently, "Thank you for being so… comprehensive."

She checked Camilla's reaction with a quick glance, but the girl only continued to silently stare at the ground.

The process was completed, cordial goodbyes were exchanged, and Neal shut the door with studied control. Mina knew he would rant later. They'd spent every waking minute together either ranting or, in her case, grieving. As soon as the necessary but odious guests had been shut out, Mina crouched to Camilla's level. Her skirts poofed around her with the quick movement.

Mina had run this scenario over in her head countless times. What was the best thing to say to a child who'd just lost her mother and been abandoned by her father? Mina had mentally played out noble speeches and self-gratifying tirades about the contemptible William-ratbag-Hawkins. Now faced with the real situation, only one thing occurred to her to say.

She took Camilla's hands in hers. "I love you, darling. Your uncle Neal and I love you so much, and we're going to take care of you. Alright?"

Camilla nodded at her shoes. Mina was pleased her voice hadn't cracked—she'd determined she would be strong for Camilla —but that little gesture from her niece nearly broke Mina's resolve. Thankfully, Neal squatted down next to her and joined the cause.

"Are you hungry, Camilla? Miss Esther is making something really nice. She wouldn't tell me what, but I think it's going to be delicious."

Camilla shook her head. The lump in Mina's throat grew. Camilla didn't want some of Esther's cooking? That had never happened before. *Ever*.

Whether she'd been waiting in the wings or simply knew when she was needed, Esther suddenly emerged from the back hallway like honey and roses. "Hello, my lamb." She plopped a kiss atop Camilla's flaxen-haired head. "Hungry or not, why don't you come back to the kitchen with me? You can make some new dough people. How's that sound?"

Esther held out her hand. After a long, silent moment, Camilla took it and allowed herself to be led back to the kitchen.

"Thank the stars for Esther." Mina stared at the door they'd just disappeared through. She stood again and turned back to her husband. "We must help Camilla feel some sense of normalcy." Neal wrapped an arm around Mina and pulled her close. "Did you find out anything about Adelle? How she's doing?"

Neal shook his head. "No one seems to have access to prisoner information. I even tried chumming up to Magistrate Harding. The man is a human canker sore."

"He can't be worse than William Hawkins." Mina practically gagged on the name. "I'm still tempted to march down there and ask him myself." She sagged. "Not that it will do me any good."

Neal kissed her head. "We'll manage. We have to."

Kieran opened the little door to the cellar and crouch-walked out. There really wasn't anything for it. The door was hidden beneath the stairs, so Kieran bore the daily silly walk with dignity. Or as much dignity as possible. Since Camilla had arrived, he'd waited each night to emerge until well after her bedtime. Only when he'd shut the hidden door behind him and turned did he scent her. A second later, she spoke.

"Is there a whole room back there?"

Kieran did the first thing he could think of. Still crouched, he closed his eyes and covered his mouth with a hand. A long silence passed, but he knew Camilla still occupied the cellar with him. By the sound of her voice, she was about ten feet away.

"Are you alright?" she asked.

"Yes, thank you," Kieran replied from behind his hand. As one might expect, it came out a bit muffled.

Another pause. "Are you going to be ill?"

"No."

"Then why are you doing that with your face?"

"Because I don't want to scare you."

Another pause. Then Kieran heard Camilla draw closer. He debated going back into his room, but Camilla could easily watch him unlock the door. She might not follow him in—she'd been raised with all the standard rules of propriety—but he didn't trust her not to go exploring when no one was watching. He had once been a child himself after all. And he really didn't feel like babysitting his own room. That being the case, still hiding his Vampyre features, Kieran waddled out from under the stairs. He blindly felt his way around them and started the ascent. Camilla's footsteps followed.

"Why do you think your face would scare me?" she asked.

"Because I have a scary face." He hoped his clothing disguised the gauntness of his frame as well. Kieran abruptly found the door to the kitchen with his nose. He started back when it smashed into the old wood and barely swallowed down the curse that tried to follow. He found the door handle and fumbled through.

Once up the rest of the stairs, he asked, "Where are your aunt and uncle, please? Or Miss Esther? And shouldn't you be in bed?"

"Your face doesn't look scary." Camilla, unsurprisingly, had meandered her way around Kieran to look at him.

Kieran heaved a sigh and wondered if there was any way out of this pickle. He checked his belief in Camilla's curiosity waning and found his faith very weak indeed. Therefore, candor would have to win the day… he hoped.

"Camilla, let's go find Mina and Neal, shall we?"

He heard her foot scrape on the floor. From the sound of it, she'd worn her slippers, which were probably less than pristine now after visiting the cellar.

"How do you know my name?"

"Because Mina and Neal told me who you were."

"How do you know? You didn't look at me. And we haven't been acquainted before today."

"Camilla, are you stalling because you're not supposed to be out of bed?" More foot fidgeting. "Tell you what. You go back to bed *and* to sleep like you're supposed to, and I won't tell Mina and Neal about this little encounter, hm?" He had every intention of telling them about it as soon as possible, but Camilla didn't need to know that.

"Alright." Kieran was frankly impressed. He'd never heard anyone sound so put upon in his entire life.

He listened as Camilla left. She wasn't particularly good at sneaking, he noticed. She must have simply gotten lucky tonight. It made sense when he found Mina and Neal all the way up in Mina's study—an oddly shaped room tucked up in the manor's only tower. Keeping an eye out for a certain little eavesdropper, he related what had just happened.

Kieran could leave that night, and Neal and Mina could refuse to tell Camilla who the strange man in the cellar was.

"I don't think secrets between us would help anything at this juncture. We're all she…" Mina's voice caught in her throat. She cleared it away. "She needs to feel she can trust us."

"I know, but is a ten-year-old mature enough to keep Kieran's secret?" Neal turned to the man himself. "How would you feel about her knowing?"

Kieran rubbed his chin. Right before he was turned, clean-shaven had been briefly in fashion. "If I stay, she will eventually find out. She's already inquisitive, and you two are hardly the people to discourage that." He was pleased this comment produced small smiles. "If I go, however, it only delays the issue. Unless—"

"Oh no," Neal said. "Out of the question." He softened. "At least, we'd like you with us anytime you're in the city."

Kieran smiled at his friends' consideration. "You two know Camilla better than I. If you feel she can be trusted to keep my existence a secret, then I trust your judgment."

The conversation went on from there. They weighed options and offered alternative ideas, not that there were many sensible ones of those. In the end, they decided to have a family meeting the next evening. If it went well, they'd bring Kieran in for a proper introduction.

Neal's heart pounded in his chest. It wasn't that he didn't believe Camilla to be sensible or trustworthy. It was that he remembered how *he* had been as a child. And now he was expected to raise one himself? He'd made some pretty boneheaded decisions even as a young man. Still did now and then, if he was honest. Had he made different choices years back, they might not have even needed this meeting. Kieran might not have been turned.

Neal refocused. He'd hashed out his mistakes a long time ago, with both himself and Kieran. The latter took a rather high road and disagreed that they were even mistakes. In any case, this was no time to revisit them.

Camilla sat on the sofa in the conservatory. She looked very serious. Then again, she and Mina were having a very serious discussion.

"So you understand the difference?" Mina was asking.

She was to be commended. Neal, for whom words didn't come as naturally as they did for his wife, had been mostly listening for the last fifteen minutes. Mina explained to Camilla, in somewhat simplified terms, the nuanced difference between a secret and respecting someone's private information. She'd used her position as a doctor for examples, and Neal was infinitely grateful she had taken up this task. He would have flubbed the entire thing. Even with Mina and her impressive skills, however, he couldn't help but wonder if he was helping bar his best friend from ever coming back to Springhaven.

Camilla nodded, and Mina briefly quizzed her to prove her comprehension. In the end, she passed the test.

"There's someone we want you to meet." Mina turned to the butler's pantry, which led to the kitchen. "Esther, will you and Kieran please come in here?"

Neal's heart picked up its pace. Esther and Kieran, with their arms entwined, walked into the conservatory. Kieran's eyes were shut and his lips pressed together.

Camilla studied the Vampyre. "He has personal information I need to keep private."

"Very good," Neal said. His heartbeat slowed a little.

Esther patted Kieran's arm. "Camilla, this is Mister Kieran. He's been a good friend of your uncle's since they were knee-high."

"Why does he…" Camilla trailed off when her aunt gave her a look.

Mina added, "Remember your manners."

Camilla shifted on the couch and waited. Neal had found one of the most difficult lessons as a child, especially given his proclivities, was that not everything was his right to know. He suspected Camilla was experiencing the same struggle.

"Camilla," Mina said, bringing the girl's attention back to her. "Mister Kieran has given us permission to tell you about a condition he has. It makes his eyes and teeth look different from ours. We're telling you so you won't be surprised when you see them."

Neal was watching Kieran, but from the corner of his eye he saw his niece nod. Esther patted Kieran's arm again, and he peeked one eye slowly open, revealing solid black hiding beneath his eyelids. Camilla cocked her head to the side. He let his jaw relax next, and the tips of his fangs just showed. Mina had never shielded her niece from medical diagrams and other doctorly accouterments.

Perhaps that was why Camilla was taking this revelation in such stride.

She folded her hands in her lap. "Do you live here, Mister Kieran?"

He nodded. "When I'm in Springhaven."

Camilla's brow puckered. "Does that mean you're sometimes not in Springhaven?"

"Sometimes, yes." Kieran smiled at Neal.

Neal suspected he and the Vampyre's thoughts were similar. This was going far better than hoped. He turned back to Camilla. "Sometimes he goes all the way down to Bone Port. And other times, Mister Kieran travels as far north as the Bladed Mountains near Duskwood."

Camilla's cherubic face pinched into a scowl. Without another word, she got up and strode out of the conservatory.

Damage control was quick and effective. Mina and Neal impressed on Camilla the importance of keeping Kieran a secret. They never actually said he was a Vampyre, nor did they tell her most everyone thought he was dead. They were, however, very straightforward as to the danger of telling others about him. Camilla, oddly enough, didn't put up a fight. She was obedient as ever to her aunt and uncle, if not a bit surly about the whole thing. Whenever Kieran was around, however, she was downright rude. Mina, Neal, and Esther all had to scold her for poor manners on more than one occasion. After Esther took away Camilla's dessert one night, the girl resorted to the silent treatment. And she refused to tell any of them why she was so cross with Kieran.

Thankfully, school and private lessons afterward consumed more of Camilla's time now that she was settling more into living with the Allens. A few nights a week, however, were stilted and

cold. And then came the evening Neal and Mina had to go out.

"You shouldn't have to attend this fundraiser," Kieran heard Mina fuss. "Magistrate Harding didn't actually help you."

"No, but I traded a favor for the pleasure of learning he wouldn't help me," Neal replied.

Kieran paced the hallway outside his friends' bedroom while they dressed for their evening. Esther was immovably engaged elsewhere, leaving Kieran as caretaker. He would be lying if he said he wasn't avoiding the child at the moment. Neal had expressed feeling inadequate to the task of taking her in—not that it stopped him from doing his duty. Kieran knew precisely how Neal felt.

"At least he's only pushing some tax reform," Neal added.

"So your integrity remains unsullied," Mina said. "Here, you're crooked."

Kieran suspected Mina was fixing Neal's cravat for him. Once upon a time, she'd done the same for Kieran, back when they'd been courting. Before he'd been turned. Kieran wandered back down the hallway. Facing Camilla's icy glares seemed preferable to wallowing.

He found her sitting in the front parlor. Inside a lap-mounted embroidery square stretched a lacy white handkerchief. Camilla didn't look at him as she stitched what looked destined to be an "H" onto the corner of the kerchief. He could see an "A" and a larger "C" traced before the "H." Kieran took up residence in an armchair nearby and tried to be as inoffensive as possible. Eventually, Neal and Mina appeared. They told Camilla to behave for Kieran, asked him a multitude of questions, and threw concerned looks over their shoulders as they left.

Not three minutes after the Allens' departure, Camilla asked, "Why couldn't Aunt Mina have stayed home tonight?"

"Because it's proper for her to join her husband. Besides, he needs the support. By all accounts, it's going to be a terrible party."

"I think that's asinine."

Kieran wondered where she'd learned the last word and if she was using it because it sounded like *ass*. His only reply, however, was, "So do I."

Camilla offered no retort as she unthreaded a stitch she'd just made. Her tongue stuck out in concentration, or maybe frustration, as she tried it again. And again, she had to undo it.

"Would you like help?" Kieran offered. She still said nothing, so he added, "I'm actually a rather dab hand with an embroidery needle."

Camilla set the square aside and stood quite decidedly, only to begin aimlessly wandering the room. She stopped near Kieran and examined a bowl of wax fruit.

"I don't think they're ripe yet, do you?" he joked. Weak, he knew, but he was trying.

Camilla glowered at his sheepish smile. Then, to Kieran's utter bafflement, she popped one of the decorative grapes into her mouth. She stared at Kieran and chewed like she was trying to intimidate the rest of the fruit. Kieran saw the moment she realized her folly. Camilla's face twisted, mouth opened, and tongue ejected.

With superhuman speed, Kieran whisked a small rubbish bin beneath her chin. The grape, now gooey and mangled, dropped harmlessly into the bin. There it could glom onto the bottom instead of into the carpet. Camilla stared daggers at Kieran.

"I wasn't the one who thought that was a good idea," he said before he thought better of it.

The daggers sharpened. "Are you a criminal?" A low, suspicious note rang in Camilla's tone.

The question hurt Kieran. It dredged up memories from when he'd first been turned. Inexperienced and alone, he'd never feared for his humanity more than during those long nights.

"I am not," he said, a shade too insistently.

She had the look of someone about to take a dangerous leap. Kieran silently willed her not to. Then she said, "I bet you are."

"Camilla Hawkins—"

"Don't call me that name!"

A voice so small shouldn't be able to hold that much anger. Kieran pressed his lips into a thin line and walked the rubbish bin back to its proper place. From behind him, Camilla let out a squeak.

What now? he thought as he turned back.

Camilla's arms were crossed over her chest, her expression crumpling. Kieran softened.

"Camilla, what's wrong?"

"Nothing," she snapped. A few tears slipped down her rosy cheeks.

Kieran raised his hands in surrender. "Very well. Nothing it is."

"You wouldn't understand anyway," Camilla muttered.

"How do you know unless you ask?"

"Because you can leave. You can go anywhere you want. *I* can't." She jammed her fists down next to her sides and stamped her foot. "And I don't want to be here!"

In a moment of utter exasperation, Kieran mimicked her movements. "Well, neither do I!"

"Then leave!" Camilla was properly sobbing now.

"And go where? I'm a Vampyre, Camilla! If people see me, they'll try to kill me on sight. I'm just as stuck here as you."

Camilla's tears slowed. She sniffed and wiped her nose on the back of her hand. Then she began hiccupping. "A… a Vampyre?"

Kieran groaned inwardly. They—the adults—had agreed they didn't need to explain that part to Camilla yet. She'd likely figure it out in her own time, but it was better not to throw too much at her all at once. Well, he'd blundered that fairly spectacularly.

"Yes, a Vampyre."

Camilla screwed up her face, probably trying to figure out what that meant, or maybe what that meant for her. "Doesn't that mean you drink blood?"

Kieran nodded before flopping onto the couch. Best to assume the most nonthreatening pose possible, so he laid himself down with his legs hanging off the cushion's edge.

Camilla said, "That's your condition." He nodded again, staring at the ceiling. He heard her come closer. "You're on my project."

Kieran looked and saw his head had indeed shoved her embroidery square against the armrest. He handed it back to her. "Apologies." Camilla sat on the end of the couch. The silence pressed on Kieran's throat. "I wasn't supposed to tell you I'm a Vampyre. We worried it would frighten you."

"I'm not—" *hiccup!* "—frightened."

"I can see that."

"I don't really know what a Vampyre is."

Thank the stars for that. Adelle never was much interested in the Old World, not like Neal.

Kieran lifted his head to look at Camilla. She was stroking the bright pink stitches she had made in the handkerchief. He dared nudging her foot with his. "If you don't like the name Hawkins, why did you put it on your kerchief?"

"It's not for Hawkins." Camilla sounded angry again. "It's for Husselbee."

"Ah." Husselbee was Mina and Adelle's maiden name. Kieran sat up. "Camilla, I know it probably doesn't help, but I am truly sorry about your mother. I knew Adelle. She was... *is* an incredible person."

Camilla nodded. Kieran waited. Finally, with tears streaming again and a squeaky voice, she said, "She didn't do what they say she did."

"I know she didn't." Kieran's voice was the strongest it had been all night.

When Mina and Neal returned home that night, they were shocked into silence by the sight of Kieran and Camilla sitting together on the sofa. Kieran was showing Camilla how to do an especially complicated stitch on her embroidery square.

He didn't look up, though he'd surely heard them come in. "I didn't master this one until medical school."

"You had to practice a lot of stitches?" Camilla asked. Her eyelids drooped. And no wonder. It was nearly midnight, but she watched Kieran's precise needlework with rather impressive focus given the late hour.

"Millions of them," he said. "Now, here's the tricky part."

As Camilla bowed her head closer to watch, she smiled. "You weren't joking about your embroidery skills."

THE BUTTERFLY EFFECT

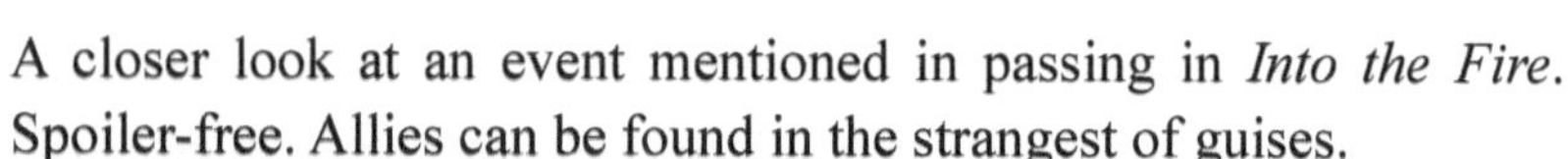

A closer look at an event mentioned in passing in *Into the Fire*. Spoiler-free. Allies can be found in the strangest of guises.

~~~

Yara's stomach growled and twisted on itself. After her usual haunt installed an ingenious new security system—an ill-natured dog with slavering jowls and teeth so large they jutted over its lips—she'd been forced to scavenge for food elsewhere, which had resulted in several harrowing brushes with even more ill-natured restaurant workers. The pain in her stomach pulled her inside the underground market, and her eyes darted like dragonflies, taking in everything at once. First observation: The rumors Yara had heard were right. It was busy now, which gave her hope.

Some of the patrons wore dark cloaks to hide their faces, while others strolled down the aisles as if browsing a shop in the Copper district and not a dilapidated warehouse in Char. Many of the vendors chatted or haggled with their customers, and in the low petrolsene light, all manner of goods glinted on tables or loomed within crates of all sizes. A stand with exotic fruits and vegetables
~~~

from frigid Duskwood and scorching Bone Port made her stomach tear at itself, demanding whatever she could nick from it. Thankfully, the padding strapped to her midsection muffled the noise.

A nearby man with a ragged scar down the side of his face twisted his forked and braided beard between his fingers, and Yara mimicked the action with her own false handlebar mustache. Leading with her cane, to affect the persona of a disgruntled gentleman, she clomped towards the stall next to the fruit and veg one—a weapons dealer—grumbling to herself the whole way.

"I say," she wheezed at the merchant like an asthmatic walrus. "Bit of a disappointment, this place. The way everyone goes on about it, I expected polished marble. Not this oversized lean-to." She banged her cane on the aged but well-maintained floorboards for emphasis.

The weapons vendor smiled coldly. "And yet you wouldn't be here unless you had a very good reason."

"Wanted to see what all the hubbub was about."

"Of course."

Yara pretended to look over the daggers, throwing blades, and other stabbing tools, while the proprietor watched with half-lidded eyes. She sweated beneath her disguise, both from the closeness of the room and her water-thin excuse for being there. She'd observed other criminals talking together. There was an art to the language that escaped her, and hunger had driven her to the market before she could create a convincing character. Another patron bumped into her generously padded backside, and she took her opportunity to create a scene.

Spinning towards the unlucky person, she flared her enhanced nostrils and rumbled, "Watch yourself there, pup!"

The other market-goers around them swiveled to watch whatever drama was unfolding. Yara had to school her expression as she saw none other than the bearded man with the scarred face turn in response to her insult. He bared his teeth, looming over her squat, portly form, and flexed his mainmast-sized arms. She switched tactics and pointed at another table nearby.

"You there! You've got to pay for that!"

The eyes around her followed her outstretched, gloved finger, and she took the opportunity to snatch a yellow star-shaped fruit from the neighboring produce vendor. Unfortunately, both her gloves and the fruit were slick, and she fumbled with it, attracting the attention of its owner, a beefy woman who looked as if she indulged more in rich meats than plants.

"Oi! You tryna steal from me!" Yara opened her mouth to reply, but the woman was already shouting and waving. "Got us a thief over here! Come'n get this lout!"

Rook was standing at the tinted window of his office when the ruckus began on his market's floor. The office jutted a story above, giving him a perfect vantage of everything that happened. Strict display regulations ensured no one did anything outside of his sight. He watched with interest as the fat old lump accosted Salt—the man with the braided beard—and then very quickly changed his tune. The change made Rook zero in on the fat man, and he saw the entire starfruit blunder.

"Marlowe, go see what that's about," he said, jerking his head towards the hullabaloo. "I'll follow along in a moment."

Marlowe, his second in command and main thug, gave a silent nod, headed out of the office, and stomped down the metal stairway to the market floor. Rook watched as the crowd parted around him, a barracuda through a school of minnows. Agnes, the woman who owned the exotic produce stall, spotted Marlowe, and even through the distance and thick glass, Rook could hear her shrieking her displeasure. He chuckled and turned for the door.

The market-goers penned Yara in, snatching away every opportunity for escape. She dared not get too near them and was a little surprised no one had tried to lay hands on her yet. Keeping one eye on the mob and one on the approaching thug, Yara trembled. She tried to make it appear she instead shook with livid indignation, but doubted her performance. The man, built like a tree, stared down at her with empty eyes. Meanwhile, the crowd around her grew more bloodthirsty.

"Come on, Aggie, thump him in his rotten face!"

"Gonna get what's comin' to ya now!"

"Gut the filthy thief where he stands, Marlowe!"

Yara swallowed hard but didn't break character. It would be worse if they saw her as she truly was. "Now see here! You've got this all wrong. I was merely catching the fruit as it fell, for which you are very *welcome*, madam!" She tried to inject venom into this last statement, but it came out more strangled than scoffing.

Marlowe reached them, and Yara stopped wondering why no one had fought her outright. Cracking his mallet-like knuckles, he looked to Agnes.

"Let's hear it, Aggie," he growled.

"This good-for-nothin' was tryna steal my product! Cost me a pretty penny, those starfruits." She then gave a gap-toothed smile and cooed, "They's some of your favorites, if I recall, ain't they, Marlowe?"

He swept his gaze to Yara, and she felt it thump against her. "And what do you say?"

"I was trying to help the lady," Yara replied, puffing up her chest. "I see now this establishment lacks the distinguished honor I was told it held."

Marlowe glared down at her, his stare pinning her in place. She licked her lips, her mouth suddenly dry, and more plump beads of perspiration sprang up to replace what had just disappeared. The crowd seethed at her words, buzzing and humming as if she stood within a hive of furious hornets.

"I'm sorry to hear you think so ill of my little business."

The sound of slow, heavy footfalls on metal rang from Yara's left, and she looked up to see a man with a too-cool expression descending from the owner's office. He leisurely rolled his sleeves up to his elbows, straightened his already perfect waistcoat. Around his eyes smeared thin lines of black. She heard someone nearby hiss the name Rook. She recognized it and instantly believed everything she had heard in conjunction with it. He glided through the crowd like a shark through the ocean—confident, determined, superior.

"What seems to be the problem?" His voice washed like a tranquil wave over the entire room, shushing every other noise. It was the voice of a man with all the power and time in the world.

"This one's been shoplifting, sir," Marlowe replied.

"I see."

He'd already known; Yara could tell by his tone. She glanced up at the owner's office, hanging a story above them and overlooking the entire market, and then around her again. She almost broke down then, but the sneering faces on all sides drove her to continue the ruse. Better a fat old man than herself. They would only beat her in this guise… hopefully.

"What would you like done with him?" Marlowe asked.

Rook's eyes remained cool as he considered the question. Yara watched him wait, drawing out the onlookers' suspense. He kept his gaze on her as he replied, "Standard punishment."

Before Yara could wonder what standard punishment entailed, something solid connected with the back of her head. She stumbled forward, the extra bulk strapped around her front dragging her forward, but she jabbed her cane forward and caught herself. Fear made her cling to her persona more tightly than ever.

"See here!" she half croaked.

In the blink of an eye, Rook snatched the cane from her hands. She'd barely gotten her feet under her, but a second later a kick to the back of her knees sent her sprawling to the ground. In her periphery, she saw Rook examining her cane as leisurely, as if he was inspecting berries along a country lane. In a move so futile as to be laughable, she reached for it, and he responded with an arched eyebrow. She curled into a ball when Marlowe kicked her in the gut, realizing with relief how beneficial her padded midsection secretly was. She groaned and pretended to be in agony, and Marlowe, apparently excited by her reaction, delivered a few more blows. Her cries turned real when one of the kicks caught her in the face.

"That's enough." Rook's words settled blissfully in Yara's ears, and she swallowed a sob that had been crawling up her throat. "Up to my office. I have some questions for our guest."

Yara's eyes popped open. No longer caring about what the crowd might do to her, she scrabbled across the floor in the direction of the exit. She hadn't made it more than a few inches when Marlowe hauled her to her feet and shoved her forward. She caught herself against a table—barely—and watched as blood dripped onto it in heavy splotches. She felt her false mustache slipping as warmth ran down her face, and she pressed a gloved hand beneath her nose to both re-stick it and stem the flow. She tried to break away once more, but Marlow merely reached out and caught her by the back of her collar before half dragging her up to Rook's office.

"*I wasn't stealing!*" she spluttered again and again.

Rook leaned against the door of his office and examined the cane in his hands. From a distance, it had appeared of very fine make, but up close he saw it for what it really was: a costume prop. The grip was nothing more than molded and painted clay, and the shaft a stick of cheap lacquered pine. The portly thief stood a little ways off, wobbling like a bowl of New Year's gelatin salad, while Marlowe leaned against the opposite wall.

Rook spun the cane skillfully before him. It tumbled back and forth over his agile fingers like a circus acrobat. "Why the deception?" His voice was calm, soothing, mirroring the soft diffused light pooling throughout his office. "People of all backgrounds are welcome here, and we are hardly in a position to judge."

"I demand you let me leave this instant!" The man's hand at his mouth muffled the words a little, but their intent rang out all too clearly.

"You stole from one of my people," Rook replied, walking forward and still spinning the cane. "That cannot stand." The man opened his mouth to object, but Rook cut him off. "I watched the whole thing. Now, I have a lot on my plate today, so can we hurry this along, please? Why the deception?"

The man lowered his voice, clearly straining to hang onto his composure, eyes flicking towards the closed door behind Rook. "I don't need to answer to you."

Rook sighed. "Just remember, I did say I'm in a hurry."

With that, he swung the cane back like a cricketer and his bat and whacked the old man across his jiggling belly. Fabric and skin split open as the gent stumbled back, legs flailing in the air as he fell.

"What the blazes?" Rook exclaimed, taking in the new scene before him.

From the man's bloated, injured stomach spewed not blood but snowy white stuffing. His legs had partially… come apart, one skewed at a horrendous angle and the other sitting a few feet away from the body. And, as the bizarre cherry on top of the entire baffling tableau, his mustache slid down his bleeding face like a grotesque slug.

"What the blazes?" Rook said again.

His usually sharp, unflappable self had wandered off like it needed a quick drink before tackling the situation at hand. He looked at Marlowe and saw twin feelings in the thug's gawping expression.

Yara's eyes rolled back and forth between the two men, mind racing for what to do now. Slowly, she reached up and stuffed her stomach padding back into place, as if that might replace some of her character's lost dignity. The mustache, however, refused to stick back onto her face and just slid down again and again.

"Bit late for that, don't you think?" Rook said, shrugging off his astonishment like an out-of-fashion jacket.

He wasn't wrong, and a new type of terror rose up in Yara. Eschewing her character all together, she left behind her raised platform shoes—the "legs" Rook had seen come off—and crept back like a cat towards the desk, peeling off her gloves as she did. She snatched a gleaming, gold letter opener from atop it and brandished it towards the men before cutting away her encumbering bodysuit with a few, deft strokes. Rook and Marlowe exchanged a look she read perfectly. She was being stupid. Yes, she knew that, but the time for deception had fled screaming. They could easily subdue her—she was tiny even for her age—but she was determined to take as many pieces of them with her before they did.

Rook drew a small square of fabric from his waistcoat pocket and held it out to her. "Kerchief? You've got a bit of blood just there." He then indicated the entire lower half of his face with the grip of the cane, which he still held in his other hand.

Yara shook her head and saw drops of blood follow the movement. Blazes! How much could a person's nose bleed? She shot an acid glare at Marlowe.

He shrugged in response. "Sticky fingers, doll."

"Don't call me that!" she snarled, spitting blood and words together.

Rook looked thoughtful as he tied the kerchief in a loose knot around the end of the cane. His voice matched his looks as he said, "I never once suspected you weren't what you appeared."

Deep down, the words pleased Yara. Not that it had done her much good in the end. She stiffened, ready to dodge as Rook stepped carefully forward and extended the now be-kerchiefed cane towards her. She skirted behind the desk, eyes glued to the infamous crime lord as he continued his slow progress towards her. He laid the cane across the desk, keeping it between them, and stepped back with his hands in the air. Right, like he was ever really unarmed.

"Two against one," Rook said, his voice soft again, but entreating this time too. "Seems only fair you should have another weapon."

Yara narrowed her eyes and reclaimed her cane with much quicker fingers now that she'd discarded her gloves. She snatched the kerchief off it and pressed it to her bloody nose, wincing when she did so with perhaps a bit too much zeal. She watched for how Rook would react to her despoiling the fabric. If she had to guess, it cost more than most families made in a week.

"Come work for me."

Yara shook her head, certain Marlowe had booted her so hard her ears had gotten scrambled. As she did, her eyes caught sight of a table in the corner of the office. Behind it sat a cabinet full of various liquors and other alcoholic beverages, but what tugged at her attention were the crystal containers of nuts, biscuits, and other snacks. Though it had gone to hide while she was getting the stuffing knocked out of her—in every sense—Yara's hunger came roaring back so loudly both Rook and Marlowe looked at her scrawny midsection.

Rook motioned towards the table. "Please, be my guest. We can discuss the details of your contract over breakfast." He snapped his fingers at Marlowe. "Bring us a full Springhavian brekkie. Spare none of the bells and whistles."

While Marlowe left to comply, Yara turned back towards Rook, disbelief sparking in her wide eyes… and a touch of drool at the corner of her mouth. "You're really offerin' me a job?"

"Protection, pay, I'll even throw in a side of beef each month if you'd like."

Yara's stomach spoke up again, making a smirk of amusement curl Rook's lips. She skittered over to the cabinet, never turning her back on Rook and being careful not to corner herself. She threw the bloodied kerchief onto the table and grabbed the closest thing at hand—a packet of table crackers. Ripping it open, she shoved no less than four into her mouth at once.

"You're on." At least, that's what she meant to say, though the crumbly wad of crackers in her gob garbled most of it.

Rook's smile widened. "I'm glad to hear it. First thing's first, what can I call you?"

Yara swallowed and gifted him her own hesitant smile in return. "Chrysalis."

SALTY SIBLINGS

During *Into the Fire*, Rook mentions that Dmitri had been introduced to Kieran at some point. This is that story, set a little past halfway through *Out of the Shadows*. Contains some big spoilers as to the events from *Out of the Shadows*.

~~~

"**K**ieran is like a big brother to me."

That was what Camilla had said when she'd proposed tonight's dinner party. She'd also explained that, not only was Kieran a member of the family, he was a *secret* member, and thus Dmitri couldn't tell anyone about him. It was by far the strangest setup for a meeting he'd ever heard, but he would have agreed even if Camilla had said they were going to dive to the bottom of Cobalt Bay and dine inside a giant clamshell. He'd agree to go to the moon for her if it came to it, though their dining location was nothing and nowhere more interesting than the Allens' manor. And he assumed that Kieran was perhaps another wanted criminal, or at least person of interest in the same way Lenore was. When Dmitri had begun asking, however, Camilla had refused to answer and instead promised that all would be revealed during the
~~~

introductions. Nevertheless, he had a plan for meeting Kieran, and was looking forward to impressing Camilla with it.

The midsummer sun had just set when Dmitri walked up the long drive of the manor and knocked on the front door—three crisp raps of the greyhound door knocker, which hung hidden behind a wreath of real geraniums and oak leaves. He found Neal's enthusiastic decorating to be rather silly and cringed at what the wreath must have cost, to say nothing of where the money could have gone instead. He smiled pleasantly, however, when Esther opened the door and gave her a courteous bow.

"Mister Sawyer, welcome," she said, bustling him inside. "Come in, out of the heat. Let me take your things. Miss Camilla and Lenore are just through there in the parlor. Neal's got his air cooler gadget going, and I've got some nice cold lemonade coming out in just a moment."

Dmitri was glad to lose the flat cap and sack jacket he wore. Though the manor had been designed to facilitate good airflow in order to cool its rooms on hot days such as this one, there was no way to escape the long trousers, waistcoat, tie, and long-sleeved shirt he wore. But he was grateful, for once, that they were all made from cheaper, thinner materials than the finer, thicker ones Neal would be wearing this evening. He resisted the urge to pull at his collar and instead dodged Esther's offer to hang up his cap for him.

The idea of servants made him uncomfortable, and he'd unequivocally drawn the line at being called "Master." Esther, however, never failed to make Dmitri feel warm and fuzzy inside. Quick and efficient, he whisked his hat into his opposite hand and hooked it onto one of the hat pegs jutting out from the wall. He then gifted Esther a small, rare smile. She smiled back, and held out her hands for his jacket.

It was a kind of silent compromise between them, and as he relinquished the garment, Dmitri basked in the aura of comfort the old woman gave off. He thanked her as she hung it up, and then she shooed him affectionately into the parlor. His eyes alighted on Camilla first, and his expression softened. Then the not-quite-openly hostile look Lenore was giving him cooled it again.

He bowed to them both. "Good evening, ladies."

"Dmitri," Camilla cooed, coming over to hold his bare hands in her gloved ones. "Thank you for coming. I realize this is a strange situation, but it's important to me."

"I know," he replied. He lifted her hand to his lips for a delicate kiss.

In background, Lenore looked as if she might vomit.

Propriety demanded that he shake Lenore's hand in greeting too, though Dmitri knew Lenore would rather gnaw off said hand than touch him. He was surprised she hadn't invented some excuse to be absent tonight, or at least feigned sickness. She still blamed him for Rook turning himself in for purging, and probably always would. But here she was, and he wanted tonight to go smoothly, so he squared up to her next, stuck out his hand, and exchanged the quickest handshake he could possibly get away with.

"Lenore," he said.

"Dmitri," she scowled. As the formalities ended, she looked as if she was considering burning her glove.

In the corner of the room, a contraption sat like another guest. It was a sort of bellows, slowly pumping air in and out, like a single lung. It sighed softly with each exchange, and Dmitri noticed the air here in the parlor did feel markedly cooler than it had in the receiving hall.

"And what is this?" he asked.

"That's Neal's air cooler," Camilla said.

"Copper's, actually," Lenore put in, her words clipped. "Neal asked to borrow it especially for tonight." The sharp glint of her eyes added, "For *you*, you undeserving, twaddling git."

He nodded and waited. Awkward silence crept into the room, and Dmitri looked to see Camilla looking towards the entrance to the dining room. Anxiety drew tiny lines between her brows. She really was concerned about him meeting this Kieran fellow. Smoothing situations over had never been Dmitri's forte. Being an Enforcer had granted him the privilege of not even having to try. It allowed him to be an imposing wallflower throughout the few social engagements he attended, and he tried to not attend as many as possible.

Dmitri had a look at his pocket watch, a battered old thing on a plain metal chain, but he kept it wound and shining. "When should we expect Kieran then?"

Straight to the point, *that's* what he was good at, though it certainly wasn't earning him any points with Lenore. Not that he was particularly concerned with her opinion, insofar as it didn't affect his relationship with Camilla.

"He's working on it." Lenore didn't quite snap, but it was a near thing.

The thing that stopped her was likely the sound of Esther's slow but steady plod towards them. She appeared with the promised lemonade a moment later, and Lenore was already moving to assist.

Esther must have heard Dmitri's question, because she said to no one in particular, "Kieran's just finishing getting ready. In the meantime, you three enjoy."

Dmitri clocked five drinks in total on the round, silver tray. "Does Kieran not take refreshments?"

He hadn't meant for it to sound accusatory. That was his Enforcer training. And Enforcers didn't need to apologize for asking rude questions, so rather than fumble an apology, Dmitri left the question hanging. Even Esther paused at that, clearly not certain how to respond, while Lenore and Camilla exchanged looks. Camilla was grasping, while Lenore glared like she wanted to set fire to something. Possibly Dmitri himself. What was with all the intrigue around this one person?

"Oh my stars, what a numpty I'm being. Must be from all the heat in the kitchen."

To her credit, Esther's rather weak cover almost convinced Dmitri. Her brow shone with sweat, and he could just see darker patches beneath the arms of her midnight-blue work blouse.

The lines on Camilla's face deepened, but Esther was already bustling back to the kitchen before anyone could say anything else. Though he remained as unmoved as a statue on the outside, inside, Dmitri groaned and squirmed. He was royally buggering up what should be a nice evening. Camilla was good with social situations, but Dmitri wanted to both support and impress her, instead of making her bear the entirety of tonight's social labor on her own. Because fat lot of help Lenore was being. And where were Engineer and Doctor Allen anyway? The air cooler sighed in the background, and he latched onto it like a buoy in a storm.

"This air cooler, how does it work?"

Again, it sounded like a demand, but it would do. Not that Dmitri expected to understand the answer, and he didn't. Not in the least, as Lenore began to point and rattle off part names and functions, explaining how it did whatever technological things it had been designed to do. He understood that ice was involved in the cooling of the air it expelled, and that was about the extent of it. But the mission had been accomplished. As Dmitri stood there and made all the appropriate noises of acknowledgment, Camilla relaxed beside him.

"Bit of a faff to move, though," came a voice from the entrance to the dining room.

Dmitri turned to see Engineer Allen—Neal to all except Dmitri this evening, because Dmitri couldn't bring himself to be that casual with either him or his wife. He wandered in, his sleeves rolled up to his elbows like he wasn't late attending his own dinner party. Dmitri bristled, mostly because he envied the look. The air cooler helped immensely, but he was still braising low and slow within his own clothes. And he suspected he'd never feel comfortable enough here to follow suit. And why was Engineer Allen coming in from the direction of the dining room? What had been so important at that end of the house to keep him away?

"You have to be really careful with the bellows," Neal went on. "One little hole, and the machine's work efficiency goes right out the window. You can patch it, of course, but you've got to find the bally spot first." He turned from the contraption towards Dmitri with a welcoming smile. "Good to see you, Dmitri."

They shook hands. "Thank you for having me this evening."

"Sorry for the wait," Neal explained. "Kieran doesn't keep quite the same hours as the rest of us."

That, of course, didn't explain why Neal had been late, nor where he'd just come from, but Dmitri didn't say any of that. He just nodded silently. Meanwhile, like a good hostess, Camilla began handing out the glasses of lemonade. Dmitri had to suppress a sigh of relief as the sweet, tart, cold liquid hit the back of his throat and cooled all the way down. Stars, he wanted to swim in a pool of the stuff just now.

Neal took a seat with his glass in hand, and Dmitri looked to Camilla and Lenore to do the same before he did. Lenore stood near the dining room door and looked to have no intention of joining in. Camilla did, however, and gently pulled Dmitri towards the sofa to join her there. For the next few minutes, Neal, Dmitri, and Camilla exchanged the required pleasantries that Dmitri so abhorred: How was work going for each of them? Fine for Dmitri. Camilla had performed her first solo compound fracture resetting. And Neal had recently narrowly avoided getting roped into joining a public relations committee at the museum. Lenore's only contribution was that she had helped Neal pull that maneuver. How were their families doing? Again, Dmitri said fine, though his younger brother, Boris, had scored well on a recent exam. Lenore's and Camilla's families were rather off-limits subjects, and Neal supplied that he'd had a letter from his brother in Duskwood to say that he couldn't possibly come visit while the weather was so hot, and the holidays would be far too busy for such things too. And all the while, Lenore remained positioned at the door to the dining room as if standing guard. Eventually, *finally*, with the mention of family, they moved onto the subject of this evening.

"I understand Camilla has told you that Kieran is a member of this family." Neal's tone was surprisingly cautious. It made Dmitri even more convinced this Kieran fellow was someone the Enforcers would love to get their hands on, in the worst way possible.

Dmitri gave a curt nod. "Yes, and I haven't told a soul about our meeting. It's fine if he…" Dmitri paused here and risked a glance at Lenore, who stared daggers at whatever he was about to say next. He gathered his words. "I have no problem if his background is similar to Lenore's."

She rolled her eyes, but Dmitri ignored it.

Neal, on the other hand, looked relieved. "I appreciate that. We all do. We couldn't bear to lose Kieran as much as anyone else here." He looked affectionately at both Lenore and Camilla. Turning back to Dmitri, he grew serious. "You should know, however, Kieran looks different than you might expect. He's given us permission to share that with you beforehand so you're not shocked."

Dmitri made a pacifying gesture. "I've seen plenty of things in my time, sir. I'm sure I'll behave perfectly appropriately." He didn't need to specify that those "things" he'd seen had been while carrying out the duties of his job. He'd even inflicted some of them.

"Does that mean you're ready for us?" That voice belonged to Doctor Allen—Mina.

Dmitri's mind boggled at the need for all this secrecy and preamble and preparation. They were all going to feel very foolish over how very nonplussed he was going to be over their mysterious friend.

Neal looked to Dmitri, who allowed himself to loosen up enough to shrug. "I'm great," he assured Neal with a rare show of levity. He even smiled. His plan was going to be so much easier than expected.

"Yes, we're ready for you," Neal called in the direction of the dining room.

From the candlelit dimness of that room, Mina appeared with a young man in tow. He looked no older than Dmitri or Camilla or Lenore, with longish dark hair that he'd pulled into a knot atop his head. The style was unlike anything current fashion would approve of, but it worked well on the man's angular features. He was tall too, taller even than Mina, who was tall for a woman to begin with. And though his suit was of fine make, Dmitri could tell it was straight off the rack and had not been tailored to fit Kieran.

What made Dmitri stare, rather, were Kieran's eyes. Solid black. And when he smiled, the fangs grabbed Dmitri's notice by the lapels and refused to let go. He'd risen at hearing Mina's approach, but now stood speechless and still, uncertain what to do. That is, until a single word fell from his mouth.

"Vampyre."

Dmitri hadn't been calling Kieran a Vampyre, though that's what he inarguably was. But rather because Dmitri was answering a question in his own head. All evening, he'd been wondering what all the fuss about Kieran was. And now it was clear. He wouldn't have even known that's what Kieran was if it hadn't been for Boris' penchant for Old World-based adventure novels. Of course, in many of those, Vampyres were slavering, half-dressed, bat-eared monsters living in caves, instead of finely dressed dinner guests politely making new acquaintances.

To this extremely rude declaration, Dmitri lost any sense of his usual collectedness and said, "Bugger me, that is not what I meant. I apologize. What I should have said was, 'How do you do?'"

Behind Mina and Kieran, Lenore was looking as smug as he'd ever seen her. To Dmitri's surprise, Kieran smiled at him.

"Dmitri, lovely to meet you. I've often heard you're one for directness. It's nice to see it borne out."

"It's a trait I admire as well," Mina agreed.

Lenore looked less smug at that, but she said nothing.

Neal had gotten to his feet at some point during these strange proceedings and gestured between the two. "Dmitri, meet Kieran, my lifelong friend. And Kieran, meet Dmitri. This is the gent Camilla has told you so much about."

It was an odd thing, the way polite society never liked directly calling someone a young lady's beau. The closest it ever came was referring to a couple's status as courting. Dmitri found it maddening, but now wasn't the time for such quibbles.

"Very pleased to meet you as well," Dmitri said, shaking Kieran's hand. It was warmer than he expected, given that Kieran was supposed to be a walking, undead, blood-drinking corpse. Then again, you could never trust those fiction writers. He looked over Kieran's youthful face again. There was a gauntness about it, he now saw, but the hairstyle and clothing had helped to disguise it. "You and Neal have been friends… *your* whole life?"

Kieran chuckled at that and exchanged a teasing look with Neal. "I'm actually older than he is."

"Only by a week," Neal said with a grin.

Dmitri sensed this was a long-standing but good-natured rivalry.

"Vampyrism keeps one young," Camilla joked.

She'd stood by him the whole time during introductions, and Dmitri was very pleased to see the little lines between her brows had disappeared. He gave her a smile to show just how at ease he was. And it was mostly true, though getting caught out on the back foot like that never felt good, but he was already taking steps to make up for that lost ground.

"Camilla tells me you're like an older brother to her," Dmitri said.

At this, Kieran absolutely beamed. "Indeed. She's like a younger sister to me as well."

Perfect. It was time for Dmitri to make his move. He stood up straighter, if that was even possible. "In that case, if you don't mind my saying so, I know how this sort of thing tends to go."

"Oh?" Mina asked.

She was still standing beside Kieran, and Dmitri realized just then that she was being protective of *him*. The loyalty of this family warmed Dmitri's heart, though he wouldn't go so far as to reveal a nugget of information *that* personal. He did smile, though, while Kieran blinked at him, waiting for more.

"I know how protective older brothers are of their younger sisters. As well as how they like to torture any young men those younger sisters bring home."

"But not other young ladies, you notice," Lenore muttered from her post by the doorway.

Dmitri actually felt prepared for this too. He peeked around Kieran to say, "I think it's fair to say we all know, by and large, men are the real problem."

Lenore actually, shockingly, granted him an unabashed expression of agreement at that.

Back to Kieran, Dmitri continued. "All this to say, let's not have any such theatrics between us. I care for Camilla deeply and never want to hurt her."

"I appreciate your candor," Kieran replied, not unkindly, "but Camilla is both intelligent and a grown woman."

Dmitri's plan, his masterful control of the situation, evaporated in a puff of smoke to the sound of the air cooler sighing in the background.

"I know she is," Dmitri said. How was it that suddenly he was in the wrong here? "I wasn't saying…" He stopped himself. What was he trying to get out? "I just want us to understand one another."

Kieran's smile turned indulgent, which made Dmitri feel very stupid indeed, though he wasn't certain why.

"Dinner is served."

Esther's cracked voice broke through the moment, and suddenly there was a murmur of excitement all around. Camilla joined up with Kieran, asking him how he'd slept. That made sense, because Vampyres slept during the day, didn't they? Now, *everything* made sense, except Kieran's reaction. Had he subtly been implying something about Dmitri?

Lenore of all people sidled up to the baffled Enforcer. "You were right to confront him."

Dmitri turned to her, but kept his face impassive, an old trick for both buying time and waiting to see what others might reveal. It seemed to have worked, because she carried on.

"Kieran *is* planning something for tonight. For *you*."

She made some very meaningful eyebrow motions at him, but for the life of him, he couldn't read what she meant by them. He considered asking outright, but he didn't want to appear like he needed the help, not in front of Lenore. And he certainly didn't want to owe her something. He waited again. She performed one final jig with her eyebrows, winked, and then walked away.

Well, that answered precisely nothing, he thought to himself.

Except that he'd been right. Now he had the advantage. Kieran must have thought he'd outplayed Dmitri with that innocent act. But now Dmitri was onto him a second time. Yes! Now Dmitri would be on the lookout. He'd heard tales of what other older brothers had done to put the fear of heaven into their younger sisters' beaus. Itching powder in the underpants. Laxatives in the dessert soufflé. A midnight beating with a pillowcase stuffed full of boots. Well, Dmitri wasn't planning on spending the night, and he planned on keeping his dessert close and his underpants even closer.

When they sat down to dinner, he took special notice of where everyone sat. Neal and Mina shared the head of the table—their dining room was big enough to seat a dozen and a half—while Lenore sat on one side, next to Kieran, and Dmitri and Camilla mirrored them on the other. Good. So Kieran couldn't try slipping a scorpion or anything into Dmitri's lap. Esther was already serving the soup course, a bright green affair made with peas and asparagus. It was all coming from the same tureen, so no danger there, but he took a quick glance down into his empty bowl. Or rather, almost empty. A trio of leaves sat within. It certainly *looked* like mint. Camilla's bowl contained some too, but were they *really* the same?

Dmitri actually knew a bit about plants. Well, herbs anyway. He had a little collection growing at home in some empty, cracked jars. And an interesting little fact he knew was that stinging nettles looked very much like mint. And that stinging nettles were covered in tiny, stabby hairs, which would attack all over the inside of his mouth if he ate it raw. And Esther was just about to pour soup over it!

Before he knew what he was doing, Dmitri yanked the bowl out of the way, similar to the way he'd whisked his hat earlier from one hand to the next. Except that a porcelain bowl had quite a lot more heft than a cloth hat, and he entirely missed the other hand, making it look like he'd just purposefully thrown his bowl away. It shattered into pieces on the polished wood floor.

The room went silent, save for the sound of dripping pea and asparagus soup. Esther hadn't realized what was happening fast enough and plopped a ladle full of the stuff onto the pristine white tablecloth.

"Uuuuuuuh…" It took Dmitri a moment to realize that idiotic noise was coming from him. "There was a spider."

It was a terrible lie, but it was also the only thing he could think of just then to explain what had to look like lunatic behavior.

"You don't like spiders, Dmitri?" Kieran asked. Shock still painted his features, but was that an act?

He knows I know! insisted Dmitri's panicking mind. Then it did a complete one-eighty and thought, *Or! Or, or! It hasn't occurred to him that I knew about the stinging nettle, but now he's just thinking about how he can get me with spiders. Probably going to try to drop them into my hair or down my shirt or something.* Too bad for him, Dmitri's tie was nice and tight and his shirt would remain neatly tucked in.

For the moment, however, there were more pressing issues to deal with. He said quickly, "Esther, I am so sorry. I'll help clean up right away."

Esther, however, was already on it. The second she'd recovered from her shock, she'd flown into action, using shortcuts learned from her long life as both a professional mess-maker in the kitchen and one who cleaned them up there and elsewhere. She already had the drippy mess contained and was making short work of that which had reached the floor.

"Don't you worry about it, Dmitri," she soothed. "Nothing a broom and a little elbow grease can't solve."

Neal, Mina, and Camilla were also already engaged with the cleanup, making Dmitri essentially useless in the process.

"And I'll make sure no nasty spiders get you, my dear," Esther added with a cheeky wink.

Dmitri's insides turned in on themselves, but he couldn't protest. Not after that. So he did the most helpful thing he could in that moment and fell in line. Which basically meant staying out of the way for the next few minutes. Kieran and Lenore jumped in where they could, but with so many hands, the job was very nearly already done. The party repositioned slightly and all moved down the table, beyond the soup spill—the table cloth was one of those ridiculous one-piece affairs, making it impossible to remove without taking everything else off, which no one was about to do.

As they shuffled, Camilla caught Dmitri for a private word. "Are you alright? You're not afraid of spiders."

Dmitri took in a breath. There was no way to explain it, not here and now, so he said instead, "It surprised me, that's all. And if I'm honest, I'm feeling pretty embarrassed about the whole thing."

"Oh, Dmitri," she cooed.

She gave his arm a comforting little squeeze, and he summoned a smile just for her.

He tried to catch Lenore's eye as well. She might be able to provide confirmation that the maybe-mint, possibly-stinging-nettle debacle had been the sabotage Kieran had been planning, but she seemed to always have her back to him as she helped get dishes and whatnot re-situated. At last, they all settled back down at the table. This time, Mina and Neal were across from the three young people and the young-looking Kieran. On one side of Dmitri sat Camilla, on the other Kieran. They ate their soup, chatting about the latest city news, and Dmitri was grateful to move on. Esther's cooking was, of course, delectable. And Bitsy, Lenore's devoted and opportunistic ringcat, made an appearance, peeking around the doorway first and then beginning to sniff around the table.

Dmitri eyed Bitsy, who just looked back at him with his large, deep black eyes, innocent as could be. He wasn't actually sure what category Bitsy fell into—cat or weasel or squirrel or something else. He looked a bit like a cross between all three, with a head and ears shaped like cat's, but a longer, pointier snout. And, of course, a long, fluffy black-and-white striped tail.

Not looking away from the ringcat, Dmitri asked, "Your… creature won't be trying to steal food off our plates or anything, right, Lenore?"

"Of course not!" she replied. "Bitsy's very well behaved, for people he likes anyway."

Dmitri didn't miss the unspoken insult in her words. She might as well have said, "For likable people, which excludes *you*."

147

"I found a pile of hairpins I'd been missing in his nest," Camilla put in. "They were some of my best ones."

"Oh?" Lenore asked. Her tone was suddenly as falsely innocent as Bitsy's look had been.

Camilla replied, "The ones with the little blue jewels."

"I gave you those hairpins," Mina said.

Lenore grinned sheepishly. "He likes shiny things."

As the discussion went on, so did the courses, and Neal helped clear the soup dishes away. Oysters came next, which Dmitri quite enjoyed. His paternal grandparents and maternal grandmother, all of whom lived with Dmitri and Dmitri's parents and brother, had often spoken of how plentiful oysters used to be, and thus they had been readily available for those with little money. The three older folks had numerous recipes for preparing the little filter feeders, and—no surprise—Esther had been listening well when Dmitri had told her about them.

As he enjoyed what was now considered a lavish indulgence, given oysters' relatively recent scarcity, Dmitri observed, not for the first time that evening, Kieran's nonexistent place setting. The man didn't even have a water glass.

"Kieran," Dmitri began, "are you not having dinner?"

Kieran smiled pleasantly. "I'll be eating later, thank you. In the meantime, I'm happy to watch all of you eat."

That stopped Dmitri mid-chew. Had Kieran done something to the oysters? To one of the other dishes yet to come? Lenore was sitting next to Kieran, and Dmitri caught her giving him the barest of eyebrow wiggles behind the Vampyre's back.

"I keep telling you," came Neal's voice through Dmitri's growing paranoia, "that's a very strange turn of phrase you insist on using."

Kieran laughed, and Lenore chipped in from the side: "I think he keeps doing it because it bothers you."

Kieran laughed harder. "Never! I would never. Not to my

oldest friend in the world."

That only served to confirm that Kieran was full of mischievous potential and very likely, nay *predisposed*, to pull a jape or two at Dmitri's expense, ne'er-do-well that he was for ever darkening Camilla's door. Thankfully, though, the fish, or rather oyster, course came and went without further incident. This time Mina and Lenore helped with the clearing up, and Dmitri decided next time around he would volunteer. True, he was their guest, and his hosts would probably never hear of it, but he wanted to show his willingness.

Next came the main entrée, roast chicken with Duskwood pudding—a buttery poof of baked batter with mixed-in herbs that was covered in gravy—and roast vegetables. Esther carried this out on a giant serving platter, which looked heavy enough to topple the woman. Neal and Mina attempted to assist, but Esther shooed them away, and Dmitri decided between carrying huge platters and kneading bread, some pretty impressive biceps must hide beneath the old woman's doughy form. He wasn't concerned about any adoptive-big-brother tomfoolery happening with this dish, and for a while was able to simply enjoy his meal in peace.

That was, until he felt… it. He didn't know what *it* was, but it was wrong and unwelcome. It was something prickly at his ankle, poking through his sock. He shook his leg, and it went away. For a few minutes anyway. As Dmitri ate his chicken, dipped his Duskwood pudding in the savory juices and gravy, the feeling returned. And when he tried to shake it off again, the thing learned that wasn't really the threat it had initially seemed. It brushed soft, tickling hairs over the skin of his leg. He kicked, but caught Camilla's leg in the crossfire.

"Ow!" she exclaimed.

"Sorry," Dmitri said, eyes wide. He paused, looking for words. He couldn't explain why he'd been kicking randomly at the dinner table, though. He could feel other eyes on him. Kieran must have released something small and precocious. Could he have even planted something on Dmitri to make him an attractive target?

Still feeling eyes on him, he refused to look at them. In a quiet voice, Dmitri asked Camilla, "Are you alright?"

She nodded, and the little lines of concern from before reappeared on her forehead.

He nodded, knowing it was inadequate. "I apologize… again."

He then looked back to his food, the only comfort in this battle of psychological warfare. The thing lurking beneath the table didn't return, however, and Dmitri could only hope he'd scared it off. He tried a time or two to get a peek beneath and identify the whatever-it-was, but the tablecloth wreathed the underneath in darkness.

"Are you quite well?" That was Kieran's voice. It hummed low and careful next to Dmitri's ear one of the times he was trying to suss out whatever the Vampyre had planted to torment him.

Dmitri sat ramrod straight in his chair. "I'm fine. Thank you. Just wonderful. This is a lovely evening, don't you think?"

He caught himself. *This* was why he preferred to remain taciturn. Too many words and one started to sound… well, not how one intended anyway. Dmitri's voice was so stern, he sounded as if he was telling Kieran that he too had better think the evening was bloody lovely, or else.

Kieran smiled mildly. *What was that smile for?!*

"It really is. I'm glad we were finally able to meet."

He's definitely plotting something, Dmitri reaffirmed to himself. *He's far, far too pleased about meeting me.*

Was it possible, just possible, Dmitri was being irrational? No. What older brother worth his salt was happy about meeting a younger sister's beau? Precisely none.

Finally, it was time for dessert.

Just as he'd planned, Dmitri offered, "I can help with the dishes."

And just as expected, a chorus of objections went up. The

hospitality was comforting, though he wasn't comfortable enough with the entire family to smile. He gifted one to Camilla, however, and his whole body felt warm when she smiled back.

Dmitri felt he was of two minds. On the one hand, he was enjoying the food immensely. And the company was fine too, though social occasions for him were rather more something to get through, a necessary part of a smoothly functioning society, rather in the same way taxes and dental care were. And on the other hand, there was the constant, looming expectation of whatever shenanigans Kieran was plotting.

Once everyone was content that Dmitri wasn't going to do anything so ludicrous as help, Lenore leaned back in her seat and looked at Dmitri, a silent request for an away-from-the-table conference. Or at least, as away-from-the-table as a hard lean in a chair got one. He leaned too and waited.

"I'm going to spoil a surprise," she whispered.

"Please do." Stars, Dmitri hoped she was about to ruin whatever Kieran had up his sleeve.

"Esther's made you Nesselrode pudding. It was Kieran's idea." And with that, Lenore returned to sitting properly at the table.

Odd, and not what he'd been hoping for, but still good news nonetheless. Esther had really outdone herself tonight. Nesselrode pudding was a molded, frozen custard confection with currants, raisins, cognac, and a sweetened chestnut purée. It was fussy to make, not to mention labor intensive. The only reason Dmitri knew he liked it was because he'd once, and only once, had an opportunity to try it at an Enforcer propaganda function. But it was yet another dish that came out as one big whole. And he was safer than ever with a dish like Nesselrode because there was a good bit of pomp and circumstance around its de-molding step, which was always being done tableside.

Dmitri hadn't even been concerned about the fact that Kieran had been the one to help Esther clear away the dinner plates, taking the tricky Vampyre out of Dmitri's sight. That is, until Kieran had the gall to reappear carrying a serving tray with *five* plates. Not one big pudding as was the usual method. No. Atop each plate was a unique copper mold, yet to release its sweet, formed dessert. Dmitri's heart sank as Kieran placed one in front of him.

"We really wanted to treat you tonight." He gave Dmitri a fanged grin as he did.

All around him, the rest of the family were oohing and aahing over the decadent dessert, excited to each have their own personal reveals. Dmitri's mold had a leafy sort of motif, while Neal's had a sort of interlocking braid, Camilla's flowers, Mina had a sort of angular swirl, and Lenore's had scales.

Dmitri wanted so badly to say he couldn't eat it, that he didn't trust it, but how would he ever be able to face Camilla again? This was it. He was just going to have to swallow—literally—whatever awful prank Kieran had planned. To prepare himself, Dmitri began to imagine the possibilities and rank them from least terrible to most. He'd just decided that a laxative treatment of some kind topped the list when The Thing That Came from Beneath the Dining Table returned for revenge. This time, it skipped straight over tentative exploration and leapt onto Dmitri's trouser leg, digging tiny, sharp claws through the fabric and into his skin, skittering up his calf, over his knee, and across his thigh.

Dmitri yelped and leapt to his feet, knocking his dining chair over. He flailed at himself, trying to catch the thing, but it was so fast. And nimble! As soon as Dmitri went for it on his front, it was on his back.

"What is it, Kieran?!" he demanded. "What did you sic on me?!"

"Dmitri, stop!" Camilla cried. "It's just Bitsy."

As if one cue, now that he'd caused mayhem, Bitsy leapt from Dmitri and safely into his mistress' arms. Dmitri patted himself down, ensuring that it really had only been Bitsy. Those little weasel-like claws made him feel creepy crawly all over.

"Why would you think Kieran sent something after you?" Camilla pressed.

Dmitri locked gazes with her, and the disappointment in her blue eyes crushed his soul.

"I… Because… He's protective of you," Dmitri managed. "You said he was like an older brother."

He risked a glance around the room. Mina, Neal, and Kieran were all staring with varying degrees of confusion and apprehensive expectation. He looked to Neal, who was the closest to maybe understanding. It was Kieran, however, who responded.

"I explained about Camilla being a grown woman capable of making her own decisions, did I not?" Kieran's tone was sincere and, more importantly, open. "Was something not understood in that?"

Dmitri sighed. He couldn't retreat to his old standby safety net and simply abstain from speaking, so he relied on the facts.

"I formed a conclusion based on my own preconceived ideas. I assumed you were bluffing somehow. Not about knowing Camilla is capable and smart and responsible; we all know that. But I assumed you were using that as a cover to trick me into letting my guard down. Because *all* brothers, everywhere, do that sort of thing for their sisters, yes? And then Lenore…"

Realization dawned on Dmitri like the morning light that reveals devastation. He and everyone else looked to Lenore. She was holding Bitsy, stroking him like an evil mastermind from a yellowback novel. And Bitsy was holding Dmitri's pocket watch in his greedy little paws.

A smile like thorny, entangling vines stretched across her face. "You forgot about sisters."

Dmitri opened his mouth, but no sound came out. He *had* forgotten about sisters. He'd been so focused on how brothers everywhere behaved that he hadn't even thought to wonder if sisters might not pull the same antics. And she had done it using Dmitri's own trick of saying as little as possible against him.

"Young lady." Those two words broke the shocked silence that had fallen over the dining room. Unsurprisingly, they came from Mina.

She didn't look nearly as angry as Dmitri initially expected, however. Though initial expectations had been what had gotten him in this mess in the first place. Rather, Mina looked… a little impressed, though clearly something had needed to be said. The Allens were too hospitable to allow their guests to go around getting tormented without a word said about it. Neal looked downright proud, but he was trying to hide it under a cough.

"We really shouldn't let Esther's hard work go to waste," Kieran suggested.

Esther had been standing in the background, watching this whole scene play out. She nodded approvingly. "That's probably the perfect amount of thawing time to get them out clean."

Dmitri wondered what she would have said if all her hard work had been in danger of being ruined. She was just as much a member of the family as Kieran or Lenore, blood or no. He would have liked to see it, but was also grateful it hadn't come to that.

As Esther predicted, the little detour had been just the time the molds needed to release their perfectly formed desserts. Each Nesselrode pudding slid straight out from its copper confinement, and the first bite cleared away any bad taste the evening's events might have otherwise left in everyone's mouths. As the party enjoyed their treats, and Lenore returned Dmitri's pilfered pocket watch, a thought occurred to Dmitri. He considered carefully how to ask. He took a deep breath before addressing the party as a whole.

"Would it be alright if we didn't tell anyone about this evening?" he began. "The finer details, I mean. It's not my best showing, and I've certainly learned from my mistakes."

He exchanged a meaningful glance with Lenore, who smugly licked her spoon in response.

He didn't need to specify that the only person they could possibly tell was Rook, given the secrecy of Kieran's existence, but he felt better having an understanding in place about it. Plus, whenever Rook completed his purging—and Dmitri wholeheartedly believed Rook would, if for no other reason than spite—it would really rankle not getting to hear how Dmitri and Kieran's introduction went.

"I think that's acceptable," Kieran agreed. And so did everyone else, because they knew, in the end, it was Kieran's decision. The Vampyre looked to Dmitri and smirked, showing just a hint of fang. "It's been delightful making your acquaintance this evening, Dmitri. This quiet, uneventful evening."

"Excellent," Dmitri said simply, in the direct, succinct way he liked best.

Surprise Party Planning

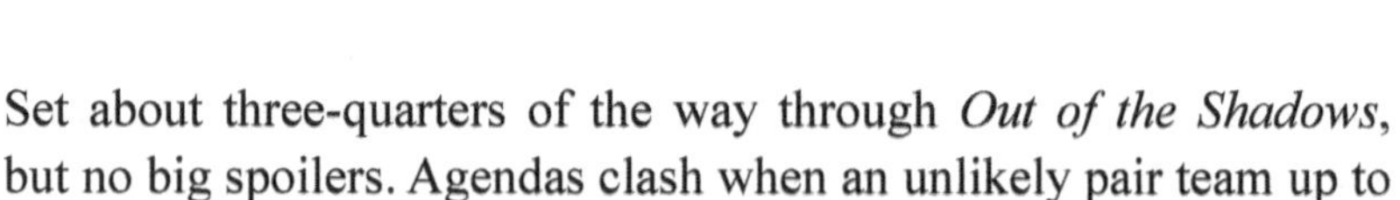

Set about three-quarters of the way through *Out of the Shadows*, but no big spoilers. Agendas clash when an unlikely pair team up to try and plan a party for Lenore.

~~~

Rook twirled the crisp, cream-colored card between his slender fingers. The delicate, looping handwriting matched the lace trim on the card perfectly. Rook mentally calculated how much money he would bet if anyone put up stakes on "lace-like" being part of the request when Camilla—or perhaps Mina—had ordered the cards. Not an obscene amount, he decided, but enough to hurt a little if he lost, which he suspected unlikely.

How long had it been since someone had sent their card round to him? Rook thought back to his childhood and early adolescent years. Coming from the highest echelon of society, he and all his friends had sent cards to each others' homes for play dates since they could write. He rolled his eyes as he looked back on the absurdity of it. Still, why Camilla of all people had sent hers to Gadget's furniture shop for him was a mystery. At the bottom of the card in handwriting just as lovely as the calligrapher's, she had
~~~

added to the standard invitation language an enigmatic, custom message:

This is a secret! Tell no one you're coming, not even Lenore.

Rook had immediately suspected something nefarious, but relaxed when he considered the rest of the situation. It was the middle of the day, the meeting was to take place at the Allens' manor, and he had seen Camilla's cards during a previous visit to the house. Even still, he'd swung by the museum to check that all seemed well with Lenore before heading over to the manor. Satisfied, all that remained was to discover the reason behind this meeting.

The door opened, and Esther's round, cheerful face greeted him. Rook smiled automatically at seeing the plump, elderly housekeeper.

"Good afternoon, Master Pendragon," she trilled. "Please, come inside. Miss Camilla's expecting you."

"Thank you, Esther," Rook replied, tipping his head to her as he slid into the receiving hall.

Herding Rook like a mother hen, Esther explained, "She's just back here in the dining room. I hope you've brought your thinking cap, as you've got quite the task before you."

"Do I?" Rook asked, grinning at Esther's warmth.

They entered the dining room, and Rook's eyebrows rose slowly. One side of the long dining table was covered in papers, rolls of streamers, fabric swatches, and bowls of various foodstuffs. At the end stood Camilla, staring down at the mess like a captain planning an attack. Her eyes flicked to Rook when he walked in, sizing him up.

He gave her a cocky smirk, and Camilla made a disgusted noise in her throat.

"Miss Camilla, where are your manners?" Esther scolded. "I

know that's not how we raised you."

Camilla lowered her eyes. "You're absolutely right, Esther. My apologies." She approached Rook and curtseyed, saying, "Please forgive my terrible behavior. I'm afraid all of this has me a bit out of sorts."

Rook's smirk melted into a perfect, gentlemanly smile as he bowed in return. "Think nothing of it. What, if I may, is all of this exactly?"

While Camilla smiled demurely at his response, Esther bobbed her head in approval and said, "I'll just be off to get the tea."

As soon as she was gone, Camilla's smile vanished, and Rook's smirk returned.

"This is the planning station for Lenore's birthday," Camilla said, her sweet voice incongruous with the distasteful expression on her face. "At least, that's what I'm trying to make it into."

"It looks rather more like an explosion. A very colorful explosion, mind you."

Camilla checked her tone, pasting on a false smile and forcing her words through gritted teeth. "I'm doing my very best, you know."

"I'm sure of it," Rook replied, leaning back against the mantel. "I'm still unclear as to what this has to do with me, however."

Camilla glanced at the doorway that led to the conservatory, which led to the kitchen. Rook didn't know if Esther knew Lenore's real back story, but he figured she had to know the tale Lenore and the rest of the family sold to everyone else was pure fiction. The woman had been housekeeper here since Neal was a child and would have heard about his "cousin" Lenore long before last fall. From Camilla's look, Rook guessed they hadn't told Esther the truth, at least not all of it. For everyone's protection most likely.

"You know more about Lenore's… background than the rest of us," Camilla replied at last, turning back. "I need your help organizing her party."

Rook tilted his head, scrutinizing Camilla's expression. "Why?" Straightening back up, he added, "Don't get me wrong, I'm flattered you deigned to call on my expertise, but you all already threw her a birthday party earlier this year."

Camilla raised an eyebrow at him and replied, "I know you know that wasn't for her real birthday, just appearances. This will be a private event for her, us, and Eamon."

"Not me?" Rook shot the words like a dart, his eyes glinting with something darker than mischief.

Camilla opened her mouth to respond, but Esther's footsteps approaching from the conservatory stopped her. Both she and Rook looked to the doorway and watched as Esther walked in, an enormous tea tray balanced on her arms.

"Let me help you," Rook offered, striding forward.

"Thank you, dear, but I... oh, Master Pendragon, you needn't..." Esther objected gently as Rook took the tray from her.

"Nonsense," Rook crooned, turning with the tray towards Camilla and the table. "It's the least I can do since you're all being so good to include me in this shindig of yours." He flashed Camilla a shameless smile as he set the tray down.

Camilla's cheeks colored a soft pink as she shot a glare at Rook. A second later, she replaced her false smile and batted her eyelashes at him and Esther.

"Oh, is Master Pendragon to join you as well?" Esther asked.

"Varick is fine," Rook replied before Camilla had a chance to. "Wait, won't you be here for it?"

"Mistress Mina and Master Neal have kindly given me the night off. It's my fourth grandbaby's birthday that night. Don't you worry, though. I'll be cooking up a storm all day before I go."

"Ah," Rook said, reevaluating his play.

Esther served the tea and asked Rook how his new job at Miss Annabelle's furniture shop was going, whilst deftly avoiding any mention of his recent purging and all that entailed. As Rook gave his neutral, safe answers and half listened to Esther's replies, he watched Camilla out of the corner of his eye. Camilla was leaning on the table and gazing at the papers spread out before her, but Rook saw her eyes flick towards Esther now and again.

"If you all need anything else, just let me know," Esther said at last. "I'll just be in the kitchen."

"Thank you so much," Rook said, lifting a teacup and taking it to Camilla, who looked up and smiled, taking it with graceful movements.

Esther left again, and Camilla sipped her tea.

"You think you're very clever, don't you?" she asked in a low voice.

"I know I'm very clever." Rook fetched his own teacup and took a seat next to where Camilla stood.

"I really think you should reconsider crashing Lenore's birthday party. It would be very unseemly."

Rook picked up one of the fabric swatches and started in on his own tea. His voice was mostly light when he spoke again, but it retained a shade of a sharpened edge. "And what about it would be unseemly? I'm Lenore's friend, am I not? Everyone knows it now. Wouldn't it be a jolly good way for her to get to know me better as her 'new friend'? And after all, we still don't know who tried to kill her or why, remember?"

"I am acutely aware Lenore's life is under threat, Mister Pendragon, but I think it's highly unlikely anyone is going to attack her while she's surrounded by people. They, whoever they are, want it to look like an accident, if you recall."

"I recall perfectly, *powderpuff*. And you haven't answered my question."

Camilla's eyes were chips of azure ice when she turned her gaze onto Rook. "Don't you think she has enough to worry about without you pouring petrolsene on the fire? You and Eamon haven't yet been acquainted." Rook sniggered to himself, and Camilla scowled. "What?"

"Oh, nothing." Rook stroked the fabric between his fingers, a heavy chenille with floral stripes.

"In case you hadn't noticed, Lenore isn't wild about you two meeting, and I can understand why."

"Because you know I'll outshine the—"

"Because you are determined to cause trouble!" Camilla hissed, snatching the fabric from between Rook's fingers. "Nevermind. Leave. I don't know why I thought you'd be helpful."

"Nor do I," Rook shot back, standing.

Esther's voice suddenly floated from around the corner, and Camilla looked down at the table again, letting her flaxen hair fall around her face, hiding it from view. Rook followed suit and, for the first time, ran his eyes over the papers before them. There were lists of foods, many of which matched the dishes on the table; sketches of room arrangements; a guest list, which was abysmally short; and activity ideas.

"Everything alright in here, dears?" Esther asked, poking her head around the doorframe.

"Peachy," Rook replied, lifting his teacup to the old woman.

Camilla barely lifted her head and gave a tight smile, nodding too quickly. Esther left again, and Rook listened as her footsteps retreated.

Before they were completely gone, Camilla whispered, "I asked you here because you knew Lenore's parents."

"I knew her father, but not well," Rook said, glowering at her.

Camilla met his gaze evenly, drew herself up, and flipped her hair back over her shoulders. "Even so, this is bound to be a difficult event for Lenore. With her…" Camilla's eyes flicked to Rook as her breath caught in her throat. "With her parents gone, Mina and Neal and I want it to be extra special for her. I am taking great pains to avoid potential pitfalls. I think you know her adjustment with us has been difficult."

Rook rolled his eyes at the insult. "I do, but I'm surprised you're aware of it."

Camilla's face twitched like she wanted to sneer back at him, but she took a deep breath and smoothed her already perfect skirt instead.

"She hides it fairly well, but the clues are there."

Rook logged this away, making a mental note to inform Lenore about it later.

"Besides," Camilla continued, "how could she not have trouble adjusting? What with everything she's been through."

Rook nodded but said nothing for a long moment. While he hesitated, Camilla turned back to the page with *Activities* written across the top. He read over the list. Bobbing for apples inspired him to reach for the bowl closest to him—stuffed, bacon-wrapped figs. He popped one into his mouth and pointed at a line.

"If you're going to play Blind Man's Bluff, don't make Lenore be it. Not once," he said.

"Why not?" Camilla said, reaching for the bowl of candied almonds. Rook gave her a look, and she added, "But she's going to be among family."

"You said yourself she's had a hard time adjusting."

Silence fell between the two again, and Esther's voice rang out again.

"Cake, my darlings!" A moment later, she came through the doorway carrying another large tray, this one laden with a dozen slices of cake.

Rook's eyes widened, and he looked between the tray and Camilla. "With all due respect," he chuckled, "how are you all not eight hundred pounds?"

Camilla giggled and said, "We would be if it weren't for walking."

"I've baked six different options," Esther explained proudly.

"Lemon, queen's sponge, Duskwood forest, spotted Richard, gold with boiled icing, and almond. Try them and let me know what you think."

With that, Esther swept out again. Rook's mouth hung open as he stared at the tray.

"What does Esther think she's cooking for exactly?"

Camilla picked up two of the plates, the lemon cake, and handed one to Rook.

"The one-year anniversary of Lenore coming to stay with us, plus a month or so," Camilla replied, before taking a bite of her cake. She smiled at her plate like it had just given her a gift.

"That's not quite what I meant, but good to know." Rook paused, thought, and said, "And Esther of all people is willing to miss that?"

Camilla shrugged in a very unladylike way, still focused on her cake. "The timing didn't work out. A lot of her grandchildren were born in the autumn."

"Well, what else is there to do in the winter but—"

"Cake!" Camilla cut in, jabbing her fork at his plate.

Rook smirked at her, but she was already on her fourth bite. When Camilla finished, she dabbed at her mouth with a napkin and folded her hands before her.

"So will you help me plan this party for Lenore?" Her voice grew serious as she added, "We want it to be special, to show her how dear she is to all of us."

"Without making her think about her parents?"

"No," Camilla said, shaking her head. "I know firsthand that's impossible. I'm sure this birthday will bring a fresh, new kind of pain for her, but we want to be balm for it at the same time."

"But I'm not welcome to participate. Not when it counts the most."

Camilla sighed. "We have our differences, Rook. Quite a few, but I hope you'll believe me when I say, where Lenore is concerned, I'm doing my best to put them aside."

"So I can come?" Rook pressed, not smiling.

"Don't you think that should be Lenore's choice?"

Rook leaned back in his chair and started in on his lemon cake. He barely registered the sweet icing melting in his mouth as he chewed.

"I should mention this is a surprise party," Camilla put in, "so asking if you can attend will need to be done with care."

"That's a terrible idea," Rook replied, pointing his fork at Camilla.

"But she'll object if we tell her about it, especially after the lovely, big party we threw for her a few months back."

"Come on, powderpuff. You know Lenore better than that." Rook shoveled another bite into his mouth and added, "Wud'll ya think'll happen if ya jumf out an' stert shotting ad'er?"

"Charming, *Varick*," Camilla drawled, raising an eyebrow at Rook.

He added more cake to his gob and gave her a stuffed-cheek grin. Camilla turned back to her planning station.

"You're right, even if you are an uncouth boor. Let's do a soft surprise then, one in which she gets clues along the way so she's not blindsided. And we won't jump out and shout at her."

Rook swallowed and said, "Let's? As in, let us?"

Camilla gave him a mischievous smile and answered, "I suppose we could build in time for you to celebrate with her. *Apart* from Eamon. Just don't abscond with the birthday girl."

"Would I do such a thing?" Rook asked, feigning indignation and pressing a hand to his chest.

"Without a moment's hesitation," Camilla parried.

They smiled at one another, and Esther returned, joining them at the table and pouring herself a cup of tea.

"Finally getting along are we, my dears?" she tutted.

Rook and Camilla exchanged a look. Before either could say

anything, however, Esther flapped her hands at the remaining cakes.

"You'd best get a move on if you want to finish before Miss Lenore gets home." When Camilla and Rook just stared back at her, she added, "Go on then."

Rook and Camilla exchanged another look and reached for new plates.

"I have a good feeling about this Duskwood forest cake," Rook said, waggling his eyebrows at Camilla. "I think it might be the one."

Camilla grinned back. "Only one way to find out."

O HARRIED NIGHT

Just a silly little romp for the holiday season. Bitsy gets some of the rest of the Broken Gears crew into a pickle. Takes place between the events of *Out of the Shadows* and *Into the Fire* and before the events of another short story, *New Year's Gifts*. No spoilers.

~~~

ook hunched into his greatcoat, the collar pulled up around his face. Even though he and Lenore were officially out as friends publicly, he didn't like anyone seeing him go visit her. His old friend darkness surrounded him at the moment, though, which eased his concern considerably. Checking that no one was watching, he scaled the Allens' fence and headed for the kitchen door of the manor, slowing to gawp at the mountains of tacky oversized bows slapped onto every intersection of house beams, masses of conifer boughs tied together like great green mustaches beneath every window casing, and glittery gold and silver stars sprinkled everywhere they could go. Neal really did enjoy his New Year's decorations, and Rook chuckled. A scream from one of the upper rooms of the house yanked his attention from the tacky décor and sent him running the rest of the way.

~~~

When Rook burst through the kitchen door, Esther spun, flour covering her hands and apron.

"Master Pendragon!" she scolded, holding a hand to her heart. "What's gotten into you?"

"I heard a shout," he replied, taking the short stairway up into the kitchen two steps at a time.

Esther flapped an unconcerned hand at him. "Oh, yes. Just a spot of bother upstairs. Why don't you go see if you can't help the younger ladies sort it out?"

Rook's expression folded into quizzical Vs. If there wasn't an axe murderer in the house, then what did a doctor's assistant and an engineer-in-training need from him? He looked around like the answer might present itself, but only streamers of red, green, gold, and blue waved cheerily back at him. Good gracious, Neal really didn't do anything by halves. Some of the festoons hung alarmingly close to the cooking appliances, but nothing looked in danger of catching fire… yet.

"Off with you now," Esther shooed. "If you want any of this apple crumble then you'd best let me get back to it."

Rook most definitely did, so he hurried out of the kitchen, skidding around corners and following the sounds of panicked cries up the stairs to Neal's drawing room. The sight that met him made him stop in his tracks. Camilla and Lenore, both with harried flyaway hair, held out handkerchiefs around one of the taller bookshelves as if to catch something. Atop it sat Bitsy, Lenore's beloved little ringcat, holding a small bottle of liquid, though Rook couldn't tell what it was from this distance. Kieran leaned against the doorframe, which was strange since last Rook knew he'd been off on some kind of mission for Neal.

The Vampyre turned towards the newcomer, amusement pulling at the corners of his mouth, and gave a nod.

"Welcome back," Rook said, returning the gesture. "What have you done?"

"Oh, this isn't me," Kieran replied, barely suppressing a laugh. "This is entirely down to Lenore's little squirrel."

"He's not a squirrel!" Lenore called over her shoulder before turning back to the creature. "Bitsy, darling, please drop it. I'll give you a lovely treat."

"How long has this been going on?" Rook asked.

"About fifteen minutes," Kieran replied.

"Rook, if you're going to be here, you're expected to help," Camilla said, her tone sharp.

Rook would have liked to see someone argue with her just now, as he suspected it would be hilarious to watch, but he was not so foolish as to take that blow. Instead, he replied, "Yes, ma'am. What are we doing exactly?"

"The grabby weasel has stolen a rather dear bottle of cologne Mina bought for Neal. She asked me to wrap it, and he swiped it when my back was turned!"

"He's not a weasel," Lenore put in.

Camilla took a deep breath before saying, "In any case, I need it back *unbroken*."

"Ah, that explains this fetching little dance you two are doing with your kerchiefs," Rook replied, sauntering over. "Let me see what I can do."

Rook made a bit of a show with his sinewy arms as he easily clambered up the bookshelf and reached for Bitsy. "Come on now, mate. Let's just give me the pretty bot—ow!"

One minute Bitsy had been hunched against the wall, the next he was taking a flying leap across the room, using Rook's face as a launch pad and smacking him in the nose with the cologne bottle as he went.

"You're letting him get away!" Camilla cried, chasing after the creature.

Rook growled and turned slowly as Kieran belted out laughter.

"Oh goodness, that's the best entertainment I've had all week,"

the Vampyre said.

"What are you even doing here?" Rook asked, trying not to snarl.

"I'm to make sure Bitsy doesn't leave this room," Kieran explained. "The poor thing is quite terrified of me you see, and Lenore has asked I not intercede unless absolutely necessary."

"I rather think the little rat could do with a bit of a scare," Rook grumbled.

"He's not a rat," Lenore said from the other side of the room now.

"Well, he could do with a bit of training anyway."

"He's not a dog either."

"Fine, cat."

"Not a cat."

"Then why is he even called a ringcat?!"

"Rook!" Camilla snapped. "If you could focus or leave, please. One or the other."

"Apologies," he said through gritted teeth.

Bitsy now occupied the inside of a pine wreath hanging high up on the wall. He set the cologne aside and started tearing into one of the attached pine cones to get at the delicious seeds within. Lenore climbed up onto a nearby chair and pulled an orange slice from her pocket. Leaning towards the animal, she spoke in soothing tones.

"Bitsy, honey, look what I have for you." Bitsy lifted his head from his work and wiggled his little nose. Stretching his neck, he reached for the treat, but Lenore pulled it back, reaching with her other arm and offering him a path down. "There we go, just a little farther."

"It's falling!" Camilla cried.

As Bitsy tried to grab the orange without leaving his perch, it wobbled beneath him and shook the cologne bottle loose. At the same time, Bitsy leapt for his mistress, who overreached to catch him and began to tumble just like the cologne bottle.

A crash.

The sound of shattering glass.

A squeak.

Then nothing.

Rook looked down at Lenore, who he'd caught. She held Bitsy cradled in her arms, who was nibbling away at his orange without another care in the world. Beside him, Kieran stood still as a statue with the cologne safely cupped in his palm. The two men exchanged a look and released twin nervous laughs.

"Oh dear," Camilla said from behind them. "I hope that wasn't expensive."

While Lenore steadied herself and stroked Bitsy's head, Rook looked down to a broken whiskey bottle at his feet. He waggled his hand in the air, saying, "Not irreplaceable, but not bottom shelf either." Camilla grimaced, and he added, "I've got one stashed away. I'll bring it by tomorrow." She looked genuinely surprised, and he gave her a cheeky wink. "Happy New Year."

Kieran handed the cologne bottle to Camilla, who clutched it possessively to her chest, glaring at Bitsy.

"Why don't you all go down and get some of Esther's lovely crumble," Kieran suggested. "I'll stay and clean up."

"No, we can help," Lenore said.

"Don't let go of him!" Camilla and Rook said together.

They exchanged a look and smiled before going to work on the broken whiskey bottle, all while the scrumptious apple-y scent of their future reward wafted up from below.

NEW YEAR'S GIFTS

Set during New Year's Celebration week between *Out of the Shadows* and *Into the Fire*. Rook attends a holiday party put on by the Allens. Mostly just vibes, and a few spoilers for relationships and events that occur during *Out of the Shadows*.

~~~

Warm. That was the best word to describe the room around Rook. People were packed around the dining table, chatting and laughing and eating. He leaned back into a corner, avoiding the press of them all. The petrolsene sconces and liberally scattered candles washed away every shadow, bathing the guests in pools of golden light and glinting off the gilded dishes and stemware. The mélange of scents wafting up from the table—succulent meats, roasted vegetables, pies fit to burst with filling, hot apple cider, and mulled wine—were all generously spiced, no small expense to be sure. Rook had brought a variety of tinned spices packed in an ornately carved box as a gift for the family. They didn't need to know it had come from his latest shipment of smuggled goods, and he was glad of his choice. The Allens certainly had splurged for tonight's event, and Rook smiled at
~~~

having been invited at all.

When Lenore had pressed the thick creamy envelope into his hand, she'd beamed and bounced on her toes.

Rook examined the intricate silver scrollwork that flowed across the paper and shimmered like mercury. Holding the invitation between two fingers, he raised an eyebrow at Lenore.

"If this is what I think it is, dare I ask how you convinced your family?"

Lenore clutched her hands to her chest dramatically. "Rook, think of the absolute *scandal* if we snubbed you during this most generous time of year." She winked.

He smiled and gave Lenore a florid bow. "I most humbly accept this kind invitation."

"But you haven't even opened it to see the details," she replied.

"Doesn't matter. For this, I'll make arrangements."

And so he had. It was nothing so serious a bottle with a bow couldn't smooth over. Now, surrounded by the Allens' coworkers, Lenore's and Camilla's friends and their families, and Eamon and his lot, Rook wondered if this had been such a good idea.

He had endured the purging, paid his debts to society, and was therefore absolved. Seeing an Enforcer dressed in street clothes at the other end of the room, however, caused unease to curl up in his chest like an unwelcome cat. He'd seen the lad a few times on patrol in the city and at the Allen manor as the investigation into Dmitri's whereabouts continued. Rook was pretty sure he'd even seen him at least once during his stay at the Halls of Justice.

Taking another sip of his cider, Rook pushed himself off the wall and headed in that direction to introduce himself.

"Varick!" came a voice from off to the side.

He turned and smoothed his plum brocade waistcoat. His fixed smile grew without him realizing it.

"Varick," Lenore said again, touching his arm. "I want to introduce you to someone. This is Engineer Cooper Richmond, my

other mentor at the museum."

"Call me Copper," he said, thrusting his broad hand into Rook's free one.

Rook had to check himself as he felt the bones of his fingers grind together under the strength of Copper's handshake. He returned as much force as he could, and Copper's bristly grin widened.

"Varick Pendragon," Rook said, still hanging on. He let go only after Copper did. "Pleasure to meet you. Lenore's told me so much about you."

"Did you happen to see the lass' demonstration earlier this year?" Copper asked. "Bloody impressive it was."

Rook did not miss the way Copper had sidestepped the standard return of the sentiment. He wanted to chalk it up to pride given the way Copper's chest puffed up as he spoke about Lenore, but everyone in the city had buzzed about a Pendragon turning himself in as a criminal.

"I did indeed. Incredible stuff. And might I say, fantastic work with those model wings."

Copper threw back his head and guffawed so hard his belly shook. Rook allowed himself to chuckle in return. They chatted for a few more minutes, mostly about Lenore's progress, before one of Copper's children came tugging at his jacket with small, eager fingers.

"Are you enjoying yourself?" Lenore asked after Copper had left.

"I'm enjoying the free food and drink," Rook replied, lifting the silver cup to his lips again.

Lenore's brow creased, dand Rook furtively brushed his fingers against her wrist. His eyes took her in again as he had when he'd first arrived that evening, drinking in the sight of the evergreen silk dress, which was edged with snowy lace against her fair skin. The emerald feathers of her fascinator bobbled merrily, contrasting against her dark tresses. Her cheeks were rosy in the warm room, and the green of her eyes gleamed in the golden light washing over everything.

He lowered his voice to a whisper, repeating the motion. "I'm having a lovely time, little bird. I'll be sure to thank Mina and Neal again later."

She turned him towards the table. "Have you tried everything? Esther's outdone herself this year, I think."

"Why don't you take me through it?"

As Lenore described each dish, Rook kept one eye on his target. The Enforcer was still talking to Camilla, though Eamon had joined their little huddle now too. From what he had observed, Camilla was the only person he knew here, though he seemed to be getting on with just about everyone he spoke to. Not in the way that prat Eamon did, with false compliments and affected manners, but in sincere curiosity about what each person did and their interests. He seemed vaguely familiar—aside from as an Enforcer, that is— but Rook couldn't place why.

"Stop working," Lenore said quietly. "We're here to celebrate."

Rook didn't see what there was to celebrate in the turning of one year over to the next, but he kept that to himself. Instead, he returned her teasing smile and kept his eye on the other end of the room.

Neal and Mina were orbiting the party like twin moons. They came around to Rook and Lenore and went through the standard pleasantries.

"Everything is exceptional," Rook said, raising his glass to his hosts. "Thank you again for having me."

"Let me top you up there, Varick," Neal said, taking the cup from him.

"How is working for Miss Wilson going?" Mina asked as her husband disappeared.

"Erm, Miss Wilson?" Rook asked, slathering charm over his

confusion with a befuddled smile and a cock of his head.

"Gadget," Mina supplied. She smiled in a way that told Rook she wasn't entirely pleased he had forgotten his employer's proper, in-public name. Or maybe she had seen through his charms. He'd long ago learned she had no patience for such things.

"Apologies," Rook purred. "She insists on the nickname. Things are very good. Busy, being New Year and all."

"That's interesting, given that I've just spoken with her." Mina indicated the woman in question with a nail that perfectly matched her cranberry-colored dress.

Gadget hovered at the entrance to the dining room. She wore gloves, undoubtedly to hide her mechanical hand. There was no way to hide her eye patch, however, and Rook couldn't help but grin with admiration at the matte gold one with which she had replaced her usual black one.

"She says you haven't been to the shop in weeks." Mina's smile remained, but her eyes turned cold and flashed a warning.

Rook opened his mouth to give one of his usual smooth replies, but Mina turned away and reached toward the table before he could. When she turned back, the ice in her eyes had melted, and she was smiling warmly at him.

"You must try one of Esther's mince pies. They're simply divine."

Mina plopped the tiny pie in Rook's hand, leaving him at a loss for words. He took a bite of the sweet and spicy treat to buy time.

"I think I'm going to need about eighteen more of these," he said at last.

"There are mountains of them," Mina laughed. "Please, take as many as you like."

Neal returned with Rook's drink and said with a wink, "I dropped a little something special into it for you."

From the smell, Neal had quite a generous hand with his addition. The two soon moved on, Rook's keen eyes following them.

"Why—"

"You haven't been around to the furniture shop?" Lenore whispered, cutting him off. "Aren't you supposed to be keeping up your cover?"

Rook leaned against Lenore, pretending to share a private joke. "I've been busy. Someone's trying to kill you, remember?"

"Oh, right!" Lenore replied, joining in the act. "I knew I'd forgotten something."

She made a face at him. Rook laughed, pushing down the concerns the conversation had stirred in his stomach.

"You needn't babysit me all evening," he said. "Go attend to your other guests."

"Are you certain?" Lenore asked. "I haven't seen you talk to anyone else here."

"If I go make a new friend right now, will that erase this little line of worry on your face?" He resisted the urge to stroke said line.

"I'll do my best," she agreed, "but I can't promise I won't worry about you at least a little."

He gave Lenore a knowing smile and watched as she filtered through the crowd, heading for Beatrice Holmes and Evangeline Bell. He drank more of his spiked cider, steeling himself for the conversation he now made a beeline for.

"He's a fine chap," Eamon was saying. "You really should speak with him. I can set up a meeting if you like."

Rook resisted the urge to do a mocking impression of him. He was annoyed he had missed the name of whomever they spoke. Probably one of the crusaders Eamon bankrolled. That could be useful information. Camilla stood beside the Enforcer in a dress of swirled silver and cream and gold, listening patiently as Eamon prattled on. Her eyes caught sight of Rook as he approached, and he was surprised the smile she gave him wasn't entirely one of well-practiced habit.

"Varick," she cooed, turning slightly away from the two gents. "It's so good to see you."

Rook's eyebrows bobbed. Varick? No Mister Pendragon? He wished he knew what exactly he'd done to get on Camilla's good list.

"The pleasure is all mine," he said, giving her a lower bow than he'd originally planned. "Thank you all for hosting tonight."

"We love it," she said, her eyes shining with joy as she gazed at the scene around them. "It's not often we get to have everyone here together and happy. This is as close to bliss as I can imagine."

Rook noticed Camilla's cup of wine was mostly empty. Perhaps she was a lightweight. Before he could respond, she gestured towards Eamon and the Enforcer.

"I believe you're acquainted with Mister Eamon Lee," she said. "Emily, from the clinic, is his younger sister."

"Indeed," Eamon said jovially, extending his hand. "We've crossed paths once or twice. Jolly good to meet up when we're not all on the go, wouldn't you say?"

Rook couldn't help but smirk as he squeezed Eamon's hand as hard as he could. It didn't feel as good as punching him had, but a spark of pleasure flared as Eamon winced ever so slightly.

"Absolutely," Rook agreed.

"And may I introduce Mister Falcon Smoke," Camilla continued. "Falcon, this is Varick Pendragon."

Oh dear, the weird bird family, Rook thought, realization dawning on him. *That's how I know him.*

Rook shook Falcon's hand as well, reciting all the correct words for the situation.

"Is this the first time we've met?" Falcon asked. "I've been acquainted with numerous members of your family, but I must confess I don't remember all of them."

"The Pendragons are rather like weeds, aren't they?" joked Rook. "Or is it cockroaches? They're just everywhere." He ignored the looks spearing at him from either side and kept his eyes locked on Falcon. "Yes, we probably attended the same to-do or other at some point in our lives. So tell me, Falcon, what do you do?"

Falcon's face was already flushed from the closeness of the room—Rook was grateful he had discarded his jacket at the door—but he detected additional color creep up Falcon's neck at the question.

His voice, though, was steady as he replied, "I'm a Fifth."

Rook had expected the constant murmur of voices to at least dip just then. Nothing. He growled inwardly. The onus was on him to continue the conversation.

"Varick, Falcon's parents work at the museum with Neal and Lenore," Camilla broke in.

Rook fluidly pushed away the impulse to look surprised at this brazen deviation in social protocol and schooled his features into polite interest.

"Different department, mind you," she continued, "but isn't that interesting?"

He sipped his drink. "Indubitably. What a small world we live in."

When the time to sing New Year's songs came along, he was surprised again as Camilla took his hand in hers. Rook had planned on escaping to the kitchen when this time inevitably approached, perhaps snaffling whatever homemade goodies he could get his hands on.

"I can't sing," he protested immediately.

"We don't mind," Camilla replied. "This isn't about impressing anyone."

He held her eyes, willing her to let go of his hand and exerting as much distaste for the upcoming torment as possible. She smiled wider at him.

"Please stay. You might find you enjoy it."

"I never have before," he said, edging his voice with sharpness.

He flexed his hand.

"Can I scooch in here, please?"

Rook's eyes flicked towards the voice and softened as Lenore maneuvered between himself and Camilla. He scanned the room and saw Eamon on the other side with his family while Mina and Neal gathered the growing circle around them in order to lead everyone. Lenore hugged Camilla and made a happy little peeping noise, scrunching her face with a huge smile, and Camilla squeezed her adopted sister in return.

"Hello again," Lenore said as she took Rook's hand in hers, excitedly bumping her shoulder against his arm. "I've never heard you sing before. This will be so much fun!"

Rook glanced over Lenore's head to see Camilla. He answered her smug grin with a small harrumph but flashed a smile at Lenore when she looked up towards the sound.

Neal and Mina began the song, Neal's rich baritone blending with Mina's smooth alto notes. Camilla's soprano voice reminded Rook of a bird, while Lenore's was something else altogether.

"You didn't tell me how terrible you are," he whispered in her ear.

Lenore burst into laughter, and she whispered back, "Oh, you think you can do better?"

"All well-to-do children are forced to endure voice lessons," he smiled against her ear. "Of course I can do better."

With that, he began to sing along, Lenore joining back up a moment later even louder than before. A gift exchange game was played afterward, and everyone opened their various candles and wee pouches of money and fine teas together. As Rook traded the package of chocolates he had received with Lenore's miniature bottle of whiskey, he let his hand linger on hers for a moment.

"Thank you for finagling an invitation for me, little bird," he whispered. "I've never been to such a nice New Year's party."

"Never?" she replied.

Behind her eyes, Rook could see Lenore compiling the snippets of information she knew about him and his family. Even just his surname would have informed anyone as to the lavish events he must have experienced growing up.

"Never," he said. "Nicest. One. Ever."

Lenore rewarded him with a beaming smile. "Happy New Year, Rook."

His mouth couldn't help but mimic hers when he heard his name, his proper name, on her lips for the first time that evening.

"Happy New Year, little bird."

DEATH CULTS AND TAXES

Am I intentionally keeping some details of Rook's new business a secret? You bet I am! Though I will mention {SPOILER ALERT!} that at the end of *Across the Ice* he did say he was going to open a clothing store {/end SPOILER ALERT}. A fun, silly story wherein Rook discovers the pitfalls of doing business legitimately. Fun fact: Most of the tax language in the story is taken verbatim from some tax forms I regularly have to deal with.

~~~

Rook looked down at the box distastefully, trying his best not to curl his lip. He looked back to the man standing before him, the one who had brought this plagued package into his shop.

Though the man was a mite taller than Rook, he gave the impression of being smaller. He hunched and kept his arms close to his body, rather reminding Rook of an overlarge tortoise, doubly so with the thinning layer of hair on the man's head and the pince-nez resting on his generous nose. The name he'd given upon entering—Mister Gomble—seemed rather fitting.

Rook looked at a small clipboard sitting next to the package on the counter between them. All down it on a plain form were
~~~

signatures, and Rook was expected to leave his next, to confirm that he'd received this package. He wasn't signing anything until he had a thorough understanding of what *exactly* was being left with him.

"Could you possibly explain in a different way?" Rook asked. He tried giving the man a winning smile, but tortoises were apparently immune to such charms.

Mister Gomble removed his pince-nez and cleaned them with a somewhat rumpled handkerchief. "This is your taxes kit."

That was precisely what he'd said before, and something in the man's manner grated at Rook. He decided to try humility and raised his hands in a helpless gesture. "I'm afraid I don't understand. When Magistrate Allen granted me my permit to open a business, I thought all those expenses had been taken care of."

"They were." And that was all Mister Gomble offered by way of an answer. Maybe it was his voice that irritated so. It was a touch nasally, and got worse when he replaced his pince-nez.

Blazes, and Rook had been having such a lovely morning before this. It was the one day a week the shop was closed, the sun was shining, and he'd just finished his first cup of tea. He knew he should have ignored the ringing of the shop's delivery doorchime, but if he had, either Dmitri or Chrysalis—if she was even awake yet—would have answered.

Rook spoke slowly, keeping his voice even. "So what is this for then?"

"Taxable business expenses."

Beneath the counter that separated the two men, Rook's hands tensed. He suppressed a growl. Even more slowly than before, he asked, "Business expenses for what?"

"For the establishment of your business."

Alright, that was something, though that wasn't saying much in this situation.

"I have to pay taxes on money I spent to establish my

business?" Stars, he missed being a criminal just now.

Mister Gomble shoved the used handkerchief into his pocket, and Rook felt a twitch in one eye start up. He had to remind himself now wasn't the time for a style consultation, especially as the man seemed to be gearing up for an actual explanation.

"That all depends."

Or perhaps not.

"Depends on what?" Rook asked through gritted teeth.

"On how much profit you've earned. It may turn out that the city owes you a credit."

Rook's ears perked up at that. "Oh? What's the tipping point for that?"

The man folded his hands before him primly. "That also all depends."

Rook had a vision of launching himself across the counter and wringing Mister Gomble's wrinkled neck. He didn't, of course. But a man could enjoy his fantasies.

"The forms will explain everything," Mister Gomble offered, as if that was any kind of help.

Rook considered his options—going round and round with the human-tortoise hybrid for a few more rounds, or trusting his own abilities. When he put it like that, the choice was easy. Rook had run a business before; he could handle a little basic accounting. So he scrawled his signature across the form staring up at him, all but ushered Mister Gomble out of the store, and took the box containing his taxes kit into the back room.

Rook looked over the contents of the kit carefully—after the life he'd lived, you never could entirely trust a package from a stranger. Doubly so when that stranger had come calling from the municipal government wanting an account of your finances. It all looked safe enough on the surface—no hidden razor blades or strange smells or anything—but Rook got a queasy feeling in his stomach from the many lines of tiny print on the papers, their boxes for entering values, subsections, and the fact that there were so many pages, and each one was backed by no less than three sheets of carbon paper.

Also in the kit, however, was a small, slim volume entitled *The Helpful Little Book of Tax Guidance*. Most lines on the tax sheets had references to where users could find more information in the book.

"Ah, see? No reason to worry, lad," Rook told himself. "You'll be done and collecting a credit from Springhaven's coffers in no time."

After flying through the initial information, taking special pleasure in entering his recently claimed new surname of Hollow, Rook read the first question aloud to himself with a jaunty sort of tone.

Are you a marketplace provider? If yes, fill out form 7-J before completing this page. If not, continue straight onto question 2.

He blinked at it. Was this somebody's idea of a bloody joke? Rook's former business, the illegal one he'd traded for this new life, had been a marketplace.

He snatched up *The Helpful Little Book of Tax Guidance* and found the explanation for the line.

A marketplace provider is a person who, pursuant to an agreement with a marketplace seller, facilitates sales of tangible personal property by marketplace sellers, as described in STM-B-19(2.1)S.

Rook blinked again. Reread the statement. Reread it again.

"Was someone drunk when they wrote this?" he asked *The Helpful Little Book of Tax Guidance*. "And what the blazes is

STM… whatever. It sounds like a venereal disease."

A quick glance down the open page of *The Helpful Little Book of Tax Guidance* showed him every "helpful" description was written in the same circuitous, meaningless way.

Rook leaned back in his seat and placed a hand on his head. How was he ever going to complete these blasted forms, much less manipulate them to his favor?

Disgust suddenly washed over Rook. *What the blazes is the matter with you? You've felled crime lords trying to flay the flesh from your bones! And you're going to wilt when a little paperwork challenges you? Pull yourself together, man!*

He sat up again. That's right. He was *Rook*, the one and only. One of the savviest business sharks of Springhaven's criminal underbelly. Formerly, anyway.

With the determination of a champion pugilist entering the ring for round one, Rook sat back up, fixed a glare at *The Helpful Little Book of Tax Guidance*, and willed it to reveal its secret tax-y language to him. The sentence stared back at him as unsympathetic as a lump of horse dung.

Rook glared harder. "Break it down. A marketplace provider is a person who—yes, got it—pursuant to an agreement with a marketplace seller…" Rook faltered. Provider, seller, weren't they the same thing? He clenched his jaw. "Skip it! A marketplace provider is a person who blather blather blather facilitates sales of tangible personal property—alright, now we're getting somewhere —by marketplace sellers, as described in STM-B-19(2.1)S."

Blank. Nothing but muggy incomprehension filled his mind. Rook glared so hard his eye twitched. He started over. Still nothing, so he gave the page a feral smile like he would have back in his old life, to intimidate the words on the page.

The words were, unsurprisingly, unimpressed.

Rook threw *The Helpful Little Book of Tax Guidance* towards its box and pulled at his hair.

"It doesn't *mean* anything! None of it! All gibberish!"

"Rook, have you seen my—"

Rook swiveled in his chair and was on his feet before the speaker could finish their sentence. He simultaneously detested the idea of anyone catching him in such a sad state and was thrilled for a distraction from his struggles.

It was Dmitri who'd come in and spoken. Rook's desk was tucked into a far corner of the store's back room, so anyone could come find him. Well, anyone who managed to figure out or already knew how to get past the backroom's custom security features. Dmitri, of course, as Rook's right-hand man, did.

Dmitri stopped short, staring in a mixture of fear and confusion. Probably at the manic grin Rook only then realized he was wearing. He adjusted his features to something more sane and collected before leaning back against his desk, smooth as butter.

"Ah, Dmitri, how may I assist?" Alright, that might have been laying it on a little thick. Rook needed to unrattle himself, and fast, but he knew better than to try and address the blunder. That would only bring more attention to it, so he waited.

Dmitri studied Rook for a moment, but apparently thought better of questioning his employer.

"Have you seen my best waistcoat?" Dmitri asked instead. "The gold brocade one I wore at the shop's grand opening?"

A set of cobbled-together apartments nestled above the shop. Dmitri had a space of his own, as did Chrysalis, and between those squatted a common living area, kitchen, and dining room combination. Rook had a sort of halfway room up there too. Nothing more than a closet with a bed inside, really, but it worked. After all, he had several little hideaways of various sizes around the city. He stayed above when shop business kept him late, so it wasn't strange that he might have run across a wayward piece of Dmitri's wardrobe.

Rook shook his head, looking grave. "No, I'm afraid I haven't.

We'd better start turning this place upside down."

Dmitri's eyebrow ticked up a fraction of an inch. "I'm sure it'll turn up. I just wondered since—"

"Nonsense!" Rook said. And then he realized he was overdoing it again and pulled back. "Dmitri, that's a very fine garment. It deserves a proper search."

Dmitri looked to Rook's desk, eyes skimming the papers and their triplicate attached carbon copy sheets. "Aren't you in the middle of something here?"

Finally starting to feel his old verve come back, Rook smoothed a smirk over his face and waved a dismissive hand at the tax documents on his desk. "Oh, this? Child's play. It'll come together in a jiffy, so let's go find that waistcoat of yours."

Without waiting for an answer, he sauntered out of the backroom, Dmitri falling into a much more disciplined step behind him.

Two hours later found them in Dmitri's usually neat-as-a-pin room, surrounded by every piece of clothing Dmitri owned. They laid draped across the mattress, chair backs, over the door. None on the floor, though. Neither would have ever allowed it. The room looked as if the armoire had, somehow with respect for proper clothing care, vomited its contents hither and yon.

Rook gazed around at the scene before him, hands on his hips. "Hm. It really is good and missing. Shall we move onto the common area or put all this away first?"

Dmitri, who was currently trying to shift some kind of order into the trousers scattered across the bed, squared a suspicious look at Rook. "Why are you so keen to help me find this waistcoat?"

Rook held out his hands in a gesture of pure innocence. "I told you, it's a very fine garment."

"Yes," Dmitri said slowly, "but you own a clothing shop. We have some very similar to it downstairs. You'd usually just give me one from that stock. Are you trying to avoid whatever's waiting for you back at your desk?"

"No." Rook said it too quickly. He reclaimed his cool, innocent demeanor again. "Why would I? You know me. I live for business."

Dmitri did not in the least look convinced. Rook wasn't about to admit a bloody piece of paper—no, something so insignificant as a single *sentence*—was beating him. Especially at the game of business acumen.

"You know what?" Rook faked a sigh. "You're right. I really should be getting back to that." He motioned at the apparel chaos around them. "Best of luck with all this. If you still don't find it, let me know. We'll get you sorted downstairs."

And with that, Rook swanned out, ignoring the burn of Dmitri's glower on the back of his head. It was a scummy thing to do, but Rook had a reputation to keep up. For this, even before his friends.

When Rook returned to his desk, *The Helpful Little Book of Tax Guidance* stared at him from where it had landed when he'd thrown it. He imagined it simpering at him, mocking him. How did he deal with competent adversaries? That's the question he'd been pondering to himself on the way down from Dmitri's room. And *The Helpful Little Book of Tax Guidance* was certainly proving to be a match for him.

He either made a deal with those adversaries or he found something to use against them.

Well, Rook could hardly offer a book something—it wasn't like he could arrange for it to be depulped and turned back into a tree or anything—so he'd have to find its weakness. Rook opened the book to the page he'd been on before. This time, something stuck out at him.

...as described in STM-B-19(2.1)S.

"So if I find STM dash B thingy, I'll have the answer." And then, as if *The Helpful Little Book of Tax Guidance* had feelings to hurt, Rook added with a sneer, "The *real* answer."

The Springhaven Levy Center—Business Taxes Subsector was housed inside a very large, semi-open room, which was in turn hidden within a much larger building disguised as an endless path of turns and corridors that seemed reluctant to reach the locations all the signs posted around promised. With dogged determination, Rook had followed these same petulant signs, never straying off the path, eyes sharp for the door he needed. Finally, he'd made it.

Within the headquarters for the Business Taxes Subsector, a line of windowed booths protected the area where the department's employees did their complex and no doubt deadly boring work. Some sat at those windows, calling numbers and, hopefully, assisting Springhaven's business owners with their various tax challenges. Outside of that protected space was a nearly featureless waiting area, lined back and forth with chairs.

Inside Rook's jacket pocket, *The Helpful Little Book of Tax Guidance* sat, awaiting its grand comeuppance. He'd been offended by how few people were waiting their turn in seats when he'd walked in, so much so that he'd double checked the sign outside to ensure he'd walked into the right place. He had. So how come there were barely more than a dozen people in here? There were chairs enough for three times that, at least.

Rook's skin crawled, certain he was missing something simple, something nearly every other legitimate business owner in Springhaven knew. He nearly walked out right then and there, convinced the clerk who would eventually help him would question his ability to run so much as a flower cart. But then there was that blasted book in his pocket, and Rook couldn't let it win.

He soothed his injured pride with the fact that fewer people meant he'd be in and out faster. And so indeed, it wasn't ten minutes before his number was called and Rook gathered every bit of charm in his arsenal.

The man behind the window was already smiling, so that was a smashing start. A vast improvement from the testudinal Mister Gomble just a few hours ago. This one had a small name badge pinned to his tweed waistcoat that read *Mister Umberbreck*. Rook nearly winced at the sight of a pin shearing through the lovely, fine tweed fibers of the piece, but he pushed the impulse away, narrowing his focus to find his advantage with this man.

"Good morning," Mister Umberbreck said cheerfully through a small horn-looking apparatus affixed to his side of the window. Then, glancing at a small clock on the counter between them. "My mistake. Just after noon now."

Rook automatically broke into a laugh and pointed at the man. Into another horn-like device attached on his side, he said, "Ah, I see what you did there. Very droll. Very droll indeed, sir."

Mister Umberbreck laughed too, and gave a little wave that Rook suspected was all false modesty. "You'll have to excuse me. I know you probably don't have the *time* for jokes."

Oh stars, make it stop, Rook's mind begged.

For once, he was glad Lenore wasn't by his side. She and Mister Umberbreck could probably keep this inanity going for hours. Though Rook knew it would serve him well to make a pun back, his brain flat refused. Not for this grinning halfwit, so he just laughed some more instead.

"Now, how can I help you today?" Mister Umberbreck finally

got around to asking.

Rook leaned on the counter like they were old friends and pulled *The Helpful Little Book of Tax Guidance* from his pocket. Pointing to the page with the so-called explanation about marketplace providers, he asked, "Can you please help me with this?" He pointed at the listing for *STM-B-19(2.1)S* on the page.

Mister Umberbreck's smile grew. Finally, Rook was getting somewhere.

"Oh, that'll have been included in your Nubby Rub Bin."

Rook's eyes widened, and he had to force his brain to stay on task instead of venturing down any gutters. "My what now?"

Mister Umberbreck laughed again. The sound was quickly starting to grate as much as the tone of Mister Gomble's voice had. "Your New Business Regulation, Use, and Bylaw Binder. Nubby Rub Bin is just a cheeky little term we like to use here around the office."

Rook could only bring himself to chuckle this time. He had a very bad feeling he could tell where this was going. Especially because he couldn't remember having received anything like that. "Of course, yes. That. Well, you see, it was quite a hectic time back when we opened. Lots of red tape, so many hoops to jump through, and then there's the marketing to get your name out there. We, my little team and I, we're a tiny operation, but we beat the streets until even the cobblestones knew our name." It was not a good joke, Rook knew. It didn't even really make sense, but he laughed at it anyway.

Mister Umberbreck didn't return the courtesy. Just sat there with his smile pasted in place.

"Anyway," Rook went on, "I'm afraid my plucky little group and I might have misplaced our… Nubby Rub Bin." He almost couldn't bring himself to say it; it was too absurd. This man, with his insincere smile, didn't deserve the indulgence, but Rook was running out of options. "Could I please have a new one?"

"I'm afraid not." Mister Umberbreck was shaking his head and yet still smiling. Rook wanted to rip that smile right off and leave the bottom of the man's face a void of nothing. That horror would be better than the perpetual, empty smile. "There's a reason we put in big yellow and orange letters across the cover, *Irreplaceable; do not lose*." With his hand in the air, he demonstrated where the letters would go on a book cover.

"But what if some of the laws change?" Rook asked. He'd dropped all pretense, letting his frustration seep through in his voice.

"In that case, we simply send out copies of the individual pages that need to be replaced," Mister Umberbreck said. "Far more economical that way. Now, if you'll excuse me, I'm already late for my lunch break." Then, as if the prat had done Rook any sort of favor, Mister Umberbreck added, "You're welcome. Have a great day."

Rook gaped as a cream-colored canvas curtain rolled down over the window. A slit down the middle snaked its way around the horn on Mister's Umberbreck's side.

This is why they have the windows, Rook thought. *So that people don't reach across and murder them. Someone must have done it once.*

He was too shocked to say anything, to try and stop Mister Umberbreck. How did a city run like this?!

Rook returned to the clothing shop in a fog. How? How did anyone legally do business in this city with such appalling, unhelpful civil servants? Where was their pride in their jobs, their sense of good customer service?

We should just abolish taxes, he'd thought as he walked. *No taxes, everyone has to just build their own roads and maintain their own sewers. That's right. That would work, wouldn't it?*

A distant part of Rook's mind knew he was unraveling, urged him to pull himself together, but he was just too baffled. How had Springhaven not caved in on itself? What manner of administrative infrastructure was it even running on?

"You okay?"

Rook looked towards the voice. It was Chrysalis. She was sitting cross-legged atop a double-barred clothing rack, looking down on him and swallowed in a coat that was at least three sizes too big for her—it did tend to get chilly back here. Only her head and hands stuck out of the coat, and a box of what was presumably lunch rested on one knee. He'd made it back to the backroom, likely pulled there by the knowledge of his responsibility, futile though the effort was.

"I have known madness today, Chrys," Rook said.

Chrysalis sucked her teeth and nodded. "Right. Want a roll? The lady gave me an extra. I think she thought I was homeless because of the coat, ya know? I'm gonna wear it again next time I go."

Despite everything, Rook couldn't help but smile. In the weeks since they'd opened the shop and she'd moved in upstairs, she'd started to blossom. Not like a rose the way most people thought of when they used that expression. No, Chrysalis had blossomed like an ivy vine, finding all the little places she fit best and sending her roots into them. She'd leapt, literally jumped into the air, when Rook had presented her with her with her apartment, small though it was. He'd expected her to sulk when he told her she had to pay rent, which could either come straight from her wages or she could give him money. Instead, she'd given him a firm nod, chosen to pay him directly instead of garnishments, and even shook on it though Rook hadn't asked her to.

She was good with the customers too, quick and professional. She'd been eager to learn the new job, and had even begun offering her own ideas for the store. And she'd stopped hoarding food like she might be out on the streets any minute. Rook had seen her nick Dmitri's lunch more than once in the beginning. On those days, to keep everything sailing smoothly, he usually offered to buy lunch for everyone.

Rook shook his head at her offer. "Thanks, but you keep it." He tried examining her position again, but the coat prevented it. "That can't be comfortable up there. We have an employee breakroom. Why don't you eat your lunch in there?"

Chrysalis shrugged, and Rook had to admire how well she balanced the box on her knee. He wasn't certain even he could have pulled that off.

"Keeps things interesting," she said. "'Sides, this way I get to see what it's like to be tall." She grinned before popping a piece of chicken into her mouth.

That was a point. She was sitting about five feet up in the air, but her torso wasn't usually that long, was it? Rook was pretty good at guessing a person's measurements just by looking at them.

"Are you sitting on something?" he asked.

Without a word, Chrysalis scooped up her lunch box, raised herself up, and drew something out from underneath her. She sank smoothly back down onto the double bars of the rack, about four inches shorter now. In her hand, she held up a thick, black binder.

Rook felt like he might cry. In Chrysalis' small hand was the New Business Regulation, Use, and Bylaw Binder. Its yellow and orange words on the front cover, just as Mister Umberbreck had described, might have mocked Rook if he wasn't so bloody glad to see them.

"Chrys, you absolute miracle worker!" he crowed.

"I know," she replied simply.

"Where did you find that?" Rook reached for the binder, which Chrysalis handed over without argument.

"Came when we were getting ready to open. You said to keep it somewhere safe but not throw it away. Makes a good seat."

"Remind me to buy you a pillow to replace it. A really nice one!"

"With tassels?" Chrysalis asked.

"A million tassels if that's what you want." Rook could have kissed the binder, but that would look insane, so he restrained himself.

Chrysalis grinned again. "Jammy."

Having regrouped, Rook walked to his desk and set his materials out again. *The Helpful Little Book of Tax Guidance* went next to the New Business binder, and not a minute passed before Rook found the page for STM-B-19(2.1)S.

Success at last, he thought.

At the top of the page was printed the same statement as what was listed in *The Helpful Little Book of Tax Guidance.*

A marketplace provider is a person who, pursuant to an agreement with a marketplace seller, facilitates sales of tangible personal property by marketplace sellers, as described in STM-B-19(2.1)S.

Followed by…

A person "facilitates a sale of tangible personal property" when the person, or an affiliate, collects the receipts paid by a customer to a marketplace seller for a sale of tangible personal property, or contracts with a third party to collect the receipts. Persons are affiliated if…

The words began to blur together. Rook felt his brain beginning to fog in the same way as it had before. How was this possible? He was the best negotiator he knew; words were his weapons as much as, well, weapons. And what even counted as personal property? Technically, he owned all the clothing in his shop until someone else bought it, but somehow that didn't seem right. And dear heaven above, he didn't want to get his forms wrong and have to redo them.

Or worse, deal with the Springhaven Levy Center—Business Taxes Subsector again.

Farther down the page, something caught his eye.

For a definition and examples of tangible personal property, see Tax Bulletin, Quick Reference Guide for Taxable and Exempt Property and Services (BT-TS-470).

Aha! He wasn't sunk yet! This binder would be his life raft after all. And if the thickness of this binder was anything to go by, Rook suspected they covered *everything* in here. Yes!

Flipping to the correct section and then page, the words…

Whether sales of a particular good or service are taxable may depend on many factors.

…rose up to meet him. That didn't bode well, but on he read. The book directed him to yet another section for examples of personal property. Rook was starting to feel a little lost with all this page flipping. He wanted a way to trace page to page where he'd started. And that was when a new idea struck him. It might cause suspicion, though. Might make him look like he was out of his depth.

Rook craned his neck to look over the backroom again. Chrysalis had disappeared from her perch, but that didn't necessarily mean she was gone.

"Chrys?" he called. "You still back here? I found a pack of chocolate biscuits in my desk."

No response. Yes, she was definitely gone. And so Rook started his work.

Three hours passed like a blink. Or like a blackout. It was hard to tell from this far down inside a spiraling rabbit hole of lunacy. Loose page after loose page hung tacked to the wall. One after another, Rook had chased them through the Nubby Rib Bin—he'd surrendered to calling it that in the hopes of appeasing the cruel, mighty tormentor. Where the impressive bulk of it had once looked like the promise of care and safety, confidence in comprehensivity, it now represented a mad god, fattened on the promise of sowing chaos and confusion.

Each new sheet pointed to yet another Rook would need to maybe, eventually, understand. They laughed at and taunted him with phrases like "For more information about" and "A list of X can be found on…" And each time, Rook had believed them. For what else was he to do?

Not long ago, he'd opened *The Helpful Little Book of Tax Guidance* and placed it open on his head. Osmosis was a thing that may or may not exist, right? Why not try it too? *The Helpful Little Book of Tax Guidance* no longer angered him like it had, for now he recognized that it was merely a pup compared to the wolf that was the Nubby Rub Bin.

Back when he'd still thought he had hope, he'd strung twine from tack to tack, connecting the pages that referenced each other, until he had something that looked like what might occur if a very large spider got drunk and tried to build a web across a frozen lake.

Rook slumped in his desk chair, staring at what he'd created without really seeing it. His arms draped limply over the armrests while *The Helpful Little Book of Tax Guidance* rested serenely atop his head.

He was never going to finish his taxes.

His business would fail.

Rook had never failed at any business venture before, but it was happening now, before his eyes, in agonizing slow motion. He could never work for someone else. He'd have to go underground, become a criminal again.

But he couldn't. Not in this city anyway. He and Lenore would have to run away, leave Springhaven. Oh blazes! He was going to have to move to sweltering, sand-scuffing, fish-loving Bone Port, wasn't he?! That might be even more miserable than failing.

Shouting came dimly from upstairs. A distant corner of Rook's mind noted that an argument of some kind was happening, but he otherwise ignored it. It didn't sound as if anyone or anything was breaking after all. Nothing except his tether with sanity anyway, so on he stared. The argument soon came to find him, though he still couldn't tear his eyes away from the physical manifestation of his descent into madness.

"I've been looking for that waistcoat for ages!" Dmitri hollered.

The sound of Chrysalis' boots stomping against the wooden floorboards of the backroom preceded his own.

"Rook!" Chrysalis said, pounding over to his desk. "Dmitri's riffled all through my closet! Bloody wrecked everything! And he won't do anything about it."

"Welcome to the club," Dmitri shot back. To Rook, he said, "The little sneak has been pilfering my clothes! I thought I might be going mad."

Don't talk to me about going mad, Rook thought.

But something else tugged at him. His people, the ones who depended on him for their pay, needed him. And *this*, at least, sounded like something Rook could handle.

So he spun in his chair towards them, slid *The Helpful Little Book of Tax Guidance* from his head, and sized up his two employees. He caught Dmitri's glance at the web of twine and papers, but pushed it away. That was a problem for later.

"Children, is shouting how we solve anything?" Both Chrysalis and Dmitri opened their mouths, but Rook continued before they could speak. "Don't answer that. It was rhetorical." He looked to Chrysalis first. "Have you been taking Dmitri's clothes?"

Chrysalis' face scrunched into a pout. She delivered her answer like a defensive parry, sharp and hard. "So what if I have?"

Dmitri opened his mouth again, but Rook held up a hand. Dmitri's expression darkened, and Rook looked to him. "Don't worry, you'll get your chance." Back to Chrysalis. "*Why* have you been taking Dmitri's clothes?"

He noticed she was wearing Dmitri's missing waistcoat. It really was an excellent piece of craftsmanship. The gold brocade looked rather nice against her tawny skin and dark hair. And she'd paired it with a pair of wide-legged trousers that she must have altered herself—he didn't carry anything like that, nor did any other clothing shops he knew of. The garment could look like a skirt or trousers depending on how Chrysalis was standing. He also noticed that she was no longer looking at him. She looked off to the side, brows knotted angrily, but she bit her bottom lip in worry.

His voice was softer this time as he said, "Whatever it is, you can tell us. We're your family. The good kind, the kind you got to choose."

Chrysalis looked back to him from the corners of her eyes. She swallowed hard and lifted her chin.

"Some days, I don't feel so much like a girl. So on them, I don't dress like one." She took a deep breath and started to rush through her words. "That's not to say I don't feel like a girl some days too. But it's important to me to be able to express how I feel as it changes."

Rook blinked at her, unabashed surprise on his face. This was one of the most eloquent speeches he'd ever heard Chrysalis make. In his periphery, he saw Dmitri's expression mirrored his own, though Rook spared no more than a moment on that.

The Reaper, or Zoe as they'd also been known, leader of the Collective, had seen themself similarly. Though instead of both male and female, it had been neither. Rook had questions: What was that like? How long had Chrysalis felt this way? Had he done anything to make her even more afraid to share—stars, he hoped not. But now wasn't the time. Chrysalis was looking at him, waiting with fear and expectation written in the taut stillness of her body.

He threw up his hands in a gesture of easy acceptance. "You can be whoever you want. We love you no matter what. Just don't start any death cults."

Chrysalis' face broke into a huge, relieved smile, and she gave Dmitri's waistcoat a proud little straightening, lifting her head high. "No death cults," she promised.

Rook gave her his warmest smile. "Excellent. And thank you for sharing with us; that was very brave." With the way Chrysalis began to glow, Rook hated what was coming next, but it had to be done. "Now give Dmitri his waistcoat back."

Like a deflating soufflé, Chrysalis' expression fell back into petulance, and she grumbled under her breath.

"And then go pick out some pieces for yourself from the floor." A smirk tugged at Rook's lips. "That's far too big a size for you. And be sure to notate them for me so I can write them off." He turned a glower back onto the hanging sheets of tax information behind him. "I'll add them to my business expenses."

Chrysalis began scrabbling with the buttons in her excitement, and Rook had to admonish, "Is that how we treat fine garments?" Chrysalis huffed but slowed. "Better."

She then neatly folded the waistcoat and carefully handed it back to Dmitri before running pell-mell into the shopfront.

Dmitri watched her with a raised eyebrow before turning back to Rook. "She's going to clean you out. You know that, right?"

Rook gave a dismissive wave of his hand. "Let her. It's a big

day for her." Rook smiled. "I'm honored she trusted us."

Dmitri nodded. "Agreed." Then he looked at the papers pinned to the wall again and pointed. "So what is all this?"

Rook grumbled and forced himself to look at Dmitri. He might be beat, but he was no coward. "I have to file taxes for the shop and I have no idea what I'm doing."

"That's apparent," Dmitri said flatly.

Rook flapped *The Helpful Little Book of Tax Guidance* at him. "How can anyone be expected to? None of this makes any sense! It's no wonder people turn to crime. The people in charge make it too complicated to do business legally."

"My mother could do them," Dmitri said.

Rook blinked at him. "Is that supposed to be some kind of insult? If so, it's a poor attempt. I'm sure your mother's a very capable and intelligent person."

"She is," Dmitri replied. "If she were a man, she'd hold a position as an accountant. But since she's not, she hires herself out to local businesses that don't want to pay for a firm. Those that will have her anyway. It doesn't bring in much, but it's a bit extra on top of being a washerwoman." He paused, considering. "I realize my recommendation is biased, but she's very good. And I can get references from other shops if you'd like."

Rook slapped *The Helpful Little Book of Tax Guidance* onto the desk, leapt to his feet, and clapped his hands together. "Right. Here's what we're going to do. Firstly, you're going to find out what the top going rate for an accountant is. Offer your mother that." He began unpinning the papers from the wall and collecting them into a pile. "Then deliver all *this*—" He said the word with the deepest disgust he could muster. "—to your lovely mother. I'd prefer to get something back from the city after the trouble they put me through today, but I'll take what I can get at this point."

Dmitri gave him *a look*. "You might have avoided some of that trouble if you'd been honest with me earlier."

Rook sucked in a breath to argue, held it as he thought, and then let it out again. "You're right. I let my pride get ahead of me, and I'm sorry."

Dmitri nodded. "She'll need access to your financial records as well."

"Done. Bring her round for tea, whatever you need to do."

"And you're sure you don't want references for her?" Dmitri asked.

Rook looked back at him, a pin half-extracted from the wall. "Dmitri, if anyone knows what an exacting employer I am, it's you. You wouldn't have recommended her if you didn't think she could do the job."

Dmitri gave a little gesture of agreement. "True, but I have one demand."

Rook froze, turned. "A demand?"

"My room is still a wreck from earlier. I've spent all day looking for this." He held up the waistcoat. "I want you to put it back to rights."

Rook chuckled, and a small smile tugged at Dmitri's lips.

"That's fair. A fitting *tax* for my poor behavior today."

Dmitri rolled his eyes, and Rook let out a laugh. He finished collecting the sheets into a pile and plopped *The Helpful Little Book of Tax Guidance* on top of the lot.

Death Cults and Taxes (Addendum)

There's a school of thought in the writing world that, whichever character is going through the biggest emotional journey, that's the POV readers should be seeing. When I initially wrote DC&T, for the scene where Chrysalis comes out as genderfluid, I'd considered switching the POV to Chrysalis', but, from a technical standpoint, given that we hadn't had her POV at all during the rest of the story, I decided that might be a bit messy. So to avoid said messiness, I abstained. However, Chrys deserves her moment, so I've written a tangent for her here. It begins just before Dmitri discovers that she's been nicking his clothes.

~~~

Chrysalis turned this way and that, examining herself in the tall, cracked floor mirror that leaned against one corner of her bedroom. *Her* bedroom, a private space all her own. She paid for it every month with her own fairly earned money, and no one was allowed in without her permission. Just thinking about that
~~~

fact still made her smile. The gold brocade waistcoat she currently wore, however, was another story. Both in how it made her feel and it being hers. She'd stolen it from Dmitri's room a few weeks back after she'd seen him wear at the shop's grand opening.

The piece was *really* pretty. Whoever had woven all the intricate, curling, swirling leaves had chosen subtly different shades of gold and bronze; even a few brazen coppers made a cheeky appearance here and there. The problem was that it fit Chrysalis about as well as a sock on a stick. Dmitri wasn't the broadest built of gents, but he had a good pair of shoulders on him and enough thickness in his trunk to make the waistcoat sag pathetically on Chrysalis' small frame.

For weeks now, she'd been trying to think of a way to take in the garment without utterly destroying it, but she simply didn't have the skillset to tailor it. She'd done well enough on the wide-legged trousers she currently wore. But all she'd had to do for those was cut a simple walking skirt partway up the middle and then sew the two pieces into trouser legs. A waistcoat was a far more involved project. And, though he *did* have the skills, she couldn't ask Rook. He'd recognize the waistcoat in a heartbeat. He'd know she took it. She didn't have anything like as nice, though, at least not in men's clothing. She had bits and pieces she'd cobbled together and collected over the years, but *this*… this was a proper bit of finery. A power piece, as Rook would call it. And if she could alter it in a way that made it look as good on her as it had on Dmitri… gosh, that'd be fizzing. Not knowing how to tailor the piece, she'd been puzzling over ways to clothes-peg it or something into the fit she wanted—she wasn't about to commit the crime of stabbing holes into the beautiful fabric with locking pins or anything. Maybe there was something she could use in her and Dmitri's shared common area?

She peeked around the door of her room. Good, no Dmitri. With the shop being closed today, there was no telling where he'd

be. The door to his room was shut too, which meant he was out somewhere. If he came back, she'd be able to hear him coming up the stairs well before he spotted her. Like a squirrel on a mission, Chrysalis darted out of her room and begin riffling through drawers. She didn't really know how to cook beyond spreading butter over toast, so most of the cooking implements she found in the kitchen cabinets and drawers and whatnot were a mystery to her. She found some bits of twine, though, amidst blank, slightly tattered labels Dmitri had made for his small collection of window box herbs. The twine might work, but it was scratchy, and the bits were all pretty short.

"Just what the blazes do you think you're doing?"

Chrysalis jumped a foot in the air and spun, bristling like a cat, fingers crooked and ready to jab some eyeballs. Dmitri stood in the doorway to his bedroom, glaring at her.

"You're not supposed to be here," she informed him.

Her anger made her sound far more certain of herself than she felt. She was annoyed that she'd miscalculated. And more than that, hot shame rose in her neck and cheeks at having been caught in the pilfered waistcoat. Rook had taught her so much better than this.

Dmitri pointed at the garment. "Give it back. *Now.*"

"You gonna try and make me?" she snapped.

The challenge had been a knee-jerk reaction. Some habits from her life before Rook and their strange little family died hard. Dmitri wasn't like the ones who'd made her think she'd forever be fighting, but it still took her a moment to shake off the old fear.

"Fine." He was already striding away from her when he said it, his voice and gait decisive and determined.

The irritation every sibling knows all too well rushed in like a wave. Dmitri was heading towards. Her. *Door.*

"No!" Chrysalis practically yowled the word. "Stay out of my room!"

By the time she'd scampered across the kitchen and through

the sitting area, Dmitri was already inside. She could see where this was going, and more hot, sticky shame washed over her as she fruitlessly tried to shout Dmitri into submission.

He threw open her wardrobe and began, one by one, to remove each piece of clothing she owned, inspecting it for more hidden, ill-gotten garments. Fair dues, this was exactly where she stored them. So it wasn't but a matter of moments before he started discovering more bits she'd nicked from him.

"One of my blue cravats," Dmitri observed. "I'll have that back, thank you."

"*One of*," Chrysalis shot back. "Means you have some to spare."

Dmitri tossed the cobalt-colored blouse within which she'd hidden the cravat onto the bed, letting any remaining semblance of tidiness it still had unfold into nonexistence.

"You'd better put that back the way you found it!" Chrysalis hollered.

"I will *not* be doing that."

The evenness, the pure implacability in Dmitri's tone, grated against every fiber within Chrysalis. Stars, how she *hated* when Dmitri got like this, all cold and superior. When he put on what Chrysalis called his "Enforcer voice," it was like trying to convince a boulder to get up and move itself out of the middle of the road.

She growled and stamped her foot, which, aside from yelling at him, was just about all she could do. Chrysalis was no fighter. And even if she was, that wasn't what she and Dmitri did. They both knew what real, physical danger felt like, and that wasn't how they treated one another. In real scrapes, she'd fight only as much as she needed to create an escape path for herself. And then she scarpered. In this situation, though, there was nothing to run away towards. Except...

Chrysalis sucked in a breath just as Dmitri was throwing a third blouse onto the bed, where, in addition to its brethren, it joined two skirts, plus a pair of boots and a simple but fashionable feathered hat. With that breath, she bellowed, "I'm telling Rook!"

It would have been impressively loud if it had come from, say, a six-and-a-half-foot wandering tuba player, so such a loud proclamation from such a small person was quite a feat. Dmitri didn't even flinch, which rankled all the more.

He didn't respond, but Chrysalis could hear his measured tread behind her as she did her best impression of a rhinocery… rhinosisiphys… one of those impossibly big creatures with the weaponized nose she'd once seen a skeleton of at the Springhaven museum. She did her best impression of one of those on her way down the stairs, happy to drive the heels of her boots right through the wood if it came to it.

The stairs to the apartments were part of the, as Chrysalis thought of it, backstage area of the store. So it was a fairly short, stomp-filled walk to the organized but crowded backroom. Chrysalis had guessed right that Rook would still be there from when she'd seen him earlier that day, when she'd been eating her lunch and he'd been weirdly excited about a huge, excruciatingly boring-looking binder.

Rook was sitting at his desk, uncharacteristically slouched, with his arms hanging off either side of the armrests. And he was wearing a small book atop his head.

Chrysalis might have been curious, but this was clearly a much bigger crisis than whatever Rook was playing at with the string maze he'd constructed on the wall and his not-very-fashionable new headwear.

"Rook!" Chrysalis said. She was trying to sound collected and official, though her pounding feet seemed to have missed that part. In any case, shouting was definitely not how one dealt with Rook. She drew up as tall as she could before him. "Dmitri's riffled all through my closet! Bloody wrecked everything! And he won't do anything about it."

Okay, some of that might have been a *bit* of an exaggeration, but Rook needed to know how serious this was!

"Welcome to the club," Dmitri said.

She pulled a face at him, but at least he was acting like a normal human now, with actual emotions instead of a heartless automaton.

He turned to Rook and added, "The little sneak has been pilfering my clothes! I thought I might be going mad."

Chrysalis felt a little spark of pride at being called "a sneak." It reminded her that, aside from today's blunder, she'd been successful.

Rook drew in a slow breath and spun in his chair towards the two of them, sliding the little book from his head as he did. He looked them both over for a long moment. The little bloom of happiness grew in Chrysalis. Yes, Rook would sort this. He always had a solution.

"Children," he said slowly, "is shouting how we solve anything?"

Alright, *that* wasn't the sort of thing Chrysalis had been hoping for. She and Dmitri both opened their mouths to respond. Chrysalis was going to repeat her complaint, this time with more emphasis, because *clearly* Rook just hadn't understood properly the first time, but Rook continued before either could speak. "Don't answer that. It was rhetorical." He looked to Chrysalis first. "Have you been taking Dmitri's clothes?"

This was even less what she'd been hoping for. And Chrysalis was beginning to regret tattling to Rook. Didn't he see that all Dmitri had to do was take his things back? Meanwhile, Chrysalis had to refold and put away all her things that *he'd* messed up. And on top of that, she was back to not having any good-quality men's clothes. Not that she didn't like her women's clothes, but she didn't like them all the time. Having the option made her feel good, *really* good. Like she was more herself when she had the option.

Anger bubbled in her chest, mixing with shame. She knew she shouldn't have stolen Dmitri's things, but he was the one with the things! And he'd been the safer bet. Rook was actually closer to her size, but she knew better than to steal from him. Plus, he didn't keep much of his own clothing here; he'd have noticed right away. And she could hardly have asked Rook for free clothes, not after he'd given her an entire wardrobe of upscale ladies' clothing. She felt backed into a corner, and Chrysalis scrunched her face up, readying herself to argue with Rook. She didn't want to do it, but she didn't see that she had a lot of choice.

"So what if I have?" She answered as hard and sharp as she could. She needed them to see she wasn't about to back down.

Dmitri opened his mouth again, but Rook held up a hand. Dmitri's expression darkened, and Chrysalis felt some smug satisfaction at that.

Rook looked at him. "Don't worry, you'll get your chance." Then his eyes came back to Chrysalis. "*Why* have you been taking Dmitri's clothes?"

Chrysalis' bravado quavered. Rook held her employment in his hands, her apartment, and he could take it away in a snap, but that wasn't what scared her. Rook wasn't like that. Rook wasn't just a fair person, he was a *good* person, despite what some of his more jealous rivals might say. If Chrysalis said she didn't want to talk about it, Rook would respect that. She worried because she *wanted* to tell him. And while she knew he was a good person, had seen proof of that over and over again, she was frightened what her truth might change between them. Not just because he was her employer and teacher and landlord, but because he was one of the few, special people she'd allowed herself to get close to. And stars, she didn't want to lose that.

Chrysalis looked away, feeling fear pull her further from what she wanted. She wanted Rook to know this thing about her. It was important in a soul-deep kind of way she didn't quite know how to describe. She wanted Dmitri to know too, even if he did drive her batty worse than any flesh-and-blood family member could. Because he too, like Rook, was one of those few special people.

No one is entitled to know about me, said her heart. *If I share, I share on my own terms.*

The guilt she felt about stealing from Dmitri was a separate issue, though. That was about trust, which she'd broken. She cared if he trusted her. And she knew they cared about her trusting them too.

They might say you're wrong, said Chrysalis' fear. *Even though no one knows you better than yourself, and they're smart enough to know that, they still might say you've got it wrong.*

They might think she was just being silly. Or that this was some kind of phase, a self-imposed fad that would pass with time. They might think less of her for any number of reasons. They might think she was a freak and kick her out.

They are good people, Chrysalis reminded herself firmly. Rook and Dmitri had risked their own safety to save her life. They'd taken her in, mentored her, like a pair of odd-couple dads. And she didn't want to live a lie with them. Chrysalis gathered words to her. Her brows knotted together; she'd never disliked her casual relationship with language before, but the sudden struggle to pick the right things to say made her angry. Finally, she bit her bottom lip, worried she was about to say something in the wrong way when all she wanted was for things to go very, *very* right.

Rook's voice thrummed soft and warm. "Whatever it is, you can tell us. We're your family. The good kind, the kind you got to choose."

That was true. The fact that Rook understood the importance of a chosen family reminded Chrysalis that he understood the intricacies of what bound them. She looked back to him from the corner of her eyes.

I really want to tell them, said her heart.

And so she swallowed down her fear and lifted her chin.

"Some days, I don't feel so much like a girl. So on them, I don't wanna dress like one." So far so good. No one was giving her any sideways looks or anything, but she wasn't done. Eager to make herself clear, Chrysalis took a deep breath and started to talk faster. "That's not to say I don't feel like a girl some days too. I do. But it's important to me to be able to express how I feel as it changes."

Chrysalis could tell by Rook's expression this hadn't been what he'd expected. Fair enough. But she wanted a response. She barely moved, staring at him and waiting for any reaction other than shock.

"You can be whoever you want," Rook began.

I know, and I will, Chrysalis thought, but she didn't say it. She could tell more was coming.

"We love you no matter what."

YES. That was what her heart had been waiting for. The words rang inside of her like a bell made of light and stars and warmth.

"Just don't start any death cults."

Chrysalis didn't even realize she was smiling until her rising cheeks entered the scope of her vision. She gave Dmitri's waistcoat a proud little straightening and lifted her head high.

"No death cults," she promised.

Rook gave her one of his "natural" smiles. Not one of the calculated ones, one of those only very certain people ever got to see. And she was one of them, not for the first time.

"Excellent. And thank you for sharing with us; that was very brave."

He'd seen how hard it had been for her. That was even better. Chrysalis was very nearly wriggling with pride.

"Now give Dmitri his waistcoat back."

Chrysalis' expression flattened into a series of unimpressed lines.

"But it's so pretty," she grumbled under her breath.

"And then go pick out some pieces for yourself from the floor." Rook was smirking at her now. "That's far too big a size for you. And be sure to notate them for me so I can write them off." He glared at the puzzle thing he'd built on the wall next to him. "I'll add them to my business expenses."

Really?! She was really going to get to pick out nice men's clothes for herself? She doubted any of them would fit quite as well as they should, but Rook would see to fixing that. He wouldn't be caught dead letting his people traipse about in ill-fitting clothes. "Not on my watch!" she could almost hear Rook say. Chrysalis was so excited she just about forgot how buttons worked.

"Is that how we treat fine garments?" Rook scolded, but not seriously.

Chrysalis huffed, but forced herself to slow down.

"Better," and she could hear the approving smile in his voice.

Chrysalis then folded the waistcoat and handed it back to Dmitri. She hoped the care she took went some way towards repairing what she might have broken between them. Then, once it was safely out of her hands, she bolted for the shopfront.

Behind her, she could just hear Dmitri drawl to Rook, "She's going to clean you out. You know that, right?"

She grinned wider, if that was even possible, when Rook replied, "Let her. It's a big day for her. I'm honored she trusted us."

As Chrysalis trotted back and forth between racks, she began building ensembles in her head. There was a whole new world of possibilities for her. There would have been either way, but it would be an easier road with support. She wondered what it would feel like if, on the days she presented more masculine, she asked Rook and Dmitri to use male pronouns for her. Or perhaps something more in between would feel better. Maybe they and them, like the Reaper had used? Chrysalis didn't know so many things, but she was looking forward to discovering them, no longer alone and in secret.

CHECK, PLEASE

Kieran overhears of an important item going missing, so he decides to secretly intervene. Of course, things don't go as planned. A very silly story based on real events that happened to a friend of mine and named for one of her favorite series. Takes place after the events of *Across the Ice*, but is otherwise in a vacuum, so the only spoilers are relationship spoilers.

~~

"Could you have accidentally baked it into a pie?"

Kieran stopped dead in his tracks. Not only was the question full of strange possibilities, but it was awfully late for anyone to be visiting the Allen manor. Around him, night painted every surface in shades of black, indigo, lapis, and pewter. Nighttime insects chirped and sang in melodic tones, though these in Springhaven were just as nasty and evil as those in Bone Port, despite their prettier music. And, thankfully, a lot less numerous.

"I don't think so." That was Esther's voice. "I think someone would notice if they'd bitten into a sheet of paper, even if it was covered in filling."

Kieran slapped at an unidentified bug coming to rest on his

arm. Being a Vampyre didn't exempt one from being fed on by the horrible, tiny demons, and he considered it a professional discourtesy. He was just coming back to the Allen manor from visiting Calandra at the Raven's Tower and suddenly wondered if Cali ate insects during the day. Did ravens even eat bugs? Other birds did, but it was one of those things that had never occurred to him. He'd have to ask the next time he saw her.

"Do you know who it's from?"

Kieran still couldn't identify that other voice, so he gathered shadows around him, blending in with the darkness, and crept towards the kitchen door. Ah, it was Thyme. No wonder he hadn't recognized her voice; the apothecarist was usually busy running her business and didn't often come round for dinner. He understood she and Mina had lunch together now and again—when Mina could find time to actually step away from the clinic for lunch anyway—but rarely dinner. Thus, he had never had much opportunity to learn the sound of her voice. He could see the two women now, as he kept close to the side of the manor.

Thyme had her copper hair, shot through with streaks of silver, gathered back away from her face, and she wore an older, somewhat grubby-looking dress. Dust streaked her cheeks, as it did Esther's, and both had clearly been perspiring. What had they been up to?

Esther shook her head. "I can't remember. I was too shocked at the time. I hurried to send you a note, but by the time I'd sat down to write it, I'd tucked the blasted thing somewhere safe."

Thyme chuckled. "Of course. Safe usually ends up as unfindable. At least the kitchen has never looked better."

Ah, so that explained the state of their clothes. They'd been looking for something. As a boy, Kieran had hidden in and explored enough out-of-the-way cupboards to learn firsthand just how dirty even the best-kept kitchens could get.

Then Thyme's face twisted in sympathy. "Two hundred gold,

though. That's a lot to be missing."

Kieran's jaw dropped, and he almost released the collection of shadows he'd gathered around himself.

Thyme reached out and patted Esther's shoulder. "I'm sure it will turn up. Are you sure you don't want me to come back tomorrow to search some more?"

Esther gave Thyme's hand a squeeze. "No, dear, but thank you. You've got your business to run. I'm sure the promissory note will turn up."

Kieran waited, thinking, while Thyme made her way out of the garden. The rest of the family must be asleep. Esther must want to keep this a secret. Otherwise Thyme wouldn't have come through the kitchen door; she'd be leaving through the front.

Two hundred gold?! Esther must be so embarrassed. As she closed the door, his eyes followed the old woman fondly, and he heard the lock click. Instantly, he knew what to do. He'd find the promissory note and return it to Esther without her ever having known he'd been involved. And he had the entire rest of the night to do it.

Calandra often said the universe had a twisted sense of humor, and Kieran was feeling that keenly at the moment. Being able to swim through the dark at inhuman speed had been of no help when he had to individually check every nook and cranny, between every plate and bowl, inside cups and soup tureens, and between every fold of table linen, napkin, runner, and doily. *And* stack them all back nicely—he wasn't about to leave Esther's hard work a shambles, after all, no matter what he was trying to do for her.

And that was nothing compared to the books. Blazes, there were so many bloody books in this house! Cookbooks, housekeeping books, slim volumes of poetry, entire treatises on flower arranging, and the countless tomes about practical plant uses and gardening. All of this just in the kitchen, butler's pantry, and conservatory beyond. Suddenly, everywhere Kieran looked, he saw books he'd never noticed before. They were like bunnies, hiding and multiplying and returning to find new mates and start all over until they'd littered their literary progeny onto every surface. Kieran couldn't believe himself when he thought it, but he was suddenly beginning to hate books. Stars, he wanted to find this promissory note more than Esther must by now. The search was turning him batty.

By the end of the night, Kieran had decided he'd need help. And not only that, but he'd need to start right away the next evening.

After a day of sleep—his sleep was never either good or bad, it just happened whether he wanted it to or not—he felt ready to tackle the search again. Esther was still there getting some things prepped for tomorrow. He greeted the sweet housekeeper and surreptitiously slipped a few questions into his conversation to see if perhaps there was news of the promissory note. All her answers pointed to no change from the night before. Esther, of course, was cheerful as ever, but Kieran felt badly for her—she did so much for the family, was always so strong for them—and he redoubled his determination.

After bidding her good night, he slipped out to the darkened garden and drew Rook's symbol into the dirt, beneath the hosta leaves where the symbol always went. Kieran also left a note he'd written the night before. It was sealed with wax and only addressed with a large "R" on the front. Leaving an actual note had been a risk—there was a chance any one of the household might accidentally stumble across it and then have questions—but he didn't know how else to tell Rook *not* to go clambering straight up to Lenore's window. And it would waste time if he stayed out here waiting for the former crime lord to show up.

So, having left his message, Kieran headed for the empty rooms of the house and re-commenced with riffling through every possible hiding place. Mina, Neal, Camilla, and Lenore were scattered to the winds of the house, each engaging in their own activities, and Kieran smiled to himself as he worked to avoid them. This was rather fun.

It wasn't long before Rook showed up. Kieran had been so involved with looking through Mina's vanity table that he hadn't heard Rook approach.

"Burnt Berry really isn't your color. Too daring."

Kieran spun, a stick of the aforementioned dark lip color in his hand. Rook was already shaking his head at the Vampyre.

"A pink would be better to offset the dark of your eyes," Rook went on. "And something as dark as this will wash out your already pale skin. Unless you *want* people thinking you're one of those overly romantic types who reads too much poetry and questions the meaning of life at every turn." Rook looked him up and down. "I could see that, though."

Kieran was about to respond, but Rook started in on a new tirade.

"And, by the way, if you're going to ask someone to help you with a clandestine operation, you might leave a window or something open for them. It's just shoddy partner work…"

While Rook nattered on, Kieran whipped out his hand in a moment of petty revenge and rubbed the Burnt Berry color stick over Rook's lips.

He grinned, showing his fangs. "I see what you mean about the color. Very daring indeed. The drama of it fits you much better."

Rook's mouth gaped, and every feature pointed down into a V, as if he couldn't believe someone had dared to pull such a stunt, on *him* of all people. Then Rook's expression transformed to one of manic joy. Quick and precise as if he were handling one of his daggers, he snatched up another lip color called Azalea's First

Bloom and swiped it across Kieran's lips, catching one of his fangs as he did and gouging the waxy stick.

With a wide, cassis-colored smile, Rook said, "Told you pink would serve you better."

Without a word, Kieran grabbed a powder puff from atop the vanity table and whapped it over Rook's face. Rook returned the attack by adding lines of the Azalea's First Bloom to Kieran's cheeks, serving as blush. This started a frenetic but short-lived cosmetics-based war. The sound of Mina's voice called an immediate cease-fire.

"Just *what* is going on in here?!"

Both men turned to see her standing there in her dinner dress, eyes goggling and too confused for anger. Neal stood just behind her, his own expression matching hers.

Rook pointed to Kieran with a brow brush. "*He* started it!"

A sparkling clip-on earring attached to Rook's ear swung back and forth. A matching necklace sat around the top of Kieran's head like a diadem, the jewels resting between his brows. Both their faces were painted in a way that would embarrass even the silliest of clowns.

Kieran affected a nonchalant manner as he leaned against the vanity table and motioned to Neal and Mina. "What brings you two here?"

One of Mina's eyebrows crept upward. "This is *our* bedroom."

Neal seemed to be having a harder time gathering his wits. To be fair, he wasn't used to overseeing and triaging catastrophes the way Mina was. He held his hands out before him helplessly. "Someone… explain… something. Please."

Rook turned to Kieran. "I was summoned. And then ruthlessly *attacked* without provocation."

Kieran locked unimpressed eyes onto him. "You'll survive."

He then surrendered his goal to keep his idea between himself and Rook. He'd planned on having Rook sneak about with him and help, but they'd blown that up in a cloud of facial powder. After explaining the situation to Neal and Mina, the Allens, of course, immediately agreed to help. Though Neal looked to Mina.

"Could Esther's mind be… you know, starting to go?"

Mina waved a dismissive hand at her husband, something both he and Kieran knew she'd never do lightly in a situation like this. "As her doctor, I can assure you Esther is every bit as sharp as she's ever been. Shock is quite a drug, and two hundred gold is nothing to sneeze at. I'm not surprised she's forgotten after a surprise like that."

Neal broke the house into quadrants and then smaller components in the same way he would an archaeological dig site and then began assigning jobs based on abilities. Rook and Kieran would take the high spots, as they were both more skilled climbers than himself and Mina.

Mina, meanwhile, claimed some of the more sensitive areas of the house because, as she put it, she didn't want Rook "riffling through our personal business like the busybody you are."

Rook stuck his overly powdered nose into the air and affected deep offense. "My busybodying serves a purpose, thank you!"

As he began to swan out, Neal followed with, "You aren't to bother either of the girls either."

Rook looked back over his shoulder with a cheeky, color-stained grin. "Don't two eithers cancel each other out? So I *should* go bother them."

"Go on then," Mina challenged. "I think Camilla's retired for the night. Bother her while she's sleeping. See what happens. It'll be fun for all of us."

Kieran chuckled, knowing Camilla's scalpel and other medical tools would never be far from her. And he also knew Rook knew her proficiency with said tools.

Rook gave a surrendering bow, and was nearly to the door when Mina called after him one last time.

"I expect you to replace my ruined cosmetics as well. With good ones, mind you. None of those horrible cheap things."

This time Rook really did look offended. "As if *I* would buy cheap cosmetics."

Mina bobbled her head thoughtfully. "Fair point. I apologize."

Rook tipped an imaginary hat in thanks and left.

Three hours of searching had passed and still nothing. Mina had been correct; Camilla was already in bed when their concerted effort began, and Lenore was busy in the cellar with an improved velocipede project. She'd be easy to avoid so long as she stayed down there. Mina and Neal, meanwhile, had taken on the task of searching Mina's tower and the drawing room, respectively, before teaming up in the library. With four people on the case, they'd made far more progress than Kieran had by himself, but he was really beginning to worry the promissory note was well and truly lost forever.

"We need more help," Rook declared.

He was standing in the conservatory, downing a cup of lukewarm tea. Kieran had brewed up a pot for his non-nocturnal friends. He felt it was the least he could do since they didn't have the advantage of a full day's sleep like Kieran did. Rook's lips left a black currant-colored stain behind—it really spoke to his dedication to the cause that he hadn't taken time to wash up yet. He might be a smarmy git, but he was true to those he considered his. He even had the grace to school his features as he gulped down the over-steeped swill Kieran had whipped up—brewing tea wasn't something the Vampyre had much experience with. Even so, Kieran wasn't comfortable with bringing more people into the plot. When he said as much to Rook, however, Rook flapped a dismissive hand at the Vampyre.

"S'already done, mate. Too late for second guessing."

Kieran blinked at him. "Excuse me?"

"I sent a message to Dmitri and Chrysalis as soon as I read your plea for help—"

"An ordinary request for assistance," Kieran corrected.

"Desperate supplication," Rook shot back. "But have it your way. Po-tay-to, po-tah-to—"

"Literally no one says potahto."

"—and all that. In any case, they're already outside, merely waiting on a word from me."

Kieran paused. "I heard Lenore leave out the kitchen door earlier."

Now it was Rook's turn to blink at Kieran. "Come again?"

Before Kieran could explain, sounds floated towards them from beyond the kitchen door. Sounds of a shout, a crash, and more shouting. Without a word, Rook and Kieran raced from the conservatory through the butler's pantry, through the kitchen, and out to the garden beyond.

Outside, they came upon a scene of thin, mangled wheels spinning atop a bush; a broken velocipede frame, which was wielded like a comically large sword by a very angry Lenore; and an equally angry Dmitri, who was gesticulating wildly and ranting about Lenore's "rolling death machine." Chrysalis, meanwhile, was standing a little ways off to the side with their arms crossed and rolling their eyes.

Since revealing their fluid gender disposition, Chrysalis had experimented with different pronoun combinations and settled on using "they" and "them."

The moment Rook came into view, they stamped their foot and pointed at Lenore and Dmitri.

"Make it stop," Chrysalis demanded.

Lenore and Dmitri apparently didn't hear them—or perhaps didn't care—as the two continued to bicker.

"Hours and hours of work, gone because you felt the need to play hide-and-seek," Lenore railed.

Dmitri snapped back, "I'm not playing—"

"Oh, so you're in a *professional* hide-and-seek league then?" Lenore cut in.

Rook chuckled and trotted over. He tried snaking his arm around Lenore's waist, but an angry jab of the velocipede frame towards Dmitri almost took Rook's head off.

"Steady on, little bird," he said, not quite as chuckle-y now.

She looked at him as if she'd only just realized he was there, and Dmitri followed. The anger drained from both their expressions and was replaced by pure confusion.

"Your face," Dmitri said.

"It's, um…" Lenore added.

Her eyes drifted to Kieran, who stood behind Rook. He too had not taken time to wash his face. She turned back to Dmitri as if he might have a word for what they were witnessing. Kieran smiled, which Lenore returned. Rook and Chrysalis both smirked—Kieran suspected the latter might have picked up that particular habit from the former. And Dmitri, well, he didn't smile, but he relented… grumblingly.

"What have you two been up to?" Lenore asked, finally letting Rook give her a sloppy, cassis-colored smooch on her cheek. She at least had the wherewithal to immediately wipe it away with her handkerchief.

Kieran explained the situation, which led to Rook explaining how he, and then subsequently Dmitri and Chrysalis, had ended up here, finishing with a terse account from Dmitri as to how he'd been hiding behind the nearby bush when a rolling, steam-powered monstrosity had come careening towards him.

"Ah, you're confusing careening with a leisurely stroll," Lenore snipped.

"I could have died!" Dmitri insisted.

"And if you had, my prototype might still be alive." Lenore turned to Kieran and Rook. "When he popped out from behind the bush like a bloody jack-in-the-box, I had to swerve and, well…" She motioned towards the wheels in the bush. "…things got messy."

"Don't start it up again," Chrysalis grumbled.

Kieran decided it was time to take charge. Given that no one was injured, he volunteered to stay outside and help Lenore clear up her broken prototype. Rook did as well, ordering Dmitri and Chrysalis to go inside, fortify themselves with tea, and await further instructions. He then turned a loving eye onto Lenore.

"You go inside too. The night stalker and I will sort this while you clean yourself up."

"I need to check the pressure in my velocipede's engine. I don't know if it's still running." Lenore looked around. "Though I'm not certain where it went."

Rook flapped an unworried hand at her. "I'll take care of it."

Raising an eyebrow at him, she said, "But you're rubbish with machines."

"I think I can handle one little engine," he chuckled.

Lenore made a noise like she didn't agree, but said, "Alright. It's probably stopped working anyway."

She then headed inside too, and Kieran looked at Rook.

"Was there a reason you wanted me alone?"

"Have you thought about what you'll do if we can't find the promissory note?" Rook asked. "It's hardly as if you can walk into a bank and arrange one for her."

Kieran's mouth turned down, as the limitations of this nocturnal life he hadn't chosen for himself reared up to laugh at him. In a single sentence, Rook had made him feel simultaneously like a dirty little secret and utterly powerless.

"I'm sorry." Rook's words invaded the sticky miasma of feelings just as they were beginning to take form. Sincerity, unadulterated by guile or any other kind of agenda, stitched through every syllable. "I didn't mean it like that. You're a good person, and you deserve better than what you have."

Again, so much said in such a small package. Kieran had neither a way to earn any means of his own nor a way to move through the world as everyone else did. Cali understood a good bit, being cursed as she was, but she still appeared every bit an ordinary human once the sun set.

One corner of Kieran's mouth changed direction. "It's getting better, now that I have Annabelle back in my life. And she's offered for me to meet Rowan, when I'm ready."

Rook smiled too, a soft, easy thing. "You'll like her. She's got a lot of spunk. And she'll like you too." Rook seemed to think for a moment. "I know you always dreamed of being a doctor, but if you ever wanted to try your hand at something that allows for anonymity—perhaps some kind of art or other—I'd be happy to offer assistance. I do have a bit of experience with marketing and distribution, and banks don't necessarily need to hold your money. There are other ways of managing it."

Kieran smiled properly now. For years, Mina and Neal and even Camilla and Lenore had made similar suggestions, but none of them had the same experience as Rook, nor the same networks. And none of them could ask for help from one of their more connected friends without risking Kieran's discovery. Rook, however... Rook knew how to function in both the dark and the light, and now that he was suggesting it, the possibility seemed more real than it ever had.

"I'll keep that in mind, thank you," he said.

"Of course," Rook replied, and his voice had that same purity as it had before, giving weight and meaning to those two little words.

Kieran then returned to the subject of their original conversation. "Mina and Neal mentioned obtaining a banker's check as well, but their names would be on it, and Esther would never accept it."

Rook nodded. "Yes, that is a tricky little snag. I know people who could probably produce one, completely cashable, that will appear to have come from wherever we want it to, but that is *technically* fraud, even if the money came from a legitimate source. That sort of thing isn't done much. Once the jig is up, the whole operation has to go to ground for a while. Bankers are as vindictive, tenacious, and power-obsessed as the Enforcers. It'd probably cost us more to get the job done than the note is worth. Plus, I am on the straight and narrow now." At the end, he muttered distractedly, mostly to himself, "Much as I adore Esther, and as much as she deserves the money owed to her, I'm not going to risk Lenore or the life I'm trying to rebuild."

Kieran could see, as Rook rubbed his chin, that he'd been working through the problem, looking for possibilities. And he was pleased at the conclusion he'd seen Rook come to. There were times Kieran worried that Rook either couldn't or wouldn't give up his old criminal life completely. And it was positively endearing the way Rook's brow crinkled in frustration at having reached a dead end. He cared as much as the rest of them about taking care of Esther.

"We'll figure something out," Kieran said. "For now, let's focus on finishing the search."

Rook agreed, and the two went inside having completely forgotten about Lenore's crashed velocipede.

Dmitri and Chrysalis, it was decided, would be best suited to the more public areas of the house. Thus, Chrysalis took the dining room and Dmitri the front parlor. They were warned to be quiet as they worked, given that Camilla was still asleep, and Mina had

prescribed that at least someone in the house should get a full night's rest. Kieran suspected that Camilla would have been all too happy to assist and couldn't help but wonder if Mina wasn't being more than a little protective, given that Camilla had classes the next day.

Unfortunately for Mina, a house full of moving people, even people all endeavoring to be as quiet as possible, will make noise, and the directive turned out to be for nothing. Less than two hours to go until dawn, just as Kieran was listening to a conversation in the library between Neal and Chrysalis, he heard the near-noiseless *whish* of Camilla's door opening. He poked his head down the hallway, watching her reaction and waiting for the questions he knew were invariably coming.

Camilla took in the sight of him looking alert and cosmetics-painted but unalarmed and available before turning her sleepy attention to the library. Neal apparently had forgotten to quite keep his voice down, though to be fair, he'd been fielding Chrysalis' questions for a solid couple of minutes now.

"Why do you need so much, though?" Chrysalis was asking Neal. During their search, they'd found the Allens' silverware collection, which included fish forks, salad forks, meat forks, dessert forks, bread knives, meat knives, fish knives, soup spoons, teaspoons, dessert spoons, and more.

Neal was handling the situation like a well-meaning but extremely tired secondary school teacher. "So that you can switch between foods without contaminating one flavor with another."

"But why can't you just lick your utensils clean?" Chrysalis asked this like it was the most obvious solution in the world. "Everything tastes like your own spit anyway."

Camilla turned back to Kieran, looking confused. "What's going on?"

"Licking isn't really considered proper dinner behavior," Neal was explaining.

"What, do people at fancy dinner parties pretend like we don't have tongues?" Something must have dawned on Chrysalis because they then added excitedly, like they'd just made a profound connection, "Is it like the way people pretend girls and women don't have legs?"

"What?" came Neal's baffled reply.

"That's why they have to wear skirts and not trousers, because people don't like knowing that females have legs."

Kieran chuckled to himself—Chrysalis had a point, in a strange sort of way—and turned back to Camilla. "If you want to go back to bed, now's your chance."

She gave a tired little shrug. "I'm up now."

"I'll explain over tea," Kieran said. "I think we're going to need another pot anyway."

Downstairs, as Camilla fixed a fresh pot of tea—much better than Kieran's attempt—he explained the situation. Camilla, unsurprisingly, was immediately onboard. Chrysalis appeared soon after, just as more biscuits were laid on.

Camilla paused in her biscuit arrangement, eyes taking in the petite figure who poked their head around the doorframe before scampering towards the biscuit plate. Camilla looked to Kieran and then back to Chrysalis.

"Hello," Camilla said. It was very nearly more of a question than a statement.

Chrysalis bobbed their head in return. "Evening."

Camilla waited, but no further response seemed forthcoming. At last, she said, "Apologies, but... who are you?"

With a swig of tea, Chrysalis chased the mouthful of biscuit they'd just shoved into their gob, and then held out a crumb-speckled hand. "Chrysalis. Pleased to meet you. My pronouns are they and them."

Camilla shook the offered hand, clearly confused, but she followed Chrysalis' lead. "Thank you. I use she and her. I take it you came with Rook?"

Chrysalis bobbed a nod. "Yup."

And that was the only explanation provided. Camilla waited a moment, and then a moment more.

"Well, we appreciate your efforts in helping us," she said at last.

Chrysalis shoved another biscuit into their mouth and saluted.

They drank more tea and ate more biscuits while Kieran and Camilla strategized. Camilla's room had not been searched yet, of course, but Kieran wanted to bounce ideas off her before dawn came. No one else had thought of any good alternative solutions, but there was always a chance Camilla might come up with something too.

"This is probably a silly question, but have you checked the rubbish bin?"

"In every room," Kieran replied.

"I mean the big one outside," Camilla clarified.

Kieran blinked. He hadn't. The idea that the promissory note might have accidentally ended up all the way out there hadn't occurred to him. Though Esther still preferred to buy by weight from her trusted specialists—butchers, bakers, greengrocers, and the like—rather than the prepackaged, branded sort of products that were becoming so popular, a household like the Allens' still produced a good bit of rubbish. Thankfully, Springhaven's regular refuse pickup service hadn't come round this month, so if the note had ended up in the large metal bin, it should still be there. Less thankfully, Kieran realized if it wasn't there, it was still possible it had gone into the *other* place for which decomposable refuse was bound.

The composter.

The Allens might be eccentric, but even they didn't want a loose pile of offal just sitting out on their grounds. Thus, their compostable bits and pieces were kept in a beehive-shaped, tiered, stackable structure. And Kieran knew it was full because Esther had spent all winter adding to it in preparation for spring planting.

He sighed, knowing it was better to "eat the frog," as the saying went, in one go. He looked to Camilla and Chrysalis.

"Would anyone like to refuse rummage with me?"

Chrysalis was already heading out the door. "Still searching through all those plates and stuff," they threw back over their shoulder.

Kieran looked to Camilla, whose face was a mixture of disgust and determination.

"If I must," she sighed. "For Esther."

"For Esther," Kieran agreed.

They decided to divide and conquer. Kieran, being a gentleman, offered to take the composter. Camilla insisted she should take it, given that Kieran didn't create as much household waste and therefore he should have the easier job. In the interest of fairness, they played a round of frog, snake, and slug to decide. Camilla's slug beat Kieran's snake, and she lifted her chin before bravely heading for the beehive. Kieran, meanwhile, made for the rubbish bin, vowing to assist Camilla as soon as he was done.

He soon learned that the compost bin might have been the better choice. Given that Esther handled most domestic duties at the Allen manor, and the fact that, before he'd been turned, Kieran had grown up with household staff, he hadn't the foggiest what went into a refuse bin. It turned out quite a lot of undesirable items could not be composted, from coal and charcoal ash to dairy products to meat bones—after, of course, Esther had used the latter to make stocks and broths. And, worst of all, Majesty's little "packages" that she left around the yard. The regal wolf was currently curled up on a sofa inside. Just because the rest of the household had decided to start keeping nocturnal hours, that didn't mean she had to.

Kieran groaned, held his breath, and began to sift through the metal refuse bin. As it was only collected once a month, the bally thing was as deep as Kieran's arms were long and as broad as his shoulders. Methodically he picked through the contents, but as with the rest of his searches, he was coming up empty.

A noise tickled his ears. His hearing was better than the average human's, but even this was faint. Kieran leaned back from his gruesome task and listened. It was a sort of groaning, a faint metallic creak. He followed the sound, which came from deeper in the garden. The noise was growing, but Kieran couldn't see anything, and his nose was overpowered by the scents of his rummaging. A faint hissing noise had joined the groaning, which had gotten worse. It sounded almost painful somehow.

At last, he tracked it to a large boxwood. It hemmed in along the little path near where Lenore and Dmitri'd had their run-in earlier. Pushing aside some branches, he spied... a... well, *contraption* was the only word he could think of. A small, metal cylinder attached to some boxes—some wood, some metal—of unknown purpose, all well-cobbled together, but cobbled nonetheless. The metal cylinder was the thing that was groaning, and a thin, angry stream of steam jettisoned its way from a seam along the bottom where Kieran couldn't see.

Hadn't Lenore mentioned losing an engine? And hadn't he and Rook been meant to...

"Oh dear," Kieran uttered.

Worst of all, he hadn't the foggiest how to handle the thing. It looked terribly unhealthy, that was certain. And, while Kieran knew very little about technologics, he did know that too much pressure in a steam engine was, as Neal had once described it, "Extremely bad."

"Lenore!" Kieran called, backing away from the machine like a dangerous animal. It was unlikely that she'd hear him from all the way out on the grounds as he was, but he wanted to try. No telling how much time they had before he learned firsthand what "extremely bad" entailed.

Not Lenore, but Camilla's voice answered his call. Quick as a flash, he swam back through the darkness towards the sound of her voice. Humans weren't nearly as hardy as Vampyres, after all. Predawn light had begun to tinge the horizon in hues of purple and pink, and he wasn't able to move as fast as he liked, just faster than a human's normal running speed, but it was enough.

He appeared before Camilla as a sort of darker blur misting through the dusky shadows of the garden. She started at seeing him, but at least she stopped in her tracks.

"Kieran, what's—" she began.

"No time." He began to usher her towards the house, his soiled hands leaving stains on the casual dress she'd donned for their work. "Inside, now."

Just as they were nearing the kitchen door, the hissing reached fever pitch, followed by a terrific *KABOOM!* to rival even the nastiest springtime thunderstorm. Kieran ducked, pulling Camilla down with him and shielding her far more fragile human body with his. Behind them, something shattered into what sounded like many tiny pieces. Neither moved save for their breathing, but the sounds had stopped, which seemed a good thing.

"What in heaven's name?" came the familiar sound of Mina's voice.

Kieran looked to the kitchen door. Silhouetted in the petrolsene light behind her stood Mina's tall figure. She headed straight for them, already volleying questions their way, one after another.

Kieran looked back the way he'd come. All seemed at peace now, save for a statue a long ways off behind them. It had been thoroughly decapitated by a metal plate, which now sat embedded in a nearby tree trunk.

More voices arrived—Rook, Dmitri, Lenore, Neal, and finally Chrysalis—but Kieran was still listening out for danger. As soon as Lenore arrived, he started asking her pertinent questions about the danger being gone, ignoring whatever else everyone was asking. Through the swarm of his friends, all buzzing, he gained the information he needed: Yes, the engine, having exploded, was now inert, though Lenore advised against anyone touching anything, as it was likely also quite hot.

"What are you covered in?" Mina was asking.

"Erm," Kieran replied eloquently. "Better you don't know." He looked sheepishly at the stains on Camilla's dress. "You're going to want to change. Now, probably."

While Dmitri and Lenore started up another quarrel about the latter's "rolling death machine," Neal went to inspect the now-headless statue.

"This was a great-uncle of mine. He commissioned this so that he'd always be able to keep an eye on everyone and keep them in line." He smiled. "Never did like him much. We moved this from the receiving hall out here when I took possession of the house."

Mina had moved on from checking Camilla and Kieran for injuries to doing a headcount of who had been inside during the explosion. Lenore and Dmitri both briefly paused their argument to confirm before picking right back up where they'd left off. Meanwhile, Chrysalis had skulked over to the statue, and they and Neal were admiring how much better it looked now.

"Well, isn't this a pleasant early morning gathering," came a spry yet cracked voice from the kitchen doorway.

All eyes turned to see Esther stepping down into the yard. She carried her handbag on her arm; she must have only just arrived to begin her work for the morning. Her eyes took them all in—Kieran's and Rook's cosmetic-attacked faces; Camilla's refuse-stained dress; the tired, puffy eyes on Neal and Mina; Lenore and Dmitri frozen in mid-squabble; and Chrysalis, who was half-hiding behind the decapitated statue. Kieran couldn't begin to imagine what the housekeeper must be thinking.

"I can explain," he started.

"Can you, though?" Rook teased.

He was wearing a smirk made of pure mischief. Alright, so the full story wasn't quite so simple as that. Rook then gave him a little shrug that perfectly mirrored what Kieran felt. They'd been caught out, and there was nothing to be done but own up to the truth. Even if he did try to spin a tale for Esther—though what tale could possibly explain the tableau they created?—it was all too likely she'd know it was a lie. And besides, who really wanted to lie to Esther of all people?

"The promissory note you received," Kieran said. "I heard you talking to Thyme about having lost it. I wanted to help find it, but I knew if I told you, you'd tell me not to trouble myself."

Esther nodded, gifting them all a smile as warm and soft as the dinner rolls she made. "And I suppose you called in everyone else to help."

"Eventually, yes," Kieran admitted. "Though only as a last resort."

Neal raised a hand, "And some of us flatly refused to be left out of it once we learned of the issue."

"I know what you're probably going to say," Mina put in, "but we'd like to recompense you for the loss of the note. You deserve it, and so much more."

A chorus of agreement went up from the rest of those gathered. Esther's smile grew.

"Well, aren't you all just so thoughtful." She pulled a tightly folded slip of paper from her purse. "That won't be necessary, however. You see, the safe place I tucked the note was right inside my bag, in a little pocket on the inside. I found it after arriving home last night."

Kieran rubbed his face tiredly and looked around at his friends, a sheepish smile on his lips.

Neal came up and clapped him on the shoulder. "Don't worry about it, old friend. We had a jolly adventure anyway."

Dmitri grumbled something under his breath and Lenore stuck her tongue out at him.

Then, with a beckoning hand and the tone of a shepherdess herding lost little lambs, Esther said, "Come along, my dears. I was planning on making sweet buns this morning." To Chrysalis, she called, "You too back there. Don't think I can't see you hiding behind his preeminence Lord Eustace Allen."

Chrysalis popped their head out from behind the headless marble man and pulled a face, mouthing the name, "Eustace."

Rook hung back, waiting to make sure Chrysalis followed, and Kieran waited for him. With his eyes on the approaching figure of his petite protégé, Rook spoke to Kieran.

"Aren't we getting quite a bit past your bedtime?"

"Quite," Kieran replied. "But I wanted to say thank you. You and Dmitri and Chrysalis, you all didn't have to come out and help us."

Rook turned to look sideways at the Vampyre, a smile playing at his lips. "That's what family does."

Kieran smiled back. "Indeed. Now, if you'll excuse me, I'm going to bed."

"Do you sleep in a coffin?" Chrysalis had just joined them, and their eyes sparkled with curiosity. "Like in the Old World stories?"

"Chrys," Rook warned lightly.

"Oh, right," they amended quickly. "Only if you're okay with sharing." They looked to Rook for approval, and he gave them an affirming nod. Chrysalis then looked back to Kieran and explained simply, "Boundaries."

Kieran flashed a fanged grin. "Thank you. And I don't mind telling you, it is a coffin, but any wooden box with a bit of dirt is comfortable."

As they walked back inside, Chrysalis asked, "Why?"

Kieran shrugged. "I don't know. It just is. You can see it sometime, when I'm not about to pass out anyway."

"Next time Lenore and I spar maybe?" Rook suggested.

As they entered the light of the manor's kitchen, the smell of dough and yeast hit their noses. Chrysalis scuttled away to where food was happening.

"Have a good sleep, night stalker," Rook said.

Kieran tipped an invisible hat to him, and made his way down into the cellar. He was so tired, he didn't even bother washing off the makeup still smeared across his face. Instead, he fell asleep to the gentle murmur of chattering and yawns and storytelling above his head, the happy, sometimes chaotic sounds of his ever-growing family.

A Modest Proposal

Rook has a lot to get done for a special event, and the universe seems bent on stopping him. ***Huge spoilers*** for events that took place during *Across the Ice*.

~~~

"Dish ish bad. Dish ish reary bad."

Rook chewed thoughtfully and paced the little employee breakroom of his clothing store. It didn't really compare to what he'd had before at the underground market. There he'd been able to offer his people an entire lounge with couches and dartboards and even an icebox for keeping wine and other goodies cold. Here, he was lucky to have space for a little stove and tea-making accouterments. Then again, he'd had over a hundred employees at the market. Here, he only had two—Dmitri and Chrysalis each occupied an armchair and sipped their tea while Rook paced.

Having swallowed at last, he repeated, "This is really bad."

Chrysalis shot an angry look at Dmitri. "Told'ya you shoulda eaten the baby cake."

"*Cup*cake," Dmitri corrected them.
~~~

Chrysalis shrugged. "Still a tiny cake."

"I trust people to do their job right. Why do you think you have so much free rein?"

Despite their bickering, both Dmitri's and Chrysalis' attention remained on Rook. They'd known how important this mission was, and they'd royally bollocksed it up. Rook sighed and rubbed his face. No, that wasn't fair. Or at least it wasn't helpful right now.

"Consider it a lesson for the future." He tried not to growl as he said it, though was only partially successful. "How do we fix it?"

Chrysalis and Dmitri exchanged guilty glances.

"The bakery's closed for the next week," Chrysalis explained. "Taking a holiday now that New Year's is over." They paused. "Want me to track 'em down? It shouldn't be hard."

Rook very much wanted that, but it wasn't how he dealt with things anymore, how any of them dealt with things anymore. They were on the right side of society now. They had to deal with problems like any other everyday pleb. He shook his head.

"No, let them have their holiday. We'll file our complaint once they're back open."

"I'll take care of it." Chrysalis gave a firm nod. "Maybe even get you a refund."

Rook took in their attire for the day. They and Dmitri had posed as brother and sister for the cake pickup. Smirking, Rook suspected Chrysalis might even put on a good waterworks show to get their way. He looked back to his right-hand man, who still only mildly sipped at his tea.

"You're being awfully quiet, Dmitri. Copper for your thoughts? Any ideas for what to do about this kerfuffle?"

Dmitri met Rook's eyes coolly. "Not to punch a hole in your plan, but you could *not* propose to Lenore."

Rook raised an eyebrow at Dmitri. Old memories they could laugh about now—well, maybe not laugh, but look back on as a bonding experience—surfaced in his mind. "What are you suggesting?"

"Don't be stupid." Dmitri rolled his eyes at being goaded. "I wouldn't suggest you breaking it off with her." Rook's eyebrow crept higher. "I wouldn't suggest it *now*, after everything."

Rook allowed himself to chuckle. Chrysalis shifted in their seat, pulling their knees to their chest and resting their teacup on top of them.

"Why d'you even need to get married?" they asked. "Everyone knows you two are mad for each other." They pulled a face.

Rook's smile returned properly now. "Thank you, though I don't *need* to. Society's the one that insists on it, and you know how daft they can be. Something for you to remember, my young protégé."

Chrysalis made another face.

In truth, Rook found the whole concept of marriage somewhat idiotic and baffling. You have a party in front of your family and friends, make a few declarations, and *then* suddenly two people will be wholly committed to each other for the rest of their lives? Nevertheless, the world was what it was, and Lenore already had enough challenges facing her as a woman in what most saw as a man's profession. On top of that, to protect her reputation and not make her career progression any harder, he was still sneaking her into his place when they wanted time alone. Despite what he'd once flippantly said to her in anger, he wanted to make her life easier. And perhaps the grand gestures that came with proposals and weddings and all that suited his flair for the dramatic.

If I was proposing marriage, believe me, you'd know it.

That was something else Rook had once said to Lenore. When he'd first met Kieran, actually. And Rook intended to make good on that promise. Which led them back to the cake problem. He scowled down at the baked good like it was intentionally trying to thwart him.

Lemon and rhubarb, what a disaster. The only reason he'd

chosen the bakery he had was because it was the only one that said they could get him a strawberry cake with lemon frosting. Rather, that was all Dmitri and Chrysalis had been able to find.

"You're sure no one else might be able to make what we need?" Rook asked. Dmitri and Chrysalis shook their heads. "Remind me why so many said no."

"Seasonality," Dmitri explained succinctly.

Rook looked to the ceiling. Of all the idiotic schemes of fashion. As if food tasted any different based on what clothes someone was wearing that season.

"Why not ask that woman who works for the Allens?" Chrysalis asked. "I bet if you say it's for Lenore, she'll snap right to it."

"That woman has a name," Dmitri scolded. "It's Esther, and you'd do well to learn it."

Chrysalis scowled at the admonishment and pulled their knees closer to their chest. They slurped loudly on their tea, staring hard at Dmitri. Rook made a mental note to set something up soon. Chrysalis didn't trust anyone easily and had rebuffed every offer Rook had extended so far to have Chrysalis back over at the Allens' manor—one brief morning over sweet buns after a harried night had not been enough to do the trick. Knowing Esther would do Chrysalis good, as knowing her did everyone good, but that was a problem for another day.

He shook his head. "Esther is too close to the Allens. Someone would notice her baking a cake, someone would ask too many questions. I can't risk the surprise getting out."

"But don't you need to talk to Doctor and Engineer Allen anyway?" Dmitri asked.

Rook flapped his question away with a hand. "One thing at a time."

Dmitri emptied his teacup, looking skeptical. Rook didn't want to talk about the fact that he'd put off that particular detail, nor why. Instead, he looked back to the treacherous, erroneous cake.

"You two man—and person—the shop while I'm gone this afternoon. There's only one person who can help me with this, and I need to go alone."

Getting into Felicia and Lowell's manor with a boxed cake under one arm was trickier than Rook had initially anticipated. He insisted on sneaking in because, well, most people in his new life would complain if he entered through their windows instead of the front door, and he wanted to keep up his sneaking skills. Felicia and Lowell never asked questions, or at least not questions about that, and only complained when he didn't bring gifts. What made the operation trickier still was that he needed the mistake cake in pristine condition for presenting to Felicia. For both the gift factor and also to serve as an example of what he wanted Felicia to do.

Rook hadn't ordered anything too ornate. Lenore was, after all, a sensible person and cared far more about how something tasted than how it looked. Still, he wasn't about to present a shoddy-looking engagement cake. He managed, at last, to unlock a window while perching the cake box where two perpendicular gables met. A gust of early springtime wind tried to knock the thing to the ground, and only Rook's quick reflexes saved it. He took a moment to release his tension by swearing under his breath before, holding onto the box with one arm, pushing the now unlocked window up and sliding on his belly into a spare bedroom.

He stopped to listen. He hadn't seen any signs that Lenore was coming here after work—he still kept tabs on her; old habits died hard—but he needed to be certain.

Lenore had been given an opportunity to become a ladies' companion to Felicia, which would have meant her moving in with the twins. She might have too, given her feelings on moving back in with the Allens, if not for the residual tension from when Lenore, Lowell, Rook, and more had nearly died in the Reaper's catacombs a while back. Felicia had not rescinded the offer, though the two ladies had gone back several steps in their relationship. Lowell, however, had not let go of the idea, and, without asking anyone, set up a permanent room for Lenore and stocked it with ensembles for all occasions.

Rook smirked as he thought of it. Lowell, he suspected, was being every bit as crafty as Rook himself was capable. Lenore, therefore, rather lived with a foot in each house. Thus why Rook was taking particular care not to be heard until he was sure Lenore was not in the Thorne manor.

No Lenore, but Rook did come upon a raven in the hallway. He swallowed hard as it—or rather, she, as he remembered Lowell saying once—pinned him in place with her beady black eyes. He wasn't certain—he had yet to see hard evidence anyway—but he was fairly sure the bird was not all she seemed.

He tipped his hat to her. "Just passing through. Don't mind me."

The raven cawed in reply and followed him from room to room as he silently searched the house for Felicia. He needed to avoid Lowell too. The bird did nothing but loom behind him, but that was enough to make Rook nervous. Once, he tried offering her a piece of candy from a dish and then tossing said candy into the corridor, in an attempt to get her to fly after the treat. The raven just narrowed her eyes at him and croaked. He was pretty certain she had just called him a very rude name.

At last, he heard humming from the kitchen. The raven flew ahead, cawing and sounding every bit like she was tattling on Rook. He carefully peeked in. Thankfully, Lowell wasn't here, just Felicia, who was shaping a soon-to-be loaf of bread. Since Lowell and Lenore were coworkers now, Rook figured that must be where he was, but again, he wasn't taking chances.

"Are you coming inside, Rookie?" Felicia asked. "Or are we just lingering in doorways today?"

Rook smiled at the nickname; today was a day for buttering Felicia up. "A thousand pardons. I'm on a rather secret mission today."

"Are you indeed?" She paused, and Rook could feel her sizing him up. "Something you need me and only me for. What could it possibly be?"

She gave him a smile that promised, whatever it was, it would cost him dearly.

"Nothing so serious as you might be thinking." Rook set the cake box on the counter next to where she was working. He opened the top. "Just one of these."

Felicia looked in and raised an eyebrow. "A lemon cake? Whatever for?"

"Lemon and strawberry, actually," Rook explained smoothly. "Just like this one, but correct. You see, my baker made a mistake. And, of course, it was just before they went on holiday. This one's lemon and rhubarb and—"

"OUT!" Felicia roared. She snatched up her bread and carried it to the other side of the kitchen, holding it like a baby and glaring at Rook. When he only gaped at her, she jabbed a finger at him. "I said out! Are you trying to kill me?"

Rook blinked stupidly. Without thinking, he replied, "Not today, though there was a time—"

He was cut off as the raven dove, for him or the offending cake, he didn't know. Rook snapped the lid back over the box and covered it with his body. He felt his hair ruffle as the raven buzzed over his head. She made the most horrible rasping noise, over and over again.

"I am *deathly* allergic to rhubarb!" Felicia snarled at him. "Imagine, claiming to be such a fearsome crime lord and not even knowing *that*. How did you even get on top?"

Rook gritted his teeth. The bird was still behind him, making her racket, and he was still bent over his cake. "Perhaps I didn't want to kill you as much as I should have."

He'd meant for it to come out as a compliment, but the raven apparently didn't see the humor and nipped at his ear with her beak.

"Ow! Sorry!" Rook said. "Only joking." It was all he could do not to turn and try to swat the raven out of the air.

He looked up to see Felicia make a placating motion at the bird. Looking back, the raven settled on the back of a chair sitting against the wall. Then Felicia looked down at the dough in her arms. It had stretched down the sides while Felicia had been lecturing Rook and looked rather floppy now.

"Oh dear, it's lost too much air." She sounded genuinely disappointed. "Probably for the best. I wouldn't want to risk eating it after you brought that *poison* into my kitchen." She shot a glare at Rook.

"Genuinely, I wouldn't have brought it into your house if I'd known." He was serious now. Felicia was as capricious as they came, and this was no laughing matter. He didn't want to risk his relationship with her for games. Nevertheless, not knowing what else to do, he held onto the box. "I do need your help, though."

Felicia grunted as she dropped her bread dough into the rubbish bin. "After all that, you still *dare* to ask me for my help?"

"I wouldn't if it wasn't important."

Their eyes met. Rook thought about his plan, and Felicia's eyes widened as whatever strange ability she possessed went to work. She allowed her shock to cool as quickly as it had come, however, and crossed her arms over her chest.

"I'll pay whatever you want," Rook said.

Felicia pointed at the cake. "First, you'll dispose of that. Then you'll clean my kitchen from top to bottom to ensure not a crumb has escaped." Rook looked down at the box, to which Felicia said,

"Don't insult my talents by acting like I can't recreate it from your description." Then, surprisingly, she softened. "Worry not. Your beloved will not be disappointed." Rook raised surprised eyes to her. "Oh, don't get sentimental on me, Rookie. You're paying for a service, remember. Paying very well, I might add. Call it professional pride."

Rook smirked. That was the Felicia he knew so well. "And Lowell? I can't have him finding out. He won't be able to keep it from Lenore."

"You let me handle Lowell. Now, you have a lot of work ahead of you." She pointed to the cake again and then to the rubbish bin.

Rook nodded, and his smile grew wider. "I'd shake your hand on it, but—"

"Don't even think about it. Not until you and my kitchen are clean."

It was evening by the time Rook had finished cleaning. Felicia had gone off to change clothes and refresh herself, but not before insisting that Rook would need to change as well. A set of Lowell's clothes did tolerably well. They were similar sizes, and Lowell had good taste, though he didn't keep up with the latest fashions as much as Rook did, which was disappointing. Finally, though, peace had returned to the house. Even the raven had gone. Rook decided it was best not to ask after the bird. He was looking forward to finalizing plans with Felicia when she informed him Calandra would be joining them for dinner that evening.

"Calandra of the Raven's Tower fame?" Rook asked when Felicia made her announcement.

Among other curiosities, he mentally added.

By this time, he was helping Felicia put said dinner together—a simple affair of seasoned bits of dough atop a dish of stewed chicken and vegetables. *Helping* in this case meant running and fetching whatever Felicia needed from moment to moment.

"The very same," Felicia replied. "Is that a problem?"

"I had rather wanted this affair to stay as secret as possible." He tried to sound casual, but his patience was already stretched too thin for such miracles.

"And why wouldn't it remain that way if Cali knows about it?"

Rook resisted the urge to make a strangling motion in the air. Felicia knew what she was doing. She *loved* needling him. Instead, he settled for giving her an unimpressed look.

"Calandra knows both Lowell and Kieran, facts *you* failed to inform me of, by the by."

"Pass me the pepper, would you please?" Felicia interrupted.

Rook turned to do as she'd bid, keeping his eyes on her. "How do I know Calandra won't blab to them about you making a cake for me?" He finally looked to where the pepper was meant to be stored and instead found himself face-to-face with the woman in question.

Calandra stood in the kitchen, holding the pepper grinder, dark eyes locked on Rook. He jumped, and his hands automatically went towards the dagger in his belt. He stopped just short of actually grabbing the handle.

"Blazes, you are sneaky," he blurted. "You could make a killing offering lessons. I didn't even hear you come in."

Calandra's mouth quirked up in a smile. Handing over the pepper grinder, she said, "I don't suppose that makes you feel better about my ability to hold my tongue."

Rook gave his winningest smile, knowing he was letting his frayed edges show. "My apologies. Important mission and all that, you know. Very sensitive information."

"I've had experience with such things." She did not expound beyond that. Instead, Calandra sidled up to Felicia and began chopping vegetables like they'd worked side-by-side plenty of times. Rook began to feel rather unnecessary at this juncture and leaned against the wall. "I understand Felicia is making a cake for you," Calandra said conversationally. She looked back over her shoulder and winked. "A sensitive cake. What's the occasion?"

"A lemon and strawberry cake," Rook returned, trying to avoid the question.

"Strawberry?" Felicia turned away from her cooking. "At this time of year?"

Rook's brow furrowed. "I did mention that previously."

"Pardon me if I was distracted by the fact that you nearly *killed me in my own house*," Felicia snapped.

He threw up his hands. "What is so bloody difficult about getting a strawberry cake?"

"Because they are not yet in season," Felicia replied. When Rook gave her a quizzical look, she explained like he was simple. "It is a matter of them not having grown yet. You cannot harvest what doesn't yet exist."

Rook's face fell. "That's what seasonality means?"

"You ran a market that offered difficult-to-acquire produce," Felicia shot. "How do you not know this?"

"I'm not a farmer!" Rook replied. "I just approved the purchasing. If something was scarce, I turned it into an exclusivity scheme."

"You two bicker worse than Felicia and Lowell as children," Calandra put in. Felicia turned a withering glare onto Calandra, who just shrugged from where she'd taken over for Felicia. "You do." Turning to Rook, she added, "You could probably source some from farther south, but it'll take a few weeks."

Rook ran his hands through his hair. He was so frustrated, he didn't even bother to think about the implications of what Calandra had said about the twins as children. "I don't have a few weeks." He motioned to the rows and rows of jars lining the top of the kitchen shelves, which he'd dusted earlier that day. "Can't you just use preserves instead? You've got plenty."

"Hmm, that is a thought." Felicia gazed up at her stocks of preserves, pressing a thoughtful finger to her lips. "The liquid ratio is all wrong, though. Cali, would Laura at the Tower be able to manage the conversion?"

Calandra shook her head. "Cakes have never been her forte. You know who could manage it, though?"

Rook let his head hang back. He could guess what was coming.

Felicia actually looked at him with sympathy. "I'm afraid, one way or another, you're not getting what you want."

Rook tried the rest of that evening to think up alternative solutions.

"Half of Springhaven is going to know my plan by the time we're done," he complained, truth be told, over a really rather scrumptious dinner. It made him feel annoyingly warm and hopeful when what he really wanted was to wallow in his misfortune.

"Why is it so important this strawberry cake happens sooner rather than later?" Calandra asked.

Rook waved his fork in the air as he explained. "There's a meteor shower or some such thing happening in a few days. It's all anyone at the museum can talk about. Apparently it's the sort of thing that only happens once in a great while. I'm planning on doing it then."

"Ah," Calandra said. "That's really rather romantic."

The front door opening and closing sounded, followed by Lowell's voice ringing through the house.

"In the dining room," Felicia called.

Rook cocked his head, listening for footsteps besides Lowell's. He heard just the one irregular set, and relaxed… slightly. Lowell entered, looking positively sprightly.

"Evening, all." He took a seat across from Rook. "And what

are we discussing this fine evening?"

"The upcoming meteor shower," Calandra replied.

"Oh! What a magnificent display it's going to be. Did you know we've only known about this phenomenon for about thirty years? Rather, we've only been tracking it for that long. I imagine we noticed before, but everyone was rather, 'Horror and despair! The sky is falling!'" Lowell did a dramatic reenactment while he spoke.

Rook looked to Felicia and held a hand towards her brother as if to say, "See what I mean?"

"I'm guessing the Allen household was all abuzz?" Calandra asked, ignoring Felicia and Rook.

"Were they ever! Engineer Allen and the other department heads are all co-leading a late night, outdoor celebration for the community. It's going to be quite the to-do."

"Are they?" Felicia asked. She turned mischievous eyes onto Rook. "Did you know about this?"

"Yes, in fact, I did," he retorted.

"Then you'll have *arranged things* so no plans go awry? Lenore is Engineer Allen's right-hand woman."

Rook's expression flattened in annoyance. "I have it well in hand."

Lowell's eyes darted between Felicia, Calandra, and Rook. "What's going on?" Felicia immediately took up humming a soft tune, at which point Lowell leaned towards her. "What are you hiding, o sister mine?"

Still humming, Felicia looked to Rook. Clearly, the next move was his to make. He took a deep breath. "Lowell, if we tell you, you have to promise not to tell anyone."

Lowell flapped a dismissive hand at him. "Oh, please. I am the very soul of discretion."

Rook narrowed his eyes at the man. "*No one.* Not even Lenore."

Now Lowell paused. "But what if… or I… Rook, she is *my person*. Surely you understand the deep bond of best friends."

"Lowell," Rook said very seriously, "if you tell her, I might never forgive you."

Lowell pressed a hand to his chest. "What has you in such a tizzy, my good man?" He covered the side of his face with a hand to whisper conspiratorially across the table. "It's not something *untoward*, is it?"

Rook took a deep breath, praying with everything in him he wasn't making a huge mistake. "I'm going to propose to Lenore."

Lowell's jaw dropped. He flapped his lips, searching for words, which formed slowly. "I'm… You're… Oh… Oh my stars and garters." He reached halfway across the table, pulled back, turned to Felicia, back to Rook, and saluted rather dramatically. "You can count on me. I won't let a single syllable fall from my lips that might ruin my tinker belle's perfect moment." Rook smiled, but it fell with Lowell's next word, "Provided…" Lowell paused, ensuring he had Rook's attention. "Provided I get to help plan the wedding." Rook gave him a puzzled look, at which Lowell practically exploded. "I barely got to attend last time! And you know it'll be a sensitive topic given horrible history and all that ugliness. Lenore will need all the support we can offer, and who better than her mechanical marvel, hm?" Lowell pressed his hands together. "Oh please, Rook. I only want to help."

Rook stared unblinkingly at him. Now it was his turn to search for words. "It's a little early to be—"

Lowell gasped and asked, "Do you think she'll say no? I don't, personally, but—"

"No!" Rook insisted. He caught movement out of the corner of his eye and saw Felicia and Calandra shaking with silent laughter. Rook collected himself and turned back to Lowell. "No, I don't. I just don't think it's my place to say who gets to plan what."

"He hasn't even finished telling you what he needs." Felicia's voice oozed with amusement.

"There's more?" Lowell asked. He practically vibrated in his seat.

So, over the rest of dinner and dessert, the cake situation was explained to Lowell. While the two men worked on washing up together in the kitchen, Lowell assured Rook he could make it happen with jam instead. He also very solemnly swore by his cravat that he would keep everything a secret from Lenore, though there was a new problem to consider.

"Engineer Allen does have her assigned to quite a few tasks for the community education night," Lowell explained.

"Then could you…" Rook's voice trailed off as Lowell shook his head.

"He's given me my own workload for the event." Rook's face twisted unhappily, and Lowell spoke gently. "You haven't spoken to Engineer Allen about your plans, have you?"

"Lenore is a grown woman." Rook nearly snapped as he said it. "She doesn't need anyone's permission to do anything." When Lowell opened his mouth again, Rook cut him off. "Or their validation or blessing or any of that other rot."

Lowell tipped his head to the side inquiringly. "Why so spiny about this, chum? What do you think will happen if you talk to Engineer Allen about your proposal beforehand?"

Rook gave him a sour look. "Suffice to say, it'll cause a problem. He and Doctor Allen aren't exactly my biggest fans."

Lowell sucked in air through his teeth nervously. "True though that may be, you might be inviting more trouble by trying to avoid it. Methinks you need to arrange things beforehand or risk your entire plan."

Rook only grumbled a sort of half assent at that.

The next day found Rook standing at the door of the Allen manor and wishing he were getting into a knife fight rather than what he was about to do. At least he'd been able to co-conspire with Lowell to keep Lenore occupied that afternoon—one less thing to worry about. Esther answered the door and greeted Rook with her usual butter-toffee sort of warmth, which managed to pull a smile from him.

When Rook explained he was there to see Engineer Allen, Esther said, "Of course. He's just in the library. Will you be long? I'll bring up some cinnamon buns if you're staying a while."

Rook wanted this over as quickly as possible, but only an idiot would turn down one of Esther's baked goods, so he simply said, "Cinnamon buns sound heavenly."

When Esther led Rook into the library and announced him, Neal was, unsurprisingly, surrounded by books. Not as many as Rook imagined the engineer regularly surrounded himself with, but that might have been down to the subject matter. Rook spied from the titles embossed along the spines and on covers that all these volumes had to do with stellanomy. An especially large volume with a depiction of the night sky spread across two pages sat open before Neal, who looked up and smiled, though the expression did not reach his eyes.

Before Esther left, Rook said, "If it's not too much trouble, Esther, Doctor Allen should be here for this too."

"Of course, Master Hollow." Esther bobbed a little curtsey. "I'll send her down if she's available."

Both Neal and Rook thanked the housekeeper but made no other move until she was gone. Only after she'd disappeared did Neal speak.

"Should I be worried?" A sort of candid wariness crept into Neal's voice.

The tone only served to pull the knot of tension coiled between Rook's shoulder blades tighter. "Why would you think you need to be worried?" He tried to keep his voice pleasant but, it came out sounding like a threat instead.

Neal raised an eyebrow. "Because you look ready to kill someone."

Rook let out a mirthless chuckle. "Ah, that. Sorry, old chap." Rook was trying to channel Lowell's usual congenial ease. He failed spectacularly. Rook couldn't decide if the foppish act made him look moronic or if it made things look like Rook thought Neal was the moron.

Only then did Rook realize he was still standing in the doorway, one foot forward in a fighting stance.

Come on, man, get a hold of yourself! he scolded himself. *You've done plenty of negotiations before.*

Lenore isn't a product to be negotiated for, you great dolt, scolded yet another voice.

Fantastic, this whole ordeal was turning Rook barmy. And he was still standing there, saying nothing, like a clod. He pulled his business persona back together—or at least tried, though it suddenly didn't fit him right. Because, as he'd just reminded himself, this wasn't a business transaction. Wearing the persona poorly, like a suit that was two sizes too small, Rook tottered over to the nearest chair and set himself down. Neal said nothing, just eyed the man. Fair dues; Rook had been the one to invite himself over and invade Neal's space.

Rook tried to regain control by making small talk and nodded to the various tomes littered around Neal. "What's new in stellanomy then?"

Neal's expression tightened, a sure sign he was resisting making a face. It passed after a moment, and he schooled his features into pleasantness. He was certainly earning points for trying.

"Nothing new really," he explained. "Well, if current theories are correct. Heavenly bodies are thought to be extremely old."

Rook was already bored, but he tried not to let his eyes glaze over. When he smiled, though, it felt more like the corners of his mouth were being pulled up by marionette strings. "Fascinating. Do go on."

This time, Neal failed to catch himself. He gave Rook a look that said he was questioning whether the former crime lord sitting in his library had perhaps been replaced with a bizarre doppelgänger from another world.

"Good afternoon, Mister Hollow."

Mina's voice breaking through the silence was like bells. Albeit, stern and somewhat unforgiving bells. The fact that she still called Rook Mister Hollow—not to mention *that particular way* she said it—was all too telling. Still, he jumped to his feet, overjoyed to see the flinty doctor. Enough of this slow torture.

Rook gave a smooth bow. "Always a pleasure to see you, Doctor Allen."

She gave him a narrow-eyed once-over. "What's happened?"

This Rook could deal with. He flashed her a grin. "That's why I like you, Doctor. Always right to the heart of the matter." And that was when he noticed the blade in her hand. Oh alright, it was a scalpel, but a blade was a blade. Strangely, though, it made Rook feel even more comfortable. He was suddenly in old, familiar territory. Until he remembered what he was here to do. He gulped. Right to the heart of the matter indeed. Mina might carve out *his heart* before all was said and done. And Neal might bludgeon him with all those books. Stars, what sort of mess had he gotten himself into?

"Shall we sit?" he asked. His voice cracked like a pubescent schoolboy caught being naughty. "Ahem, apologies. Just need something to wet the old whistle, I think."

Mina's eyes were trained on Rook as she sat without responding. Neal gave him an unimpressed look, and his tone was equally flat. "Esther should be bringing some tea soon."

Rook's mouth had gone dry, and he swallowed again. Did Neal think Rook had been sneakily asking for a drink? As if Rook would be some kind of passive-aggressive coward about it.

Great, add that to his already poor estimation of me.

Rook managed a smile. "Of course." He'd fulfilled the societal expectations for catching up with Neal—barely—so he turned to Mina. "Everything well with you, Doctor Allen?"

Mina placed the scalpel on a little table next to her. "Well enough. I was just practicing my incisions and stitching." She turned to Neal. "That reminds me, we're having lamb roulade for dinner."

Rook wondered if she'd only brought the scalpel because it had been him of all people who needed to speak with her. He hoped she'd washed it. It looked clean, shining brightly on the small table and well within Mina's reach. He began to feel nervous, of all things. Too quickly, he said, "That sounds delicious!" Mina turned an appraising look back on him. Blazes, he had done it again. Then, to make matters worse, Rook, the man other cutthroat crime lords hadn't dared to cross, began babbling. "I wasn't angling for an invitation. If I wanted one, I could always get one from Lenore. No, wait, that didn't sound right. I mean to say, you're always such lovely hosts. No, that still sounds like I'm angling. I'm really not. Not that I wouldn't be happy to join you all for dinner."

Mina exchanged a look with Neal before cocking her head to the side and very clearly assessing their guest's mental state. Rook pulled at his collar. It was getting bloody hot in here.

Succinctly, she asked, "Mister Hollow, are you quite well?"

He gawped at her like a fish. After flapping his lips with equal fishiness, he replied, "Why would you think otherwise?"

Neal came around the book-laden worktable and stood next to Mina's chair. For protection or curiosity, Rook didn't know. In either case, he couldn't blame him.

"You came here today to speak with us about something?" Neal asked. "What is it?"

Rook took a deep breath. He'd tried to think up speeches, arguments, reasons why Neal and Mina should give him and Lenore their blessing. Not that he needed it, but it would make Lenore happy. And maybe prevent an argument or two in the future. To be honest, he had nothing. There was no reason the Allens should support a match between Lenore and Rook. They already didn't like the relationship, so why had he thought this had even a whisper of a chance of going well? Curse Lowell and his sodding insistence. Anger welled up in Rook. He wanted to tell them to forget it, that he'd made a mistake. Rook closed his mouth and looked away, covering himself with cold resolution. Then the mantel over the fireplace caught his eye.

An image-still of the family sat right in the center. It spoke to Neal and Mina's priorities that they'd spared the expense for such a pricey memento—or momento as certain dolts were fond of calling image-stills. It spoke even more to their characters that each person in the image was smiling. It was traditional for subjects to look austere and brooding during the process, but the Allens were hardly a traditional family. And they made Lenore so happy; Rook could read it all over her in the image-still, from the relaxed fall of her shoulders to the puff of her cheeks as she smiled. He sighed, releasing his anger with it, and turned back to Neal and Mina.

"I came here to ask for your blessing," he confessed, without any ounce of attitude or guile. And then, because he was who he was and just couldn't help himself, to be perfectly clear, he added, "I'm going to propose."

Neal looked like he had just been slapped. He shook it off a second later and seemed to grow taller in his spot. Yes, he was definitely going to grab a book, probably an especially heavy and boring one, and beat Rook to death with it. Meanwhile Mina's features all sharpened as keenly as the scalpel next to her. Before anyone could say another word, a delighted cry trilled through the room.

"A proposal! Master Hollow, how marvelous!" Esther scuttled over to him, momentarily leaving her tea tray and grabbing his hand. She pressed it between hers, which were warm and doughy. "Lenore is ever so fond of you. Be sure to think of me when you're planning a menu for the reception." She gave him a wink before returning to her tea tray.

The old woman continued to natter while she served cinnamon buns and tea. Rook, however, was too flabbergasted to say anything in return. Esther was practically bouncing. Only when he nearly drooled on himself—the cinnamon buns did smell divine—did he realize his mouth was hanging open in shock. A quick glance told him both Mina and Neal were keeping an eye on him, but most of their attention was on Esther. And Rook suddenly found he didn't care as much about the near-drooling incident. *Esther* was happy for the match, and it drew a wide grin from him.

With some of his usual charm back, he said, "I had rather meant for it to be a secret. You'll understand if I ask you to keep this under your hat?"

"Of course, Master Hollow. Of course. Not a word shall pass my lips." Esther made a jolly little pantomime of locking her lips and throwing away the key. "You just better tell me everything when all is said and done. I do so love engagement stories."

"You'll be the first I tell." Then, in a stage whisper, Rook added, "And I'll bring some of that special almond liqueur you like."

"Then I shall make a special dessert to go with while you regale me with the tale."

Rook's smile stretched so wide it nearly hurt. Stars, he might love Esther almost as much as he loved Lenore. In a precious grandmother way, of course.

"Now, dears, you all just let me know if you need anything else." And with that, Esther bustled back out.

Rook met Mina and Neal's eyes with greater hope this time, but needing to hear their answer still withered his confidence.

"So?" he said, trying to move things along.

"Why are you asking us this?" Neal wondered evenly.

Because Lenore's real parents are dead and you're the next best stand-in, Rook thought. *No, don't actually say that.*

"Because Lenore's real parents are dead and you're the next best stand-in," he said.

No! What are you doing?! Why was this process making him so stupid?

To Neal and Mina's incredulous expressions—and also possibly murderous; it was hard to tell in his panic—Rook hurried to explain. "What I mean to say is, Lenore sees you two as surrogate parents. Surrogate? Is that the right word? Anyway, she cares for you both deeply, and I know what your approval means to her. You're her family."

Rook felt like he'd just sprinted a mile with that admission. It took every ounce of his willpower to remain sitting up straight instead of flopping back into his chair. He decided to restore his strength with Esther's tea and cinnamon buns.

Neal and Mina visibly softened. They exchanged one of those looks that Rook had observed before—a sort of silent understanding between two people who had been close a long time. It made him nervous, and he took another big bite of cinnamon bun to distract himself. Maybe, no matter how this went, he'd see about taking a few more distraction buns with him on his way out.

Finally, Mina spoke. "We've only ever wanted happiness for Lenore. If you can provide that—"

"As well as safety," Neal put in. "Apologies for the interruption, my dove."

"Not to worry, darling. Mister Hollow and I have already had *that* discussion." As she spoke, Mina's hand came to rest suggestively on her scalpel. "Yes, her happiness and her safety. If you can provide that for her, then I suppose we have no room to argue." And, because Mina was who *she* was, she added, "Despite any personal reservations we might have about your character."

Rook smiled at her and stood to bow. "Thank you, Doctor Allen." He tipped an imaginary hat to Neal, as he'd doffed his real one at the door. "And to you, Engineer Allen." Still standing, Rook shoved the rest of the cinnamon bun in his mouth and drained his teacup. "I'd stay longer, but…"

He didn't need to say that no one really wanted that. Neal granted him a small smile. "Perhaps we'll share a congratulations drink after this is all said and done?" When Rook raised an eyebrow at him, Neal added, "It is rather the done thing."

Rook gave him a cheeky grin. "Why, Engineer Allen. I fear I may be growing on you."

"Like Sphagnum moss," Mina quipped.

She too gifted him a small smile. Rook had no idea what the moss reference meant but decided to get out while he was ahead. He gave them a playful salute and left, bent on hitting the kitchen next.

The sun had just dipped below the horizon by the time Rook made it back downstairs. He was fairly walking on air through the back corridor to the kitchen when something slammed into his side, making him stumble against the wall. He was about to react, hands already on a dagger hilt—he still kept a few scattered around his person, just in case—when he felt the tip of a blade against his throat. He froze. His other senses were just behind, and Rook nearly laughed at the sight that greeted him.

Camilla, gentle, sweet Camilla, was glaring up at him. Honestly, what was she playing at? Though, credit where credit was due.

"Where'd you learn to tackle like that?" he asked.

"It takes an impressive amount of force to crack open a ribcage," she replied coolly. It sounded as if they were discussing the weather. "I know how to concentrate my bulk."

"Impressive. Gruesome, but impressive." Why did her blade feel a little bit wrong? He glanced down. That was why. "That's a letter opener."

"So?" She was clearly not to be deterred. "A lady is always ready to improvise."

Rook's throat bobbed against the sharp, silver tip as he squelched a chuckle. "Do you even know how to use that, powderpuff?"

"I've had no problems getting into my mail thus far." Camilla pushed the letter opener's tip harder into Rook's throat.

Rook decided against telling Camilla she wouldn't stab him. She might be tender and sweet to most people's eyes, but Rook had seen steel in her before. And besides, Camilla had a special place in her spleen for him. Instead, he held out his hands in a peaceful gesture. "Is there something I can help you with? I do have things to be getting on with."

"What's your plan for a ring, hm?"

His brow furrowed. "Beg pardon?"

Before Camilla could answer, a form made of solid shadow emerged from the growing darkness of the corridor and took form —Kieran. He looked curiously between the two. Camilla was all bubbles and sunshiney smiles for him, though she still didn't move.

"Good evening, Kieran," she greeted. "Sleep well?"

He smiled back placidly at her. "Like the dead."

Rook groaned and rolled his eyes, but neither Camilla nor Kieran paid him any mind.

Kieran motioned blithely to the scene before him. "What's all this then?"

Still holding the letter opener to Rook's throat, Camilla explained, "Rook is planning to propose to Lenore."

"Is he?" Kieran grinned, showing far too much fang for Rook's comfort.

"Indeed," Camilla went on. "I was just asking him about his plan for a ring."

Kieran pointed at Rook. "Very important detail."

Rook was so baffled, he shook his head. Camilla, thankfully, had already begun retracting her weapon, and he goggled at them both. "Like I don't know that." He began to regain his usual composure and raised placating hands towards the two. "Relax, I have it well in hand."

Camilla and Kieran exchanged dubious looks. It was Camilla who began the interrogation. "And how much do you know about gemstones?"

"Color? Cut? Clarity? Carats?" Kieran shot his questions like darts.

"Do you even know Lenore's ring size?"

"Does she prefer square, round, or pear shapes?"

"Have you considered how the type of metal will look?"

Rook looked quizzically at them both. "What, do you two run a jewelry business I don't know about?"

Kieran gave a little shrug. "I did my own bit of ring shopping back in the day."

Camilla did not so much shrug as gave a graceful yet nonchalant little bobble. "I like shiny things."

Rook raised his eyes to the heavens. "Stars, save me from sassy sisters and uppity Vampyres." The other two exchanged a grin, and Rook added, "As I said, I've got it well in hand."

Camilla crossed her arms over her chest, clearly waiting for more explanation. Kieran leaned back against the wall, also waiting.

Rook felt far more confident about this than he had about his chat with Mina and Neal. "I did some digging and tracked down what happened to Twila and Edgar's possessions."

Camilla softened, but Kieran looked suspicious. "Did this require criminal activity?"

Rook made a dismissive gesture at him. "Calm yourself, night stalker. Just some light breaking and entering. I didn't even steal anything. Anyway, I found Twila's engagement ring." He turned to Kieran again. "And I *bought* it back."

When Springhavian citizens became denizens of the Halls of Justice, their valuables were given over to city hands and resold as a way for those arrested to "repay" Springhaven for their crimes. Rook didn't mention he would have stolen the ring without a second thought if he'd had to. Happy coincidence he'd been able to acquire it through legal means… minus the breaking and entering.

Kieran and Camilla exchanged looks of agreement.

"Fair enough, that is pretty good," Camilla confessed.

"True," Kieran added, as if Rook needed their approval. "I suppose our work here is done."

Rook smiled and tipped the same invisible hat from before at them. He said nothing more as he continued down the corridor and to the kitchen. He didn't think Esther's cooking could get any better, but apparently so when it followed such a complete and devastating win.

Cake, check. Family blessing, check. Ring, check. The night had come, all the pieces were in place, and Rook was dressed just so. He did not want to clue Lenore into something being up, so he'd chosen a suit in slate grey—just dark enough for an evening event but light enough for early spring. Chrysalis had even pressed it for him. They were a dab hand with an iron, and Rook's collar points looked sharp enough to cut. Now if he could just remaster words.

As Rook made his way down the road, heading to the museum for their educational night, he practiced his speech in his head. He'd written the thing down, performed it in front of the mirror again and again, but somehow he kept flubbing it. And then changing things. And then re-flubbing and re-changing. Nothing sounded right. How did all those writer types not go mad? He gave it another thought. Actually, writer types all seemed a little bit insane, so maybe that was the secret. It was clearly a type of madness Rook didn't possess, though he might be on his way there. And all the while, he rubbed the ring in his pocket between thumb and forefinger like a good luck charm.

Edgar had apparently had a romantic streak, as he'd purchased a ring with both his and Twila's birthstones—topaz and ruby. Rook pulled it from his pocket to examine again. The gems flashed like fire in the dying sunlight. Maybe intertwining something about flames into his speech would help. He kept staring at the ring as he walked, hoping it would grant him poetic inspiration.

He was so wrapped up in which words where, emphasis, pauses, and so on, he failed to see an approaching pothole. The cobbles fell away beneath Rook's feet, he did a funny sort of jig in the air trying to find them again, and ended up tripping himself on his way down. Rook's hands flew out to catch himself, the ring still grasped between his fingers. He watched in slow motion as his fingers splayed on instinct, as the ring went flying through the air. And as it flew, things sped up hideously.

Rook's quick reflexes had him from the ground to back on his feet in seconds. The glint of sunlight on metal guided his eyes. He leapt towards it. The ring bounced and skittered along the road and

—

"No, don't!" Rook cried, as if the ring would stop and turn back to him.

Of course, it did no such thing. The ring tumbled across a storm drain and down between two of the grates. Rook threw himself onto the ground again.

Please don't have fallen far, he begged.

Springhaven's sewer system was impressive, complex, and above all, extremely smelly. Rook knew from personal experience it was a good way to lose pursuers if one had the time and strength to lift a manhole cover and slip down into the tunnels. Unfortunately, he also knew from personal experience that many of the sewers were full of stinking sludge. And that anything that fell into those putrid depths was likely lost forever.

Rook's eyes raked through the growing darkness, darker still beneath the grate. Sometimes there was a ledge… Success! A few feet below, near the edge of the hoped-for ledge, the ring reflected evening's waning light. And there was even an opening in the curb just large enough for Rook to snake his arm through. His fingertips hovered above the ring, so he pressed himself flatter against the street. When that wasn't enough, he squashed his face against the curb and wedged his side against the opening. He made no quick moves, terrified of knocking the ring into the darkness below. He'd dislocate his arm if he had to. He could still propose with a dislocated arm, right? The glinting from the gemstones mocked him.

How could you be so stupid? the ring seemed to say. *You know there's only one of me, right?*

Rook pressed himself so hard against the street, he thought a passing hansom cab wouldn't feel more than a slight bump if it ran him over. His fingers extended against the edge of the ledge, forming a barrier. And, groaning with the extreme stretch, he hooked his thumb into the ring and secured it against his fingers. Thank the stars! Safe in his closed fist, which he clenched like his life depended on it, Rook extracted his limb and stood.

"Hah!" he gloated to the universe at large. "Think I'll give up that easily?" With his free hand, he drew a small box from his jacket pocket and carefully, ever so carefully, nestled the ring inside and snapped the box closed. "Now, stay there."

Rook picked up speed, wanting to make up for lost time, but he watched the ground closely for any other sneaky tripping hazards. So when he was just a few blocks from the museum and someone reached out from a dark alley, Rook was snatched off his feet and sailed back into said alley. He might have stumbled again if the figure had not held onto him like it did. Rook spun, daggers drawn, ready to strike.

"Just what do you think you're doing?" came a familiar, foppish voice.

Rook's eyes caught up with his ears, adjusting to the darkness of the alley. He immediately assumed the worst. "What's gone wrong with the cake?"

Lowell gave him a scathing look. "The cake is perfection. Which is far more than I can say for *you*." From head to toe, he raked his eyes disapprovingly over Rook. "What *have* you done?"

Rook looked down at his clothes. The crisp white of his shirt was stained with dirt—at least he hoped it was dirt. It was rumpled too, along with his waistcoat. And his trousers. He remembered the way he'd smushed his face against the pavement and was afraid to see what sort of damage had been done there. Lifting his fingers to his neck, he found his collar points had bent terribly. Stars, he was a mess. Rook took a deep breath.

Very well, so he wasn't going to look as perfect and pressed as he wanted. Lenore wouldn't mind. She was good like that. But Rook minded. He minded very much. And that condescending way Lowell was shaking his head wasn't bloody helpful.

"Could you stop that please?" Rook grumbled.

Lowell either hadn't heard him or, far more likely, was ignoring him, because he clicked his tongue and said, "This will never do. Imagine, my little tinker belle being proposed to with you looking like that. You're positively scruffy."

Rook narrowed his eyes, but before he could say anything, Lowell started unbuttoning his own waistcoat.

"What the blazes are you doing?" Rook asked instead.

"Fixing this. Now hurry up, we don't have much time."

"I..." Rook didn't know how to continue as Lowell shed his

waistcoat and held it in one hand while he began to undo the buttons of his shirt with the free one.

"Daft man," Lowell scolded. "We're switching clothes. I can claim I fell out of a tree trying to get a better view or something."

Rook felt strange about the offer, but he preferred to look dapper for Lenore and so began to unbutton his own garments. Trying to take his mind off how uncomfortable he felt disrobing in an alley, he asked, "Will anyone believe that?"

"You let me worry about that," Lowell said.

They exchanged shirts and vests and redressed their top halves quickly. Rook looked to the alley entrance before starting on his trousers. He averted his eyes from Lowell and got down to business.

"You know," he joked, "if anyone catches us, they're going to think we're engaging in an entirely different proposition."

"Please." Rook could practically hear Lowell rolling his eyes. "You're hardly my type. I prefer a man with far more intellectual proclivities."

Rook blinked. "Did you just call me stupid?"

"Now's hardly the time, Rook. Focus."

Minutes later, both men were trousered again, though Rook could hardly say he felt fresh. Body warmth from someone else inside an outfit was a rather uncomfortable sensation. At least Lowell had dressed well for the evening. His collar points even rivaled the glory that Rook's had enjoyed, short-lived though that glory had been. Lapis was a bit too ostentatious a color for Rook's taste, but it wasn't near as bad as some of the other options out there. Not that Rook could muse on that for long, as Lowell suddenly attacked Rook's face with a handkerchief. Rook sputtered, but Lowell backed away before Rook could push him off. The handkerchief was soiled, and Rook understood that Lowell had been cleaning his face.

"That will do," Lowell said approvingly. Then he began

practically shoving Rook back out of the alley. "Off with you now. There's a lovely lady out there needing to be swept off her feet. So go forth and *sweep!*"

Rook trotted on, wondering about some of the finer details of this mad plan. Had Lenore already seen Lowell that evening? Would she recognize his clothes on Rook? And why had he even been in that alley? Rook decided to let it go. He trusted Lowell enough not to fret about it.

Finally, he reached the museum. Sandwich boards with helpful arrows showed him the way. The directions led him through the building, past refreshment tables, along exhibits and galleries of interest, and finally to the outdoor section of the museum's Zoology area. A passing scholar walked by with a regal wolf on a lead. Not Majesty, Lenore's specimen of the same litter, but one of Majesty's siblings. Lenore had decided to keep the beloved creature instead of turning her over to the Zoology department. Rook and Lenore would have to figure out how to fit a regal wolf into what would be their new life together, but they would get there. For now, he had to get through this without accidentally swallowing his tongue or something equally embarrassing.

He followed the flow of people to a wide-open space the Zoology scholars used as a training and demonstration field for the animals. Tall torches had been stuck into the ground around the field to provide light, which Rook appreciated. It created a nice ambiance for what he had planned. Though his pace had slowed, his heart sped up the closer he got. When he saw Lenore, it practically galloped.

She wore a practical outfit with a high-low skirt and trouser combination and a pair of strange-looking goggles on her head. The lenses were thick and multilayered, making Lenore appear as if she had a pair of stubby horns growing from her skull. She smiled when she saw him, though she was busy directing a group of spectators and handing out programs. Rook smiled back and approached, keeping enough distance to appear as if he was simply waiting his turn. The ring box in his pocket suddenly felt huge and bulging and like it was glowing brightly within the fabric. When the spectators moved on, Rook sidled up to Lenore, who handed him a program.

She began to go through her spiel, but Rook didn't hear any of it. He wanted nothing more than to pull her close and kiss her. Of course, with her working, that was out of the question.

"And thank you for coming," she added. "I thought this sort of thing might bore you."

He grinned. "Not at all. I think tonight's going to be fantastically exciting."

Lenore's smile widened, but her attention was caught by a family coming up to join the festivities. Rook began to sweat. She *was* going to be free soon, yes? Both Lowell and Neal were aware of what he had planned for this evening. As if magically summoned, Lowell came trotting up, looking more than a touch worse for wear in Rook's clothes. With impressive deftness, he nipped the programs from Lenore's hands and ushered her away.

"So sorry for the delay. Got into a bit of a biff with a tree. All's well that ends well, though, yes? So you two are free to go enjoy yourselves."

Lenore began to protest. "Are you sure I can't… Lowell, what happened to… I can… If you want…"

Lowell batted every objection away like a champion badminton player. "Go, go, my little tinker belle. I've got things well in hand."

Rook helped to gently pull Lenore along, and soon they were making their way towards a slightly more secluded spot. Well, as secluded as one could get in a crowd. Lenore was still looking back at Lowell with a curious expression on her face. Rook decided distraction was his best weapon now.

He tapped the strange goggles on her head. "So what are these for?"

She gave a little peep of excitement and explained, "They're magnification lenses. One of the stellanomists lent them to me, so I can see the meteors in clearer detail." She pulled them down over her eyes and suddenly looked like a very happy owl. "They're really something, aren't they?"

Rook managed to stifle a laugh, but he couldn't squelch his smile. "They really are."

Lenore removed the goggles back to the top of her head. "Oh! Did you know Felicia was coming tonight? I saw her and Calandra walking by earlier. They looked very suspicious."

"Suspicious?" Rook asked. His voice cracked a little, traitorously. He cleared his throat. "Apologies. Suspicious how?"

Lenore didn't seem to notice the gaffe and said, "They just kept smiling. I don't know Calandra very well, but I think Felicia only smiles like that when she's up to something."

It took a great force of will for Rook not to look around. Instead, he decided to up his distraction game and turned the conversation to that night's big event. Lenore immediately latched onto the subject and started bubbling over with explanations and theories about stars and the sky beyond and the universe's creation. Rook didn't understand most of it, but he nodded and smiled and kept an eye out for other possible surprise-ruiners. Sure enough, he spied Camilla and Mina not far off. Thankfully, they were hidden behind a cluster of other families. Felicia and Calandra strolled nearby once like a pair of orbiting moons. And, Rook noticed, Lowell was never far off. He even spied Esther, though she was with a huge group that was likely her own family. Rook would have to go meet them, having heard so much about them from Esther, but first things first.

The meteor shower's arrival was heralded by a growing "ooooh" of wonder from the crowd. Lenore gasped and pointed up, babbling stellanomy terms at Rook. He grinned so hard his face hurt. It really was rather breathtaking. One after another, what looked like new stars fizzed across the inky sky above, trailing ribbons of light. He pulled Lenore close, grateful to be able to share this moment with her.

It went on for about twenty minutes before the spectacle let up. According to Lenore, things would pick up again after a short break. That had been part of her little welcome spiel from earlier, and Rook had decided that's when he would act. He suddenly found that his mouth had gone dry.

To try and loosen up his tongue, he joked, "Awfully considerate of the universe to provide us with an intermission."

Lenore faced away from him, but he could see her nod as she looked around. Her mind was clearly elsewhere. "It seems like everyone came out tonight. We should go say hello to some people."

"No!" Rook said too quickly.

Lenore looked back at him, and he realized she was wearing those ridiculous goggles again. He let out a laugh, and Lenore pulled them onto her forehead, giving him a smirk. Worry swam in her eyes, though. Rook's heart pounded. He couldn't tell if he was sweating because he felt both hot and cold all over. Is this what it felt like right before one fainted? Just in case, he decided it would be better if he got closer to the ground and practically threw himself down to one knee. He held Lenore's hand in his, and he realized he was shaking a little.

Oh bugger, here I am, he thought. *It's happening.*

Lenore was staring down at him, but suddenly, for the first time ever, he couldn't read her expression. Was that fear or surprise, or did she just think he'd gone mental? This *couldn't* go wrong, so he plowed forward before she got the wrong idea.

"Lenore, I love you. I want to spend every day with you. No matter where your career takes you or what new adventures find us, I want to be there with you. By your side as your partner. Will you marry me?"

With his free hand, he pulled the ring box from his pocket and opened it. Lenore sucked in a breath, eyes growing wide, as she took in the sight. Tears began to glitter in her eyes, and she reverently reached out to touch the gemstones on her mother's old ring.

"Is this really…" she murmured.

"It really is," Rook replied.

He stood, still holding the ring in place between them, and brushed a hand along Lenore's face. Standing close to her, he spoke in a low, gentle tone. "Tell me what you're thinking, little bird."

She looked at him, and her green eyes almost seemed to glow in the soft torchlight. "I'm thinking I can't wait to marry you."

If it could have, Rook's answering grin would have stretched beyond the bounds of his face. While he wanted to take her in his arms and drown in kisses, he remembered they were surrounded by her colleagues. Instead, he brought his face close to her ear and planted a small, gentle kiss on her cheek and whispered a promise into her ear.

"I'll show you just how happy you've made me later."

She grinned back at him, and Rook slid the ring onto her finger.

Lenore looked at it again and said, "Thank you."

Rook understood everything she meant with those two little words. Before he could reply, though, a new voice broke in.

"I guess she said yes to putting up with you forever."

Rook and Lenore turned to see Dmitri and Chrysalis approaching—the latter had done themself up today to match Dmitri's usual disguise, appearing like his younger sister. Chrysalis carried a glass cake platter in their hands, topped with Lowell's beautiful cake, and Dmitri followed close behind, clearly ready to fly in for a rescue in case they tripped. Rook couldn't help but smile at them, but Lenore was the one who spoke.

"I did. And quite happily, mind you."

Dmitri rolled his eyes, but he was smiling. "Thank goodness.

He would have been more impossible than usual if you'd said no."

Lenore turned warm, loving eyes back onto Rook. "Never."

Chrysalis made a gagging sound in their throat. "Can we eat cake already?"

"There's cake too?" Lenore seemed to only just notice the cake under the stand's gleaming glass cover. Her eyes lit up even brighter.

"Cake makes everything better," Lowell said, trotting up to join them. He took Lenore's free hand in his and pressed it affectionately. "Congratulations, my tinker belle."

Camilla, the Allens, Felicia, Calandra, and Esther all came round and joined the celebration. There was equal ooing and aahing over Lenore's ring and the cake—Lowell really had outdone himself with handmade sugar flowers and edible pearls. Lenore's coworkers came over to see what all the fuss was about, and more congratulations were shared. Copper shook Rook's hand so hard he thought his whole arm might pop off. Felicia produced a second cake, far less ornate but much bigger, for the growing crowd to share as well. Gadget and her daughter Rowan glided over, and Gadget whispered to the happy couple that even Kieran was lurking nearby. When the meteor shower began again, Lenore and Rook were surrounded by their found families.

Rook released a breath that felt years in the making. "I'm so glad I never have to do that again." He turned to Lenore and added, "But I would every day if you asked me to."

Lenore laughed, pecked him on the cheek, and ran a hand down his sleeve. Then she pulled back, a curious expression on her face. "Rook, are you wearing Lowell's clothes?"

He couldn't help but give a sheepish smile and squeeze her hand, which now bore the ring that blazed brighter than the shooting stars above.

~*~

If you enjoyed this book, please consider leaving a review on StoryGraph, Fable, Goodreads and/or Amazon, etc. Even a single line is massively helpful. Thank you in advance for taking the time to share your thoughts.

To get more goodies from Dana, consider joining her Patreon at https://www.patreon.com/wordsbydana

You can also sign up for early updates, cover reveals, and exclusive content by joining her VIP newsletter. You can sign up for that on her website: https://www.wordsbydana.com/

AN EXCERPT FROM FALCON'S FAVOR

CHAPTER 1

The flat was… well, it wasn't that bad, right?

Falcon looked around the parlor, his new parlor. Though "new" by any measure other than it being his—well, partially his—would be laughable.

"It has Old World charm," Beatrice had said of the place.

Literally, Falcon thought to himself now.

Beatrice had been the one to find this "hidden treasure," for him at a bargain monthly rate. Being the daughter of a well-to-do politician came with gaggles of connections, which had come in rather handy given Falcon's sudden limit in resources. He was forever impressed by but could never understand how the socialite bore traversing the complex web of favors and politics with the grace she did.

Like the entire row of houses all along this street, and the next, and the next, the building he stood in now had been constructed just over a century ago after the cataclysmic War of Light, and in short order no less. So much in the city of Springhaven had been destroyed then, and these row homes had been a quick fix for much-needed housing. Walls covered in stained, peeling wallpaper tried to liven up the old place, while windows with ratty wooden frames and thin glass radiated cold against the warmth of the room.

A brick fireplace sat inside the back wall, squashed beneath the stairway to the second level and giving off some fantastic heat against the early spring chill pressing in from the outside. Falcon could see through the back of it to the kitchen on the other side of the wall. A hook for hanging cookware and other fireplace accouterments peeked through the sooty opening.

Mismatched furniture gathered around this side of the fireplace —a long sofa, a battered wingback chair, and what looked like a trio of dining chairs from different sets. These had been provided by his new roommate. Falcon had yet to meet the chap, however, as beggars—thankfully not literally—couldn't be choosers. The scuffs all over the timeworn wooden floor made it look as if this set or previous furniture had often taken lively turns about the room. Petrolsene sconces dotted the wall at intervals, though the wan but persistent sunlight coming in through the grimy windows was filling in for them at the moment. Falcon didn't need to know much about architecture to guess that every other row home along this road shared the exact same floor plan.

Falcon was grateful for the warmth of the fireplace, as the cold made his service injuries ache—injuries that made him feel much older than his nineteen years. Those same injuries were the reason he was currently leaning on a telescoping cane, one he was still getting used to. The handle probably needed some adjustment, but the last few weeks, full of moving preparations as they'd been, hadn't left much time for such things.

Falcon ventured further inside the house and leaned through the open doorway that led into the small… could it even be called a corridor? Whatever its proper name, he looked around the space which served as both a corridor and landing for the stairs, neatly tucked between the door to the sitting room and the kitchen door.

Gazing up the harrowingly steep and narrow staircase to the second floor where the bedrooms must surely be, Falcon grimaced. *Not sure how the movers will get my bed and things through there.*

A knock at the front door made him turn. He felt his cheeks flush with embarrassment as he once again took in the motley crew of furniture and tatty decor, and he hurried to stand up straight on his own power rather than leaning so heavily on the cane. For which his body rewarded him with a gentle warning twinge.

"Hello," trilled Beatrice Holmes' voice as she pushed open the front door with nothing more than a finger's touch.

Seeing how easily she pushed open the door, Falcon wondered if he'd failed to close it or if it had been contrary when he wasn't looking. In either case, he took control now and ensured it was shut before taking Beatrice's proffered hand in greeting.

"I trust you found the little gem of a place all right?" she asked.

Beatrice began to stroll about the room with the same poise and charm as if entering a garden party thrown in her honor, and nothing in her manner showed any disagreement with their rough surroundings. Though her burgundy satin visiting dress, with its ruffles and bustle and ruching and all, couldn't help but make every inch of the flat seem even more tired and washed out.

Nevertheless, Beatrice's composure put Falcon at ease, and he returned to leaning on his cane. At that, he heard his grandfather's voice in his head, remonstrating: "Don't slouch. It makes you look soft." Falcon banished the thought. Given that he was no longer on speaking terms with his grandfather—both a blessing and a curse— he didn't appreciate the reminder, thank you very much. Even so, he stood up straight again. They were familiar with one another, true, but Beatrice was still a lady.

She carried on with her perusal of the flat. "Rather quaint, being tucked away back here, isn't it? It's a sweet little hideaway, which I imagine will serve you well given your newfound celebrity."

Falcon swallowed down no less than three different responses, failing to decide on one. By "tucked away," Beatrice had referred to the fact that this particular set of joined-up homes were down a side street—barely more than an alley, really—which came off a forked road, which was, thankfully, attached to a main thoroughfare.

"Quaint," of course, also referred to the size of the place, which was a mere splinter compared to the family manor in which he'd, until very recently, lived his entire life. That manor, as with so many homes like it, was located in Springhaven's Rose district. This "little gem" was in the Cobalt quarter, which was, well... Cobalt played by its own rules. It was different things to different people, sometimes changing for the same person within a single day. On the way here, Falcon had seen a large, grimy steamworks repair shop next door to a tiny, shiny, high-end watchmaker's and a bustling cafe next to that with people from all walks of life seeping in through and spilling out the entryway as they came and went.

And finally, "newfound celebrity" was about the fact that he was the Enforcers' new poster boy for their recently-formed emergency response unit—literally; his image graced posters all over the city. The detachment had been created partly in response to the fact that, previously, Springhaven had no unified team trained and available to deploy in the case of crises. But also as an attempt to clean up the Enforcer order's public image, which to many was not much better than a gang of thugs who happened to be on the right side of the law.

It had been a little over a month since the harrowing raid on Springhaven's catacombs, during which Falcon had assisted the city's so-called peacekeeping order with taking down a strange syndicate of criminals called the Reaper's Collective. Operative word being "assisted," though the fact that he'd had to take leadership of the operation when his C.O. had gone down—not dead, thankfully, just injured—had rather propelled Falcon to career stardom. Which had then turned awkward when he'd publicly defamed his grandfather, who'd been a well-respected Second in said order—a high rank indeed—but who had grossly abused his power for years.

That brought Falcon back to today, to his new flat. His family was… disappointed wasn't the right word, but these last few weeks since the scandalous revelation had been tense. He could have gone to live at the Enforcer barracks, but ratting out a brother in arms made that an even less welcoming place than his family's manor. At least his parents still liked him enough to pay for movers. The thought made Falcon's cheeks go from hot to cold. Beatrice knew this place was the only one he could afford on both such short notice and his civil servant salary, so he wasn't quite as embarrassed with her as he might have been with someone else. But the thought of movers seeing this place, of them bringing his grand furnishings in here… it made him want to catch them in the street and send them back from whence they came. And he absolutely refused to think of his family coming to visit. In fact, he'd told them not to. At least not until he'd settled in, he'd said. Not that his parents nor either of his sisters, both of whom were younger, had volunteered to come round for tea.

A long silence had passed while Falcon was lost in thought, and Beatrice gave the appearance of not having noticed as she sedately took in their surroundings. She went on. "I admit, it's a bit of a fixer upper, but I'm sure you and Keene will spruce it up in no time."

Ah, yes, the mysterious roommate known only as Keene. All Falcon knew was that Keene was about his age and, as Beatrice had put it, "In need of new lodgings as soon as possible."

"Having you here already does half the sprucing job for us," came a smooth response from the corridor.

Falcon turned toward the voice, and the sight of the young man leaning against the doorframe made him freeze.

The man was, in a word, radiant. Thick black hair more than a touch longer than current fashion dictated brushed around his shoulders in loose waves. It was the perfect accent to his warm medium brown skin, which peeked scandalously through his shirt, a button or two of which he'd apparently forgotten to button. His dark eyes glittered from a kind, open face, made kinder by the pearly white smile he flashed at Beatrice. The smile was what caught Falcon's gaze for longer than anything else. It was not the ambitious smile of a man who'd decided—foolishly—that he was a match for Beatrice. Nor was it the insincere bearing of teeth Falcon saw so often among the Enforcer order, which was full of backbiting and vitriol. No, this man smiled at Beatrice with pure, unadulterated joy.

Falcon's Enforcer training kicked in then, always on the lookout for trouble. Not that he was worried about Beatrice in particular; he'd seen her decimate powerful men with naught but a single word. But he shouldn't risk underestimating this newcomer. Then again, was he new? No, he'd come from further inside the house. He must have gotten here before Falcon even, so why hadn't he come out before? Was that suspicious? To be fair, Falcon hadn't been here more than a few minutes.

The man certainly didn't appear threatening. His movements were easy and relaxed, fluid like a stream, as he walked fully into the room.

"Keene!" Beatrice sang upon seeing the man.

When they met, they took one another by the arms, grasping each other at the elbows, and popped kisses into the air on either side of the others' face. Falcon suddenly wondered if the man— Keene, apparently—was one of Beatrice's paramours.

"I knew you'd arranged for your furniture to be here, but I didn't think you were coming until tomorrow," Beatrice said in surprise. That was a rare sight indeed; she was almost always a step ahead of everyone else.

Keene gave a nonchalant shrug, as if moving house for him was as easy as changing waistcoats. "My old roommate didn't mind if I left ahead of schedule, so I did."

Blazes, Falcon envied the way he moved. Falcon knew enough of society to know he himself was fairly attractive as such things went. He was tall, taller than Keene anyway, and had his own handsome mane of hair, though it was much shorter than Keene's, always budging against Enforcer regulations, which allowed no more than two inches of length. Falcon's hair was a rather drab walnut color, however, and liked to piece itself into straight, spiny factions, despite his best efforts to tame it. His own skin, which, before last year, had always carried a healthy wheat hue about it, looked sallow now. That, along with his uncertain mobility, was thanks to some misadventures from last year, which included but was not limited to having been blasted into a tree during an attack on the Enforcer headquarters, the Halls of Justice, by the Reaper's Collective. Falcon had subsequently spent some time in a coma and had since then fought an uphill battle to regain his previous vigor. He suddenly wanted to hide the cane he leaned on, to prevent this lithe, beautiful man from seeing his greatest flaws. The saving grace in this shadow of his former self Falcon had become was his eyes—such a bright light brown they were nearly golden.

Something in Keene's previous statement raised a flag in Falcon's brain. "Old roommate?" Falcon asked. And then the upper class gentleman in him mentally cringed. He hadn't even been introduced to the man and he was asking impertinent questions. The Enforcer side of him, however, told the gentle born side to shove it.

Before Falcon could even begin to consider how to recover, Beatrice was smoothing things over, as she was so adept at doing. "Oh dear me, how very rude of me. Falcon, darling, come here. I'd like to present Mister Keene Kohli. And this is… apologies, Falcon, what's the shiny new title you just received?"

Falcon was grateful he'd managed to almost completely hide his limp as he approached—it was something he'd been working hard to accomplish. The current formalities, though, made him feel just as uncomfortable.

He cleared his throat before answering, "Steward of the Sage, but Falcon is fine, thank you."

Keene tipped his head to the side in a way that made Falcon feel he was definitely being assessed. The man's smile, though genuine, didn't hold nearly the same amount of warmth it had for Beatrice. "I should hope so, given that we'll be sharing the same house. Bit of a mouthful saying the whole title every time we see one another."

"Yes, I suppose so." Falcon rubbed the back of his neck. "And not a nice mouthful at that." The sentence he'd just uttered seemed to turn back on the air and stare at him in the face, questioning why it existed in the first place. "Not that…" he began, trying to recover before realizing he had no idea where he was going.

Stop before you make it worse, said his inner filter. *Please!*

Falcon coughed once before finishing, "Lovely to meet you. I'm sure we'll get on very well."

As they shook hands, Falcon got a whiff of spices from Keene. He didn't know cooking well enough to know what kind, but the scent was warm, as warm as Keene's chestnut skin, and reminded Falcon of pies during New Year's week.

"Rough hands," Keene said as the handshake ended. "Is that from holding a truncheon so much?"

That drenched the warm feeling like a bucket of ice water. Keene's tone hadn't been sharp, but Falcon couldn't tell if he'd just been making idle conversation either. The Enforcers had earned their reputation for cruelty hundreds of times over, true, but Falcon had always tried to be different. He strived to be better, to be a force for good from the inside. If Keene did despise Falcon simply on the basis of his job, then Falcon couldn't blame him. But the barb hit a tender spot inside and stung like Keene had been wielding a truncheon of his own, a verbal one.

I can fix this, Falcon automatically thought to himself. *Say something helpful.*

But before Falcon could think of anything, Beatrice put in, "Steward of the Sage is the name for the head of the Enforcers' new crisis response unit." Her tone made it sound as if she was dropping an interesting little factoid into the conversation over luncheon. Falcon couldn't decide if he wished he'd thought to say that or was glad he'd had the wherewithal not to. His new title did sound a bit self-aggrandizing.

"I know," was Keene's only reply.

Very well, I won't fix it by talking about work, Falcon decided. *But I* can *still fix this.*

Before he could venture down that path, however, a knock rapped against the front door. It obligingly opened under the force, which had not sounded particularly forceful, and Falcon scowled at the stubborn door. It seemed all too happy to let anyone just walk right in.

"Hello?" called a gruff but professional voice into the house. Whoever was on the other side was clearly confused but too polite to step inside. "Is there a Mister Falcon Smoke at home?"

"You're right on time," Beatrice chirped, sweeping over to the door.

The movers! Falcon had completely forgotten to think up an excuse for turning them away, what with being all distracted by handsome new acquaintances and all. Perhaps he could fabricate some tale about… *Oh, I don't know, floor gophers or something.*

He made a strangled sort of noise before blurting, "Never thank you!" He had meant to say, "no, thank you" before his mind switched to, "nevermind." His mouth hadn't been able to keep up, however, and thus he'd smashed the phrases together instead.

Both Beatrice and Keene gave him quizzical glances. Falcon

rubbed the back of his neck again, mumbled an apology, and traipsed over to the door. Why, he didn't know. She was already taking command of the situation and giving the movers orders. Falcon stood by, however, wanting to be helpful and equally wanting to slink away as the pieces of his grand bedroom set were heaved into the house and up the stairs… or merely attempted to, in some cases. In the end, getting the headboard, a huge, solid piece of carved hardwood, up the skinny stairway was beyond both human ability and physics. Given that the rest of the four-poster bed would be tragically sloped without it, the movers set what they called chocks beneath the frame to level it. It turned out that "chocks" was just a fancy word for "hunks of wood," and Falcon thanked the stars for the dust ruffle, which would cover them. He also cursed the dust ruffle because the fine, hand embroidered fabric looked positively ridiculous against the chipped and pockmarked plaster walls and dusty wood floors of his new bedroom.

While everyone got to work—or in Falcon's case, watched everyone else get to work—Keene put on a pot of tea and laid on some sinfully buttery biscuits. Falcon took the opportunity to offer a hand, rough though it may be from truncheon swinging.

See, I'm helpful, and not a thoughtless lout.

But Keene seemed perfectly in his element in the kitchen and politely declined, barely sparing Falcon a glance. So then Falcon went and stood by Beatrice. Not that she needed the help. Beatrice was the kind of person who… well, if a steamroller was made of flowers and charm, that was her. It was best to stay out of her way and let her get on, but Falcon stood by, ready to assist should she call.

See, Keene, I know when to stand down, and I'm happy to do so. Falcon did have to remind himself not to stand quite so much at attention, though. That was at least made easier by the fact that standing at attention made his injuries complain. *See, I can relax too. I'm just as easygoing as you… alright, that might be a stretch.*

And when the tea was ready, Falcon jumped at the opportunity to serve the movers theirs.

Just look at how I think of others first.

They, in turn, happily took a break and removed themselves and their teacups out to their moving wagons. Falcon expected Keene to object, as it must have been Keene's drinkware the movers had absconded with—albeit, not far—but the man just sat next to Beatrice with his own refreshment in hand and left them to it. Only then did Falcon realize he'd fallen prey to one of the twisted beliefs his grandfather had tried to drill into him:

"The poorer classes are a drain on society. They'll steal from you as soon as look at you. They ought to put forth a little effort and better their situations instead of asking for handouts."

Falcon mentally shook himself. He'd worked hard to shed those so-called "lessons" and was grateful his parents, who had far better hearts and more sense, had, over the years, helped to undo the damage. Though any direct battles with the family's patriarch were few, far between, and carefully chosen, for it was he who controlled the Smoke family wealth.

Thus, with his moral compass realigned, Falcon too settled into the mismatched furniture of the sitting room. He must have been more drawn than he'd realized because he nearly groaned with pleasure as the restorative brew washed over his lips.

"This might be the best tea I've ever had," he said, unabashedly relieved by the reminder that there were still some reliable things in this world, things like good strong tea and rich biscuits.

"It's my own signature blend." Keene took a sip from his own teacup. Chipped, Falcon noticed, but Keene did not elaborate.

"I'd have had the chipped cup," Falcon said. Why he'd thought to fill the void with that, he didn't know. Clammy horror washed over him. Why was he pointing out the shabby state of Keene's teaware?!

Finally, blissfully, Keene granted Falcon a small smile. It was

not as luminous as the one he'd given Beatrice earlier, but it was warm and genuine and made Falcon's clammy embarrassment evaporate like dew in the sun.

"What kind of host would I be if I'd served you a chipped cup?"

In a less than genteel move, Falcon shrugged. He immediately heard his grandfather's voice in his head, admonishing him for such a flippant gesture: "A man does not shrug. A man makes a strong answer."

"Given that we're roommates now," he said, ignoring his grandfather's voice, "I'd hardly hold it against you."

Beatrice smiled at them both and steered the conversation into amiable waters—the latest fashions, some new plays that had recently premiered, and other easy subjects. Falcon wanted to ask Keene a million questions. The man's manners implied he was gentle born as well, but why then was he living here with Falcon? Falcon's self-inflicted downfall had been painfully public. He had a feeling Beatrice knew the answer, as she kept their conversation neatly reined inside what were apparently safe spaces for the both of them.

The movers meanwhile were jolly pleased by the treats and all had a new spring in their step after they'd partaken. Maybe they weren't even judging Falcon as harshly as he'd imagined. It, and Keene's warming regard, gave Falcon a new lightness of heart. He wasn't even bothered when the head mover reported that some of the neighbors had come out and were sniffing around Falcon's fine things. The man had, in no uncertain terms, told them to shove off. Falcon knew his was a strange situation, but it was a situation he didn't expect to remain in. Once he was back on his feet and had saved up a little money, he'd move along to something more permanent… and far less dingy.

By the time the sun was going down, Falcon's bedroom set had been unloaded as best as possible. Beatrice had made her apologies and left by then, citing another engagement but promising to return soon to see how the two were getting on. Falcon's writing desk was upstairs with the bed now. And given how much room just those took up, he'd opted for his favorite chair to join the gathering of furniture misfits in the sitting room. Unwilling new denizens to the collection were Falcon's headboard, which he wasn't sure what he'd do with just yet, as well as his stately wardrobe, which had been even more of a lost cause than the headboard. Both had been painted in the striking blue-grey shades of a peregrine falcon, making them stand out like sore thumbs even more than they otherwise might.

The mover's payment had already been arranged, though it was apparently customary to tip. Falcon's funds, after putting down his deposit on the house, were severely diminished. Also, what was an appropriate tip after a gaggle of lads had just heaved your ridiculously oversized furniture from one place to another? Falcon had always hated tipping. It was such an odd affair—"Yes, let me pass judgment on your performance via this arbitrary amount of money and we'll both steep in the awkwardness of this moment together."

Just as Falcon was standing before the foreman and dithering, Keene glided over and pressed a tin of biscuits and a packet of his tea blend into the foreman's hands. A card was attached to the tin's top, and Falcon read just quick enough to catch the words "events catering."

"We're a bit light on funds, but I hope this shows our appreciation," Keene said, bearing another one of those magnificent smiles. He then lifted a hand to the side of his face and said in a stage whisper, "I've included some of my special chocolate and orange biscuits too."

The foreman thanked them both and left without seeming upset about the lack of extra payment. Again, why not just charge what you want to earn? That thought, however, was quickly replaced with a new realization: For the first time in his life, Falcon was *alone*. On his own in this new environment with no safety tether. Not even socially, and he looked at Keene, the stranger with whom he now lived. Falcon suddenly felt as if he was treading water and possibly or possibly not surrounded by sharks. If there were sharks, were they going to attack? Maybe, if he said the wrong thing.

No, Falcon assured himself, *You're being dramatic. All will be well.* No imagined real or nonexistent sharks existed… no, wait, that didn't make sense. He decided to leave the shark analogy for now.

"So, Keene, here we are," he said, and then immediately felt stupid for such an obvious statement.

"We are." Falcon got the distinct impression a different expression was hiding beneath Keene's easy countenance, but he couldn't guess what it might be. "Not for long, though. I'm heading out. Nice meeting you and all. Best of luck unpacking your things. If you need it, I've gotten some of my cookware set up in the kitchen already. It's not my good stuff, so don't feel like you need to be too precious with it."

Falcon swallowed a strangled noise of alarm. He hadn't even thought about the fact that he'd have to cook for himself, something he'd never done, not once, in his entire life. With everything else that had been happening, that hadn't occurred to him. No need for Keene, the blender and brewer of spectacular tea and creator of peace-making biscuits, to know how feckless he was in that area, though. Not yet anyway.

"Mind if I tag along?" he asked instead.

He didn't know if he had the funds to go out, nor even how expensive Keene's little excursion might be, but he didn't fancy spending the evening alone with his lack of cooking skills and surrounded by reminders of all he'd lost in the pursuit of doing the right thing. Falcon could always learn how to boil an egg or something tomorrow.

Keene gave him a sheepish smile—the first time Falcon had seen the man lose his cool and collected air—and Falcon knew the answer before it even came out. "Sorry, chap, but it's sort of a prearranged thing."

Falcon was already nodding, "Of course, of course. Apologies. It was rude of me to be so forward."

He'd broken eye contact, looking for anything in the flat that might provide even a halfway graceful escape. Maybe he could slip out a window or something without Keene noticing. Right, that seemed plausible. A warm tone in Keene's voice brought Falcon's attention back.

"Perhaps we can do something together tomorrow?"

Had Keene actually noticed how earnest Falcon had tried to be? He dared to hope that it had improved his new housemate's opinion of him.

Keene added with a kind half-smile, "We can make dinner and get to know one another."

The whole cooking affair was still very much a problem, and a part of Falcon couldn't help but wonder if Keene was avoiding introducing him, the horrible Enforcer, to his friends, but it was a start. Besides, how long could it take to learn to cook? And showing Keene he wasn't, in fact, horrible would happen along the way. Falcon would just pick up a cookbook on the way home, give it a skim, and problem solved.

He felt a smile bloom on his own face. "Tomorrow will be great."

To find out what happens next, you can purchase *Falcon's Favor* from anywhere that sells books. Available in ebook, print, and audio.

Enjoy More of the Broken Gears World

Out of the Shadows

Pride and Prejudice meets HG Wells with a dash of *The Hunger Games*

* The beginning of Lenore's trilogy
* Adventure | Light Romance | Some Fantasy Elements
* Chronology: followed by *Into the Fire* and then *Across the Ice*

Raven's Cry

A dark retelling of *Swan Lake*

* Standalone
* Dark Fantasy | No Romance | Fairytale Retelling
* Chronology: precedes all other Broken Gears books

Rook's Gambit

Ocean's 11 style steampunk heist

* Standalone
* Heist | Light Background Romance | No Fantasy Elements
* Chronology: precedes *Out of the Shadows*

Falcon's Favor

A queer, cozy mystery romance full of food, cravings, tea, and found family

* Standalone
* Cozy Mystery | Sweet Romance | No Fantasy Elements
* Chronology: follows the events of *Across the Ice*

Death Cults and Taxes

For those who want more from the Broken Gears world

* Assumes you've read Lenore's trilogy, but any spoilers are mentioned at the beginning of each story
* Chronology: stories take place during various points in history

ACKNOWLEDGEMENTS

Writing acknowledgements for this book is weird. Mainly because it's grown so slowly over five years. I'm sure there's a metaphor for this kind of slow growth… something about plants or trees or fossils possibly. But, though I don't know what that metaphor is, I do know that I'm never alone in this very solitary process. Thus, in no particular order…

Thank you to my editor, Rachel Oestreich of The Wallflower Editing. I became so comfortable with you as an editor after *Falcon's Favor* (our first book together), I did a complete 180 and email-spewed all the things this weird little book needed, with all its various caveats. And you, incredible professional that you are, totally rolled with it.

To Sally, Heather, Mike, Scout, and Shannon—a.k.a. my High Counsel. You are all, as Lowell puts it, *my people*.

To my amazing Patreon patrons for their incredibly generous, continued support: Doug Peterson, Zack Jones, Shannon Lee, Murky Master, Rebecca Williams, Arbor Winter Barrow, and DJ Gray.

Thank you to Bruin, the best little fluffy coworker anybody could ever ask for.

A.E. Gill, who is also a fantastic author, is everything I could ever ask for in both a critique partner and a friend. You are always so encouraging and helpful. I cannot tell you how grateful I am to have you as a friend on this crazy industry we're a part of.

Thank you to my mom, Dr. Zack, Nikki, and all the rest of the folks I've forgotten to mention by name (or those whose names I don't actually know). Thank you for listening, for advice, for support, for coffee, for rest, and so much more.

And last of all, but certainly not least of all, thank you, dear reader. If you're reading this book, you've probably been a reader

for some time now. Thank you, immensely, for your time and your readership. You have no idea how much it means to me and how much I appreciate you—it's a *lot*. Like, *so much*. I don't have strong enough language for it, and I hope this works.

Oodles of gratitude to all of you. I continue to wish each and every one of you nothing but the best for your lives.

About the Author

Dana Fraedrich is a three-time Kirkus Star recipient, dog lover, self-professed geek, and author of the steampunk fantasy series Broken Gears, which includes the Amazon bestseller, *Out of the Shadows*. Dana's books are full of secrets and colorful characters that examine the many shades of grey that paint the world. When she isn't busy writing or attending conventions and book festivals, she can be found co-hosting the podcast *Steam-Powered Movies*, playing D&D and video games, and exploring new interests.

Even from a young age, she enjoyed writing down the stories that she imagined in her mind. Born and raised in Virginia, she earned her BFA from Roanoke College and is now carving out her own happily ever after in Nashville, TN with her husband. Dana is always writing; more books are on the way!

If you enjoyed reading this book, please leave a review. Even it's just one line, that really helps authors.

⚙ Find Dana online at www.wordsbydana.com and sign up for her VIP Newsletter, where you can read new short stories as they're released and keep up with her adventures

⚙ Facebook: https://www.facebook.com/wordsbydana/

⚙ @danafraedrich on Bluesky, Threads, and Instagram

⚙ Follow Dana on Goodreads, BookBub, or her Amazon Author page

⚙ Or you can get goodies and support her on Patreon - https://www.patreon.com/wordsbydana - Thanks!